ATTACK FROM THE '80s

Edited by Bram Stoker Award-Winning Editor

Eugene Johnson

Acknowledgements

All stories are original to this nonfiction anthology except where noted, and have been used with permission:

When He was Fab © 1992 by F. Paul Wilson first published in *Weird Tales* #305—Winter 1992/93
Taking the Night Train © 1981 by Thomas F. Monteleone first published in *Night Voyages*, Spring, 1981
Top Guns of the Frontier © 2021 by Weston Ochse
Snapshot © 2021 by Joe R. Lansdale and Kasey Lansdale
The Devil in the Details © 2021 by Ben Monroe
Return of the Reanimated Nightmare © 2021 by Linda A. Addison
Catastrophe Queens © 2021 by Jess Landry
Your Picture Here © 2021 by John Skipp
Permanent Damage © 2021 by Lee Murray
Slashbacks © 2021 by Tim Waggoner
Munchies © 2021 by Lucy A. Snyder
Ten Miles of Bad Road © 2021 by Stephen Graham Jones
Epoch, Rewound © 2021 by Vince A. Liaguno
Demonic Denizens © 2021 by Cullen Bunn
The White Room © 2021 by Rena Mason
Ghetto Blaster © 2021 by Jeff Strand
Haddonfield, New Jersey 1980 © 2021 by Cindy O'Quinn
Welcome to Hell © 2021 by Christina Sng
Perspective: Journal of a 1980s Madman © 2021 by Mort Castle
Mother Knows Best © 2021 by Stephanie M. Wytovich
Stranger Danger © 2021 by Grady Hendrix
The Garden of Dr. Moreau © 2021 by Lisa Morton

Dedication

To my family Angela, Hannah, Bradley and Oliver. To my best friend
Luke Styer who helped make this book a reality.

Contents

Introduction by Mick Garris...1
Top Guns of the Frontier by Weston Ochse...3
Snapshot by Joe R. Lansdale and Kasey Lansdale...18
The Devil in the Details by Ben Monroe...37
Return of the Reanimated Nightmare by Linda Addison...49
Taking the Night Train by Thomas F. Monteleone...51
Catastrophe Queens by Jess Landry...65
Your Picture Here by John Skipp...79
Permanent Damage by Lee Murray...85
Slashbacks by Tim Waggoner...101
Munchies by Lucy A. Snyder...113
Ten Miles of Bad Road by Stephen Graham Jones...129
Epoch, Rewound by Vince A. Liaguno...137
Demonic Denizens by Cullen Bunn...141
The White Room by Rena Mason...149
Ghetto Blaster by Jeff Strand...157
Haddonfield, New Jersey 1980 by Cindy O'Quinn...164
When He Was Fab by F. Paul Wilson...169
Welcome to Hell by Christina Sng...185
Perspective: Journal of a 1980s Mad Man by Mort Castle...189
Mother Knows Best by Stephanie M. Wytovich...197
Stranger Danger by Grady Hendrix...212
The Garden of Dr. Moreau by Lisa Morton...231
Biographies...241

Introduction
Yin and Yang:
the Eighties

BY MICK GARRIS

In the words of Charles Dickens, it was the best of times, and it was the worst of times. Though perhaps not so potent as in 1859, when Dickens published *A Tale of Two Cities*, that phrase easily sums up the world of horror entertainment in the Reagan Era.

It was the decade of the double-edged sword, years of a penny with tails on both sides. In Hollywood, though, there were unique voices in terror making themselves known with iconic, intense, literate genre films, like David Cronenberg, John Carpenter, Stuart Gordon, Tobe Hooper, Wes Craven, Tom Holland and others, their work was overshadowed by the cookie-cutter slashers that were cheap, didn't require name actors or even good ideas to make box office revenue. If you were lucky, they offered creative kills and impressive effects, but the thrills evaporated once you left the theater.

But then, the theater wasn't really the point. It was the era of the videocassette, the movie as merchandise, cheap and disposable, and Blockbuster had a insatiable appetite for new blood in their Horror sections for the weekend. It didn't have to be good to make money: teens and trauma were enough for the adolescent audience that clamored for holidays celebrated in blood.

For every *Scanners*, there was a dozen *Pieces*. For every *Re-Animator*, there was a six-pack of hockey-masked Jasons. For every *Nightmare on Elm Street*, there were summer camp slashers ad infinitum. As always, there was a lot of good, original work to be found on screens big and small, but they were shouted over by the cheapjack imitators who measured quality by body count.

On the other hand, it was a boomtime for horror literature, in particular, short horror fiction. Stephen King was offering up bite-size collections of his short fiction. The self-proclaimed Splatterpunks—David J. Schow, John Skipp and Craig Spector (working separately or as a team), Joe Lansdale, and Richard Christian Matheson—were shaking things up in a huge way.

Clive Barker and his *Books of Blood* blew up the horror shelves in a huge way. The Lisas, Morton and Tuttle, brought the feminine perspective to a heretofore testosterone-infused genre, and showed that they could tell us a thing or two about sex and violence.

Tom Monteleone and Douglas E. Winter were authors and anthologizers extraordinaire, who not only created original horrific worlds of words on their own, but brought together other like-minded authors and presented them to an eager, downright begging audience.

It was a fiery and creative era, hot-headed and light-fingered, unafraid to explore the taboos. This new army of authors had broken the rules like Romero's original *Night of the Living Dead* had shaken up the Hollywood horror film. There were no boundaries that withstood these eager entertainers. The horrors were human, which made them much more dangerous and relatable, rather than werewolves and vampires and demons and ghosts. Oh, those tropes of a bygone era of chills still made their occasional cameo appearances on the written page, but usually thrust into a much more modern world of psychological depravity.

The horror stories of the eighties actually *hurt*…and they were *meant* to. But it was because a new generation of authors found their bliss in horror stories that were personal, that made us feel, to ache in a newly conservative world that needed shaking up.

Many of those authors who came of age in the eighties are to be found in this fine collection. Though most of the stories within these pages are not *from* the eighties, they are most definitely *of* the eighties. This literary time machine will transport you to a time when we discovered that horror was never meant to be comfortable.

The writers collected in this volume remember the eighties…and sometimes the worst of times made for the best of times to be a reader.

Mick Garris
20 February 2021

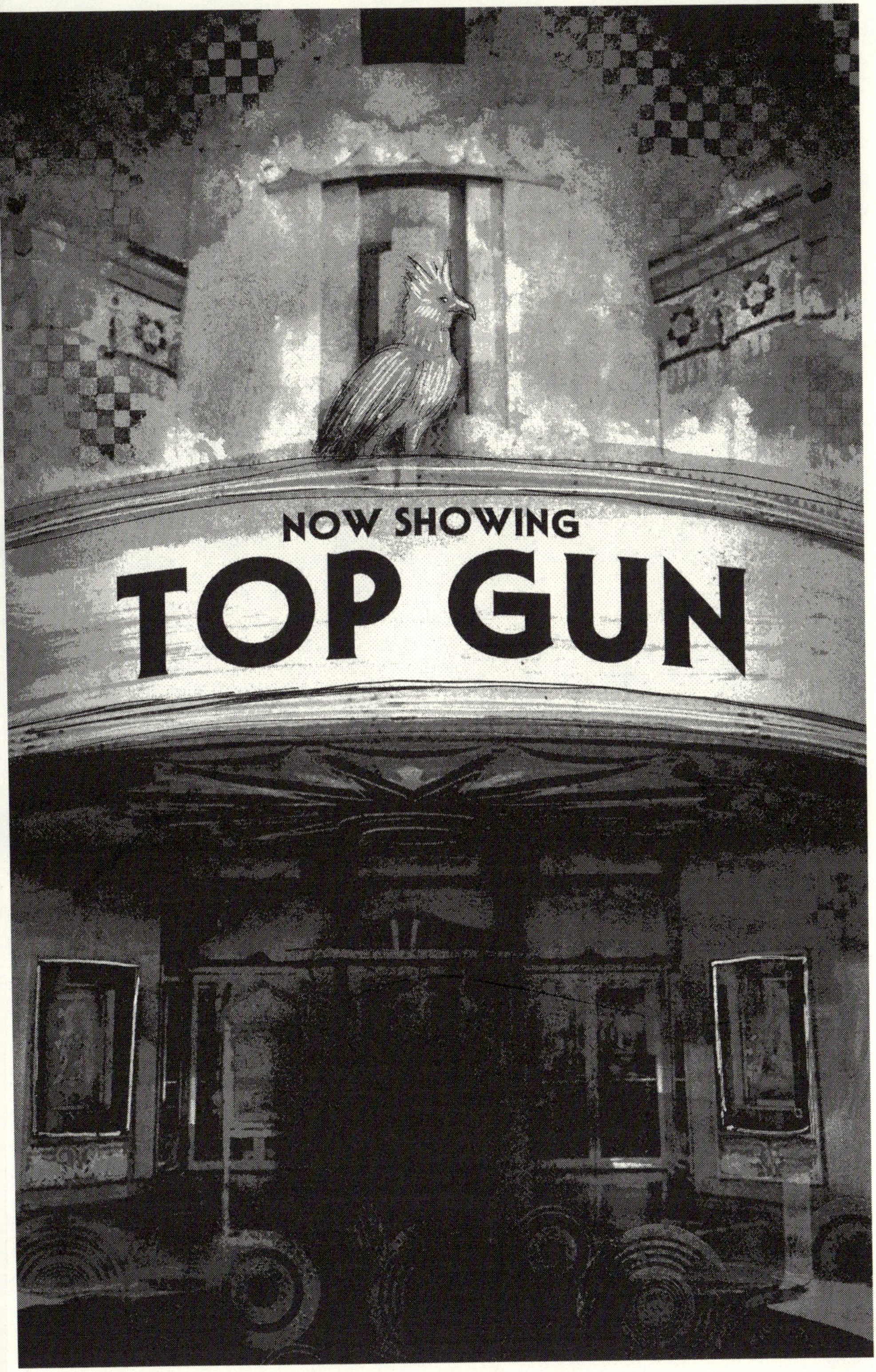
NOW SHOWING
TOP GUN

Top Guns of the Frontier

WESTON OCHSE

We'd never wanted to join the military, but then when we'd seen *Top Gun* last weekend at Eastgate Mall, we could think of nothing else. We all wanted to be Maverick. Doug wanted to be Maverick. I wanted to be Maverick. Everyone in the theater wanted to be Maverick. I mean, who wanted to be Goose? He died. We wanted to best Iceman so we could punish him for killing Goose. We memorized the song "Loving Feeling" and planned on using it when we were old enough to go into bars, which was a crazy three years after we'd become old enough to kill people, which was another three years away for us.

In the meantime, Doug said that we needed to practice. Not practice killing people, but in shooting, and in Signal Mountain, Tennessee, there was plenty enough to shoot. The town was nothing but a sprawl along Highway 127, high above the Tennessee River and the city of Chattanooga that greedily hugged its banks. So, we took to the woods as often as possible, strapping our .22 rifles across our backs with duct-taped slings, and riding our bikes deep into the trees. We'd shoot everything that moved. Squirrels. Rabbits. Crows. We'd even shot a deer once, but not the right way. It had slung itself through the brush, stumbling as it bled out. When we finally found it, its eyes were wide and terrified, as if it knew death was coming. Doug had started to cry just then, saying how it wasn't fair for the deer to know it was going to die. It needed to be a surprise to be right and we'd done it all wrong. So, I shot it in the face, just like Doug would do to Betty Sue later on that summer of 1986.

When we weren't shooting, we liked to hang out at the Alexian Brothers Nursing Home where they had an actual monastery with honest-to-God monks. My father worked there as a janitor and Doug's father worked as a groundskeeper, so we had the run of the place. The building was from the early 1900s and had been some grand hotel with hundreds of rooms, high ceilings, marble columns, and a wraparound porch. There the monks would play

3

shuffleboard with us. Sometimes gin rummy. Or sometimes just tell us stories, like Brother Roy, who had been in World War II and had lived a whole life as a husband and father before he decided to become a monk.

We'd talked to him about *Top Gun*. He hadn't and couldn't see it, his vow of poverty not allowing him such "vain extravagances," as he called them. So, we'd told him about the movie. He then explained to us that it was a homily about good and evil and how even when one is trying to do good things, evil things could happen.

Doug had asked, "Why can't the good just do good?"

"Why can't the bird just be the bird? It can, but to a worm the bird is evil. To another bird the bird is just a bird."

"But Maverick is a good guy," I argued.

"Was he a good guy to the Russians? Was he a good guy to this Iceman?"

That was Brother Roy all over. He never spoke to us directly. It was all questions and quotations. But we still liked it. He treated us like adults or as near as one could two fifteen-year-old boys who couldn't be stopped from making up their own religion.

Then he said something perplexing. "Only on the frontier can the good be truly good and the bad be truly bad."

I'd heard the Wild West called the frontier and said as much.

"Not that frontier, although it might have been one a long time ago. There are boundaries between things. Boundaries between places. When you're on one you can see the world as it truly is and recognize true evil."

"What does true evil look like?" Doug asked.

Brother Roy had gazed hard at us before he said, "You're never going to have to ask that question, but I can tell you this—evil can recognize itself."

And then it was time for him to go to Vespers.

We also wanted to lose our fear of guns. When we eventually did become top guns, as we knew we would, we didn't want to have someone point a weapon at us and then freeze, so we devised a way to conquer our fear. Doug had found a stash of last year's Chattanooga telephone books. We leaned one up against a tree and fired into it several times. Our bullets never got past the Ss, so we felt pretty safe in the idea that we probably wouldn't die. We'd duct tape a telephone book to our chest and play a game. We'd take turns where one of us leaned against a tree and aimed, while the other walked through the woods towards the other, usually shooting each other when we got within ten feet of each other.

The first time was a surprise at the way the impact felt. I'd laughed nervously, but Doug had actually cried. That was only the fourth time I'd seen him cry. Once had been when he'd found out that he was diabetic and could never eat the things other kids could eat. The other was when his mother passed away in

4

a restaurant down in Hixson, a chicken bone lodged so firmly in her throat it had to be surgically removed after her death. The third was when we messed up killing the deer. And then the fourth was when I shot him in the chest. He said it felt too real. He said he could imagine dying.

I felt no such thing. To me it was no different than old time knights wearing armor and practicing war. Only our war had guns and phone books and Maverick's F-14 and the Soviet Union out there somewhere as badass as the evil Empire from Star Wars.

But to see Doug cry was always an astonishing thing. He was the all-American kid. Blond hair, parted in the middle. High cheekbones and full lips. His body was long and lean, taller than me by several inches. Where his shoulders looked like the knobs of logs, mine looked like the bend of branches. We'd once gotten into a fight and he'd taken me down easily, punching and kicking me until I begged him to stop. He looked more like Billy Zabka, the bad guy from *Cobra Kai* who beat up Ralph Macchio in *The Karate Kid*, except that Doug was preternaturally good and would never hurt anyone, except that time I made fun of his dead mother, which was stupid anyway.

We started wargaming. We knew how dangerous it was, but we didn't care. We were basically invincible. We'd bicycle to the woods, strap phone books over our chest and abdomen and back and stagger around seeing who could hit who. I missed getting shot in the head by an inch once. I put a long wound down Doug's left arm that he had trouble explaining to his dad. It wasn't like he could say, "Sebastian shot me with his .22 and the bullet just grazed me instead of hitting me in the chest where it should have."

We might have continued wargaming except for the Pickett family. One day past Julia Falls, we came upon them, us dressed in phone books and them dressed in old worn dungarees. They were just leaving what we'd come to find out was their still cabin when we stumbled across them—Billy, his dad, his brother, Natty, and his sister, Betty Sue.

She'd been crying, but brightened up when she saw us, a tearful laugh escaping her.

The brothers sneered.

Mr. Pickett's frown deepened so his weathered and sunbaked face was almost all shadow, dark and evil and mean. "Whatchu boys doing here by our place?" He asked it fast, like the end of a bullwhip slicing through the air.

"Wargaming," Doug said. "We're going to be top guns like Maverik."

I winced. Somehow, I felt that the truth shouldn't have been our best choice on this occasion.

"What the hell is a top gun?" Mr. Pickett asked.

"It's a movie, Pop." Billy spat tobacco at my feet, just missing the toe of my Keds. "That boy in the underpants in *Risky Business* is in it," only it came out "isinit," as if it was one squashed word.

"And they wear phonebooks in this movie?" Mr. Pickett asked, clearly thunderstruck at the prospect.

I lowered my head and stared at the ground, feeling like an idiot in front of kids my age who I knew were making Ds and Fs in school, and that made me feel like even more of an idiot.

"You boys just make sure you stay away from me still," the father said, inventing a new word called "mestill."

We both nodded.

I backed away and grabbed Doug. Soon we were almost running towards our bikes. We left the laughter and incredulity behind us, but we also left a mystery. A mystery I promised myself I'd ignore, but by the time I'd gotten home and removed all the telephone books, it loomed impossibly large in my imagination. After all, I'd never seen a still.

That night we took our dinner in the wide nursing home cafeteria. Doug's dad had to work late and couldn't cook—not that he did much of that—and I just invited myself along because I wanted to talk Doug into going back that night.

We sat with Brother Roy, eating fried chicken, okra, mashed potatoes and gravy, and some red beets—all fixings meant for the old folks who lived at the home, but with enough to spare for the help and a few wild kids like us.

Doug surprised me when he interrupted the mundane conversation about each of our day's activities with the question, "Did you see one of these frontiers in World War II?"

I stopped eating, my fork halfway between my plate and my mouth.

I noted Brother Roy hesitate ever so slightly, then continue eating, taking his time to chew the mashed potatoes which he could have easily swallowed.

"I saw Auschwitz. I was there when we freed the prisoners. That was a frontier. I saw shadows I weren't sure were human or monster. I don't know what else happened there, but there was a reason for it besides meagre inhumanity."

That night I convinced Doug to join me. His father had taken a night shift from a friend at the aluminum plant, so there was no one to check up on him. My father and mother had a movie night and after a bottle of wine, they retired grossly to their bedroom, not even a thought of me on their brains as they made noises I never wanted to hear.

We were on our bikes by nine-thirty, our .22s slung across our backs, pedaling furiously down the mountain paths towards the Picketts' still house. The half-moon was more than enough to light our way. I wore my dad's green U.S. Army hat with the Army logo on the front. Doug wore his father's old, dirty white Tennessee Vol's cap, that had VOLS in orange across the front. Every time I glanced back, his head looked glowing, the moon reflecting off the white of his hat. I knew then that we'd succeed, but I'd yet to learn how much it would cost.

The still house wasn't much to look at. It seemed to be more of a shack than anything else. Although there wasn't any space between the boards, it looked like a house that should have been about to fall apart. The boards looked as if they'd weathered enough seasons that even Brother Roy would call them old. But it was surrounded by triple strands of rusted barbed wire with a sign that said Keep Out in mean crooked letters.

We'd dumped our bikes a hundred yards up the path and were on our stomachs as we stared at the darkened still house.

"What are those?" Doug asked, pointing to something I'd seen but ignored. "They look like little figures."

I looked closer and Doug was right. They were little figures affixed to the outside of the building. I could make out the arms and legs but the torsos looked all wrong. My mind had earlier discarded them as some twisted twigs. I had no idea what they really were or why there were there.

"I don't think it's a still," Doug said, totally unconvincing.

I didn't either but I wanted to hear Doug's reasoning, so I asked. "What do you think it is?"

"Did you notice the smell? It smells like an animal."

I tried to figure out what sort of animals it could house, but was at a loss.

"Plus, the way the Picketts acted—it was just weird."

We found a space beneath the barbed wire, and twisting our bodies, managed to low crawl to the side of the building with only a few scrapes. Close in, I could now see the small figures for what they were. Red-painted pinecones with the plastic arms of action figures attached to them. I couldn't see how they were affixed, but they were at all levels. There had to be dozens of the creepy things. Along their chests, if that's what they were, was a jagged black line. The more I looked at it, the more it seemed to allude me. I became nauseous the more I concentrated on the blackness so I was forced to look away.

We heard rustling from the inside of the cabin and I smelled what Doug had smelled, but the sounds were more animal than human. Scratching, as if there was something that wanted to come out. Crunching, as if something was eating.

We crouched there listening for several minutes until we heard the words, "You know you look silly."

We turned to the voice at the same time.

Betty Sue stood at the corner of the still house, staring at us. Her hair was pulled back into twin pigtails.

"Pa thought you might come back so he had me stay here jusincase." Another new word.

My face red with embarrassment, I stood first, brushing my pants and shirt free from leaves and insects.

Doug did the same, but slower, as he peered out and into the night.

"Are those real guns on your back?" she asked. "They look awfully small."

I removed mine and held it. I'd never thought it small, but now that I looked at it, it did have a thin quality about it.

"What is it you're doinere?" she asked.

I couldn't really see her eyes in shadow, but her blonde pigtails glowed like angel wings in the moonlight.

"We've never seen a still before," Doug said.

I nodded, still trying to make out her eyes which looked like black holes.

"Well, you're not going to see one now," she said cryptically, then added, "At least, not yerexpectin."

"You're not going to let us just get a peek?" Doug asked, trying to pour on the charm, but too nervous for it.

"You ain't gonna see one because there aren't one here," she said. She stepped forward a few inches and the moon caught her eyes and they glowed like her wings. "We juss tell people cuz they know to stay away. Peoples get shot at stills if'n it ain't therown."

"If it's not a still, what is it?" I asked.

She regarded us for a moment, then stared off into the night, her head cocked, listening. Finally, she nodded. "Y'all can come see. Just know you might not like what happens after."

"What do you mean what happens after?" Doug whispered.

"It's a line," she said. "You cross it. That's it." She turned towards the door.

I started to follow, but Doug grabbed me. "What if this is a frontier?"

"This isn't a frontier," I said.

"But it feels like one, RayRay. It smells like one." His eyes were bright, feverish. "I'm not sure I want to cross that line."

I sniffed the air. "It smells like a barn."

"With no animal I've ever smelled before."

Both veterans of the woods, he was right. I sniffed again. The rankness of it made my insides squeeze into itself, the stench like earth and sweat and animal hair and sulfur.

"Are y'all coming?" she whispered.

I glanced back, then nervously pointed at one of the pinecones with the action figures. I couldn't look directly at them. They made me feel nauseous. Still, I wanted to know. "And these?" I asked, pointing to a figure.

She grinned tightly. "Those are my netties. Leave them be and they'll leave you be." Then she slid inside.

I followed her in, Doug scooting close enough behind me, then when I stopped he bumped into me.

Darkness held the inside of the cabin in a clenched fist. I couldn't make out anything once the door closed behind us, just the heady stink of some animal.

A rustling from a corner startled me and made me jump back, pinning Doug to the door.

He squirted out from behind me and grabbed my arm.

"What is it?" he rasped.

The sound of a match was followed by the whoosh and sizzle of a Coleman lantern, the mantle going from yellow to white as Betty Sue turned the adjustment. She held it up and placed it on an old table that held two chairs around it. On the table were bowls that glowed red in the light as if they'd once held blood.

"'Lectrcity don't work inhere. Neither does batt-ries. Got to go old school," she said.

Why wouldn't something with batteries not work in here, that's just—For the first time I noticed a strange figure in the far corner of the room. Not a figure but a thing. Its face was in shadow, but it was the face of a woman. An older woman, heavy brow, stern face, staring right through me. I lowered my eyes for a moment, then when I raised them, I noticed in the shadows it had wings and the long taloned-legs of a raptor. I didn't know what it was, but it stared at me with hollow eyes the same way Betty Sue had stared at me outside.

"What is it?" I asked in an awed whisper.

She strode over to it and placed her hand on the back of its head. I was transfixed by her standing beside the creature. She was like a Pippi Longstocking of the Evil Forest standing with a lantern in one hand and a monster in the other.

"Harpy, my pa calls it. Theys hard to find, so when we do get one, we have to save it for a while."

"What does that thing eat?" Doug asked, finding his voice,

"Hate," she said. "It eats hate."

"Then what was in the bowls?" I asked.

"Baby blood," she said. "People baby blood."

My heart dropped in horror. I tried hard not to look at the bowls. "Why—why the blood?" I asked.

She grinned wickedly. "To feed the hate, of course."

I laughed but it wasn't really a laugh—more of a croak—as I tried to bite back my nervousness and failed.

"I don't get it. Feed hate?" Doug asked.

She pointed with her left hand at the ground beside her. "There."

For the first time I saw the hole in the ground. I'd been so intent on the harpy that the circle of black nothing had gone unnoticed. Old, worn rounded bricks surrounded the hole. From inside came a deep bellow like a foghorn far away. Sulphur seeped from its depths.

Doug glanced at me nervously.

I gave him the "let's get the fuck out of here" look but he was always bad at reading faces. Fine, then I'll play the game, I thought. Seems like she wanted to play show and tell but make it twenty questions. Fine!

"What's down there?" I asked.

"A new frontier," she said, then she grinned, as if she dropped the mic and knew what her words meant to us.

The next morning found me biking to the library to look up "harpies." I needed to know more. Something was going on and I didn't know if I needed to stop it or not. When I reached the library, I slung my bike against the metal bike bench, and hoofed it up the stairs. I'm not sure what bothered me most about last night. The harpy. The horror about the babies. The pit with something called "hate" inside of it. Or her answer when I asked, "Why are you telling us this?"

She'd laughed and I could have sworn her eyes glowed when she said, "Pa needs more hunters. He needs more people outchere who can get things for us. We're doing something special here. The world is changing. Lives is changing. Everything is changing and you will be changed along with it."

The library inside wasn't what one would call large, but the librarian seemed to know where everything was. When I mentioned harpy, her eyebrows had arched, but she hadn't said anything other than guide me to a section about mythology, and then a section about rare species of birds. I soon found out that the mythological harpy was probably based on the harpy eagle, which had a face that looked disturbingly like my grandmother.

I scribbled notes for Doug, then biked to Brother Roy. On the way, I thought of the scene in *Top Gun* with Meg Ryan and Goose, where she screamed, "Take me to bed or lose me forever." Such joy in those words. Such a vocal embrace. I dialed up the image of Betty Sue and tried to make her fit the Meg Ryan ideal, but found it impossible. It was more than just the wrong-shaped puzzle piece. It was the wrong puzzle. For some reason, I felt that Betty Sue didn't belong in my reality and the thought disturbed me enough that when I saw Brother Roy, he knew something was wrong.

"Why do I smell sulfur on you?" he asked.

I was still wearing my dad's old Army hat. I snatched it off my head and stuffed it into my back pocket.

"Sulfur by itself is not bad, but it can be associated with things you don't want to be part of, son," Brother Roy said.

I hesitated, but then just blurted it out. "Brother Roy, does everyone know what a frontier is?"

"That's a weighty question that begs the idea that you've met someone who has."

"A girl. My age. From the woods."

"A girl in the woods?"

"Yes. I know her from school. She's from the woods."

"The woods. Many of their traditions stay the same while ours fall victim to civilized inventions such as MTV."

It dawned on me that Brother Roy was actually being forthcoming instead of mysterious, but I didn't say anything because I didn't want to ruin it.

"The woods are a frontier unto themselves. A demarcation from who we were before civilization decided that it needed to be replaced and who we are now."

I wanted to tell him about the harpy eagle, but was afraid that if I did, he'd tell my dad out of worry for my safety, so I held my tongue.

We talked for a while longer, then Brother Roy had to leave for prayer, and I wandered off into the side of the property where the manicured lawn met the forest line. Where old times met modern times. I could look back and see where the shuffleboard court was and I could look in front of me where the shadows gathered in the trees like they probably had for a million years.

What Brother Roy had tried to get me to understand was that frontiers were meant to be destroyed. Not that one should seek out a frontier, but when they discovered a frontier, by the very motion of crossing over, they destroyed it. Yet, to destroy one frontier created another. There would always be a line between what we were, who we are, and what we could be. But some lines are thicker. Some frontiers are more permanent than others.

As if reading my mind, he told me that the frontier between mythology and reality was the foundation of universal knowledge. Once we gained that knowledge, the mythical frontier was shattered, but if one were to be able to resurrect that frontier, one might have significant power.

It was at that moment I decided to save the harpy.

When I told Doug of my decision, he was all in. Not only because of what I'd said, but because of what he'd stolen. He pulled a nettie out of his back and showed it to me. It was tied to a brick for some reason.

"This thing is pure evil," he whispered. "I had nightmares all night because of it."

The arms looked like they'd been ripped off a G.I. Joe and the legs seemed to be borrowed from a Barbie. The body was a large pinecone that had been spray-painted a candy-apple red. It didn't have any other features except for the sliver of black that ran almost the length of its body. Even as I looked at it, I began to feel sick, my heart beating furiously, sweat beading on my brow.

"Why'd you tie it to the brick?" I asked.

He put the brick on the ground and said, "Watch it."

My eyes popped wide as the arms and legs began to move.

"What's it doing?" I whispered.

"I chased it around my room for an hour when I got home. I think it's trying to get back."

I stared at it, then shook my head and closed my eyes. I bit back bile that was trying to crawl up my throat. "What are you going to do with it?"

"I think I need to let it go," he said. Then he knelt, pulled out a pocketknife, and cut free the twine that had lashed the arms and legs to the brick.

The nettie's arms moved, then its legs as if flexing. At once, it climbed off the brick, stood and faced us, then ran off into the woods, its Barbie legs pumping crazy fast, its G.I. Joe arms held out in front of it as if reaching.

"I-I'm not going to touch one again," Doug said, shaking his head. "I don't know what it is, but I don't want any part of it."

We'd been invited back to the cabin for a ceremony at midnight, but we found ourselves there by nine. We had no interest in the ceremony. Saving the harpy eagle was our goal.

We'd geared up and were ready for war. Pieces and parts of all the area phone books had been duct taped to our triceps, thighs, calves, back, chest sides and even abdomen, the latter making it hard to ride. We even wore old football helmets from Doug's brother's room. The helmets were white, but we'd found black spray paint and made them as black as possible. Then we'd argued for almost an hour about who would be Maverick and who would be Goose. In the end, after I lost at roshambo, Doug became Maverick and I became Goose, our names written in white house paint with our fingers on the back of each helmet.

We approached the cabin from a different direction this time. We'd seen enough war movies to know how to move silently through the forest, flitting from tree to tree, careful of the brush and leaves. We even found one of their traps, a wire with tin cans to alert them if someone were about to come around either accidentally or intentionally. That should have been our indicator that someone was always there, but we weren't thinking straight. We were like Maverick wanting the ace and trying too hard.

Light shuddered inside the cabin.

We glanced at the netties, worried that they might come alive at any moment.

Doug pulled himself up to the windowsill, then beckoned me over. I slid along the side of the building without touching it. Then when I got even with the window, I peered inside.

The Coleman lamp sat on the table, lighting the inside of the cabin. Four people stood around the open hole in the floor. Betty Sue's back was to me. Beside her stood her two brothers, Billy and Natty and across from her was her father. The boys held a strange wooden cross with the harpy eagle affixed to it as if it were crucified, wings outstretched and held in place. They lowered the eagle into the hole, so that only its head was visible. It began to struggle and scream, the face of the old woman agonized and angry. Its head thrashed left and right as it tried to snap at the boys with its raptor beak. When they began to lift the eagle back up, its claws were enmeshed in what could only be a blanket of shadow—a darkness darker than anything else, like the squiggles on the netties. Only this piece was huge and made me think of nothing but hate.

Seeing it, I wanted to kill it. I wanted to make it cease to exist. I was so overtaken by the desire to be rid of it, that I was at the door and opening it before I knew what I was even doing.

The father saw me and cursed, his hand on a bone-white knife the size of a small sword. He'd been cutting away at the shadow when he saw me at the door. Natty turned to see what his father was looking at and in doing so lost part of his grip. The shadow slid and curled around Betty Sue's left leg.

Her panicked and shrill scream would stay with me for the next thirty years. She'd been holding a silver bucket where pieces of the shadow coalesced inside. She swung it at the darkness that had attached itself to her leg and succeeded in breaking it free, but the contents of the bucket latched onto her arm and surged towards her face.

Billy reached for her and grabbed a hold of the darkness, trying to wrestle it free.

His father screamed, "No!", and hacked away the part of Billy's arm that was already being eaten by the hatred—for that's what I knew it to be, hatred, or pieces of hate—cut from a never-ending shadow of hate, all lured from the hole by the presence of the harpy.

Billy couldn't hold onto the wooden contraption through his pain and let it go, causing Natty to stumble as he took the weight. The wood crashed onto the side of the hole, freeing the eagle, who immediately went for the nearest soft tissue, which happened to be Natty's eyes.

Now, everyone was screaming, even me and Doug as we were locked in our positions, watching the terrible transpire.

Betty Sue spun towards me and lurched, her face gone, replaced by a darkness with a single terrified eye. A mouth opened up from where her mouth might have once been, but this was ear to ear and looked like it was torn free. A low-pitched creaking emanated from her throat, followed by a scream that was equally low-pitched.

Something slid to the ground beside me as I stood in the open doorway.

Then another.

Then another.

It was the netties, running towards whatever Betty Sue had become. They swarmed over her, causing her to spin and flail. She crashed into her father, who slammed his head against the wall, before falling into the darkness of the hole. He caught himself and screamed. Somehow, he managed to pull free a pistol, raised it and shot me in the chest.

I flew backwards from the impact, my head crashing into the earth, just outside the door.

I heard a window breaking, then a rifle shot.

From the corner of my eye I saw Betty Sue's head jerk back as a bullet from Doug's rifle smashed through her face and out the other side.

But it didn't do a thing. The hate had her and wouldn't let her die.

She surged towards me and I rolled out of the way as she stumbled off into the woods, scraping the netties away who seemed to be trying to save her or kill her or save us or whatever they were doing, their little slices of darkness eager to bring the larger darkness back.

I climbed to my feet and drew my rifle shakily on Mr. Pickett, fumbling with the safety.

He'd managed to hang onto the edge of the hole, even as he screamed in terror, his whole body jerking as if something were snagging at him. One hand still held the pistol, the wavering barrel smoking from where he'd shot me.

Shot me!

I glanced down and saw the hole in the phonebook. Dead center. But I didn't feel anything.

Then the hate took him and his screams.

Silence filled the room.

It was only later that we realized what had happened.

I'd been shot, but the bullet had only managed to make it to the Zs, stopping right at Zebrowski.

Natty told us how to keep Billy from bleeding out.

Billy told us how to keep Natty alive.

They told each other that they would survive this, but their eyes said otherwise—at least Billy's did—the wide-eyed panic of the deer we'd shot, knowing it was going to die and unable to avoid it. In the end, they both succumbed to their wounds sitting there in the backwards place that distilled hate, but not before they shared a little of what they'd been doing. The darkness got to them. As did the netties. What became of them I can't say under the light of the sun. Such things are held for fuzzy moments between sleep and nightmares and waking, but the place was indeed a still. Only, instead of moonshine they sold hate, bottled, and sold around the world for prices that would make you weep.

Hatred had many powers, they said.

Hatred had many uses.

Just a little hate went a long way.

Doug didn't go on to become a top gun. He became a Ranger instead and spends his years in places most would never want to go, trying to save people who didn't always know they needed saving. So, I guess he did become a Maverick in his own way, except instead of flying into the face of an enemy, he runs there.

I didn't become a top gun either. Or at least, not the normal sort. I went off to seminary, then joined the monastery the last year of Brother Roy's life. He explained to me something about what he'd been doing there all this time, watching the woods, tending the frontier. When he passed that became my job.

That's my own version of being Maverick, I suppose.

I have a mated pair of harpy eagles now. I raise them because the hate can't hurt them. Sometimes Betty Sue comes around, pushing at the edges of the frontier, but she's known as the Screaming Girl, now, her low-pitched screams just on the edge of hearing when the wind comes and the boughs bend and the thunder promises to shake the heavens.

And then there are others that the hate has touched.

Others who are bound by their own dark frontier.

And I sit atop my mountain, watching, tending, waiting.

A top gun of the frontier, so you don't have to be.

Snapshot

JOE R. LANSDALE AND KASEY LANSDALE

DEEP EAST TEXAS, NINETEEN EIGHTY-EIGHT

THE HOUSE

They came along through the night, the small camper running near silent over the red, damp, clay road, the shadow-bathed trees close on either side.

At the wheel, Trevor said, "Maybe we can find a good place to park that isn't muddy."

"Good luck with that," Gracie said. "Comes another rain like that, I'm going to start watching for Noah."

The headlights showed them a bend in the road, and at the bend there was a gravel turn around.

"Perfect," Trevor said.

"I prefer a hotel."

"Too far out tonight. Maybe the next night, couple towns down the road."

"We just left a town," Gracie said.

"Yep, and some houses in that town are missing some jewels, some money, and a kid's science project."

"That was mean, Trevor."

"A little. I always wanted one of those volcano things with the lava that comes out, and now I got one."

"Jesus."

Trevor parked the camper, and they were about to slip to the rear of it, crawl into bed, when he said, "Look there."

Gracie looked. They were on a bit of a rise, and through the trees, she could see the moon shining on water. A large pond, and across from the pond there was a light on a tall pole. The light showed them a house, not exactly a citadel, but the best construction an upper middle-class income could buy. Oaks grew strategically about the yard, and there was a large satellite dish on the roof.

18

"Thinking what I'm thinking?" Trevor said.

"Not unless you're thinking about going to sleep."

"You know what I'm thinking."

"Yeah," Gracie said. "I know.

THREE DAYS EARLIER

"Hurry it up, would you?"

"You want to be sure it gets there, don't you?" Trevor asked.

"Not really."

"Well I do, and I didn't hear you complaining when you found that ruby bracelet."

Gracie instinctively touched her wrist, said nothing. Trevor used his finger to smooth down the stamp in the corner a final time, pulled open the blue metal door and dropped the envelope inside. It made a squeaking sound in protest, followed by a loud clang. He turned to her, pushed back a tendril of dark hair from her face.

"The only way we are going to make a name for ourselves is if we let them know who we are."

"I think we've made a name already. Well, no one knows our name actually."

"Sure they do. Our moniker, anyway."

Gracie glanced next to the mailbox where local newspapers were contained in a bright red newspaper rack. Through the plastic front, she could see the title headline. "THE SNAPSHOT BURGLARS STRIKE AGAIN."

"Let me see that," Trevor said, pointing at the stack. Gracie slipped a coin in the slot, a paper dropped, and Gracie pulled it free from the chute.

Trevor held it up and began to read aloud.

"The Snapshot Burglars have struck again, making themselves known to their unsuspecting victims by sending Polaroid pictures of stolen items to said persons following the incident." Trevor let the fold of the paper fall away and continued reading from the bottom half of the page. "The Snapshot Burglars seem to target houses in middle class neighborhoods, and are adept at entering and leaving quickly undetected. In some cases, victims of theft were only made aware that someone had been in their homes and taken possessions when an envelope containing the snapshots arrived in their mailboxes.

"It's judged there are at least two burglars. Sometimes, other than the snapshots, they rearrange household items. Frequently, the burglars take time to prepare themselves a snack, and sometimes steal food items. No fingerprints have been found. The fact that food items are removed, suggest that the thieves live on the road, moving from one town to the next. Law enforcement is looking for any information that might be provided by the public that will lead to the apprehension of the burglars."

Trevor folded the newspaper, looked at Gracie. "We're unknown and famous."

Back in the camper, Gracie reread the article while Trevor drove. When she was finished reading, she positioned her seat back so she could rest. They drove all through the day, stopping only to buy gas and snack food, cruising in a big circle through East Texas. Pretty soon they'd have to expand their territory. Oklahoma, Louisiana, maybe move on out to Santa Fe where the sun was bright and so was the rich folks' jewelry.

Gracie had always wanted to be famous, and this was the next best thing. The Snapshot Burglars. They were like Bonnie and Clyde without the murder, and without being known by name.

Gracie remembered her mother's remarks about how she would never need to amount to much. "You got looks, girl. You don't need smarts or skill. Look what it's done for me."

Gracie didn't like what it had done for her mom, a trailer home full of ceramic chicken knickknacks, the trailer positioned on a sunbaked concrete slab just outside a little town where the greatest excitement was watching the red light change to green. Then again, there had been that bit of insurance money from her mother's last husband, ole Stan, who worked in maintenance but seldom found much to maintain, outside of putting batteries in a TV remote, keeping his weight up by guzzling beers, and reaching for peanuts in a plastic bowl on a coffee table made of an electric wire spool. One day he reached and his heart said no, and that was it for Stan. He ended up on the floor between the couch and the spool, his hand still clutching a wad of nuts.

Yeah. Her mother was living the life, all right, though that insurance money did provide for a larger trailer, a double-wide, soon filled with more chicken knickknacks and a new boyfriend named Clyde who worked at the chicken plant, which was perfect for her mother's collection. If she couldn't have a life-sized chicken, she could at least have a life-sized man that worked at a place where real chickens were handled, dressed, and sent to market. Her mom was living the dream.

And for a while it looked as if Gracie would be living the same one.

Then she met Trevor and the world got brighter and more exciting, and she developed skills that he taught her. Trevor's skills didn't come from community college, but he had gone to the school of burglary, and appeared to have graduated with honors.

In short time, he told her, "My daddy was a professional burglar, and he was at it for years, anything from lawnmowers to cars to roadwork machines. He stole and sold and made a good living, and then he messed up, tried to steal a Corvette from a carport and was shot by the owner. Never served a day in jail, but is now serving an eternity in the ground."

Trevor had helped him steal a number of items, but was fortunately not with him that day. He remembered advice his father gave him only the day before his death.

"Got to tell you, Trev, stealing this big stuff. It's got a good pay off, but you got to hide it, deal with a specific buyer, change VIN numbers, all that shit, and it's tiring and easier to get caught. You continue in the family business, I suggest you steal small but rich. I think jewelry and the like would be the ticket, and except for this car I got my eye on, come next week, I'm changing my method of operation. If I can't carry it out in a bag from now on, I'm not bothering."

With his father's death, and him being so young and surviving on shoplifting, he was picked up by the cops. He ended up in an orphanage, but it felt more like a prison. When he was old enough to leave, he found that, like his father, he had a knack for theft. And he followed his father's advice. Steal small.

One day his knack failed him. Got picked up for shoplifting, placed in a program to put juveniles on the right track. It was silly. There was no way a thing like, some stupid program, could make a person change that didn't want to change. But there was one plus. Another shoplifter was there. Gracie. Given room and board and daily lectures for stealing ceramic chickens from a knick-knack store.

THE HOUSE—THE PRESENT

They slipped on backpacks and left the car among the trees and walked through the dark using moonlight, arrived at the house a little after nine. There were no lights shining from inside. There was only the pale lemon-yellow light on the pole outside. All three stories were enveloped by the wind-weaved shadows of tall oaks and the sawing sounds of cicadas. There were no cars in the drive. Trevor moved to a window and peered inside. It was hard to see much more than his own reflection.

Gracie took gloves from her pack, handed Trevor a pair, slipped on the other pair. "Alarm goes off," Gracie said, "run like hell."

"As always," Trevor said.

She jiggled the knob gently. No alarm. She took out her tool kit and went to work on the latch. She was done quickly, and the door snicked open.

"Did you remember the Polaroid?" Trevor said.

"Of course," she said, swinging the pack off her back, reaching into it to remove the camera. She handed it to him, then repositioned the pack on her back.

Trevor took the camera, slipped the strap over his neck, let the camera rest against his chest. Gracie, silent as a silhouette, moved inside. Trevor followed, both moving stealthily through a kitchen rich with the smell of garlic, and from somewhere came a heavy pine fragrance—air freshener perhaps. Trevor remained there as Gracie slipped down a hallway that opened into a large living room with nice furniture and the intensified sick-sweet smell of that pine air freshener. Gracie stood in the gap, one shoulder against the wall, and studied the room.

The wallpaper looked new, its pink and blue flowers bright and freshly painted. There were a few unique sculptures in a cabinet, behind glass. They were cool looking, but they were too distinct to try and sell. Someone would trace them back pronto. You had to stick to jewels, folding money, a special item or two, but all stuff that was easy to move quickly and didn't require special expertise for the fence.

Gracie's eyes traced a slightly worn path in the wooden floor from the living room couch, and followed it. It was another entrance into the kitchen. A noise startled her as she entered the room.

In the light of the open refrigerator, Trevor stood, looking like a kid who had been caught with a hand in the cookie jar.

In this case, a jar of pickles. It lay shattered on the floor in front of the refrigerator, pickles scattered about, the briny liquid that had soaked them now flowed over the kitchen tiles.

Trevor was about his notorious sandwich making. It had become, like the Polaroid's, a thing.

"Sorry. Jar slipped."

"I can see that," Gracie said. "No pickles on mine, please."

Trevor grinned at her, began to remove items from the fridge, place them on the kitchen counter. Various cold cuts and condiments.

"Anything?" he asked.

"Nothing jumping out at me from the living room. No fireplace, no quick-sale paintings, no safe. Some small sculptures, but too unique and difficult to carry. We need to check the other floors, search for their special hiding places."

"Let's save a bedroom for last," he said with a wink.

Gracie smiled, nodded, and watched Trevor continue his sandwich making. He opened the walk-in pantry door near the fridge, said, "Where's the bread?"

"Like I would know."

Trevor flicked on the light in the pantry.

"Don't you think we ought to rob first, snack second?" Gracie said.

"That's best all right, but I'm seriously hungry. Peanut butter and strawberry jelly, there's jars of it."

"Might be better than cold cuts. I'm sick of cold cuts. Is that a light?" Gracie said, pointing inside the pantry.

"It's something," Trevor said. He pushed aside some cans with his foot and gave the crack of light a closer examination. An economy sized bag of dog food was propped against the back wall, unopened.

"See a sign of a dog anywhere?"

"No."

Trevor pulled the bag aside, rested his gloved hands on the bare wall and pushed gently. A door in the pantry wall swung open.

It was an entrance to a cellar, larger than most, and smelled even more of pine scent than the house, and there was a scent of ammonia from what Gracie thought must be some kind of cleanser or bleach.

There were wooden steps. The walls were solid, made of concrete slabs. Gracie and Trevor took flashlights from their packs, flicked them on, cautiously, started down the steps, which creaked and bent a little beneath their weight.

"I was the owner of this house, this is where I'd hide the good stuff," Trevor said. "Maybe the bad stuff. I'd redo the stairs, though."

"It smells like pine trees live down here," Gracie said.

They made their way to the bottom of the stairs, flipped a switch there. It wasn't a bright bulb, and the light only lit up the center of the room. Tendrils of illumination drifted into and were consumed by shadows in the corners of the room.

"Look at this," Trevor said. Near the bottom of the stairs was a pool table. It looked new. The green fabric, lush and vibrant.

"Come on, Trevor, we have to stay focused."

"Fine. But you owe me a round." Trevor walked deeper into the room, touched a thick canvas apron draped over a rectangular shape. Gracie could see the bottom of it. A meat freezer.

She was proved correct when Trevor pulled the canvas aside, let it drop on the floor.

"Had time, and wanted it, bet we could cook up some venison, pork chops and such. I bet this thing is stuffed with them."

"We don't have the time to thaw and cook meat, goofball," Gracie said. "Let's grab some goods and hike. You're starting to get too bold, Trevor."

"Surely we can look," Trevor said, and touched the lid. "I want photos. I think it's perfect to send to them, show them we were in their holy of holies."

"Sure. What the hell?"

With both hands, Gracie pushed the heavy lid upwards, let out an involuntary gasp when the light inside the freezer coated the contents.

"Holy shit, Trevor."

Peering inside, Trevor said, "Whoa. What in the actual fuck?"

There was a plastic bag full of filmy eyeballs.

"Who would eat animal eyes?" he said.

Gracie gently lifted the package from the freezer, frost fading from it as she removed it, stared at the contents through the plastic. "Do animals have green eyes?"

"Cats, I guess."

"I don't think these eyeballs belong to cats."

Trevor was leaning into the freezer. He lifted a frosty package, round and firm. He turned it in his hand. He could see a man's face inside, the nose tight against the plastic.

"Oh, shit, Gracie."

"Yeah," Grace said. "Oh, shit. Trevor, the other wraps. They're more heads, body parts."

Now that the freezer door was open, and the frost had dissolved somewhat, they could see more body parts in bags, a number of heads, slack-jawed faces staring up at them, frost bitten eyeballs glinting in the freezer light. Two or three heads on the top row looked fresher than the others. Frost clung to their brows and hairline. The stumps of their necks were evenly cut and dark where the blood had frozen to a deep purple.

"Jesus, there's a sack of balls," Trevor said. "Take a picture. We need proof." Trevor dropped the head back inside as Gracie leaned over the grisly collection and snapped a photo, the flash making the room seem exceptionally eerie for a moment. The mechanical click and hum of the Polaroid echoed in the room.

"Take another," Trevor said.

Gracie flashed away with the Polaroid.

"God, Gracie, think what someone would pay not to have these photos released to the law? We could make a fortune."

"You have got to be out of your fucking mind, Trev," she said as she tucked the camera back in her pack, and hoisted the pack on her back. "These are people. Someone murdered them, someone who'll keep doing it. And do whatever it is he's doing with these body parts. Eating them, maybe. Shit, I need

24

to get out of here. I'm gonna be sick. And Jesus, if they come back, we could be in that freezer before daybreak."

"Yeah. Yeah. Sure."

Trevor closed the lid gently as they backed away as if from a poisonous snake.

As they reached the stairs, Gracie said, "That smell, under the pine fragrance, the bleach, it's rotting meat. That means it isn't just the freezer."

"It's probably everywhere. In the floorboards, under the freezer, behind things. Cutting up people like that is messy. Now, like you said, let's go."

Gracie froze in her tracks. There was an opening, previously unseen below the stairwell. It was a little door with a silver handle. "I think the stink is coming from there."

"And now you want to look?"

"Can't help myself."

"Yes, you can."

But already Gracie was moving toward the door.

There was a *clattering* sound as Gracie grabbed the door handle. Trevor moved beside her, touched her arm, whispered, "No."

Gracie shook her head, gently pushed on the lever.

It was a larger room than expected. The air was frigid and a plume of froth puffed out of Gracie's mouth. Trevor stood back, as if nailed to the floor. In the room the light bulb was pale and orange and hung centrally located over a long steel table. A woman lay on the table, her head turned toward them. Her mouth was plugged with a small stuffed animal, a pink puppy, maybe a teddy bear, and a black leather strap held it in place.

The eyes of the woman widened as they stood at the entrance to the room, and later Gracie would know that reaction was a swift flare of hope, like a firing squad victim holding tight to the possibility that the bullets in the rifles were blanks.

The woman on the table appeared to be naked, but Gracie couldn't be certain. Her body was blocked by someone standing on a step stool in front of the table, someone wearing a hood bunched up in the back, and a leather wraparound apron that fell to the tops of bare feet, but revealed a bare upper back and shoulders. The butcher, for that's how Gracie thought of the individual, loomed over its victim with a hacksaw in a leather-gloved hand.

A tattoo of a pink and blue butterfly was located on the nape of the butcher. The shoulders were smooth, brown, and wide. On the floor, next to the step stool, was a crusty-bladed hatchet.

In that same moment, Gracie took in not only the butcher and the woman on the table, but shapes in the shadows covered in tarps.

The butcher leaned over the woman and placed the hacksaw to her throat. The light glistened on a tear on the victim's cheek as the butcher began to slowly saw at her neck, one hand on the woman's jaw to hold her still. There was a thin line of red at the victim's neck, and then it was wider, and blood spurted and splashed on the butcher and the floor, which was concrete with a drain positioned under the table. Gracie could see it through the legs of the step stool. Could see the blood flow into it.

The victim jerked, but she was strapped down securely, nowhere to go. The saw bit, and within seconds, the head came loose and rolled off the table and struck the floor with a thud.

When the hooded butcher turned, she saw Gracie, dropped the saw, and stepping off the stool, she picked up the hatchet on the floor and started to rush toward Gracie.

Gracie having been frozen in place, came unstuck. She started to yell for Trevor to run. But he had already made his exit. Gracie could hear his feet pounding on the stairs as he climbed them with all the speed of a spider monkey.

Gracie slammed the door shut, pushed the weight of her body against it as the butcher banged on the other side, nearly knocking Gracie down. Gracie felt the pressure on the door increasing, and knew she couldn't hold it for long.

She gave it one last push, then wheeled toward the stairs.

Gracie emerged from the cellar, stumbling as she went over the sack of dog food. Trevor was nowhere to be seen. She could hear the butcher, tight on her heels, the stairs squeaking like mice.

She scanned the area for a weapon, reached for a plastic ketchup bottle, then decided against it. The pounding of footsteps was now only a few feet away. She scooped up the dog food bag using both arms, hoisted it onto her hip. The bag ripped slightly. Dog food dribbled out. It smelled of molasses and corn. She glanced down the stairs as her masked pursuer reached the top, and heaved the bag down the stairs with all her might.

The butcher let out a yelp as the bag hit at knee level, burst open, scattered dog food in all directions and caused the butcher to stumble backwards and fall with a sound like someone dribbling a basketball, then hitting the floor with a hollow thud. Gracie ran out of the pantry towards the back door, and then was outside, running with all her might, making good time even though she had a pack on her back.

As she ran, she glanced back and saw the butcher exit the house, trying to run in the long leather apron, or to be more precise leather robe. It was not an outfit designed for running. Gracie outdistanced the butcher, and the butcher stopped running, stood holding the hatchet, watching her. Gracie beat feet around the pond, up toward the wood line where their camper was parked. She turned her attention to that location, saw Trevor climbing the hill into the trees. At that moment she dearly wanted to coldcock him with a two-by-four. She also feared, panicked as he was, he might drive off and leave her. Something she had never considered before.

She hurried on up the hill and through the woods, was relieved to see the camper still parked beside the road. She took a moment to look back over the moonlit pond. The butcher was no longer in sight. She found Trevor in the driver's seat, both hands gripping the steering wheel. He looked as if he had been hit between the eyes with a mallet.

"You left me, Trevor!"

"I was going for help."

"You were going to save your ass."

"It was reflexes, alright?"

"No. Not all right. She had a hatchet. I had a bag of dog food."

"I never claimed to be any kind of white knight. I'm a thief, not a fighter."

Trevor started the camper, drove it onto the road.

"It's okay," he said. "We'll just move on. I'm sorry, babe. Really."

They cruised along in cold silence for a while, and then Gracie said, "We have to tell the police, someone. The butcher back there murdered a woman, sawed through her neck like she was a Christmas ham."

"We talk to the law, they'll want to know why we were in the house. We can just send them the Polaroids, give them the address."

"What is the address?"

"I hadn't gathered that information yet. I planned to."

"They'll just think the Polaroids are faked."

"We can't go to the police."

"All those body parts in the freezer. Jesus Christ."

"I don't know."

Gracie stuck her foot across the seat and put it on the brake. The camper slid, nearly turned completely around."

"Are you crazy?"

"No, Trevor. What just happened is crazy, and had I been just a few seconds slower, I'd have ended up on that table. We are going to the law, and I don't care what it costs us. You're through calling the shots. I saw what you're made of back there, and it's a pile of shit. Maybe they'll give us a pass, we tell them where a crazy murderer lives with body parts in their freezer. Do that, we might get a slide, or a short sentence. Now turn this thing around, and go back to the last town we drove through."

The sheriff's office was in a trailer on the outskirts of town. It was a double-wide on about three acres with a few outbuildings, and out front a sign that said Bryant City Sheriff's Office.

Inside the office they were seated in a row of chairs, and off to the side a partition of glass had been built. On the other side of it were a few cramped desks and three people in deputy sheriff uniforms, one younger woman in plainclothes. They were in front of their computers, typing. Gracie wondered what they were typing. A town as small as Bryant was unlikely to have much crime, and then she thought about the reason they were there. Those body parts had come from somewhere. They added up to a lot of human beings. For all she knew Bryant City might be dead center of a world class crime wave.

The sheriff, a long lean man who looked as if he had recently stepped out of a shower, polished with a rag, and given a coat of wax. He had a handsome, but not particularly flexible face, teeth that looked to have been built into his mouth by someone in a hurry. His straw cowboy hat was on his desk. Straw or not, it was expensive looking. He was probably forty, maybe even fifty years old. The little placard on his desk stated his name was Sheriff Tom Wilkie.

Behind the sheriff, on the wall, were a variety of brightly colored abstract paintings that seemed out of place. Gracie thought any art in a place like that would be a motel style landscape, or the Sheriff would have a painting of a bucking bronco or some such.

"Let me get this straight. You was robbing the place, and you're the Snapshot Bandits."

"Burglars, but yeah."

"So, you were in the house, and you found a freezer full of body parts, and you seen a person, man or woman you're uncertain, sawing a woman's head off. You kids ain't been smoking nothing, have you?"

"We saw it."

"We thought this was the right thing to do. Murder kind of trumps us stealing a few items, taking photos," Gracie said as she dropped them on Sherif Wilkie's desk.

"I suppose it does," Sheriff Wilkie said, and pushed the photos on the desk around like he was mixing cards. "These look like what you say you saw, but who's to say they're real?"

"They're real all right," Gracie said.

A knock came at the door and Sheriff Wilkie pushed the array of photos into a pile at the corner of his desk.

"Come on in."

A young Hispanic woman with a curtain of thick black hair cascaded down the shoulders of her beige uniform. A stiff black necktie and gold badge glimmered underneath the fluorescents. The corners of her wide mouth peeled back as she spoke.

"What have we here?"

"Deputy," Wilkie said, "these here kids are the Snapshot Burglars."

The deputy scanned them both. Her face didn't show much.

"These kids claim they might can help us out with those disappearances we been having, least I think if what they're saying is true, could explain them. I'm sure they would be up for a little trade. What say you? We let a few things slide, you show us where this so-called butcher lives."

"Butcher, huh?" the deputy said.

"They got photos of body parts in a freezer."

"Say they do?"

"Look real, too."

"We show you where we took those photos, how much of a favor will you do us?" Trevor asked.

"Well, you won't get off scot-free, but you might end up with shorter jail time and a smaller fine. I can say some good things about you, doing the right thing and all, and that might help."

"Might?" Trevor said.

"Best I can offer you." The sheriff turned his attention to the deputy, tapped his finger on the stack of snapshots. "Look, here, Ace."

The deputy reached for the photographs.

"What do you think?" Sheriff Wilkie asked.

"Look like the real deal, you ask me."

Gracie nodded, "They're real alright. Come with us, and we'll take you there."

"Alright," Sheriff Wilkie said. "We'll follow you."

In the daylight, there was a part of Gracie that felt it had all been a nightmare, but the thing was, she and Trevor could not have had the same nightmare.

They parked on the hill overlooking the pond and the house. The sheriff and deputy pulled up beside them. The sheriff got out and went around to the driver's window of the camper. Trevor rolled the window down, seat belt strapped tight across his chest said, "The house across the pond. That's it."

"Look here," Sheriff Wilkie said. "You two are coming with us. You're felons, and I don't like the idea of you running off and leading us on a wild goose chase."

"There wouldn't be any point to us doing this, letting you know who we are, if we hadn't seen something. You have our names."

"I got your license plate number, too."

"There you are," Trevor said.

The deputy was out of the car now, her long black hair hanging down from under her hat, the sun flaring against it like a wet crow wing. She strolled over to join them.

"Be that as it may," Sheriff Wilkie said, "you're coming with us, so get your ass out of the camper and let's go."

So down the hill they went, Sheriff in the lead, Gracie and Trevor in the center, the deputy bringing up the rear.

"So you picked the lock, then what?" Sheriff Wilkie asked.

"We went in and made a sandwich," Trevor said.

"A sandwich?" the sheriff said.

"Yeah," Trevor said. "It's kind of our trademark, besides the snapshots."

The sheriff stopped walking and looked a question back at the deputy, Ace.

"Yeah," Ace said. "That's what the reports say. The Snapshot Burglars always make a sandwich, sometimes shit in the toilet and don't flush."

"That was him," Gracie said.

"One time, and that's because there was low water pressure," Trevor said. "It wasn't a statement."

They started walking again. The sheriff said, "Okay. You made a sandwich, and then you went to the cellar and found a freezer full of body parts."

"Exactly," Gracie said. "Shouldn't you be writing this down?"

The sheriff tapped his head. "All up here. Besides, it's not like you won't be answering the same questions again."

"And again and again," Deputy Ace said. "Might even ask you two to answer in interpretive dance. And you'll do it."

"In some kind of costume if we ask," Sheriff Wilkie said.

"Do you know this place?" Gracie asked the sheriff.

"I don't think so. You Ace?"

"Nope," Ace said.

"Now show me exactly what you did to get inside."

"Don't we need a warrant or something?" Gracie said.

"Not in these parts. Not with what you found."

Gracie worked the lock with her lock picking tools. It only took her a moment, and then they were inside. The air freshener was still thick in the air.

"So sandwich, then pantry?" Sheriff Wilkie asked again.

Trevor nodded.

Wilkie walked to the pantry, opened the door. Ace stepped inside, shone her light around and pushed at the panel in the back, sliding it aside, revealing the stairs. The sick orange light from below was visible, the color of spoiled honey. The pine smell was really strong down there, so thick it turned her stomach. Gracie thought of it as a portal to hell.

"Shouldn't you check the rest of the house?" Trevor said.

"You be burglars, we'll be police," Sheriff Wilkie said. "I want you to show me the exact place you took those photos."

"I'm not going down there," Gracie said.

Ace patted the butt of the service weapon in her holster, glanced back over her shoulder at them. "You'll be fine. We'll be with you, and we're armed."

"You lead the way, Ace," Sheriff Wilkie said, stepping aside. "I'll bring up the rear. I want to keep a check on our burglars."

Before she started down, Ace lifted her hair, slipped a band over it to knot it into a ponytail. Gracie squeezed Trevor's arm. Why hadn't they searched the rest of the house as Trevor suggested? And how had Wilkie and Ace known exactly where to go, and which door was the pantry without asking them the way in?

And then if Gracie harbored any doubts, she lost them when she saw the tattoo on Ace's bare neck.

Gracie was telling her body to run, but her legs wouldn't move, and by the time the signal from the brain was strong enough to make them function, Ace was already down the stairs, and Sheriff Wilkie, seeming to take his time about it, grabbed a can of corn from a shelf in the pantry and used it to hit Trevor in the forehead.

Trevor let out a long sigh, like the sound of a dying engine on its last road trip, stumbled to his knees, a hand to his bleeding face, said, "What the hell?"

Before Gracie could fight or flee, the sheriff grabbed her by her hair and pulled her past him, causing her to fall over Trevor, and onto the stairs where she bounced down each step, cracking a stair step as she went, finally landing on the hard floor below, stunned.

Then Trevor came thumping down the stairs behind her, propelled by Sheriff Wilkie's foot. He stopped rolling, stopped moving, and lay in a heap on the bottom step of the stairs, not far from where Gracie lay.

Looking up, she saw Sheriff Wilkie walking casually down the stairs, grinning like a Cheshire Cat with a canary in its teeth. When he reached the stair step she had cracked, nestled his foot on top of it, the stair cracked again with a sound like gunfire, and his leg went through the break in the stairs. Gracie felt a slight bit of satisfaction when she saw the smile rip off his face to be replaced by a wide-open mouth making a scream so high and wild it made the hair on the back of her neck stand up like porcupine quills. He was hung there, and a jagged piece of the step had gone through his groin and blood was gushing everywhere.

Ace, who had been in some other part of the basement, came rushing out then, and Gracie barely made it to her feet in time to be on the receiving end of a mallet Ace was swinging.

The world turned white, not dark, and then there were stars for an instant, and then there was pain and blackness.

When Gracie awoke she was lying on her back, strapped to a table, and in an instant she realized it was the same place she had seen the woman strapped down before Ace took the hatchet to her. A rancid smell filled her nostrils. There was a cacophony of light and noise. Banging drums and ringing cymbals. Flashing colored lights and a strobe that blinked off and on and made the ceiling crawl with light and shadow. Flies fluttered around her face, looking for a place to land.

"You little bitch," Ace said.

Gracie turned her head in the direction of the voice. Ace stood nearby, nude except for the leather apron, a hacksaw in her hand. She hadn't bothered with the hood. Next to Ace near the table, there was a tray on a rolling platform, and on the tray were shiny sharp objects.

"I'm going to make it last on you, bitch. I'm going to saw slow. I'm going to slit a hole in your stomach and ease your guts out slowly with pliers. I'm going to clip off your toes with hedge clippers. I'm going to pull out your teeth one by one. I'm going to pop your eyeballs onto your cheeks, let them dangle on their tendons. I'm going to heat you up with a leather burning set, put my initials on your lilly-white ass. I'm going to—"

"That's quite a list," Gracie said, and soon as the words came out of her mouth, she thought, don't agitate the crazy person, but it was done. On the other hand, Gracie thought, if I'm going to die, I might as well get a few quips in. But now she went silent. The gravity of her situation hung over her like...Well, like the strange thing on cables above her, swinging slowly around and around, coated in colored and strobing lights.

It covered the entire ceiling. There were lots of cables used. There were withered, dried body parts, heads and arms and legs and feet, and they had all been stitched together with wire, making a unique artistic display. Intestines had been dried into dark ropes, and they twisted through the body parts like snakes. It all moved slowly on some sort of wood and metal rig coiled with wires. The colored lights and the pounding and clanging intensified the horror of it.

Then she saw Sheriff Wilkie's head. It was boiled pink and missing the eyes, which had been filled with red Christmas tree bulbs. His head was wearing his cowboy hat, and his sheriff's badge was pinned to his forehead. His penis, or someone's penis, had been fastened under his chin by red wire, sewn right into the lower jaw as if it were a wormy beard.

"It's to honor him," Ace said. "He had sensibilities you would never understand. We were meant to be together, but you killed him."

"Me? The stairs broke. He fell."

"Your fault, though. I have made him part of the tapestry of life we were working on. One of many of our artistic creations. He would have appreciated that. You need to see the rest," Ace said. "Our art project was private, but since you'll soon be part of it."

Ace came closer to the table, worked a crank. It raised the table, lifting Gracie's head and shoulders up. She tried to move her feet and arms, but the straps held her fast.

"Look and see what my beloved and I have created."

Ace did something else to make the table swivel, spin actually. As it spun Gracie saw propped up by old boards and wire the remainder of a nude, decaying man. His once-bloated body was ruptured and his guts, a putrid pile of goo and bones, were piled in a wash tub that was held up by a rope around the dead man's neck. There was a woman too. She hung limp on a spinning display of bone and wire. Her body was tightly wrapped in green Christmas wire and multicolored Christmas bulbs. Decaying flesh dripped from her headless frame as she moved around Gracie like a parade float.

There was the body of a young man, and he had been rigged with metal extensions that caused his arms to move. There were drumsticks in his hands, and they beat at a big drum fastened about his neck in the same manner as the man with the tub of decaying guts. Another body, the woman she had seen on the table the day before, was sawed apart and fastened back together with rods and wire. Like the drummer, she moved, pounded cymbals. Flies weaved in and out of the mess like a squadron of bombers.

All the bodies were linked by barb wire and electric wire of different colors. There were creaking hinges, rattling chains, grinding gears and pulsing lights. The corpse display moved around her as she spun on the swiveling table like a macabre merry-go-round of flesh and bone, guts and gristle. When she stopped spinning, Gracie felt sick and dizzy. The circle of decay continued its noisy, brightly lit parade as it dollied around her on its metal track. So not only had she been moving, so had the corpses.

Ace bent over Gracie, said, "I added my beloved to this, and soon, I'll add yours. Trevor. That was his name, right? Little fucker broke his neck when he fell down the stairs, so I missed having fun with him. But when I get to him, I plan to fill his mouth with shit and sew it up. I'm actually going to shit in his mouth myself."

"All of this is about an art project?" Gracie said. She didn't want to talk, but she feared not talking. Anything to stall for time.

"A masterful project, using the bodies of illegal aliens, strays and malcontents and assholes and criminals who had it coming, one way or another. The government could have given them their punishments for theft and murder, peeping toms and troublemakers, run away kids who didn't understand the meaning of respect and family. They could have, but they didn't. We wanted those losers to be our personal, artistic display of truth and justice and the American way. We love art, our first love, but neither of us were able to express it. Didn't understand our role in art until we met. Our meeting was an artistic blossom made up of human flesh, and a fulfillment of dreams. You spoiled our work together, you little bitch. So, what I'm going to do, is I'm going to remove your clothes with very sharp scissors, and I believe I may manage to poke you with them a bit. Then I'll slowly saw one of your legs off at the knee and after I'm coated in your hot squirting blood, I'll apply a tourniquet, and that will keep you from bleeding out. Give me time for more sawing and cutting. Then I'll sew your Trevor's balls between your legs, and you'll still be alive while I do it. I've learned tricks. I'll have so much fun with you the heavens will cry. Art and revenge, little bitch."

Ace had turned ecstatic, a little girl displaying her schoolwork.

Coming up behind Ace, moving slow, staggering, was Trevor. His head dangled to one side and rested on his shoulder. One of his knees was bending out to the side as he walked. He held a chunk of the broken stair step in his hand, a solid, jagged piece of wood.

Ace, hearing the drag of Trevor's shoe, turned too late.

The board fragment in Trevor's hand flashed out. The strobe light made the board look as if its descending arc was a series of stills cut from a film. There was a cracking sound as the board made contact with her head. Ace dropped the saw, stumbled to one knee. Trevor hit her again, and this time she rolled over on her side and grunted, her ass sticking out from under the raised apron like a baby head peeking around a curtain.

Trevor, even weaker than moments before, made his way to the table, unfastened the wrist strap on Gracie's right hand.

"Oh, Trevor," Gracie said. "I'm so sorry."

As Trevor reached across her for the other wrist restraint, there was a cracking sound, and his already loose head swung forward on his chest, and he collapsed across her. He made a coughing noise, then there was a gurgling sound, like someone drowning. Slowly his body weight carried him off her and he dropped on the floor.

Gracie sat up, used her free hand to unclamp her wrist, and then her feet. She swung her legs off the table, and that's when Ace hopped up from her position, like a frog leaping for a fly, grasped Gracie's throat with both hands, and pushed her back against the table.

Gracie struggled to break free, but without results. Ace was strong.

Gracie reached out and grabbed at something on the rolling instrument table. It was scissors. She jabbed at Ace's side. Once. Twice.

Ace bellowed and leaped back. There was a hatchet under the table, and she reached for that.

Gracie grabbed the rolling instrument table, pushed it hard into Ace, knocking her back, causing her to trip over Trevor's body and drop the hatchet. Gracie picked up the hatchet Ace had dropped, and turning the blade away, hit Ace with the back part of the hatchet in the middle of her forehead like she was driving a railroad spike.

When Ace awoke, Gracie was standing nearby. The noise and lights had been turned off. The bodies were no longer spinning about the table.

35

"Hey there sleepy head. Well, it's almost like you got two heads, way you're swelled up. But I got to give it to you. You took some serious blows, and you're still spry. Or would be, if you weren't held down with those straps."

Ace, as if on cue, struggled against her restraints.

Gracie held up her Polaroid camera.

"I went back to the camper to get my camera. I figured you could use a little nap. So I took my time. Had myself a peanut butter sandwich too. Blood sugar was a little low."

"You bitch," Ace said.

"Nailed it," Gracie said.

She lifted the camera then, flashed a photo.

She waited a moment as it ejected from the camera, took it, shook it, and watched as it developed.

"Oh, that's a good one. But, woman to woman, you might want to have some work done, jaw's starting to sag a little. You know, you could get the skin pulled back to make your face tighter. Oh, wait. I can do that for you. By the way. This photo, I like to call it the *before* shot."

Gracie placed the camera on the floor with the photo, stood up straight holding the hatchet. She lifted the hatchet over her head, said, "And in a moment, I'm going to take the *after* photo."

Gracie was amazed how loud Ace could scream.

The Devil in the Details

BEN MONROE

The sky over West Hollywood was a riot of orange and gold as the sun sank in the west. Tom Haggerty was inching his faded yellow VW Beetle convertible down Sunset Boulevard and thinking about how the sky would be beautiful if he didn't know it was really a filthy blanket of smog. He took a drag off the last half an inch of his Marlboro, tossed the filtered stub over the door where it hit the strip and bounced with a brief spray of sparks. Despite the light breeze, the fall air was dry and warm. He cursed himself for a damn fool for taking the top down. Could have been nice and cozy with the air-conditioning on, but now he was sweltering and sucking fumes from hundreds of other cars on the road.

He missed the East Coast. The Saturday night before Halloween there should be fall colors, the crisp tang of approaching winter, and the smell of burning leaves in the air. But in L.A. it was palm trees and sunshine and smog. Hell, he'd even spent two hours at the beach that morning.

The Beetle was the first thing he bought with his own money after moving to California for college. Tom had earned a decent scholarship, and his folks were supplying the rest for tuition, room, and board. But he also earned some money on the side teaching guitar lessons to local high school kids. He'd wanted to study music at UCLA, but his parents wouldn't have anything to do with it. His dad thought music was a waste of time, and his mom thought the rock music Tom loved was the tool of the devil. "You keep playing that rock and roll, and you'll wind up in the hot place, Tommy!" she used to scold him.

So he kept the guitar lessons to himself. His dad had asked about his money situation a few times and Tom just said he was earning a few extra bucks tutoring. He didn't even have to lie.

Marcie's going to kill me, he thought, as he popped the clutch, pressed the gas and inched forward another few feet. They had a date tonight—a big deal one, too. They'd been dating for a few months and tonight Marcie wanted to introduce Tom to some of her friends from Day Star. They were some kind of self-help group, near as he could tell. They sounded sort of like EST or Lifespring, probably into that primal scream stuff.

"Should be a hell of a party," she'd said, when she invited him. The impression Tom got from hearing her talk about them was that the Day Star people were sort of hippy-dippy, but according to Marcie they always had good dope. Real "consciousness-raising shit" as she'd said a few times before. He wanted to be at her apartment in twenty minutes. But the way traffic was snarled on Sunset, it would take at least an hour.

Fumes were chugging out of the exhaust pipe of the car in front of him, belching out under the "Reagan/Bush '84" bumper sticker. Fat chance, Ronnie-boy, Tom thought. Nobody's falling for your BS again.

Peering ahead, he saw he was approaching the intersection of Sunset Boulevard and North Fairfax. The light turned green, and the traffic inched forward. Tom saw his break and quickly zipped around the lane of traffic ahead of him, taking over the bus lane. He barreled past half a dozen cars and swerved right onto North Fairfax. Should have taken back streets, he thought. Got off Sunset before I hit the Strip and all the damned tourists. He decided to go up into the hills and take the back way.

Traffic was lighter here, and he shot up two blocks with no effort. He pulled into an Exxon station by the side of the road and parked near a phone booth on the side of the building. Tom fished in his pockets for change as he walked toward the phone, then slid a couple of dimes into the coin slot and paused. He couldn't remember Marcie's number. It was in his address book, though, which he pulled from his hip pocket and thumbed through it until he found her name. A few button presses later and the phone was ringing.

Tom leaned against the cinderblock wall of the Exxon, phone handset cradled between his ear and shoulder. Traffic flowed steadily along in front of the station, not nearly as bad as the snarl he'd been in before. Across the street was a two-story building with a little bodega on the bottom floor, windows filled with bright red strands of dried chilis, and a hotel above it. Rates by the Hour/Day/Week! a sign said next to an ominous dark staircase leading up. Tom thought it looked like the sort of place where you'd get crabs just walking through the lobby. The sun was almost down and through the gloom Tom saw a mural on the wall of the building facing him, depicting a suntanned, beach-blond California surfer dude, wearing bright red Jams with a white tropical hibiscus pattern, a pair of jet-black Wayfarers, and hanging ten over the edge of a surfboard. Automatic street lamps flicked to life as the sun set, and Tom noticed that someone had crudely spray-painted devil horns and a goatee on the surfer and the name "El Diablo!" on the board he was riding.

He started thinking about something he'd read in the newspaper a few days ago, about some dogs the cops had found eviscerated in the 6th Street viaducts. The reporters called it a satanic ritual, but they called everything satanic lately.

"Hello?" a distracted-sounding female voice said from the other end of the phone.

Tom stood up, pushing away from the wall, turning away from the strange graffiti. "Oh, hey, Marcie? It's Tom."

A pause. Tom heard muffled voices distantly through the handset. "Hey, baby," Marcie said. "Where are you? Everyone's here already."

Tom let out a long sigh, "Ah, I'm sorry. Look I got stuck in traffic on Sunset but I'm on my way. Just wanted to call and let you know I'm late, but I'll be there."

Another pause, longer this time. "Oh…oh, that's okay," Marcie said. "See you soon?"

She's out of it, Tom though. Must've already gotten started on the "good shit." "Absolutely," Tom said. "You need me to bring anything? There's a grocery across the street if you want me to pick something up."

More muffled voices. Marcie must have put the handset against her chest or covered the microphone with her hand. "Malcam says bring whatever you want."

Malcam says, Tom thought. How many times had he heard that phrase starting a sentence out of Marcie's mouth lately. "Okay, sure, baby. Be there as soon as I can."

"Rad," Marcie replied. "See you soon." With a rattle as she placed the handset back on the receiver, the phone went dead.

"Fucking L.A. weirdos," Tom muttered as he hung up the phone. He walked to the sidewalk, waited for a break in the traffic and then dashed across the street to the bodega. As he stepped up onto the sidewalk in front of it, he looked up at the mural. The surfing devil glared down at him, its gleeful smile strangely sinister in the cold yellow light of the streetlights. Written on a sign taped to the bodega's chrome-framed glass door was No Masks!/¡Sin Máscaras! in wobbly Sharpie script.

Tom entered the store, the bell over the door tinkling as he opened it. The smell of exotic spices, and the glare of neon and flickering fluorescent light overwhelmed him as he entered the bodega. A middle-aged Latino looked up disinterestedly at him as the door swung shut. Tom walked down the aisle toward him and said, "¿Cerveza, por favor?"

"Alli," the man said. He waved a finger down the aisle toward the back of the shop.

A few minutes later Tom was back outside the shop with a case of Corona under one arm, and a fistful of Slim Jims in his hand. Waiting for a break in the traffic, he looked back up at the graffitied mural, the devilish surfer suspended eternally on that tasty wave. He remembered the news, the dogs. A chill inched up his spine and he shuddered.

Over the car's radio, Huey Lewis was asking his girlfriend if that was it, and to just please let him know. And Tom was gnawing on a Slim Jim as he cruised up into the Hollywood Hills, past the homes of rock gods and movie stars. Lights glowed in houses set way back from the street. The Saturday night parties hadn't quite gotten started yet, but he knew that in a few hours they'd be going strong and hard.

As he passed a particularly large mansion, Tom imagined what it would be like to be partying in one of those houses. Rubbing elbows with Seger, Henley, Fogarty, and the rock gods who looked down over Hollywood from their Olympian perches.

He gunned the engine and tossed the Slim Jim's empty wrapper from the car. Tom had the map to Marcie's place on the seat next to him, the path traced in fluorescent pink highlighter. He'd stopped and refigured it while at the gas station, since he was going the long way to her place, a road he'd never taken before. Tom wound through the hills, the sun long since set, and saw the gleaming, glittering lights of Hollywood stretching out below him.

He began a slow descent, following the map, then a few turns, and slowed down as he approached Marcie's house. When he reached her block, he saw rows of cars parked on both sides of the street in front of her house. He drove past her little one-story blue-and-white craftsman-style bungalow. A strange orange light flooded the porch and he could see a pair of carved pumpkins next to the front door. He parked at the end of the block, Kenny Rogers' "Islands in the Stream" was just starting on the radio as Tom shut the car off. Thank the Lord, Tom thought as Kenny's voice disappeared like an afterthought.

He grabbed a pack of cigarettes from the glove box, tapped a Marlboro out and lit it up. Tom took a long drag, feeling the smoothness of the smoke filling his lungs, then let out a long stream of smoke. The street was empty aside from the cars lining the road. The cliché of nobody walking in L.A. struck Tom as somewhat amusing, yet true more often than not. He got out of the car, adjusted his thin black tie and pulled on his jacket, shoving the rolled-up cuffs up over his elbows. Grabbing the case of Corona, he walked down the center of the street toward Marcie's house, whistling "Mirror in the Bathroom" as he strolled along the sun-warmed asphalt.

He could hear the sounds of the party as he approached the address. The Eagles' "Hotel California" was floating through the night air on a haze of marijuana smoke. He unlatched the low gate and walked along the path leading to Marcie's porch. The porch light was on, but covered with a thin sheet of translucent orange plastic which gave the porch the strange glow he'd noticed earlier as he drove by. The front door opened just as he was reaching to knock.

Standing in front of him was a tall man, bald with a black goatee. He was wearing a long red robe with a high, rounded collar. Tom looked him up and down. "Who are you supposed to be, Ming the Merciless?"

The bald man scowled. "No, Anton LeVey," he said with a thick, gravelly accent which Tom couldn't quite place.

"My mistake," Tom said and moved to enter the house.

The bald man stepped to the side to block him. "And who are you supposed to be?"

Tom stopped, took a drag on his cigarette and blew a cloud of smoke in the guy's face. "Marcie's boyfriend. She's expecting me."

The man stepped back, coughing and waving at the smoke. "I see. I suppose I expected you to be a little more…festive?"

Tom walked past him. Shit, he thought, it's a Halloween party. "Yeah, well, I stopped dressing up for Halloween about the same time I started shaving." He handed the guy his jacket. "But this is working for you, man. If I see the Hawkmen I'll tell them you said hi."

Tom heard voices and music down the hall and walked toward it. He passed a dimly lit kitchen and left the case of Corona by the fridge, taking two bottles with him. Leaving the kitchen he continued down the hall until he entered the small living room with wide glass doors open onto the back patio. Black lace draped over the lamps casting strange spiderweb-like shadows onto the walls and ceiling of the dimly lit room. As he entered the room, zombies, witches, a Frankenstein monster, a few generic vampires and two Draculas turned to watch him. A wolfman looked up from his crouch over a bubbling hookah.

Tom suddenly felt self-conscious. He didn't know it was a Halloween party, just thought it was a little get-together. He'd just assumed that nobody was dressing up, because they were a bunch of grown-ups and it wasn't actually Halloween until Monday. But here he was, surrounded by pale faces, dark, kohl-rimmed eyes, and flowing black velvet and leather. "Um, hey," he said, surveying the room. "Anyone know where Marcie is?"

The wolfman stood up from his crouch, walked toward Tom and let out a cloud of marijuana smoke in his face. "Saw her out back a while ago," he mumbled around a mouthful of plastic fangs, "I'll show you," and turned to walk across the room.

41

Tom followed, soon back out in the night air. Marcie's yard was small, with a few benches and small tables. Jasmine vines crawled along the wooden slat fence which surrounded it, filling the warm night air with a heady perfume. Wolfman waved to where Marcie was sitting with three other women and two guys. "Thanks, Fangface," Tom said. "Watch out for silver bullets." Wolfman turned and went back into the house, leaving Tom outside with Marcie and her companions.

Compared to the freak show inside the house, the fashion choices of the people on the patio were sedate. Mostly denim, T-shirts with band logos. The two guys were wearing sunglasses and one had a rumpled brown leather outback-style hat pushed back on his brow. No costumes at all, unless they were trying to pull off a bunch of stoners. And if they were, they were doing a great job of it. They were sitting on low chairs around a small brick fire pit, the dying embers licking them with orange light. A boombox sat precariously on a wooden crate, pumping out AC/DC's "Highway to Hell."

Marcie was wearing her trademark black tights and off-the-shoulder sweatshirt, her long blonde hair pulled back in a side ponytail that streamed over her shoulder. They were dressed for comfort, not Halloween, in that deliberately casual way common to L.A. The group was talking quietly, laughing, and passing a small wooden pipe around. Tom almost felt guilty stepping into such an intimate gathering. Marcie was just taking a drag from it, using a neon-pink Bic lighter to burn the bowl when she looked up and saw Tom approaching.

"Hey, baby!" she said, smiling crookedly. "Glad you made it."

Tom gave her a quick hug and a kiss on the cheek. "Sorry I took so long. Sunset was a bitch, so I took mostly back roads through the Canyon." When he stood up, he noticed the others had gone quiet, and were looking at him. "Hey everyone, I'm Tom," he said, raising his hand to wave at the group.

They waved back and a half-hearted chorus of "Hey, Tom" sputtered around the circle.

He raised the two beers, "Anyone want one? I left the rest of the case in the kitchen."

"Sure man, thanks," the guy in the outback hat said, reaching for one of the bottles. He pulled a keyring from his jeans pocket. A bottle opener hung from it along with his keys. He popped the bottle open and handed the opener to Tom.

"Tom, this is Malcam," Marcie said, as Tom popped the cap off his bottle with a sputtering hiss.

"Oh, hey, man, nice to meet you," Tom said, then held out his bottle. Malcam clinked the lip of his bottle against Tom's.

"Cheers, man," Malcam said, taking a long draw from the bottle.

Tom sipped from his. "I didn't realize it was a party tonight," he said. "Thought it was just a small gathering."

"Ugh," Marcie said, rolling her eyes in disdain. "My loser roommate's having a Halloween party tonight. Didn't realize until people started showing up."

The rest nodded. One woman, a tall brunette wearing a halter top with the Aerosmith logo across it reached for the pipe Marcie was holding. "No biggie," she said. "Too nice a night to be cooped up inside, anyway."

"For sure, Debbie," Marcie said, and handed her the small wooden pipe.

Tom took another sip of beer and then noticed that Malcam had almost finished his. "Just kind of surprised me when I got here. Thought I'd stumbled into the Prom Night of the Living Dead or something."

Malcam laughed at that, a wheezing cackle. After a moment the rest started laughing along with him. "Oh, man," Malcam said, wiping a tear from his cheek. "That's rich. Prom Night of the Living Dead, that's a good one."

"Good one, man," the other guy said.

Debbie exhaled a cloud of pot smoke which wafted into the air, the smell mingling with the scent of jasmine. "What's her deal, anyway? Who knew she had so many friends?"

"Beats me," Marcie said, reaching for the pipe. "She got a bit part in the *A-Team* or something and threw a party to celebrate."

Another woman—a bottle-blonde Madonna-wannabe—turned to look back into the house. "You think she's got a good agent?" she said.

"Forget her," Malcam said to the blonde. "Your time will come. And sooner than you think."

Tom pulled up one of the patio chairs and took a seat next to her. "Well, I mean good for her chasing her dream and all, I guess."

"And how about you, Tom?" Malcam said, pausing to swallow the rest of his beer. "What's your dream, man?"

All eyes suddenly turned to Tom. He took a swig of his Corona and leaned forward. "Well, that's the ten-thousand-dollar question, isn't it?"

Marcie rubbed her hand up and down his arm, from shoulder to elbow and back again. "Tom's a senior at UCLA."

Tom nodded. "Environmental Science. Maybe someday I'll figure out how to do something about all this damn smog."

Malcam leaned forward. "But that's not your dream, is it? Smog and pollution, that's here to stay, you know that. But what's really in your head? What's the dream that keeps you up at night?"

Tom sat up, feeling a little dazed, a bit off kilter. "What...what do you mean?"

The group was staring intently at Malcam now, enraptured faces looking up at him. "I mean, man, what makes your soul sing? If money were no object, what would your heart whisper to you?"

Tom's heart pulsed in his chest, a pressure building, uncomfortable and otherworldly. "I guess…" he said, "I mean, I dabble in poetry a little." Instantly the pressure subsided, he felt a wave of release wash over him.

"The man's a poet!" Malcam said, clapping his hands together for emphasis. "I knew it. You look like someone deeper than an environmental engineer. The world burns, and the poets cry to the heavens! You got a favorite poet, Tom?"

"A few, I guess," he said. "Thomas, Baldwin, some of Plath's later stuff, I guess."

"But?" Malcam said. "You still sound like you're hiding something."

"I guess what I really love is the poetry of song lyrics."

"Hey, there it is," Malcam said, and the rest of the group nodded appreciatively. "Like me, man. See I love stuff like Milton. Paradise Lost is a hoot, you know? And Ginsberg's Howl…man. Great stuff. But these guys," he said, pointing to the boombox where the final chords of "Highway to Hell" were just fading away, "it's like they're singing just to me."

Tom smiled and then drained the last of his beer. "Rock and roll will never die," he said.

"Ain't that the truth," Malcam replied. "You're all right Tom. You've got a good head on your shoulders." Malcam took the pipe from Marcie. He sucked at it, dragging smoke deep into his lungs. "Your problem," he grunted, holding the smoke in. "Is that your mind's closed," he hissed as he released a cloud of thick, bright green smoke. It shot forward like a stream of venom, the cloud bursting over Tom's face, and invading his nose and throat. The acrid stink of sulfur mingled with the sweet funk of the pot smoke. "You just need to open it a crack. Then let some light in."

Light exploded in Tom's mind. Everything he saw was incandescent, glowing with phantom fire. The sound of pealing bells overwhelmed him, and his skin suddenly felt warm, then hot. Sweat poured from him in rivers as he slid out of his chair to the ground below him. He felt hands around his head, lowering him gently to the ground. Lights danced in his mind and before his eyes. His vision wavered, swimming in liquid golden currents. From both a distance and deep within his mind he heard Marcie's voice, slow, drawn out, "You'll be fine, baby." He gasped great lungfuls of air but couldn't catch his breath. "You'll be fine…"

Filling his vision, he saw Malcam's face. At least it was a face reminiscent of Malcam. It had his nose, his chin. But when it lowered its sunglasses, Tom saw the green, slitted eyes of a serpent staring back at him.

And then he drifted, carried away on wings of light across space and time, a mote of dust amongst the cosmos.

Golden sunlight gleamed through the windows of Tom's bedroom. He sprawled lengthwise across his bed, still in the same clothes he'd worn to Marcie's. His mouth was dry and his head throbbed. Tom opened his eyes slowly, as they too were gummy and dry. It took him a moment to realize that the light was shining in from the western window, not the north-facing one that was usually glowing with morning sun. He raised his hand, bringing it close to his face to check the time on his black plastic Casio wristwatch. His first shock was that it was 5:03 p.m. His second was the date: Monday, October 31. He didn't remember getting home but somehow between the party at Marcie's on Saturday night and now, he'd lost a day and a half.

"What the hell?" he muttered, then slowly got up from the bed. He noticed his shoes were missing when his bare feet hit the ground. Sitting on the edge of the bed he saw them tucked next to the door to his bedroom. He stood and walked across the room, out into the hall past the small bathroom and into the kitchen where he poured himself a large glass of water and guzzled it. A second glass began to slake his thirst. As he was putting the empty plastic cup down, he noticed the numeral "2" flashing a red LED pulse on his answering machine.

He clicked the PLAY button on the machine and waited a moment while the message tape rewound to begin playback. A click as it reached the end of the tape. There was a high-pitched electric beep and then, "Hey, baby, hope you're feeling okay. Hope you had fun at the party, anyway. You were pretty out of it when I drove you home. Listen, we're having another get-together on Halloween up at Leo Carrillo State Beach outside of Malibu. Malcam asked me to invite you. He seems to really dig you. Hope you'll be there. It should be really spiritual. Malcam says he's got…" The message cut out. A moment later the beep again followed by "Sorry, got cut off. Hate these machines. Anyway, be there around nine. We'll be on the beach down at Sequit Point. It's just past Mulholland on the One. There should be signs for it near the beach. See you!"

He looked at his watch again. He could be at the beach in an hour. Plenty of time. Something was definitely off about Malcam, and Tom decided he was going to this shindig.

Waves crashed against the dark beach, echoing in the mouth of a cave in the cliff wall nearby. Starlight glittered in the clear night sky, though the moon was a dim, waning crescent. In the distance, twinkling lights betrayed the passing of working fishermen and Halloween party boats.

Tom leaned against the cliff wall, watching the sandy path which led down to the beach from a small parking lot. A half-smoked cigarette wavered between his fingers, as his hand trembled. He blew a cloud of smoke out, watching it drift across the beach, and dissipate into the night sky. Then he heard voices, quiet, muttering, but approaching him. Shoes crunching on gravel and grit as people walked toward him from the lot.

Then he saw six figures approaching, their shapes dark in the nearly moonless night. But as they approached, Tom could recognize them. Malcam in his rumpled hat led the way. Tom recognized the others from the party on Saturday. Marcie was in the middle, but her usual exuberance had left her. She seemed sedated, walking with a shuffling, almost trance-like cadence. And then Tom noticed that Marcie and Debbie, the brunette from the party, were leading a pair of goats, had them leashed up with two lengths of rope.

As the six and the goats stepped off the wooden planks at the bottom of the path, Tom moved away from the cliff wall and strode toward them. The group turned as one toward his approach, and for a moment, he caught a glimmer of poisonous green light in Malcam's eyes.

"Tom," Malcam said. "So happy you joined us."

Tom stalked toward Malcam. "What the hell did you do to me?" he said. "What was that voodoo shit you blew in my face?"

The six other followers circled Malcam and Tom, taking up positions that made Tom feel nervous and threatened. Like an animal with its bloody foot caught in a trap. Marcie and the Debbie tugged on the leads to the goats. Malcam stepped forward. "I just want to help you, Tom," he said. "Help you open your mind and see that there's more to the world than you've witnessed with your own limited senses."

"This is bullshit," Tom said, turning to Marcie. He stepped toward her, and the group mirrored his action, stepping toward him. "Marcie, baby. Can't you see this guy's nuts?"

Marcie's eyes darted from Tom to Malcam and back. "You don't understand, baby," she said. She moved toward Tom, took his hands in hers. "But you will, I promise."

Tom felt strong hands on his shoulders, his arms. Dragging him down to the ground, pinning him to the damp sand. Then a voice, a rhythmic chanting in a language that Tom didn't recognize. But something about that guttural tongue sent shrieking fear through Tom's mind. Terror stirred in the small spaces at the base of his brain, squirmed like a toad baking on a desert freeway. The language was older than civilization, older than mankind.

Around him Malcam's followers threw back their heads, spread out their arms in supplication. They joined in the song, shrieking that awful primeval chant into the night. Tom tried to get up, to run away, some unseen force had him pinned to the ground, pressed to the earth as if trapped under a great invisible paw. He felt the breath pushed from his lungs, his blood struggling to move through his body.

Then as Tom watched, Marcie and the other woman pulled long, curved knives from behind themselves. The knives shone like silver in the starlight, and Tom watched, transfixed, as they quickly slit the throats of the goats. Blood sprayed across the sand, across Tom's face and chest as the goats fell soundlessly, kicking and twitching and then still.

Malcam stood before him, shredding his grimy T-shirt, raking at his clothing with cruelly barbed taloned hands. Bronze horns burst from Malcam's brow, sending rivers of blood down his face. Malcam looked down at Tom and grinned, showing a mouth full of black, serrated shark-like fangs.

"Tom," the gravelly voice said, pouring from that awful mouth. "I've walked the Earth in penance for far too long. For eons." The thing crouched over Tom, green slitted snake-like eyes staring into his mind. Tom watched as a third eye split open in the creature's forehead, forming a trinity of glaring verdant evil.

"All I ask," it said. "Is to be worshipped, to be followed." A black snake-like tongue slithered from its mouth. "Pledge yourself to me, and you'll have anything you ever dreamed of."

Tom forced his head to the side, where Marcie was swaying back and forth to the rhythm of the chanting circle. "Marcie," he said, straining his voice. "Help me! This is insane!"

Marcie broke the cadence and looked down at him. "I am helping you, Tom. Stop fighting it, just let it happen."

A clawed hand gripped his face, forcing it back. Malcam was inches away, sulfur on his furnace-like breath bursting into Tom's face, singing his hair.

"No!" Tom screamed. "No, this can't be happening!" He forced his eyes shut as he saw Malcam opening his mouth impossibly wide, rows of teeth going back into a throat that reached into infinities of time and space. Pain exploded around Tom's face as Malcam bit down. Oceans of blood and falling stars filled his mind.

The sun rose in the east, as it had done every day since the dawn of time. Shadows from the Malibu hills kept the beach cool and dim, but eventually the morning light fell across Sequit Point. By then the police had already arrived, two squad cars and an unmarked sedan driven by Detective Deborah Frost (Debbie to her friends) of the Malibu Homicide department. Detective Frost had ordered the officers to cordon off the beach while she and her partner checked out the scene. Some surfers had called it in earlier after stumbling across the carnage.

Her partner Mike Burns had seen it all over the years, but this was a new one. "Two goats, throats slit. And a guy with no head." He raised his camera and snapped a few shots of the scene. "Unbelievable."

"That it is, Mike," Frost said. She was standing at the edge of a ring of footprints, with the goats' and victim's corpses inside. She'd been taking notes, looking for anything that might give the police a clue what could have happened here.

"Dammit, Frost!" Burns scolded. "You messed up the footprints! That was evidence!"

Frost acted like she hadn't noticed them. "Sorry, Mike, my head was just somewhere else. That body…"

"Yeah, grim stuff, kiddo," he said, softening. "Nothing we can do about it now, I guess," Burns said. "So what are you thinking Debbie? More satanic cult stuff? Like those dogs in L.A.?"

Frost flipped her pocket notebook shut, and put her pencil behind her ear, under her long black hair. "Give me a break, Mike," she said. "You know there's no such thing as devil worshippers."

Return of the Reanimated Nightmare

LINDA ADDISON

"Why have you called me to this time and place?"
The Thing's scratchy voice erupted from the reborn jaw,
grimacing at the bad taste of its own bloated tongue,
its body regrowing rotting flesh, muscle, ligaments.

"We, the Children of the Deadly Night, Creeping Day,
demand to be worshipped and feared again, we need
you to be our Hand in their nightmares, ripping breath
from those who have dared turn us into objects of ridicule."

"How did you let these fragile humans misuse you?"
It asked in disbelief, coughing up cockroaches, as
eyeballs floating in ragged eye sockets, while
bleeding flesh sloughed off maggot-filled cheeks.

"We could not control the new fables they wrote, the machines
that created moving pictures for entertainment. Now, as night
approaches and thick fog lingers near their shores, they buy
popcorn and stuff to sit, unpossessed, enjoying their flickering screens."

"What of our poltergeists, hell-raisers and gremlins howling in the
shadows?" It stood ten feet tall on reconstructed legs covered in
open sores, weeping green pus. "Are you saying these children
play with our sprouting hordes from hell, as if they are pets?"

"All turned into decorative items, collected and gifted to each
other, images made into costumes worn by their children once

a year to collect candy. Their imagination, once a key used to
open their souls to our horror, now keeps Fear away. Will you help?"

The Thing swelled with bloody fluids in the timeless space of its rebirth, "Yes,"
hundreds of cracks burst over its skin, becoming gaping mouths, "I will," each
mouth sprouted jagged teeth, purple pointed tongues, "Oh, I will create such
new, unimaginable terror to feed their minds as they sleep, and haunt their days.
They will run, screaming, back to You for reprieve."

Taking the Night Train

THOMAS F. MONTELEONE

It was after 3 a.m. when Ralphie Loggins scuttled down the stairs, into the cold sterility of his special world.

Holding the railing carefully so that he would not slip as the November night wind chased him, he entered the Times Square subway station. Ralphie always had to be watchful on steps because the elevated heel on his left shoe was constantly trying to trip him up. He fished a token from the pocket of his navy pea jacket and dropped it into the turnstile, passing through and easing his way down the last set of stairs to the platform.

Ralphie walked with his special clump-click-slide to a supporting girder by the tracks and waited for the Broadway-Seventh Avenue local, noticing that he was not alone on the platform. There were few travelers on the subways in the middle of such winter nights, and he could feel the fear and paranoia hanging thickly in the air. Turning his head slowly to the left, Ralphie saw a short, gray man at the far end of the station. He wore a tattered, thin corduroy jacket insulated with crumpled sheets of the Daily News.

To Ralphie's right, he heard footsteps approaching.

Just as he turned to look, he felt something sharp threatening to penetrate his coat and ultimately his kidneys. At the limits of his peripheral vision he was aware of someone tall and dark-skinned looming over him, the stranger's breath heavy and warm on his neck.

"Okay, suckaah!" came a harsh whisper, the words stinging Ralphie's ear. "You move and you dead! Dig?"

Ralphie nodded, relaxing inwardly since he knew what would come next. When he did not move, the man pressed his knife blade a little more firmly into the fabric of the coat, held it there.

"Now, real easy like…get out your bread, and give it up…"

Ralphie slipped his left hand into his back pocket, pulling out his wallet, and passed it back over his shoulder to the mugger. It was snatched away and rifled cleanly and quickly. The tip of the blade retreated, as did the tall, dark presence of the thief. His footsteps described his flight from the station, and Ralphie was alone again. He looked to the end of the platform where the gray old man still stood in a senile, shivering daze.

A growing sense of loss and anger swelled in Ralphie. He felt violated, defiled, hurt in some deeply psychic manner. The mugger had reinforced his views of life in the city and all the dead hours within it. A silence pervaded the station, punctuated by a special kind of sadness and futility. Stifling his anger and his pain, Ralphie smiled ironically—it was most fitting that he be robbed in the subway, he thought.

Time seemed to lose its way beneath the streets of Manhattan, flowing at a rate completely its own, and it seemed to Ralphie that there might be a reason for it. He felt that there was something essentially wrong about the subways. As though man had somehow violated the earth by cutting these filthy pathways through her, and that the earth had reacted violently to it. Ralphie believed this, because there was a feeling of evil, of fear, and of something lurking beneath the depths of the city that everyone felt in the subways. Ralphie knew that others had sensed it, felt it, as they descended into the cold, tomblike stations.

His thoughts were shattered by the approaching roar of the train. A gust of warmer air was pushed into the station as the local surged out of the tunnel, jerked to a halt, opened its doors. The old man shuffled into a distant car; Ralphie entered the one closest to him. As he sat on the smooth plastic seat, the doors sighed shut, and the train rattled off into the darkness, under the belly of the beast, the city.

The only other passenger in Ralphie's car, an old woman in a ragged coat, a pair of stuffed shopping bags by her high-topped shoes, looked at him with yellow eyes. Her face was a road map of wrinkles, her lips so chapped and cracked they looked orange and festering. Ralphie kept watching the old woman, wondering the usual thoughts about members of her legion. Where did she live? What did she carry in those mysterious bags? Where did she come from? Why was she out riding the night trains?

The rocking motion of the cars was semi-hypnotic, soothing, and Ralphie felt himself unwinding from the tension of the robbery. He allowed himself to smile, knowing that the mugger had gotten nothing of value—his left pants' pocket still held his money clip and bills, whereas the wallet had contained only some pictures, business cards, and his library card.

He had not been counting the local stops, but he had been riding the train for so many years that he had an instinctive feeling for when his station would be coming up. It was not until the train reached Christopher Street-Sheridan Square that Ralphie began staring through the dirty glass into the hurtling darkness. Houston Street would be next.

Then it happened.

The lights in the car flickered and the motion of the car slowed. The old, shopping-bag lady seemed to be as still as a statue, and even the sound of the wheels clattering on the tracks seemed softer, slower. The warm air in the car became thicker, heavier, and Ralphie felt it was becoming difficult to breathe. He stood up, and it felt as if he were underwater, as though something were restraining him. Something was wrong. The train seemed to be slowing down, and he looked out the windows, past the reflection of the interior lights, to see something for the briefest of moments—a platform, a station with no sign, no passengers, only a single overhead bulb illuminating the cold beige tiles of its walls.

For a second, Ralphie imagined that the train was trying to stop at the strange station, or that something was trying to stop the train. There was a confluence of forces at work, and time itself had seemed to slow, and stretch, while the train struggled past the place. Then it was gone, replaced by the darkness, and the train was gathering speed, regaining its place in the time flow.

The air thinned out, the old lady moved her head, gripped her bags more tightly, and Ralphie could move without interference. The train was loud and full of energy once again. Ralphie felt a shudder pass through him. It was as though something back there had been reaching out, grasping for the train, and just barely failing. The image persisted and he could not stop thinking about it. He knew that the image of the stark, pale platform and the single naked bulb would prey upon him like a bad dream. He knew he had passed a place that no one ever saw, that no one even knew existed; yet he had seen it, felt its power...

The local lurched to a halt, its doors slamming open. Ralphie looked up and saw the Houston Street sign embedded in the wall tiles. Jumping from the car, he hobbled across the deserted platform, wedged through the turnstile, and pulled himself up the steps. The cold darkness of the street embraced him as he reached the sidewalk, and he pulled his collar tightly about his neck. The street was littered with the remnants of people's lives as he threaded his way past the overturned trash cans, discarded toys, heaps of eviction furniture, stripped cars, and empty wine bottles. This was the shabby reality of his neighborhood, the empty shell that surrounded his life.

He walked to the next corner, turned left, and came to a cellarway beneath a shoe-repair shop. Hobbling down the steps, he took out his key and unlocked the door to his one-room apartment. He flipped on the light switch and a single lamp illuminated the gray, tired room. Ralphie hated the place, but knew that he would never escape its prison-cell confines. Throwing his coat over a straight-backed chair, he walked to a small sink and medicine chest, which had been wedged into the corner of the room. His hands were trembling as he washed warm water over them, chasing the stinging cold from his bones. In the spotted mirror he saw an old face, etched with the lines of defeat and loneliness. Only thirty-one and looking ten years older: his sandy hair was getting gray on the edges, his blue eyes doing the same. He tried to smile ironically, but could not manage it. There was little joy left in him, and he knew that it would be better to simply crawl beneath his quilt on the mildewed couch and sleep.

That night he dreamed of subway trains.

It was late in the afternoon before he awakened, feeling oddly unrefreshed. He could not forget the baleful image of the empty station, and he decided that he would have to investigate the place. When he took a train up to midtown, he asked the trainman about it. The IRT employee said he had never heard of that particular platform, but that there were countless places like that beneath the city: maintenance bays, abandoned stations, old tunnels that had been sealed off. Somebody must have left a light on, that's why Ralphie had seen it at all. The trainman seemed unimpressed, but Ralphie had not told him how he had felt something reaching out from that place, trying to take hold of the train...

After having coffee in a small shop off 52nd Street, Ralphie walked the streets aimlessly. He knew that he should go to the public library and get a new card, but he felt too restless today. His mind was too agitated to read, even though it was one of his only pleasures. When he had been a child, living with his uncle, the old man had taught him the wonders of books, and Ralphie had educated himself in his uncle's library. When the old man died without a will or an heir, Ralphie was turned out on the street, a victim of New York State Probate Court at the age of seventeen, with nothing. A string of odd jobs leading nowhere, combined with his crippled leg, had beaten him down until he didn't seem to care anymore. He identified with the desperation of characters from Dostoyevski and Gogol, the self-inflicted terror and pain of characters from Hawthorne and Poe. The world had been different when those writers had lived, he often thought, and people knew how to feel, and think, and care. In the city, Ralphie wondered if people even cared about themselves anymore.

Evening crept into the streets, and Ralphie worked his way toward Times Square, watching the faces of those he passed on the crowded sidewalks. Some said that it was an unwritten law that you did not look at anyone you passed in the city, but Ralphie knew that was untrue. Everyone looked at everyone else. Only they did it furtively, secretly, stealing glances at one another like thieves. They walked behind masks of indifference playing the parts assigned them in the mindless dollhouse of the city. It was like a disease, thought Ralphie, which had infected us all.

Down Broadway, he turned left at 42nd Street, already ablaze with the flashing lights and colors of the theaters and porn shops. The crowds of tourists and theatergoers mingled with the panhandlers, the hustlers, and the legions of blacks and Puerto Ricans carrying suitcase-sized radios at full volume. Dealers hung in doorways or strutted and leered at passersby. The sidewalks were speckled with trash and dark wet patches that could be any number of things. In the middle of the block, Ralphie entered the glass, satin-lined doors of the Honey Pot, to be swallowed up in the sweaty darkness and loud music of the bar. The lyrics of a song pounded at him, and he listened to the words without wanting to:

I want to grab your thighs…
I want to hear your sighs…
M-m-m-make luuuuuv to you…!

Ralphie shook his head sadly to himself, took off his coat, and walked past the bar, which was already half-filled with patrons. Behind the bar was a light-studded runway, backed by a floor-to-ceiling mirror where the girls could watch themselves while they danced. Brandy was strutting back and forth across the runway, wearing only a pair of spiked heels and a silver-sequined G-string. She was short and lithe, with stringy dark hair, boyish hips, and pendulous, stretch-marked breasts that seemed absurdly large for her small frame. She half-walked, half-pranced to the beat of the music, causing her breasts to bounce and loll in what to Ralphie was a most unerotic manner. Once in a while she would smile at the patrons, or lick her lips and pout, but it was an empty, hollow gesture. Ralphie had seen all the girls pretending to like the customers and he hated the whole game, hated that they were trapped in it, as was he. Empty exchanges, devalued emotions, flensed of meaning and feeling.

When he reached the end of the bar, his boss, Mr. Maurice, spotted him. "Hey, Ralphie boy! You're early tonight…"

"Hello, Mr. Maurice. You want me to start anyway?"

Maurice, a broad-shouldered, overweight, and balding man, smiled and shook his head. "Naw, there ain't nothin' out there yet. Go on in the back and get a coffee. I'll call ya when I need ya."

He dismissed Ralphie with a turn of the head, resuming his conversation with one of the new dancers, who was sitting on a barstool by her boss, clothed only in a bra and panties.

"Okay," said Ralphie, walking into the darkness beyond the bar, and through a door to the girls' "dressing" rooms, to a small alcove where a coffee maker and Styrofoam cups could be found. As he poured the black liquid into his cup, someone entered behind him. Turning, he saw it was Brandy, completely nude, going to the dressing room.

"Hi, Brandy. How are you?"

The girl looked at him and smiled, but said nothing, then disappeared behind the door. She treated him as all the girls did—like a mascot or a pet dog. Funny, he thought, but he had never grown accustomed to the way people treated him. Just because he was a short, dough-faced cripple didn't mean that he had less of a need for warmth and a little caring. Ralphie shook his head slowly, embarrassed that he could indulge so easily in self-pity. He walked from the back room to one of the vacant tables farthest away from the bar, sat down, and sipped his coffee.

A half hour passed under the haze of cigarette smoke and the sheets of loud music as Ralphie ignored the laughter and the whistles from the bar patrons. His thoughts kept returning to the Broadway local, and that abandoned station—there was something about the place that would not leave him. It was as though there was something down there, waiting. Waiting for him, perhaps…He knew it was a crazy thought, but it felt so strong in him that he could not get rid of the idea. He had felt something, damn it, and he had to know what it had been.

Maurice appeared by his shoulder, slapping him in mock friendliness. "'S after eight…Ya better get out there and bring in some rubes, huh? Whaddaya say, Ralphie boy?" Another slap on the arm.

"Yeah, okay, Mr. Maurice." He stood up from the table and pulled on his coat, wrapped his scarf about his neck. Ralphie hated his job, but it was by far the best-paying gig he had ever had. If he didn't need the money so badly, he would have quit long ago.

Walking past the bar, he saw that Chrissie was dancing now. She had long legs which seemed too thin when she wore a dress, but looked all right when she was nude. Her face was long and thin, making her eyes look large and forlorn. She was not what you would call pretty, but she had, as Maurice phrased it, "a big rack," and that was what the guys liked.

He pushed through the glass doors and felt the wind sting his face, the brilliance of the lights cut his eyes. Even in the cold November night, there were thousands of people, mostly men, out looking for warmth—or whatever could be passed off as the same. Ralphie held open the door to the Honey Pot and began his spiel, the words so automatic that he never thought of them anymore: "All right, fellas! No cover, no minimum! Take a peek inside! We got the best show in town! Young girls for you! All nude, and that means naked!"

He would pause for a moment, and then repeat his message to the ever-changing surge of topcoated bodies. Sometimes he would stare into the men's faces, especially the ones who listened to his patter, the ones who slipped through the open door with heads bowed as if entering a church. He always saw the same things in their eyes. Our eyes betray us always, he thought, and he saw in their expressions a searching for something, for something lost and becoming unrecognizable. He also saw sadness. Sadness and shame.

On and on, he repeated his litany of the flesh, until the night had whipped past him and the traffic thinned out, the pedestrians disappearing. Maurice came up behind him and tapped his shoulder. "Okay, Ralphie. Nice job, let's pack it in, baby."

He entered the bar, walked past the hunched row of men. They were the hangers-on, the ones who closed the bars, the loneliest of the lonely. This last crowd watched Jessie work through her final number, wearing only a pair of gold-glitter platform heels as she swished her hips and played with her blonde pubic hair. She had an attractive face, but it was flawed by her empty-eyed stare, her artlessly constructed smile.

Ralphie sat at the back table after getting a cup of coffee from the back room. As he used its heat to warm his hands before sipping it, more thoughts of the Broadway local ripped through his mind, and he feared that he was becoming obsessed with it. There were whispers and giggles behind him as the girls were emerging from the dressing room, putting on their coats, and preparing to leave. They filed past him, ignoring him as they always did, but this night the gesture seemed to eat at him more than usual. He knew that he should have become accustomed to the treatment, but he never did. The strange thing about it was that for the first time he felt himself disliking them, almost hating them for their lack of compassion, of simple, honest feeling. And that scared him.

Finishing his coffee, he left the bar, not saying good night to anyone, and no one seeming to notice his departure. Out in the Broadway night, fleets of cabs battled for one last fare, and the fringe people of the dark hours huddled in doorways and on street corners. Ralphie descended into the Times Square station, dropped a token through the stile, and held the railing as he went down to the platform. He was thinking that he should quit the Honey Pot, knowing that he had hung on there so long only because it was easier than looking for something better, or even taking courses during the day so that he could be qualified for something with more of a future. But that would mean getting out and interacting with the people of the day, and that might mean more pain and indignation. At least the people of the night considered him almost invisible, and did not actively hurt him. But they did hurt him, he thought, only to a lesser degree. To everyone, Ralphie was a loser, a hunched-up, bummy-looking clubfoot. He was one of the semi-human things that inhabited the shadowy parts of all cities, one who did not think or feel, but only slinked and scrabbled and hustled for an empty existence.

He would show them someday how wrong they were, he thought.

A rattling roar filled the station as the local rumbled to a stop. The train was a sooty, speckled nightmare covered with spray-paint graffiti—an old, dying beast. Its doors opened and Ralphie stepped inside, moving to a hideously colored turquoise seat. The air in the car was heavy with the smell of cheap wine and vomit, but the only other passenger, a dozing, fur-coated pimp in a droopy-brimmed hat, did not seem to notice. Ralphie took a seat near the doors and stared at his reflection in the smeared glass window across the aisle.

Penn Station. 28th Street. 23rd. The night train hurtled down the tunnel, and Ralphie felt his pulse quickening. Would it happen again? Would he see that station with no name? The questions dominated his thoughts. 18th Street. Then 14th. Sheridan Square was next, and the train seemed to be going slower already. He hoped that it was not just his imagination.

When the train stopped at the Square, several passengers boarded. Two were teenaged girls wearing almost identical suede jackets with fur collars and Calvin Klein jeans with butterflies embroidered down the legs. Rich girls out slumming, thought Ralphie, as one of them looked into his eyes and smiled. He felt something stir in his heart, and smiled back at the pretty young girl.

"You're kind of cute," said the girl. "Come here often?"

Ralphie couldn't believe what she said. He could only stare for a moment. "What?" he asked dumbly.

The girl giggled and nudged her friend, who looked at Ralphie, then whispered loudly to the first girl. "Hey, watch it, you're getting Quasimodo excited!"

They both laughed, and Ralphie looked away, feeling something shatter inside, breaking and turning to dust. The train was moving again, and he wanted to ask them why they had acted that way, but his thoughts were racing ahead as he sensed the train approaching that secret place once again. There was something new smoldering in his heart; it was a new feeling, still unrecognized. He looked past the reflections in the glass into the rumbling darkness, and suddenly it was happening again.

He felt a slowness come over him, and he looked to the other passengers, the pimp and the two girls. Why didn't they feel it too!? He could feel the train itself struggling to get past that place, that station with no name. Watching and waiting, Ralphie sensed something tugging at the fibers of time itself. There came a flicker of light beyond the car and, for an instant, an illuminated rectangle. The image burned into his mind: the single bulb, the cold yellow tiles, the empty platform.

And then it was gone.

The train seemed to be regaining its speed, the sound of the girls giggling and the wheels clacking. How could they not have seen it? Felt it? He stood up, grabbing the center pole as his vision fogged for a moment, and he fought the sensation that he was going to black out. He swayed drunkenly, fighting it, still looking out the windows. Then the train was jerking to a halt, its doors opening at Houston Street.

Forcing his legs to move, Ralphie limped from the car and stood on the concrete platform, rubbing his forehead. The vertigo had passed and the cooler air of the station seemed to help. The doors whooshed shut, and the local clattered from the station, leaving him alone, staring down the black shaft from which he had just come. It was so close, he thought. It could not be far from where he now stood...

There would be no trains for fifteen minutes. He had the time. He was alone in the station, and no one saw him ease off the platform and slip down to the tracks. The electrified rail was across the roadbed and he could easily avoid it, but ahead of him the black tunnel hung open like a mouth waiting to devour him. Driven by the need to find the abandoned station, he walked forward, into the darkness, trying not to think of what it would be like if a train rushed him ahead of schedule.

The tracks curved to the left and soon the lights from the Houston Street station were completely obscured and Ralphie was moving in total darkness. There was not even the dim eye of a signal semaphore to give him direction, and he felt his stomach tightening as he moved clumsily, keeping his left hand in touch with the cold, slightly moist, slightly slimy wall of the tunnel. He lost all sense of time, becoming engrossed with the darkness, the uneven roadbed, and the dead touch of the wall. He felt more terribly alone than he had in his entire life, and he knew in his gut that he was walking to a place where no man had ever walked before.

Something was taking shape ahead of him, rimmed by faint light: he saw that it was the outline of a support girder along the wall. Another came into view, and then another. With each step the light grew stronger, and he could see the shine of the rails ahead of him. The wall curved to the left again, and he was upon the place: a rectangle of light suspended in the darkness. It looked unreal, like a stage devoid of props and actors.

He pressed forward and pulled himself up over the edge of the platform, instantly aware of a coldness about the place which transcended temperature. It was a chilling sense of timelessness that touched his mind rather than his flesh. Looking about, Ralphie saw that the platform was not deep, nor were there any exit stairs. Only a seamless wall of cold tiles trailing off into the shadows beyond the perimeters of light from the solitary bulb.

He knew that it was into the shadows he must walk, and as he did so, he became more acutely aware of the silence of the place. The mechanical clop of his elevated heel seemed so loud, so obscenely loud. He should have felt fear in this place, but it was replaced by a stronger emotion, a need to know this place for whatever it was. Then there was something touching his face. Out of the shadows it languished and played about his cheek like fog. It became a cold, heavy mist that swirled and churned with a glowing energy of its own, and it became brighter the deeper he probed it. He could sense a barrier ahead of him, but not anything that would stop him, but rather a portal through which he must pass.

He stepped forward...

...to find himself standing upon a narrow, rocky ledge, which wound across the sheer face of a great cavern. Above him, like the vault of a cathedral, the ceiling arched, defined by the phosphorescent glow of mineral veins. To his right a sheer cliff dropped off into utter darkness; to his left was a perfectly vertical wall. Ralphie followed the narrow winding path, each step bringing him closer to an eerie sound. At first it was like a gently rising wind, whispering, then murmuring, finally screaming through the cavern. An uncontrollable, eternal wailing.

Ralphie recognized the sound—it was the sound of utter loneliness. It was a sound made by something totally alien, and simultaneously all too human. It was a sound that, until now, he had heard only in the depths of his own mind. Such a primal, basic sound...He became entranced by it, moving closer to its source, until he saw the thing.

The ledge had widened ahead of him, becoming a ridge that slowed gently upward to another sheer cliff face. Affixed to the face of the cliff, upon a jagged outcropping of rock, by great shining chains was the thing. Even from a distance, it looked monstrously huge. Its arms and legs gave it a vaguely human form, but its true shape was. amorphous, indistinct. There was a shimmering, almost slimy aspect to its body as it writhed and strained against the chains that bound it to the rock.

Moving closer, Ralphie now saw a bird thing perched upon a piece of the jagged rock, balancing and swaying, and batting the air with its leathery wings. It was skeletal, reptilian, its head hideously out of proportion to its thin body. All curved beak and yellow, moon-pool eyes.

The creature paid no attention to Ralphie's approach, continuing with its task in dead earnest—savagely tearing out the chained one's entrails. With each rooting thrust of the bird's beak, Ralphie heard each wail fill the chamber louder than the last. One foul creature feeding upon the other. Ralphie watched the nightmare for a moment and knew it for what it was.

The thing on the rock must have perceived Ralphie's recognition, for it turned away from the cause of its agony long enough to look down at Ralphie with fierce, white eyes. It regarded him with a coldness, a calmness, which seemed to say: So, you have come at last...

Ralphie looked into its eyes, human and yet inhuman, seeing the eons of suffering, millennia of pain and loneliness. And deep within the eyes he could also see the disillusionment, the brooding coals of hate and retribution waiting to be unleashed.

There was a sensation of betrayal which radiated from those monstrous eyes, and Ralphie could feel a bond with the tortured figure on the rock. Watching it, Ralphie saw it change. Less amorphous now, a head and face appeared vaguely. The emotions in its eyes seemed to alter.

When the bird swung its beak savagely into the thing's middle once again, it flinched, but there was no sound of pain this time, no agony in its eyes, which remained fixed upon Ralphie, as though speaking to him.

Set me free, said its eyes. And I shall right the wrongs.

Ralphie understood, nodding, almost smiling. Slowly he approached the bird on its perch, seeing that it was almost equal in size to him and could tear him to ribbons with razor-like talons. A man would normally fear this thing from the myth time, but Ralphie was beyond fear now. He had peered into the eyes of the thing on the rock, sharing the greatest pain, the hate, and the betrayal. Ralphie could feel these things pulsing out of the creature, especially the hate, which had been bubbling like lava for untold ages. It raged to be free upon the world that had twisted its gift, forgotten its sacrifice. It reached out and touched Ralphie, suffusing him with strength, and he stepped closer to the bird, his left foot sliding upon the cavern floor.

Hearing the sound, the bird paused, turning its skullish head, cocking it to the side, to regard the odd little creature that stood below it. As it watched, Ralphie bent to pick up a fist-sized rock. In one motion he stood and hurled it at its head, striking one of its great yellow eyes, puncturing it like the delicate yolk of an egg. The bird screamed as its empty socket oozed, then launched itself upward with a furious beating of its thick wings. It shrieked as it hovered for a moment above Ralphie, then it rose up into the darkness, leaving only the echo of its wings smacking the dead air.

Once again, Ralphie looked up to the figure on the rock, transfixed by its ravaged entrails and the stains on the stone below, where the excess of its torture had dripped for millennia. Stepping forward, he touched one of the chains; it was hot to his touch. There was a large pin holding the chain to a hasp cut into the rock, and Ralphie pulled upon it. He could hear a chinking sound as the chain fell free, and the great thing with the eyes that spoke to him surged against the remaining bonds. That wailing had ceased, replaced by a gathering vortex of excitement and power. The sensation grew like an approaching storm, filling the cavern with a terrible static charge.

Ralphie reached up and loosed another pin; the chain fell away from the harnessed body as it moved against the last two restraints. It gave out a great cry—a cry born of eons of humiliation and defeat, but now almost free. The cavern walls shook from the power of the cry and the remaining chains exploded in a shower of metallic fragments. Ralphie backed away, for the first time awed by the power he had unleashed, seeing that its face had changed into something dark and nameless. For an instant, the thing's eyes touched him, and he felt immediately cold. Then there was an eruption of light and clap of thunder. Ralphie fell backward as the great thing leaped from its prison rock, past him, and toward the entrance to the depths.

Darkness and cold settled over Ralphie as he lay in the emptiness of the cavern. He knew where the thing would be going, and he knew what terrible lessons it would wreak upon the world, what payments would be exacted upon the dead souls. All the centuries of twisted vision would soon be put aright. His thoughts were coming slower and his limbs were becoming numb as he surrendered to the chilling darkness. He knew that he was going to fall asleep, despite the rumblings in the earth, despite the choir-like screams that were rising up from the city.

And when he awoke, he was not surprised to find himself upon a rock, bound by great chains of silver light, spread-eagled and suspended above the cavern floor. The air was filled with the smells of death and burning, of unrelenting pain, but he did not mind.

Out of the darkness, up from Gehenna, there came a deliberate flapping. It was the sound of wings, beating against the darkness, closer, and closer, until Ralphie could see the skull-like face, the beak, and the one good eye.

62

Catastrophe Queens

JESS LANDRY

Hazel stopped at the edge of the creature's den, the air thick from the lit torches lining the cave walls. From under her hood, she surveyed the war-torn scene inside: skeletal remains of her soldiers lay in amidst a sea of creatures she had never seen before, creatures with elongated faces, sharp teeth; creatures soaked in hot-pink blood. It was as though they'd been halfway through a transformation before the battle broke out.

Just then, a growl echoed through the cave from behind her.

She spun around, the hem of her long, red cloak flowing with body.

It stood in the entrance, masked in the shadows, glaring at her, towering over everything in its wake.

The massive creature took a step forward. Its mouth dripped with the guts of her comrades. Its crimson claws at the ready. Its Nazi uniform had all but ripped away; only patches of the man it had once been remained. Its helmet fused with its skull, cracking at the center of the swastika patch, wild brown fur sticking through like a mohawk.

The Alpha Wolf.

They glared at one another in the firelight. Its red eyes, small, squinted, filled with an unquenchable desire to kill, focused on her.

Her blue eyes did not waver.

Then, it howled, shaking the very ground they stood on, rattling the bones and awaking the cockroaches underneath the gore.

"My, my…what big teeth you have," Hazel smirked.

The wolf cocked its head.

In a storm of fire and smoke, Hazel Hellborne tore off her cloak. It cascaded down her body like a satin sheet, revealing her skintight leather catsuit with a plunging corset held together by black lace. Her teased, fiery-red hair drifted in all directions as her blood-red fingernails found the triggers of the machine guns tucked away at her hips.

Hazel took aim.

65

The creature lunged.

"Die, Nazi werewolf scum!" Hazel shrieked. Bullet shells rained down as they charged toward one another, ricocheting off every inch of her body, forming a trail behind her six-inch black stiletto boots. Something *crunched* under her sole as she stepped.

When the gunfire stopped, so did the werewolf. It fell at her feet into a pool of its own hot-pink blood, some of it splashing onto Hazel's top, an outreached claw nicking her arm.

Hazel brought the barrels of her guns to her lips and blew, her bright-red lips curling into a wicked smile.

"See you in Hell," she smirked.

"And...cut!"

"Ugh, gag me with a spoon," Hazel muttered, leaning against a bloodied, flayed body to examine her top and her boots. The bottom of her boot was a scene of pure carnage—the cockroach had never seen it coming. "Can someone pass me a moist towelette?"

"I got it, I got it!" Hazel's assistant, Tiffany, called out, snatching a box of baby wipes from a nearby table and bringing it to Hazel. The set lights glared in Tiffany's Coke-can glasses, nearly blinding Hazel; her skinny frame was barely able to keep her high-waisted jeans in place.

"Thanks, kid," Hazel said, taking a wipe and flinging the carcass of the cockroach off her boot. She then tried to clear the hot-pink blood, but to no avail.

"Oh, totally, no problem," Tiffany blushed.

With a loud grunt, the werewolf rose behind Hazel, his body dripping in fake blood, staining the cheap-looking fur that covered his chest to the top of his poor excuse for a mohawk.

"Damn, that's grody," Jerry quipped from inside the werewolf's mouth, opening the animatronic jaws as wide as they could go so only his eyes and nose were visible.

Another roach scuttled through the fake bodies not far from where they stood.

Before Hazel could say anything, Jerry clomped past her. A *squish* sounded out, and as Jerry pulled his prosthetic foot back, a string of stinky innards stuck along with him. "Like shooting fish in a barrel," he grinned.

"Was that really necessary?" Hazel replied, only noticing the cut on her arm then. "Hey, dick-brain—when you pulled your little Rambo stunt, you nicked me."

Jerry turned toward Hazel and adjusted his wolf head to get a better look. A small stream of blood dripped from the cut and onto the ground below, mixing with the hot-pink werewolf goop.

"Shit, sorry, darlin'. Better get that checked out. Wouldn't want you catching rabies."

"Very funny," Hazel said sarcastically, then turned to the crew of *Nazi Werewolves from Mount Gore* and asked, "Can I get a medic?"

A buff dude in a tank top with a mullet munching on a three-day old donut from the craft services table motioned for Hazel to come over as he dug through his fanny pack. "I think I've got a Band-Aid in here somewhere," he said with icing sugar on his moustache.

"Thanks, stud," Hazel teased as she stepped off the stage and sauntered toward Mullet Man. "Why don't you and me go back to my trailer and you can bandage me up there?"

"Uh, yeah, that sounds…rad," Mullet Man stammered, following Hazel out of sound stage twelve, while Tiffany kept her distance.

As the stage cleared and the room fell silent, the hot pink goop slithered its way around the props, coiling slowly around everything in its path.

And when it touched what remained of the cockroaches, it began to sizzle.

Hazel stomped back onto set several hours later, a contented smile on her face, donning a Sex Pistols tank top with "God Save the Queen" emblazoned on it. Tiffany trailed behind like an obedient puppy.

Her boots skipped a beat as another cockroach skittered by.

"Seriously! This place is infested," Hazel scoffed, then turned to Tiffany. "Can you call an exterminator or something?"

Tiffany nodded. "Totally. I'll take care of it, Hazel."

"Good girl." Hazel smiled.

No one else on set seemed too concerned about the infestation: the craft services crew kept the days-old food warm and fresh-looking, the production assistants ran around while producers barked orders at them, and on the stage, a cleaner worked furiously trying to contain the pink goop which had spilled from the stage onto the ground, his acid-stained jeans soaked to the ankles. He bopped to himself with his yellow Walkman secured to his bicep.

"Hazel, baby!" Chet, the director, called out from behind one of the cameras. He donned a ball cap at all hours, even now as the sun began to set, under the guise that he was "taking cues from Spielberg" and not because he was "prematurely balding."

"What's good, Chet?" Hazel asked, coming up beside him.

"We're setting up the next scene, the one where you rip the wolf's head from its spine. Just wanted to give you some notes."

"Head ripping is pretty self-explanatory."

"Sure," Chet chuckled. "But it's all about angles. I want to make sure we get your position exactly right."

"Uh-huh." Hazel raised an eyebrow.

"Where's Jerry at?" Chet continued, speaking to no one and everyone all at once. "I called for him, like, twenty minutes ago. Someone go find Jerry. And you…" he said to the cleaner, who didn't acknowledge him, "Move on out. We've got a scene to block."

The cleaner had stopped dancing. Instead, he stood with his back to the crew, motionless, the hot-pink blood up to his knees.

"Hey, pal," Chet called out, again.

No response.

Aggravated, Chet made his way onto the stage, wading through the fake carnage.

"Buddy, you hear me?" Chet poked the back of the man's shoulder, the hot-pink blood now up to his waist.

The cleaner didn't budge.

"Hey now—"

Then, Chet screamed.

"What the…" Tiffany started.

"…fuck," Hazel finished.

The cleaner turned, the fake blood climbing up his clothes at a steady pace. The yellow Walkman on his arm had fused with his skin, his whole appendage a blend of flesh and gears and cassette tape. His headphones, the ones with the orange foam at the ear, had been consumed by his skin so only a hint of orange was visible, the metal band overtop sunk into his skull.

And his skin. It looked as though it had melted away, the meat and muscles throbbing and stained hot pink.

The Walkman Man's arm latched onto Chet, ripping his own arm off in one fell swoop.

Then, as Chet's screaming, spasming body plopped to the floor, as the hot-pink blood wiggled itself upward into Chet's agape mouth, the cast and crew collectively turned to one another, as though they needed to look into someone else's eyes to confirm what was happening in front of them.

It was only when the sea of fake corpses started to rise that everyone ran.

"Ohmygodohmygodohmygod," Tiffany screamed as Hazel slammed her trailer door behind them. "It's not possible. That's not possible. *Was* that possible?"

Hazel drew the blinds, then pressed her back against the door, her chest heaving, the screams outside growing louder. "You saw it, too, right? This isn't just my speed wearing off?"

"Whatthefuckdowedo?" Tiffany squealed, pulling at her scrunchied brown hair.

"His arm, it was…" Hazel started. "His face, it looked like it had melted…"

Tiffany chugged some air. "And he was covered in that pink mess."

Hazel and Tiffany turned to one another.

"Where did you put my corset?" Hazel asked, wide-eyed.

"I put it in the bathroom after that guy left."

They both turned their heads toward the bathroom door.

Slowly, Hazel and Tiffany moved forward, staying low and away from the windows, while doing a quick scan of their surroundings.

Tiffany grabbed a curling iron.

Hazel took off her shoes and propped them heel up.

"There's no way this is possible, right?" Tiffany asked as they crept to the door. "How could fake blood reanimate everything it touches?"

"How the fuck should I know? I'm not a scientist," Hazel whispered as they stopped in front of the door, weapons at the ready.

"It was a rhetorical question," Tiffany whispered back.

Hazel shushed Tiffany as she reached a shaking hand out and turned the knob.

Her corset, still stained hot pink, sat on the bathroom sink.

It hadn't budged.

The women lowered their weapons, a slight chuckle escaping their lips, one that ascended into laughter, which segued into a full-on fit.

"Can you believe…" Tiffany said through the tears, "that we actually thought your slutty costume was alive?"

"I know!" Hazel snorted back. "Maybe the speed *is* kicking in!"

The corset shuddered then, as though it had just been awoken after a long sleep. It rose into the air, slowly, hovering, the black laces lining the front now forming into a sadistic sideways smile, sharp teeth ready to shred.

Their laughter died out.

"You've gotta be shitting me," Hazel said.

Without warning, the bloodthirsty piece of clothing swooped down at them. Both women instantly ducked, flattening themselves on the ground.

The corset fluttered around the ceiling like a moth searching for a flame. It circled back around, opening its lacy maw for another attack, its course set for Tiffany.

"Get under the table!" Hazel screamed, but it was too late. The top swooped in, plunging its fangs into Tiffany's back, wrapping its boning around her face until it engulfed it completely. Tiffany cried out, dropping the curling iron to try and pull herself free.

Hazel was on her feet before she realized it, boots secure in her grip. She lunged at the clothing, quickly but carefully using the heel to pry it from Tiffany's face.

Finally, she pulled the corset loose, pinning it to the ground.

She brought the other heel down everywhere and anywhere, shredding at the silky fabric until it was in tatters. Pink goop squirted from the top, spraying out into the open as Hazel ducked out of the way.

The corset convulsed for a minute before it abruptly stopped.

Tiffany wiped the blood from her eyes and pulled at the boning that the corset had tried to lay under her skin, her scrunchied brown hair now flat and red against her head.

Hazel crawled over to Tiffany, baby wipes in hand.

"Moist towelette?" she asked.

Outside, the world had changed. Fire ravaged the lot. Prop creatures stumbled around, pink slime oozing from their pores. Everything that had come in contact with the blood, alive or not, now roamed the studio.

Hazel and Tiffany threw on some leggings—the only non-skimpy clothing items in Hazel's trailer—and ducked through the backlot, sticking to the shadows of each building, trying to remain as silent as possible, a much easier task for Hazel in her Nike Air Max sneakers.

"How much farther?" Hazel asked.

"We're almost there," Tiffany said.

"What kind of car do you drive? Tell me it has AC."

"Is that really a concern of yours right now?"

"It's hot, Tiffany. Everything's on fire."

Tiffany sighed as they stopped near an outdoor eating space, the picnic tables flipped over, trails of blood and guts, pink and red, splattered over every inch.

Just beyond was the parking lot.

And in the parking lot, Tiffany's '86 Dodge Omni (no AC).

Seeing the coast was clear, the two women stepped out from the shadows. Tiffany picked up her pace, swerving and swaying through the debris. Hazel trailed behind through the gore, accidentally knocking against a radio.

It buzzed on.

"This is KXYZ radio, today's greatest hits."

The women stopped in their tracks.

"And now it's time for a special request from the biggest dance movie of the year…"

"Turn if off!" Tiffany squealed. "Hurry!"

"So turn up that dial…"

"Don't spazz out, I got it," Hazel said, grabbing for the radio.

"Uh, Hazel…" Tiffany started.

"And get ready for the hits."

"I said I got it."

"Hazel!"

The radio slipped from Hazel's hands as "(I've Had) The Time of My Life" started.

Hazel looked up and followed the path of Tiffany's finger, pointing to a dark field beyond the lot. In the night, she could barely make out what was moving toward them.

But it looked big.

And hungry.

A horde of reanimated corpses drew closer, some of them props Hazel had crawled over, some of them the crew freshly reanimated as pink blood super soldiers. The horde sped toward them, jaws open wide, hot pink and with one clear intention: kill.

"Aw shit," Hazel said as the guitar kicked in.

Hazel and Tiffany ran as fast as their legs could carry them, dodging tables and fires until they cornered themselves in front of sound stage twelve; the horde circling them, waiting.

"What now?" Tiffany asked, wiping the sweat from her brow.

As the chorus began, Hazel grabbed a loose, sharp leg from an overturned picnic table and said, "We fight."

She charged at the creatures, releasing a primal scream that seemed to startle even the reanimated.

71

Not wanting to leave Hazel to fend for herself, Tiffany grabbed the only items she could find—a fork and a butter knife—and joined in.

They fought side by side, cha-chaing around the reanimated, side-stepping blows, delivering punches, ripping their assaulters apart. Blood and guts and pink goop rained down around them. The horde's numbers diminished as Hazel and Tiffany sliced and diced and Swayzed through the gore.

As the song slowed, building to its biggest moment, the women stopped to take a breath, assuming the coast was clear.

But it was not.

One final straggler rose behind Hazel, its pink goop and disfigured arm catching Tiffany's eye. The Walkman Man.

"Hazel!" Tiffany called out, sprinting toward her friend, her footsteps heavy like concrete as the creature behind Hazel lunged. "No!"

Hazel, with no time to react, saw Tiffany coming toward her, fork and knife ready. So she did the only thing she could—as Tiffany sprang to attack the Walkman Man, Hazel crouched down and caught Tiffany, lifting her body into the air.

Tiffany intercepted the Walkman Man, lodging both her fork and knife into the orange foam from where its ears should've been.

All three tumbled to the ground. The Walkman Man fell onto the radio, destroying it, the cutlery embedded deep enough into his skull that some hot-pink brains sputtered out.

Hazel, exhausted, turned to Tiffany, and stared at her in pure awe.

"What?" Tiffany exhaled. "I watched you do the same thing in *Hornball Babe Massacre*. I owe it all to you."

Hazel thought for a moment, then nodded. "Fuckin-A, Tiff."

Both women rose, brushing themselves off, and surveying the scene. They had been backed up into sound stage twelve, at least twenty bodies piled around them.

"Let's bounce," Hazel said, taking a step over Walkman Man.

"Uhh…" Tiffany began, lifting a finger, pointing behind Hazel.

"For fuck's sake, what now?"

Just then, something howled behind them, shaking the very ground they stood on.

"Oh, come on!" Hazel cried as her and Tiffany turned to see Jerry—or what was once Jerry—rise from the set of *Nazi Werewolves from Mount Gore*.

He towered over Hazel and Tiffany, the shag rug that had once been his fur now sleek and smooth, his muscled arms and razor-sharp claws now very real, drool spilling from his snarling mouth. His Nazi helmet had cracked off completely. All that remained was a perfectly coiffed mohawk, hot pink and totally punk.

"Get out of here," Hazel said to Tiffany. "Get to your car. Get somewhere safe."

"No way," Tiffany said. "I'm not leaving you."

"Seriously kid, you need to go. I'll deal with Teen Wolf here."

At that moment, the wolf charged.

And so did Hazel, pushing Tiffany aside, hot-pink-stained picnic table leg pointed toward him.

The two collided in pure powerhouse fashion, slamming right into one another, the wolf landing the first blow, knocking Hazel to the ground.

Hazel flung back up and lunged at the beast. She swung, he swung; Tiffany glanced around the room looking for another weapon.

Hazel found her way onto the wolf's back and began stabbing him over and over again with the rod, a few blows penetrating his thick skin.

But Hazel grew tired and the creature was able to get a hold of her, throwing her off his back and onto the set, just missing the pink goop, but knocking down the backdrop.

Sequestered behind the curtain were several barrels covered in the hot pink mess. WARNING! TOXIC! Was stamped on each of them, with a smaller warning underneath: Do not mix with bleach, Gak, or human blood.

"I fucking knew it," Hazel managed to say with the wind knocked out of her. She stayed down as the werewolf formerly known as Jerry stomped toward her.

He leaned into her face, his breath warm and putrid, his saliva soaking her skin.

He brought his arm up, his claws prepared to gut her, when something hit the back of his head.

"Hey…dick-brain!" The wolf turned, and there stood Tiffany, days-old, rock-hard donuts in her hands. The wolf cocked its head.

"Yeah, you!" She chucked another one at him—a Jambuster—hitting him square in the eye, the icing sugar leaving a ring on his fur.

The creature howled and started toward her.

She chucked as many as she could at him, giving Hazel enough time to come to. But before Tiffany knew it, the wolf had her cornered.

And she was out of donuts.

The wolf snarled, opened its massive jaws, and leaned in.

Tiffany cowered, accepting of her fate, her life flashing before her eyes.

Just as the wolf was about to take a bite, he suddenly stumbled and fell to the ground, yelping in pain.

Tiffany looked up to see a giant cockroach skittering by her.

Gathering all her courage, Tiffany rose from the corner and darted toward Hazel, who had come to.

"Am I glad I didn't kill that guy," Hazel said in disbelief.

Safe in each other's arms, the women watched from the stage as the wolf took a bite out of the bug's antennae.

The roach quickly retaliated by stabbing the wolf with its legs, but the wolf was fast—its grabbed hold of the bug and tossed it across the room.

That was enough for the cockroach. It seized its moment.

The bug flew up into the air, hovering over the wolf, diving toward him. With a twist, the bug expanded its wings, dodging the creature's claws, and slicing the wolf at the belly.

The wolf howled and tumbled down, still attempting to claw at what it could with its dying breaths.

Hazel, noticing her prop guns nearby covered in the toxic blood, grabbed one of them, sure not to get the sludge on her, and strutted over to the werewolf.

As the wolf slumped over, its head on the pavement, his chest rising and falling, Hazel placed a sneakered foot on its head, her Sex Pistols shirt ripped so that "God Save the Queen" now read "The Queen."

"See you in Hell," Hazel Hellborne said, shooting the creature square in the skull, brain matter splattering all over the floor. Hazel smirked down at the scene. Tiffany came up beside her and did the same.

Out of the shadows, a smaller cockroach emerged. Then, coming to the bigger bug's side, the two moved toward the set, antennae searching for something.

Both cockroaches let out an alien-like wail at the sight of the bug Jerry had crushed earlier in the day.

"Oh god," Tiffany muttered under her breath. "Was that, like, the dad or something?"

Then, both roaches scuttled over to the women, their heads down. They paused in front of them.

"I, uhh…" Hazel started. "I'm sorry for your loss?"

The sentiment seems to appease the bugs. They lowered their heads in what appeared to be a nod, then moved out of the studio. The women watched as the bugs walked away into the great unknown.

Tiffany and Hazel brushed themselves off and started toward the parking lot, the scenescape of the big city coming into view.

Downtown burned brightly in the night sky. And somewhere above them, helicopters flew by.

As they got into Tiffany's Dodge, the radio blared on.

"This is KXYZ radio, today's greatest hits. Your home of Rick Astley...and the apocalypse!"

"Never Gonna Give You Up" started to play.

Tiffany stared ahead, socked hands tight on the steering wheel. "Now what?"

"The fuck if I know," Hazel smirked.

Your Picture Here

JOHN SKIPP

Tawny was both the hottest and the coolest. Which was a pretty neat trick, you gotta admit. And we loved each other more than words could say.

So when I fed the quarters into the slot, and she appeared behind the masturbation glass, her smoky eyes went as bright as mine.

"Oh, thank God," she mouthed, already naked and prepared for the worst. It was the end of her shift at Show World, the multistory sex emporium on the corner of 42nd and 8th, and she'd already wriggled and writhed her way through several dozen peep show jackoff sessions for New York's finest—only some of them off-duty cops—since she came on duty at noon. I'd timed it in the hopes that I'd be her last customer.

But she still had to go through the motions, cuz the security cam was on her, making sure she didn't lallygag around. Show World frowned on lackadaisical performances from their employees. They didn't want the trade wandering elsewhere.

So she put on the show—grabbing her boobs, waggling her ass, galivanting around—but she had that giant goofy grin on her face the whole time. The camera couldn't see her face. Only I could. That face was for me.

The camera wasn't watching me to make sure I desperately came in a hankie instead of the floor. The poor maintenance crew would take care of that end, when the shift changed. As for me, I kept it in my pants for later.

It was Date Night.
We had a lot of fun in store.

I was smoking on the sidewalk when she sashayed out. We swept each other into a kiss that made my bootheels melt. Then she lit one, too.

"So whaddaya think, gorgeous?" I said.

She turned, scrutinizing the strip to Times Square, the endless strip of marquees blazing down 42nd, all the lost and meandering crowd.

"Hmm," she said. "I like me some Bruce Lee. But I'm kinda in the mood for more gore."

"I can do that. There's Make Them Die Slowly, if you feel like Italian. That shit looks completely insane. On the other hand, there's a double-bill of C.H.U.D. and Children of the Corn that might be fun."

"Ooooh," she cackled. "Cannibalistic Humanoid Underground Dwellers? That sounds dumber than fuck. Let's do that!"

"The other one's based on a Stephen King story I really like," I added. "So worse come to worst, maybe one of 'em might be good."

And so, hand in hand, we raced across 8th, ducking between the honking traffic and laughing all the way, finally landing in the sea of fish-food tourists and sidewalk piranha that defined the strip of 42nd Street between Port Authority and Times Square they called The Deuce.

The Deuce was a mix of porn and every other form of exploitation cinema. A lowbrow paradise, and to my mind, the centerpiece of the thoroughly rotten Big Apple that I called home. There were a bevy of little shops in between the dozen-plus theaters that lined it from either side, hawking tourist attractions and beers you could carry around and chug from a brown paper bag. But it was mostly about the movies and the sleaze. The two as hand in hand as we were.

It was a street we both knew well: she as a twenty-three-year-old working girl who'd worked it in a pinch over the year since she'd moved here, though most of her business had moved inside; and me as a street messenger, one whole year older, who sold nickel bags and the occasional psychedelic on the sly.

And though we were both open-hearted towards our prey—wished them the best, in this journey called life—we both fell squarely on the piranha side.

Tawny Willow was pure Grace Jones with a rainbow mohawk. Six-two without her heels. Which was to say, she was all legs, at least till you got to the top half, which was all sleek fashion-model curve culminating in that face and hair. So if any shoe-gazer wasn't sold by the time they hit her miniskirted hips, they were pretty much done for by the time they hit the heights.

I wasn't a bad-looking dude, from what I heard, more Gary Oldman than Rob Lowe on the cuteness scale, and a good three inches shorter in our matching hi-top PF Flyers (hers mint green, mine stop-sign red).

But walking next to her, I mostly looked like the luckiest asshole in the world, gauging by the dagger-eyes of envy I clocked from every man we passed. If they looked at me at all.

"Let's get some beer," she said, ignoring them imperiously. We grabbed four quarts of Bud and an extra pack of Winstons, just in case we ran out, stuffed it all in my messenger bag. I had four joints of the good stuff rolled, and a couple hits of acid, just in case we wanted to go there.

And then, coming out, we saw the neon banner that called to us.

A double-bill of Basket Case and Dr. Butcher, M.D.

"I think I know what I want," she said.

"Your wish," I said, "is my command."

We got our tickets free from Jonesy, the pasty lump behind the box office glass. He'd done her once, and seemed to live in the hope that he'd ever get to do that again. I avoided his watery gaze as she thanked him, blew him a kiss. And in the door we went.

It was a Wednesday night. But this wasn't a date night theater, unless you were us. Mostly greasy grindhouse enthusiasts (almost all of them black), a couple of white college students, and a trio of hand job hookers interspersed throughout the meagre crowd, because twenty bucks was twenty bucks. But maybe forty people throughout. Not bad for a Wednesday night.

We took our seats in the second-row balcony, center. Popped a quart of Bud apiece, lit our first joint, and snuggled in as the coming attractions rolled. Nobody gave a shit in here, so long as you didn't interrupt the movie. And by "interrupt," I mean shoot the fucking projectionist or set the screen on fire. Other than that, pretty much anything was fair game.

Somewhere in between the trailers for Slumber Party Massacre, Xtro, Humongous, and The Beast Within, a scrawny little white dude with a big-ass picnic basket took a seat directly in front of us. "Aw, man," I said. But once he sat down, he was short enough to not obstruct my view of the screen. Then Tawny kissed me, hard, and I forgot all about him. Hands working each other over, sliding up and down the backs and sides before settling between each other's legs. Not going in yet. Just reminding each other of all the cumming to come.

So I was surprised when someone bumped into me from the seat to my left. "Oops," they said. I looked up and around, was doubly surprised by the spindly middle-aged Korean woman settling into the seat, perching an oversized knitting bag on her knobby knees.

"Whoa," I said, surveying all the empty seats around us. "Really?"

"Don't mind me," she grinned. "I'm just here for the show. Very exciting, isn't it?"

"Very," Tawny said. I wasn't sure which show they were talking about—my boner receded like getting caught by my mom—but if Tawny was cool with it, who was I to argue? We concluded our smooch with a quick peck of delicious, then settled back in our seats.

As the feature began.

As it turned out, Basket Case was the touching low-to-no-budget story of a young man and his hideously deformed conjoined twin—violently surgically separated in their youth—now living in this very neighborhood. It was a gleeful rush to see the street we'd just walked in from suddenly blown up on the screen. I'd actually sold weed in the tenement where our main characters lived.

"Fuck," I murmured in Tawny's ear. "We're almost in this fucking film!"

She laughed, lit a cigarette. I joined her in this, was about to offer one to the nice lady beside me, but she already had one lit. Eyes intent on the screen.

That was when I noticed the little doll head poking out of her bag. Actually, not so little. Full-on baby doll sized, and pointed at the screen, like it was watching it, too.

That was when I noticed that the picnic basket in front of me was also open. And that the audience had roughly doubled in size.

On the screen, a love triangle unspooled between the guy, the unconjoined monstrous twin in the basket he was carrying around—the titular Basket Case— and a sorta-cute woman who lived in that dump with them. We could tell it wasn't gonna end well, because now the brothers were fighting as to who loved and/or wanted her more in this skeezy *menage-a-what-the-fuck*. And because it was, after all, a horror story. Increasingly so, as the violence ramped up for the thrill-packed conclusion.

Now's probably a good time to point out that the movie audiences on The Deuce were probably the best, most responsive, and absolutely one hundred percent funnest audiences in the world. Soooo into it, on the visceral nerve-end level. There was no restraint.

When I watched An American Werewolf in London with a straight-ass audience in York, Pennsylvania, everybody just sat there staring. When I watched it for the third time—right off Times Square, having freshly gone from Olde York to New—I was stunned by the difference in engagement.

If people were fucking on the screen, they went, "Oh, yeah, baby!" Were totally grooving on it. If somebody got violenced, they yelled and yipped all the way, as if they were either doing it or feeling the pain of having it done to them.

When they screamed in terror at a terrifying scene, they really let it all out.

But this screaming was different.

"Baby?" I said, as a hand grabbed ahold of my crotch and squeezed with an urgency that stunned me. "OOO!" Looking over at Tawny.

Both of her hands on another hand. A very large and malformed one.

Wrapped around her throat.

From behind.

Tawny was smart. First thing she did was peel back one offending finger and snap it like a twig. Whoever was behind us shrieked with pain, let go. As her wide eyes met mine.

And my pants unzipped.

"THIS IS OUR NIGHT!" screamed the little man with the giant picnic basket, standing now at the balcony's summit, tossing it to the side as if it were totally weightless.

And from throughout the theater came roars of triumph, almost louder than the screams.

I had no idea that Basket Case was a documentary, or at least based on a true story. Even less that there were so many conjoined twins in New York City who had somehow survived outside their host bodies.

I guess it made sense that, if they did, they'd be monstrous.

I couldn't see them all. In the following split-seconds, my focus was entirely on two.

First was the one crawling onto my lap, pulling my never-limper dick out, with tiny hands. The second was the one that grabbed Tawny with both hands, and pulled her backwards right out of her seat, into the row behind.

"NO!" I screamed as she disappeared, shrieking, those long legs dangling and kicking, then gone.

Only then did I look down at the gray-haired abomination leering up at me from my crotch. Like a fifty-year-old gray-haired baby mirror image of the woman beside me, who held a knife to my throat and said, "Let her do it. She's been waiting soooo looooong…"

I was a New York City street messenger, used to negotiating chaos at every turn. I had trained myself toward instant response to any situation.

So my first response was to karate-chop that no-longer-nice-lady in the throat with my left hand, so fast that the knife dropped before she caved sideways. My second was to grab her malformed twin by the hair with my right, yank her face back before she could engulf me, and dangle her up in the air.

Then Tawny screamed again, and I thought about the knife now on my lap, precariously close to my cock.

I tossed the horny monster as far as I could toward the balcony railing. It bounced off it, then plummeted below. Then grabbed the knife. Leapt out of my seat, messenger bag still slung over my right shoulder.

And jumped directly into the row behind me.

The thing that was grappling with Tawny was the live-action version of the cheap-but-kickass special effect we'd been watching on the screen. It had no torso beyond the hard nipples prominently on display. It was all huge arms and far too many teeth in a face no mother had ever loved.

To her credit, Tawny kept punching it in the face, even as its claws ruined her own for porn forever.

That was when I stabbed it in the head. Once. Twice. Three dozen times, in rapid succession. So many times that it finally stopped clawing her, in its own version of fondling. And its lights went out at last.

I will never forget the look in her eyes, when she realized it was dead, and that I'd saved her.

I will never forget how much beauty was left in her ravaged face.

I will never forget our last hug, so desperate and yet so connected, before we raced for the exit together.

There was one last crawling monster before us, on our way out. She kicked it in the fucking face before I could, sent it flying on our way down the stairs.

We were not prepared for the lobby full of blood-splattered doctors, waiting for the next feature.

But God, did we fuck like our lives depended on it, when we finally made it home.

Permanent Damage

LEE MURRAY

Kath pulled her Avenger into an empty space outside Trendz Hair Design. There were just four shops in the block: an opportunity shop run by the church, a mower repair store, and the corner dairy. Only the dairy was open on a Sunday, yet there were three other cars parked in the lot; Kath recognized Nicole's Suzuki Alto with its crumpled back fender, and the yellow Nissan belonged to Shelley's mum.

Kath frowned. Trust Shelley to arrive first. God knows why Nicole asked her to be a bridesmaid. She hadn't been part of their group for ages, not since they left school, going off to study accountancy or law or something in Hamilton. But now she was back and working in an office in town, as if that somehow made her special. Not that she'd changed much. Still acted like she was their class councilor, bossing everyone about. Shelley had been angling for Nicole to make her maid of honor, too. Kath snorted. It would be over her dead body. Kath's boyfriend, Rhys, was the best man, so by rights maid of honor was Kath's job. She'd be damned if she was going to let Shelley steal the show.

Her bag in her lap, Kath tilted the rearview mirror, stretched her mouth wide, and touched up her Bonne Bell lip gloss. At least she had looks on her side. Not to brag or anything. *Whoops. Better motor.*

Kath took one last look in the mirror, drawing back her lips to check she hadn't got cherry gloss on her teeth, then snaffled up her handbag and entered the salon.

The door chimed.

"Kath!" Nicole gushed into the mirror. The blushing bride-to-be swiveled her chair, lifting a champagne flute in Kath's direction and inadvertently sloshing the liquid down the front of the black hairdressing cape. "You're here."

"Good thing, too," Shelley said, pulling that twisted Nellie Oleson smile of hers. Leaning against a wash basin, she took a deliberate sip from her own glass. "We thought we might have to start without you."

85

"Not even," Kath said, glancing at the clock above the window. "Anyway, Lauren's not here yet."

"She's here," Shelley said, plucking at the skin at her throat. "I picked her up on the way."

Of course, you bloody did.

"Lauren's out back in the little girls' room," Nicole said, cocking her head towards the back room. "The salon shares it with the dairy. The stylist went with her because you need a key."

"You should probably go too, Kath," Shelley said, raising her eyebrows and throwing Kath another Nellie Oleson smile. "Save you getting up for a wee later."

Kath tightened her grip on her bag. She wasn't five years old; she didn't need to be told when to go to the toilet. What the fuck did Nicole see in her, anyway? Honestly, the woman was a total poser.

But Nicole obviously hadn't heard Shelley's little dig; it had been lost in the crinkle of raincoat fabric as she crossed to the counter. "Have some bubbles, Kath," she said, grasping a bottle by the neck and topping up her glass. "We should get in some practice before the big day."

Throwing Shelley a look that would wilt flowers, even the fake ones, Kath slung her handbag on the window seat that served as the salon's waiting area and joined Nicole at the counter. She held out a glass for her friend to fill. "Just think. In exactly three weeks, you'll be waking up to your first day as Mrs. Andrew Flynn."

Nicole giggled. She tipped her glass, clinking it against Kath's. "I know! It's so crazy. I can hardly believe it."

"She might not," Shelley said.

Kath whipped her head up. "What's that supposed to mean? Of course she will. Andy's a good guy. They've been going out for ages. He's hardly going to dump her at the altar."

Nicole clapped a hand to her mouth in mock horror. "Ohmigod, I hope not!"

Shelley pushed away from the wash basin. Stepping closer, she lifted Nicole's hair, teasing it back from where it was trapped in the neckband of the cape. "What I meant was, you might want to keep your maiden name."

"Nah," Nicole said. "Don't get me wrong. I'm all for feminism. I want equal pay and all that, but you want your kids to have the same name as you, don't you?"

Kath agreed. There were some things that men were meant to do. Like opening doors for their girlfriends. And proposing. If only Rhys would take the hint. Which was another reason why Kath needed to be maid of honor.

"Well, did you even ask him?" Shelley said. She was still having a mental about this name-thing. "You never know, Andy might just—"

Out back, a flyscreen clanged, and seconds later Lauren bounced in from the back room, followed by the stylist, who was tucking her keys into her apron.

"Yo, Kath!" Lauren said, stuffing her smokes into her pocket, and accepting a glass of champers from Nicole.

"Great, looks like everyone's here?" the stylist said.

"Yes, Kath is the lucky last," Shelley said.

The stylist grabbed a notebook from under the counter. "Shall we get started, then?" She gestured them towards the window seat and rolled up a stool for herself. "So, Nicole, why don't you tell me what you have in mind?" she said, when everyone was seated.

"That's just the problem: I don't know," Nicole said. "I want something special. Unforgettable."

"Ooh, I know! We should do our hair like Madonna," Lauren said. "The way she has it in *Desperately Seeking Susan*, all crimped and wild." Kath liked Lauren. A bit of an airhead, but nice, you know?

Nicole grimaced. "I'm not sure…"

"Aw, c'mon. It'd be wicked," Lauren said. "We could tear up scraps of the dress fabric and use it in our hair."

Shelley tutted. "For a formal wedding?"

Kath wanted to slap her. It was a mean thing to say to Lauren. Curvy-bordering-on-fat, everyone knew Lauren had low self-esteem. Not that she'd said anything, but, well, it went without saying, didn't it? Kath, on the other hand, was in the best shape of her life; she'd been doing jazzercize twice a week since Christmas.

"Well, it's not a church wedding. But she's having her reception at the yacht club," Lauren told the stylist.

"Riiight." The stylist scribbled something in her notebook. "Maybe it would help if you gave me an idea of what everyone will be wearing…"

More crinkling of the cape. Nicole grabbed her bag, rummaging around inside and coming up with the brochures she'd been toting around for months. She spread them out on the coffee table, on top of the stacks of *Women's Weekly* and *Headway* magazines, and shuffled through the pages.

"So the boys are wearing grey tails with white shirts, and cummerbunds and bowties in this vibrant teal color, and…this is my dress," she said, pulling out a photocopy of the Butterick pattern. She handed the page to the stylist. There was no need to show it to the rest of them; they'd already seen it a gazillion times.

"It's so gorgeous," Shelley said. "Like Scarlet O'Hara in *Gone with the Wind*."

"Except Nicole's dress is raw silk taffeta; Scarlet made hers out of old curtains," Kath said.

"Well, yes. I meant the style…" Shelley retorted.

"The bridesmaid's dresses are the same style, only tea-length…" Nicole droned on. They'd heard it all before. "…and in teal to match the boys' cummerbunds."

The stylist nodded. Pursed her lips a moment. "Given the style, I don't think the Madonna look is going to work."

"Aw." Lauren pouted.

"Hang on." Setting her notebook down, the stylist lifted Nicole's pile of papers and pulled out an issue of *Headway*, flicking through the pages and opening it up on a photo of Whitney Houston.

Everyone leaned in.

"How about we do a spiral perm, like this?" the stylist suggested. "Lovely soft curls falling over your shoulders. Lots of volume. I think that will give you the romantic look you're going for. Then, on the day of your wedding, all we have to do is finger dry it and pin it up at the sides."

"That'll be rad," Lauren said.

"Yeah, perfect," said Shelley.

Kath froze. All very well for the others, but her hair was short. A perm would make it frizz and boing outwards and she'd end up looking like a Brillo pad.

"Kath?" Nicole asked. "You okay with a perm?"

Sweat trickled in the crease under Kath's boobs. *Fuck.*

Smiling, Shelley took a sip of her champagne. Bitch! Wouldn't she just love it if Kath's hair turned out butt-ugly. But like people always said: one wedding brings another. There was Rhys to think about.

"Kath?"

"Of course. Whatevs. You're the bride." *Fuck.* What else could she say with those two schmoozing up to Nicole?

Leaning over, the stylist ran her fingers through Kath's hair. "Hmmm. Your hair might be a bit *too* short." *Oh thank goodness.* "Maybe we crop it on the sides here, and we use a heated curling wand on top for the curl?"

"You mean, like Molly Ringwald in *Pretty in Pink*?" Lauren asked.

"Something like that."

"Choice. Let's do that, then," Nicole said. "Sorry, Kath."

Kath covered her relief with a shrug.

"Right, then." The stylist closed the magazine. "Let's get our bride in the chair and we'll get started."

Kath had had her hair washed, cut, dried, and curled with the styling wand when the stylist finally turned the hairdryers off. By that point, she'd also heard *No Jacket Required* by Phil Collins—both sides of the tape—read every *Women's Weekly* in the salon, and finished up the champagne dregs.

"I'll be right back with the neutralizer for you three," the stylist said to Nicole, Shelley, and Lauren, each of them ducking out from under a Perspex hood as the stylist went out back.

Nicole took a moment to cross to the one of the styling stations, lifted a hand mirror, turning around to check out the blue-rod cornrows on the back of her head. "I can't wait to see what they look like."

Lauren giggled. "Me either. I hope I look like Jennifer Beals in *Flashdance*."

Kath all but rolled her eyes. There was no way Lauren was going to look like Jennifer Beals in *Flashdance*.

Pushing back the cotton batting at her hairline, Shelley wrinkled her nose and blinked away tears. "That waving solution smells god-awful, doesn't it? I hope it doesn't ruin my hair."

"It'll be fine," the stylist said, bustling in from the back room. "I'm using a new neutralizer to reform the disulphide bonds. Less harsh." She gestured to the basin. "Who's first?"

"Me!" Nicole said, rushing over, her cape fanning out behind her like she was Batman. She wiggled her fanny on the seat and leaned back, shuffling her neck into the U-shape at front of the basin. The stylist set about rinsing Nicole's hair, then she popped the lid off the neutralizer and squeezed the liquid over Nicole's head, taking care to fully saturate each rod.

"Oooh, it's cold." Nicole giggled.

Minutes later, the stylist was unraveling the rods, dropping them in the basin.

"I can't wait," Lauren said. She bounced on the soles of her boat shoes.

"Well? How do they look?" Nicole said when her head was free of rods.

Leaning over the plastic basin, the stylist blinked. She blinked again. She lifted her hands clear. "Ummm."

"Is something wrong?" Kath asked.

"I haven't…There's something…I don't…" the stylist stuttered. She scuttled backwards.

"Let me see." Shelley, the pushy cow, hustled over and peered into the basin.

Kath had to make do with a gawk over her shoulder. *Oh!* She sucked in a breath. Her heart skipped. What on earth? The contents of the sink, Nicole's hair, was heaving.

Startled, Kath took a step back.

"What's going on?" Nicole demanded. She sat up, water dribbling down the cape.

Gasping, Lauren stepped sideways, knocking over a flimsy display stand, and sending shampoo bottles flying. "I'm sorry, I'm sorry," she babbled, grappling to right the stand.

"What? Why?" Nicole said, getting to her feet. "Don't tell me it's too curly?"

Oh it was curly, all right. It was coiled and twisted and pulsing with movement. Practically *undulating*. Only, it wasn't hair anymore. Instead, hundreds of pencil-thin black snakes roiled in the air, their tiny mouths opening and closing as they writhed and twisted away from her scalp.

"Guys?" Nicole shook her head. The serpents moved with her. She glared at the stylist. "You better not have wrecked my hair…" she hissed, and she stalked over to the styling station. Her mouth dropped open. She whirled to face the stylist, who was backed up into the corner.

"What did you do?" she roared, her face ugly with rage.

The stylist gave a squeak. She lifted her arms to shield her face. "I-I don't know," she stammered. "It's never happened before."

"There are snakes on my head!" Nicole screamed, lunging towards her. "Snakes!" The little serpents hissed.

The stylist snatched up the curling wand she'd used to curl Kath's fringe, brandishing the still-hot utensil in Nicole's face. "Stay back!" she warned.

But Nicole kept coming, bringing her head of serpents with her. One of the snakes darted from behind her ear, and, ducking under the appliance, it sank two hooked teeth into the stylist's arm, biting down. When it pulled away, blood beaded in the tiny puncture holes. The snake swayed gleefully.

The stylist was less pleased. "It bit me!" she shrieked, and she slapped at the serpent with the shaft of the curling wand. The serpent sizzled, the scorched tendril searing off and dropping to the floor, where the little jaws opened and closed in futile protest.

"Nicole! Stop!" Shelley shouted. "Step back. They're only tiny. If we stay far enough away, they can't hurt us. We can fix this. We just need a minute to figure out what to do."

"But there are snakes in my hair!" Nicole screeched again, but Shelley's bossy tone did the trick because she stopped her advance on the stylist.

"It has to be the permanent wave that caused the transformation," Shelley said. "Some unexpected reaction to the perming solution."

No kidding, Einstein.

All at once, Lauren leapt onto the coffee table, teetering on the piles of magazines and knocking over an empty champagne bottle in the process. A solution bottle in each hand, she took aim and squirted them over Nicole's head.

"Lauren! What are you doing?" Kath shouted.

"Adding more neutralizer," she said, giving the plastic squeeze-bottles a final pump before jumping down. "Shelley said it was a reaction to the perming solution…"

The snakes hissed angrily.

"No, no, no," the stylist moaned, her eyes widening.

Kath turned to look. The serpents were growing, expanding. Within seconds, they were as thick as vacuum cleaner hoses and just as bendy, the tendrils spooling outwards from Nicole's head, regarding them through slitted snake eyes.

"Dammit, Lauren! You've gone and made it worse! It was the neutralizer that caused the transformation in the first place!" Kath said.

"Well, I didn't know, did I?"

Nicole rushed to the mirror. She threw up her arms. "I *can't* look like this! I'm getting married at the end of the month!" As she spoke, the serpents thrashed and twisted. No longer just black, several of them wore stripes of vivid red. Kath shuddered. More and more of them were striking out, searching for something to bite. They seemed to be feeding on Nicole's anger. Pulsing and growing along with her fury.

"Let's rinse the solution off," Shelley said quickly. "It might stop the reaction." She gestured to the basin. "Nicole, honey, come back and sit down. We're going to try and wash the solution out."

To Kath's surprise, Nicole did as she was told, storming back to the basin, narrowly avoiding the blitz of shampoo bottles rolling about on the floor. "Alright, but this better bloody work," she barked, while the serpents snapped at her. Kath spied the grisly snake stump as she plonked her bum on the seat, then leaned back and placed her neck in the hollow. "Well? Come on, then," she said.

"I just have to get some gloves from out back," the stylist said. *Too quickly.* She was going to do a runner.

"Great. I'll go with you," Kath said.

The stylist's face clouded.

"Hurry up, you two," Shelley hissed behind her hand. "I don't know how long I can keep Nicole calm."

Exchanging worried looks, Kath and the stylist hurried into the back room.

"Where do you keep the gloves?" Kath demanded.

The stylist motioned to a drawer with her hand.

Kath drew in a breath. *Omigod.* The stylist's forearm had swollen to the size of a football, the flesh around the puncture wounds stretched pink, her fingers resembling four bulbous sausages.

The stylist gawked. Realization must have hit her because her knees buckled. Kath caught her mid-swoon, just before she smacked into the wall. She gave the woman a moment to collect herself, then grasped her by the shoulders and fixed her with her best high school principal stare.

"Look. You need to pull yourself together," she said.

The stylist flicked her eyes at the bloated limb. "But my hand! It hurts! What if it's poisonous?" I could die," she wailed.

Kath had to admit, it was a real possibility.

"As soon as we sort Nicole's hair, we'll call an ambulance for your hand, okay? Right now, she's freaking out because you turned her into a gorgon. So you're going to need to hold it together."

Her eyes full of tears, the woman nodded.

Kath grabbed the gloves out of the drawer, then marched her back into the salon.

"What were you two whispering about out there?" Nicole asked. She turned her head. Two dozen snake eyes turned with her.

"Nothing." Kath struggled to keep her voice even. She didn't want to fuel Nicole's paranoia. "Gloves were in the wrong place." She went to hand them to the stylist, but the woman waved her swollen appendage in the air.

"Can't," she said. "You'll have to do it. My hand won't fit."

No way. Kath turned, holding the gloves out for the next likely victim. "Lauren?"

Lauren shuffled backwards. "You've got the gloves."

"Yes, you've got the gloves," Shelley chimed in.

Kath's heart sank. Those two! Refusing to help. Talk about a useless waste of space. Nicole should never have chosen them for her bridesmaids. She yanked on the gloves, snapping the yellow vinyl over the sleeves of her sweatshirt. Would it be enough to stave off a snake attack? If anything, the beasts were even thicker now, pumped up on Nicole's impatience. At least, the rubber fitting had a long hose. But perhaps the dousing that Lauren gave them earlier meant the snakes had a longer reach, too. There was a chance this could prove fatal…

Crouching low, she ducked in, flipped the water on, then ducked away again. The hose bucked, windmilling droplets around the room. Red and black serpents spat at the twisting plastic, several striking out. But the hose was too quick for them, their needle-teeth finding only air.

Still at a distance, Kath jumped up and grasped the end of the pipe, pointing the nozzle into the basin. *Time to do this.* "You're going to have to distract the snakes," she said to the others.

"How?" Lauren said.

"Maybe if we feed them?" Shelley whispered.

"Do you want to donate a finger?" Kath said. "I'm happy to give you the gloves."

"I saw a snake eat a light bulb on TV once," Lauren said.

"Why would it do that?" Shelley asked.

"Because the bulb was warm and shaped like an egg."

It was as good a suggestion as anything. And there was a chance Nicole's squirming mane could be sliced and diced from the inside. "Quick, unscrew one of the bulbs from around the mirror," Kath said.

"We should probably turn the electricity off first," Shelley said. "All this water. We don't want to get electrocuted."

"I can feel them wiggling," Nicole bellowed. "It's making me ill. Stop your blathering and *do* something."

"Where's the mains switch?" Kath said. She glanced around for the stylist. *If she's taken off...* But the stylist hadn't gone anywhere, although she was clearly *not all there.* Listing gently from side to side, the woman's face had turned as white as hair mousse, and her punctured arm was bulging like one of Popeye's.

"I..." She staggered forward, gripping the edge of the basin with her hand.

Distracted by the movement, the snakes turned to face her. Or maybe they'd been waiting for her to falter? Maybe they knew she was weaker than the rest of them. In any case, Kath didn't wait; she pointed the hose and drenched the seething mass, sloshing water over Nicole's scalp so each writhing viper got a thorough dousing.

The serpents ignored the water, their focus still on the stylist. One of them, as thick as Kath's arm, reared up, opened its maw and sank its needle fangs into the stylist's shoulder, pinning her upright, while a second even thicker specimen, slithered from Nicole's nape and coiled around her torso.

What was that about snakes mesmerizing their prey? Kath didn't know about the stylist, but she couldn't look away, holding her breath as slowly, inexorably, the constrictor bunched its muscles and squeezed.

The stylist gaped, a tiny mewl escaping from her lips.

The serpent tightened its grip. There was the dull crunch of bones and the coils tightened again, wrapping round and round her like a telephone cord.

Kath was as helpless as the stylist.

"Kath, stop. It's hopeless," Shelley's voice said in her ear. Her fingers tugged at the back of Kath's sweatshirt, pulling her away from Nicole.

Almost calm, Kath flipped the water off on the way past. The stylist was dead, slumped upright at the basin.

The three bridesmaids congregated at the counter. Lauren dug in her pockets then lit up a cigarette. She tossed her lighter on the counter, sucked in deep, and blew smoke into the air.

Shelley glared at her.

"What? I'm nervous, okay?"

Kath was nervous, too. What the hell were they going to do now? She glanced over her shoulder at Nicole. Still at the basin, their favourite bride-to-be was weirdly still, her eyes fixed on the ceiling while the snake at her nape crushed the stylist to a pulp.

"We have to call the police," Shelley said under her breath. "The stylist is dead. Nicole killed her."

"The *snakes* killed her," Kath corrected.

Shelley folded her arms. "I don't think the police are going to differentiate," she said.

"I don't think the police are going to come," Lauren replied, taking another drag on her ciggie. "Who's going to believe us?"

"It was an accident," Kath said. "Nicole couldn't help it."

Shelley rolled her eyes. "Come on, Kath. Get real. She's a fucking monster. What if she decides to kill one of us? What if she goes on a rampage?"

She didn't look like she was preparing to rampage. Inert, Nicole was still slumped in the chair, while the thick snake clutched the corpse in its coils. Meanwhile, the other hair-serpents were stabbing at the body, big time, puncturing it repeatedly with their fangs.

"I'm calling the police," Shelley announced. She dived under the counter for the phone.

"No!" Kath said loudly, causing a little snake to look their way. "We have to at least *try* to save, Nicole. We can't just give up. We're her bridesmaids."

Lauren dropped her eyes to the floor. She kicked at a stray shampoo bottle. But Shelley sighed. "Okay. Fair enough. What do you suggest?"

Kath thought hard. "There's a stump. Where that little snake lashed out and bit the stylist. She singed it off with the curling wand."

Lauren and Shelley looked at her blankly.

"Well, it means the heads don't grow back, doesn't it? So, maybe we could get some scissors and cut them off."

Stubbing out her cigarette on the side of an empty champagne glass, Lauren cocked her head at the corpse. "There's no way we're getting the scissors out of that woman's apron."

"Hairdressing scissors will be too small, anyway," Shelley said. "Have you seen the size of some of those snakes?"

"There's a mower place next door," Lauren said. "We could break in and get a chainsaw."

Kath frowned. "You want to use a chainsaw on our friend?"

"Let's check the drawers in the styling stations," Shelley said. "There has to be something we can use."

Their eyes still on Nicole, they sidled over to the styling stations and began rifling through the drawers. Lauren gestured to them that she was switching the curling wand on again. Kath nodded. It had worked before, and it wasn't like they had a lot of options.

"Hey, guys," Shelley said, pointing to an open drawer.

Kath rushed over. Lying in the bottom of the drawer was a fold-out razor. She nodded. That would do the trick. She was reaching out to grab it when Shelley stopped her, her hand on Kath's forearm.

"If we do this, what's going to happen to Nicole?" It was a good point. Severing the snakes might kill Nicole. She could bleed out…"We could still call the police…" Shelley said. "Let them deal with it."

"What the fuck is going on here?" Nicole screamed.

Kath raised her head and looked in the mirror. Nicole was right behind them, had snuck up on them like a snake in the grass. Now she was towering over them in full-on Medusa mode, the mass of snakes churning on her head. Then two snakes drew back to full height. They were going to attack…

"Heyaaaa!" Lauren yelled, racing in with the hot curling wand. One of the smaller snakes was blindsided; Lauren stabbed it in the eye with the tip of the wand. The smell of roasting chicken filled the air. But it seems snakes believe in the eye for an eye thing too, because the wounded appendage fired a stream of venom that struck Lauren in the eye.

"She's attacking me!" Nicole shrieked, turning on Lauren, serpents swirling around her head in a frenzy. Lauren dropped the wand, bringing her hands to her face, but not before a barrage of snakes had showered her with venom, the caustic spray making her skin bubble and lift.

Shelley charged in, slicing wildly at the snakes with the razor.

Meanwhile, Kath raced to the window seat, plunging her hand into her handbag for her sunglasses and putting them on.

When she looked up, she saw Shelley had got lucky, managing to lop off a couple of snake heads and drawing the others' attention away from Lauren. Pumping blood, the severed stumps swayed and slumped. It only seemed to make Nicole angrier.

"You bitch!" Nicole screamed and the death-crush snake burst from her nape again, whipping beneath Shelley's legs. As she fell, it coiled itself around her neck.

Frantic, Shelley plucked at her throat, her feet kicking uselessly. Slowly suffocating, she couldn't speak, but Kath caught the movement of her lips: "KILL HER."

Snatching up the champagne bottle that had landed on the floor when Lauren jumped on the coffee table, Kath smashed it against the edge of the table. She weighed it in her hand.

Kill her…

Suddenly, the door chimed and a man popped his head inside. "Hello? Is everything okay, in here? I could hear yelling from the dairy and I thought I'd better…"

Startled, Nicole jumped. She whirled to face the newcomer, the big snake at her nape releasing Shelley in surprise. But several smaller snakes went on the attack instead, erupting from Nicole's head, they opened their jaws in unison and bit down hard on the intruder's arm. Embedded in his flesh, they hung on, one trying swallow his hand.

"What the hell?" the man bellowed, shrugging his shoulder in a desperate attempt to free himself. "Get them off me!"

Kath rushed at Nicole from behind. As close as she dared. She slashed at the big crusher with the broken bottle. Its hide was as hard as a crown pumpkin. Kath leaned into it, gouging deep to sever the killer limb. Blood sprayed across the room.

After that, everything happened in slow-mo. The dairy owner hollered. The smaller snakes reared back, holding fast to the man's limb. Kath imagined the venom pumping. The man's thrashing slowed. His eyes watered. Where his arm was still visible, a blue-red vein branched. Suddenly, the skin at his shoulder broke, revealing purple muscle. Tendons stretched, white and sinewy. Fibers pinged.

The arm popped free.

Omigod. It was just like that scene out of *Cat People* when the panther mauls the zookeeper. Lying on the floor, the dairy owner stared at the ceiling, grasping at the stump of his severed arm, blood spurting through his fingers.

Kath backed away, almost losing her footing, there was so much blood. The man opened his mouth, but he barely made a sound.

Nicole clenched her fists. Her eyes flashed. "He surprised me!" she shouted. "It wasn't my fault. He shouldn't have come up behind me like that." She was hysterical. But at least she didn't know it had been Kath who'd attacked her from behind. The snakes whipped and danced in agitation. Although, they seemed...

On all fours, Lauren was flailing blindly on the floor. "Help! What's happening?" she called. Also on the floor, the dairy owner shuddered then lay still. Tinged blue, Shelley didn't move. That just left Kath. The last bridesmaid standing.

The last bridesmaid standing...

Behind her back, Kath slipped the bloody bottle into the basin. Maybe she could salvage something from the situation? She raised her hands. "Of course, it's not your fault, Nicole," she soothed. "I know things look bad, but I'm not going to let anything happen to you, okay? I've got your back. It's what bridesmaids do, right? You just sit yourself down on this stool and let me take care of everything."

A dozen eyes narrowed as Nicole sat on the stool.

Good one, Kath. Now all you have to do is tame a bunch of snakes. Duh. She was an idiot. The beasts on Nicole's head were snakes. They were *snakes*.

Kath raced across the salon, avoiding the bloody puddles and shampoo bottles, to where the tape deck sat on its shelf. She pressed PLAY. The tape crackled for an instant and Phil Collins rang out. "Sussudio" had a certain charm. Would it charm Nicole's snakes? She turned. The snakes swayed, their movement almost graceful. Crouching, Kath crept back, and grabbing up a corner of Nicole's hairdressing cape, quick as a flash she flipped it over Nicole's head, so the remaining snakes were caught in the thick black fabric, committing the creatures to the darkness. Then she tied off the turban with a scrunchy snatched from a styling station. At first, the cape bulged as the snakes writhed, but after a moment the darkness soothed them and they lay quiet. Nicole seemed calmer, too.

Just the salon to tidy now. Kath took a can of Clairol from one of the styling stations, and Lauren's lighter off the counter. Pressing the nozzle of the hairspray, she flicked on the lighter, and shot a long burst of flames at a stack of towels. The towels went up with a whump. When the fire was crackling nicely, Kath checked the turban was still secure then took Nicole's hand.

"Come on, honey. Time to go."

"Kath? Shelley? What's happening?" Lauren said. "I can smell fire." How could she still smell? Her nose had all but burned away. But already, fire was taking hold; it was licking at the walls, black smoke billowing near the ceiling.

Kath hesitated. She could just leave them. Except Shelley's mum's Nissan was parked out front. Eventually, someone would ask why Shelley and Lauren had been at the salon, and sooner or later, they would want to know why Nicole and Kath weren't there too.

Kath sighed. "Here," she said, placing Lauren's hand on Shelley's shoe. "Hold on to this. Don't let go. Nicole, follow us."

Kath picked Shelley up under her arms, and, dragging her past the dead dairy owner, she led the bridal party out of the salon.

Kath lifted the lace hem of Nicole's bridal dress as they climbed the stairs to the yacht club reception room. "Watch your step."

"Omigod, I'm so nervous," Nicole said.

On the landing, Kath let the fabric drop. "It's going to be fine. Andy adores you."

Nicole touched her fingers to her classic chignon, whispering, "Is my hair okay?"

Kath smiled. "You look beautiful."

In the end, they'd had to go to a different salon since Trendz Hair Design had been closed down due to the unexpected chemical fire. The dairy had closed down too, pending new management apparently. Little issues like these were why brides did these pre-wedding style consults in the first place.

With a blast of chatter, Nicole's dad slipped through the double doors, but not before Kath spied Rhys standing at the front of the room next to the groom, looking super-hot in his best man's suit. Everything was falling into place. Six months tops, and it would be her turn to take a walk down the aisle. She smiled. All that remained was for her to catch the bride's bouquet.

Nicole's dad offered her his arm. "Ready to go, love?"

"In a sec." She turned to Kath. "Kath, thank you. I honestly don't know what I would've done if you hadn't agreed to stand up as my maid of honour."

Grinning, Kath lifted her chin. "Don't be a ditz. Of course I'll stand up for you."

To be fair, Shelley was still in a coma in ICU and might never wake up; she couldn't stand up for herself, let alone hold a bouquet. As for Lauren, not to be mean, but there was no way she was going to be in any wedding photos any time soon. She'd got her wish of resembling someone from the movies, though: with those scars she could be Freddy Krueger in *A Nightmare on Elm Street*. Both of them were bald too; their hair, too long in the perming solution, had been burned away, although Shelley might never know it. Luckily, Lauren was blind, or she'd totally wig out.

The bridal march played behind the closed double doors.

Nicole took a deep breath. She rolled her shoulders. "Okay, shall we do this?"

"Hang on," Kath said, and, reaching out, she tucked away the tiny tendrilled serpent that had escaped from her friend's chignon.

Slashbacks

TIM WAGGONER

Dwayne Hunt was driving home from work on a rainy early evening in late August. It wasn't raining hard, but the sky was overcast, making it seem as if a premature gloomy dusk had arrived. Dwayne wasn't a big drinker, but he was sorely tempted to stop at a bar. He was still upset over what Sandra had done yesterday, and he wasn't in a hurry to see her. Spending a few hours in a bar – without her – sounded damn good right then. He'd almost made up his mind to do it, when he saw the store. Its interior lights were on, giving him a clear view of what was inside. Row after row of chest-high white shelves, filled with rectangular book-size objects.

He glanced above the store's entrance and—as if his attention was a trigger—the building's neon sign came to glowing life. In blazing red letters, it spelled out *ThrillerKillers!* All one word, followed by an exclamation point.

Dwayne meant to drive past, but the store's mystery beguiled him. He could've sworn that when he'd driven by this place on the way to work this morning, the building was empty, a *For Lease* sign taped to the inside of the glass door entrance. How could someone lease the building, move in, and be ready for business, all within a day? Not even a full day, more like nine hours. Then there was the name—*ThrillerKillers!*—all in red letters. *Blood* red.

He whipped the steering wheel of his Honda Civic to the right just as he was about to speed past the entrance to the store's small parking lot. Tires squealed in protest, momentum caused his left shoulder to slam against the vehicle's interior door, and the driver behind him laid on the horn in anger over his sudden, reckless turn. The Civic's rear end fishtailed as it skidded into the lot, and Dwayne fought to keep the car under control. If there had been any other vehicles in to the lot, he might well have hit one of them. But the lot was empty, and Dwayne managed to maneuver his car into a space close to the front entrance without incident.

He sat there for a moment, hands white-knuckle tight on the steering wheel, heart pounding triphammer fast. He sat silently for a moment, stunned by what he'd just done. He was in his thirties, for godsakes! He wasn't some impulsive, erratic teenager who acted without thinking. He was the kind of man who paid his bills on time, made sure to put a little money in savings every pay period, filed his taxes early, saw his physician regularly, ate right, and exercised (a little, anyway).

He smiled, shook his head at his own foolishness, and got out of the car. He bowed his head as he walked to keep the rain out of his eyes, and when he pushed the front door open, he heard a loud electronic tone: *bee-baw.*

He stopped just inside the entrance and looked around. He couldn't believe it.

As if the store's name wasn't clue enough, the interior décor said this wasn't just *any* video store. This one specialized in *horror movies.* Murals were painted on the walls, oversized images of horror icons – masked slashers, burnt-faced tormentors, chainsaw-wielding maniacs, homicidal dolls and puppets. The wall directly opposite the entrance had the phrase *I Love Horror* tattooed in black-ink letters on a huge painting of an anatomically correct heart.

It's revolting. What would your parents say?

My god, Dwayne. You're too old for that kind of crap.

You're an adult, for Christ's sake. Don't you think it's long past time for you to grow the hell up?

Dwayne squeezed his eyes shut and concentrated on ignoring the voices. When his mind was once again quiet, he opened his eyes.

"Can I help you?"

Startled, Dwayne turned toward the voice and saw a raven-haired woman in her twenties standing behind a blood-red counter. The woman was petite, hair short and curly, skin fair, almost pale. Her makeup was thick and – to his mind – gaudy. Bright red lipstick, crimson eyeshadow. She wore a black polo shirt with the *ThrillerKillers!* logo stitched above her left breast with red thread. A flock of bats was tattooed on her left arm, and a pair of silver earrings shaped like tiny axes dangled from her ears. She wasn't wearing an employee name tag, and he thought maybe she was the manager.

Dwayne smiled, feeling sheepish for being caught gaping at the store's interior.

"I've never seen a place like this before."

It was the woman's turn to smile. "Let me guess: horror fan?"

He laughed. "How can you tell?"

"By the expression on your face when you came in. It was reverent, like you'd just entered a cathedral. All horror geeks look like that when they first set eyes on the place. It's like Disneyland for gorehounds."

"It sure is. I've never seen anything like it."

The woman's smile widened to a grin. "That's because this store is one of a kind. Nothing like it anywhere else in the world."

Something dark and shimmering moved in the woman's eyes, just for an instant, and then it was gone.

"You been into horror long?" she asked.

Dwayne was so startled by what he saw—or thought he'd seen—that it took him a moment to reply.

"All my life. I was crazy about dinosaurs as a kid, then I started reading horror comics and religiously watching the Saturday afternoon horror movie show on TV. I put together horror models and collected horror toys, and when I got a little older, I started reading horror novels. I can't get enough of the stuff, you know?"

"I do. You're dedicated, one could almost say devout, aren't you? We appreciate that."

Dwayne frowned. "We?"

"Fellow horror fans."

"Oh." He remembered the dark glimmer in her eyes and swallowed nervously.

"Does this place work like a regular video store?" he asked. "You sign up for a membership, pick out a few movies, pay a rental fee, take them home, then bring them back in a few days?"

"Yep," the woman said. "Signing up for a membership is easy, though. All we need is your name and telephone number, and then I can issue you a passport to hours of entertainment."

Dwayne grinned. "Sounds good. Sign me up."

True to the woman's word, it only took a couple minutes for Dwayne to get hooked up with an account. The woman then filled out a membership card and Dwayne was official. When the woman gave him the card, he held it in his hands for a moment. It felt colder than it should have, as if it had just come out of a freezer.

"You're one of us now," she said.

"Thanks." He put the card in his wallet.

"Take a look around," the woman said. "I know you'll find something just right for you."

Dwayne nodded, picked an aisle at random, and began perusing the selection. He grinned the entire time, seeing well-loved favorites. The covers were all lurid variations on a theme – blood, mutilated flesh, severed limbs, screaming women, killers wielding sharp implements and dressed to reflect various slasher "themes." From time to time, he'd stop, pick up a movie, turn it over, and read the breathless description on the back. *We dare you to make it to the end of this movie without puking! The most intense shocker ever put on film! The last ten minutes will make your heart stop!* He'd chuckle, put the movie back, and continue on. After a bit, he came to a film that looked out of place among the others. There was no blood on the cover, no masked killer, no shrieking women with surgically enhanced breasts. The cover was a photograph of a middle-aged woman with frazzled strawberry-blond hair. Her glasses were perched on the end of her nose, and her narrow, pinched face was twisted into a dark scowl. The title of the movie was *Art Period.*

Dwayne didn't reach for this one. He stared at it, unable to believe what he was seeing. He knew that face, that exact expression. He'd never forget it.

"It's revolting. What would your parents say?"

Dwayne froze, too afraid to look up at Mrs. Kaufman. But he could feel the weight of her disapproving stare on him, and he shrank down in his seat several inches. His hand had reflexively moved to cover the paper on the desk before him, but Mrs. Kaufman said, "Take your hands away," in a stern voice that brooked no argument. Dwayne obeyed.

The drawing revealed was a crude representation of an ambulatory corpse – lean arms and legs, flesh rotted away from the head to reveal the left half of the skull, clothes little more than tattered scraps. The dead thing's mouth was open in a soundless cry, and its claw-like hands were raised, as if it were approaching the viewer, intending to attack.

Mrs. Kaufman snatched the drawing off the table and held it up high, as if she wanted to make sure Dwayne couldn't take it back.

"Do you think this—" she shook the drawing for emphasis—"is an appropriate subject for art?"

The other students giggled and whispered to each other as they watched Dwayne's humiliation.

Dwayne was seven, and he hated being in Mrs. Kaufman's class. She was mean, and he believed she secretly didn't like kids, had taken this job solely so she could torment them. But he looked forward to art period, which they had twice a week, on Tuesdays and Thursdays. She usually gave them an assignment and then left them alone to work on it while she graded assignments at her desk. Today, she'd told them it was free drawing day, meaning they could draw whatever they wanted to. Dwayne had been excited, and he'd chosen to recreate the cover of a horror comic his grandmother had bought for him. He'd been having so much fun drawing it, but now he wished he'd chosen a different subject.

Dwayne looked down at this desk. "I guess not."

He spoke so softly, he didn't think Mrs. Kaufman would hear him, but she did.

"You *guess* not." Her voice dripped with sarcasm. "Well, I *guess* not too."

Mrs. Kaufman took hold of his drawing with both hands and tore it in two. He felt tears threatening, but he knew if he let them come, the whole class would laugh at him. He fought hard, but the tears came anyway, as did his classmates' mocking laughter.

Dwayne shuddered at the memory and turned away from the video with Mrs. Kaufman's face on it. No, the face of a woman who only *looked* like her.

Feeling self-conscious, he glanced back toward the front of the store to see if the woman at the register had noticed how uncomfortable he'd become. She wasn't paying attention to him, though. She was working at the computer, fingers tapping the keyboard.

Dwayne was relieved. He knew it was stupid, he'd only just met this woman, didn't even know her name, but he didn't want to appear foolish in front of her. In front of anyone, for that matter. Not after that awful day in Mrs. Kaufman's class. He would've left the store right then, but he didn't want the woman to ask him why he was leaving so soon, didn't want to come up with some kind of excuse. So he continued down the aisle, pretending to browse the videos but not really looking at any of them – until he saw one with his father's face on it. The man's expression was a mixture of anger, disgust, and disappointment. The name of this "film" was *No Son of Mine*.

"My god, Dwayne. You're too old for that kind of crap."

Dwayne was lying on his bed, back propped against the headboard, legs stretched out in front of him. He'd been so engrossed in the magazine he'd been reading that he hadn't heard his dad open his bedroom door and step inside. The walls of Dwayne's room were covered with horror film posters, and his shelves displayed action figures of various movie monsters. The magazine he held was called *Gore World*, and it contained articles, interviews, and reviews related to horror films, especially the more extreme variety.

"Did your goddamn grandmother get you that thing?" his dad demanded.

Dwayne was fifteen. His father was in his late forties, already going bald, and whenever he got angry, his face turned bright pink. He must've been really pissed off because his face was a deep red.

"I bought it with my own money," Dwayne said. And then, just to make sure his father understood, he added. "I got it for mowing the McAndrys' lawn last week."

"You're supposed to be saving money for college, not blowing it on trash like *that*." He nodded toward the magazine. "Jesus, Dwayne, I'd rather have caught you reading porn instead of that thing. At least looking at porn is normal for a boy your age." His eyes widened suddenly. "You didn't jack off to any of the pictures in there, did you?"

"God, no! That's disgusting!"

"That's something to be grateful for, I guess." He walked over to Dwayne's bed and held out his hand. "Give it to me."

Dwayne closed the magazine and gripped it tight. "No." He'd meant the denial to sound forceful, but it wasn't much louder than a whisper.

Two things happened then. Dwayne's dad slapped his face with his left hand and tore the magazine from Dwayne's grip with his right. Dwayne was so stunned at being hit by his father that at first he didn't believe it had actually happened. But then he felt the pain, and he reached up and put a hand to his cheek and jaw, as if attempting to shield it from a second blow.

His dad looked at him as he curled up the magazine and gripped it like a weapon.

"Don't defy me, boy. When I tell you to do something, you *do* it. Understand?"

Dwayne wanted to tell his dad to go to hell, but he kept his mouth shut and gave a barely perceptible nod. His dad gripped the magazine tighter, and for an instant Dwayne thought he was going to start beating him with it. But then he lowered his arm to his side and let out a long sigh.

"Go out for sports or something. Get a girlfriend. Just do something *normal* for a change, okay?"

His dad left then, not bothering to close the door behind him. Dwayne looked at the empty doorway, teeth clenched, hands bunched into tight fists.

Before his dad had entered his room, Dwayne had been reading an interview with a low-budget horror film director. Dwayne had been thinking that maybe he could make horror movies too when he grew up. But after what his father had said, he did his best to forget that dream, and when it was time for him to go to college, instead of majoring in film, he went into photography. He told himself it was *kind of* like film, but the closest he ever came to making movies was recording clients' weddings on video.

Dwayne didn't realize he was holding his breath until he drew in a gasp of air. As he'd done with Mrs. Kaufman and *Art Period*, he wanted to deny that the man on the cover of *No Son of Mine* bore any resemblance to his father, but he couldn't. He didn't know what the hell was happening here, and he didn't *want* to know. All he wanted was to get the hell out of here, get in his car, and drive as fast as he could to the nearest bar where he would start pounding drinks and keep pounding them until he was too drunk to remember this store existed.

He started toward the front of the store. Dwayne didn't care if the woman at the counter looked away from her monitor and wondered why he was fleeing the store in a near panic. All he wanted was to get away from this place.

He was halfway to the door when one of the videos fell off its shelf and landed on the floor in front of him. He didn't want to look at it, wanted to keep going, but his eyes were drawn to the cover as if against his will. When he saw it, he felt a cold jolt. He stopped, bent down, and with a shaking hand picked up the video so he could look at it more closely. The title of this movie was *Grow the Hell Up*, and on the cover was a picture of his wife.

Dwayne stood in the center of their spare bedroom. This was where he'd established his version of a rec room—a large TV, a recliner, and an end table to hold drinks and snacks. The walls were covered with shelves that held his extensive collection of horror films on video cassette. Or at least, which *had* held them. They were empty now. Not a single movie remained.

He turned around. Sandra stood in the doorway, hands on her hips, mouth set in a self-satisfied smile.

"What did you do?" he asked. He had no doubt Sandra was responsible for the disappearance of his movies. She *hated* anything to do with horror. Books, films, haunted houses, spooky hayrides . . . She hated Halloween and refused to let him decorate the house. She didn't even like giving out candy to trick-or-treaters. She always insisted they go out for dinner and a movie that night. A *non-scary* movie.

His wife was a tall woman—taller than he was by several inches. Her red hair was always perfect, as was her makeup. She'd just gotten home from the bank and was still in work clothes—a white long-sleeved blouse and black slacks. Like him, she was in her mid-thirties, but she looked ten years younger. She worked hard at maintaining her illusion of youthfulness.

"You're an adult, for Christ's sake," she said. "Don't you think it's long past time for you to grow the hell up? Plus, you've spent *way* too much of our money on those ridiculous films of yours. I took off work this morning, boxed up all your movies, and took them to a used bookstore and sold them. I got pennies on the dollar, but it was worth it to have the damn things out of my house."

"Our house," Dwayne said softly.

"What was that? I couldn't hear you."

For perhaps the thousandth time since they'd been married, Dwayne wondered why Sandra had chosen him to be her husband. The answer that came to him was the same as every other time he'd asked himself this question. He was weak, and she wanted someone she could control, someone who wouldn't stand up to her – and he fit that description to a T.

"*Our* house," he said more loudly. He took a step toward Sandra. "Those were *my* movies. You didn't have a right to sell them."

"We're married. Everything we own is joint property. Of *course* I had the right to sell them."

Her tone was smug. Dwayne felt fire building inside him. But before it could become an inferno, all emotion drained out of him. His shoulders slumped and he let out a sigh.

"What do you want to do for dinner tonight?" he asked in a thoroughly beaten voice.

"That's up to you." Her smile became a smirk. "It's your night to cook."

"I haven't seen that one, but it looks scary."

Dwayne was still kneeling. He looked up and saw the woman with the silver ax earrings gazing down at him with sympathetic eyes. Embarrassed, he took hold of *Grow the Hell Up*, straightened, and put it back on the shelf. He then turned to her.

"I've got to go. Thanks for signing me up for a membership. I'll be back when I have more time to look around." But he knew he wouldn't return. Nothing could get him to set foot in this place again.

"You're not going to leave without checking out the back room, are you?"

Some independently owned video rental stores kept porno films in the back room where only adults were allowed to look at them. He'd always been curious about the movies in there, but he'd never had the guts to sneak in to take a look.

"I don't think so," he said. "Those aren't the kind of movies I'm interested in."

He started to move past the woman, but she took hold of his arm to stop him. Her grip was much stronger than he expected, and the dark glimmer in her eyes was back

"I think you'll really like what's waiting for you back there."

He realized something then. "I didn't see a back room."

"Sure you did," the woman said. "It's right over there."

She pointed past him and he turned to look toward the back of the store. Beneath the heart with the *I Love Horror* tattooed on it was a doorway that he would've sworn hadn't been there a moment ago. Instead of a door, a black curtain concealed what lay inside.

"Go on." The woman released his arm and gave him a gentle push between the shoulder blades. "You're going to love it."

He started walking toward the mysterious back room. After seeing the three videos that somehow had images from his life on their covers, he wasn't sure he wanted to see what waited for him in the room. But although he was afraid, he was excited too, at least a little. He felt as if he were living in one of the movies he loved so much. He was the hero, and he was heading toward the final confrontation with darkness.

He reached the curtain, hesitated only an instant, then pushed the black cloth aside and stepped through the doorway.

Inside was a dimly lit room. There was a steel table to the right upon which rested a number of objects. But what drew his immediate attention was the three people sitting in metal chairs bolted to the concrete floor. Their hands and feet had been bound with barbed wire, and blood trickled from the wounds. They were naked, held to their chairs with black leather straps that had been buckled tight around their abdomens. They couldn't speak – their mouths were covered by black cloth gags – but their eyes communicated their terror quite clearly. Dwayne recognized all three of them. Mrs. Kaufman, his father, and Sandra. His teacher and his father looked exactly as they did in his memories, even though both were much older in real life. He wasn't sure that Mrs. Kaufman was still alive, but Sandra looked as she did today.

They all started trying to talk to him at once, but the gags muffled their words, and he couldn't understand anything they said. He could guess, though. He'd seen enough horror movies to know what people in this situation would say. *Unbuckle us! Let us go! Help us!*

He made no move toward them. Instead, he turned to look at the objects on the table. A variety of tools were laid out in neat rows: knives of various styles and sizes. hatchets, axes, ice picks, hand scythes, bone saws, chainsaws . . . There were masks, too. Halloween masks of different kinds, sports masks, cloth masks, masks carved from wood, others forged from metal. Dwayne turned back to the captives and smiled.

"The manager was right. I *am* going to love this."

The three soon-to-be victims began shouting and screaming behind their gags. Dwayne took his time choosing, but eventually he donned a mask, selected a weapon, and went to work.

WELCOME
NANCY!

Munchies

LUCY A. SNYDER

I shouldn't be talking to anyone about this. Yes, honey, I know it was a long time ago…but those monsters still have friends in high places. So you didn't hear this from me, okay?

A pseudonym? Okay, but for God's sake don't use my drag name. People in the scene know my real name, too…it isn't safe. Wait…you can use the name Charlee Cheeks.

She was there when it all went down, but she died in the epidemic in 1989. As far as I'm concerned, Ronnie the Monster killed her and everyone else. I mean, it wasn't even four years later…that's not a coincidence. That was his revenge on us all for the "crime" of protecting our own town. So it can be her voice reaching from beyond the grave to finally tell the truth. I think she'd approve.

It all went down on Wednesday, April 17, 1984. I was seventeen years old, a junior in Lamersal High School in far West Texas. Never heard of Lamersal? Of course you haven't. *Nobody* has. You ever see a map of Texas? You know that big, empty part in the middle where there's no interstates and no mountains and no cities and it's just a flat, dry stretch of *nothing*? Lamersal is right smack dab in the middle of that. From there, it's a six-hour drive to Dallas, a twelve-hour drive to Houston, eight hours to El Paso, four hours to San Antonio…yeah, you get the idea. Kids in small towns in places like Ohio only *think* they're isolated. You'd have to go to, like, the Aleutian Islands to find an American community more cut off from the rest of the world. How do the lyrics to Lou Reed's "Small Town" go? Something like, the only good thing about a small town is loathing it

113

so much you have to leave it for a better place? That's the damn truth. Our major export wasn't beef or wool or crude oil…it was eighteen-year-olds.

Lamersal fronted really hard as this red-blooded, more Texas-than-thou, more Christian-than-thou kinda place. Football was religion. Rodeo Day was a holiday. And I think we had more Baptist churches per capita than any other town in Texas…which *is* saying something. The cops regularly raided our sole book shop, Ye Olde Fantastique Paperbacks, looking for porn.

And that cuts to this: once you scratched past the town's brittle Christian crust, you'd find the place was wearing a sequined thong under its Wranglers and bled rainbows. It's just that everyone had to be way on the down-low because of all the crusty Christians. But it's like we found out in physics lab: every action has an equal and opposite reaction. So the more the town fathers told us to be abstinent, the more we got freaky. The more money they threw into the D.A.R.E program, the more weed and LSD we had at parties. And every time a local preacher pounded the pulpit about how Dungeons & Dragons was satanic, a new game group formed up in someone's rec room.

Teen rebellion? I mean, sure, on the surface…but it was so goddamned *boring* there! If you weren't into football, weren't into church, and you didn't have cable, I mean…what else was there to do? You had a choice between alcohol, or just completely losing your mind…or you could get creative. Which is what we did. For all the theatre and choir kids who had aspirations to get the hell out of there, go to college in a big city, and become someone relevant, our down-low drag shows and Rocky Horror parties were a whole lot more attractive than getting wasted on Coors and Miller Lite down at the reservoir.

But even the people who were all onboard with the Christians & Cowboys front of the town chafed at the knowledge that they were living and working in a place that was so completely inconsequential to the rest of the planet. One of the local preachers, Billy Ray Lowder, wanted to move on to bigger and better congregations, maybe a TV show, and he needed a higher profile to do that. His wife Loretta was the main guidance counselor at our high school, and he put a bug in her ear and got her to organize a new anti-smoking, anti-drug, anti-delinquency program: Bee Aware. Our high school football team was known as The Swarm, and the mascot was a cheerleader in a killer bee costume. So of course everything at the school was bee-themed to a truly cheesy degree.

I found out years later that Bee Aware was a blatant rip-off of Tulsa's Operation Aware program, which Billy Ray had learned about when he was traveling. But none of us knew, of course, because how would we? Anyway, the Lowders got a whole bunch of buzz going and leveraged their church contacts and got a writeup in the *Dallas Morning News* and later in *Time*. Before we knew it, Nancy "Just Say No" Reagan herself was flying in to Lamersal's tiny airport to honor the school—and the Lowders, of course—for their totally plagiarized program.

This was by far the most exciting thing that had ever happened to Lamersal High School…Principal Wiley probably had to pass out Depends to the whole faculty and staff. Anyone who wasn't wetting themselves over Reagan swooping in to hand out a plaque, a check, and deliver a soundbite to the local stations was losing bowel control over all the chaos her visit promised to bring.

I and my cousin—I'll call him David—had gotten busted for skipping Mrs. Bellum's American History class. Bellum actually said out loud that emancipation was the worst thing that ever happened to black people in this country. Only she said "negroes." And she was looking right at Levon Jones when she said it. Like she was *daring* him to contradict her. He'd already backtalked her a bunch and the principal had warned if he did it again he'd get suspended. But Levon just sat there, poker-faced. We took him with us to costuming that night and let him take all his frustrations out on a couple of gowns I'd messed up. Ripping up fabric is pretty damn satisfying. Levon talked about the history he knew from his college professor uncle, and we realized the enormity of the bullshit Bellum was teaching us. We decided to just skip her class after that.

Our vice principal Mr. Lopez was sympathetic to why we'd skipped, but he said rules were rules and we had to be punished. He gave us a choice between after-school detention or working in the school cafeteria before school, during study hall, and during special events. We picked the cafeteria because we had costuming sessions and rehearsals right after school and couldn't miss them…the big School's Such A Drag ball in the second-floor dance hall of The Red Bandana was in just a month and a half, and neither of us had our costumes together and we hadn't really settled on songs, either. David, like most drag performers, was gonna lip-synch. But I had a pretty good falsetto and I wanted to try live singing. Work what you got, right? Besides, I haven't met a queen who wouldn't sing for real if anyone gave her half an excuse.

So anyway: at 6 a.m. the day Nancy Reagan visited our school, David and I were mixing up brownies and cookies for her reception. We were both barely awake, and Bernie the head cook wasn't even there yet…and if he had been, he would have warned us away from using the two pounds of butter we found in a covered steel bowl in the back of the refrigerator. He would have let us know that he'd infused nearly a half-pound of Maui Wowie in it. Normally he'd never have anything like that at school…except that the local police station had brought his cop brother in from Odessa because they needed extra officers on hand for Reagan's visit. And so the cop brother unexpectedly needed to stay at Bernie's apartment, and the butter was way too precious to just dump down the toilet.

But he wasn't there, so we didn't know, and we used Bernie's weed butter to make three pans of brownies and at least one batch of the four dozen snickerdoodle cookies. But it was the brownies that mattered.

The press arrived to set up several hours before the event. It was ridiculous. Lamersal only had two radio stations, a CBS affiliate, and a newspaper, but I counted fourteen TV broadcast vans out in the parking lot along with a whole bunch of strange cars. Principal Wiley told all of us to park around back behind the gym to leave room for visitors. Sheriff's deputies patted folks down and searched cars and bags before they let any of us onto the school grounds; a couple of seniors who forgot about the deer rifles in their truck racks got sent home. That morning was just a huge pain in the ass for all of us, really.

Billy Ray Lowder had put on his best blue suit and snakeskin boots and was right in the middle of it all the moment the first reporter arrived. Because of course he was, right? Glad-handing everyone, giving interviews…you could just see the visions of fame and fortune dancing behind his eyes. This was the day that was gonna make all his dreams come true.

But of course the reporters totally ignored him and swarmed onto the front sidewalk as Nancy Reagan's motorcade pulled into the traffic circle. About a dozen Secret Service guys were there along with twice that many deputies holding the press and rubberneckers back as Reagan got out, looking surprisingly cool and collected considering she was wearing a long-sleeved red suit dress in the eighty-five-degree weather. Me and David had to wear dark suits because we were serving refreshments at the reception, and we were both sweating like pigs.

The teachers herded us all over to the auditorium for her speech. She only talked for like a half an hour, first about how special the month of April is because of Easter, and then she talked about how drugs steal the dreams from children's hearts, and some bullshit story about how some kid could only see in black and white when she was strung out on drugs but now that she was clean she could see colors again. David and I were trying so hard not to laugh. But I guess there were probably kids in the audience who believed her because how would they know any better? Then Reagan handed the Lowders an appreciation plaque and gave the school an oversized check to fund Bee Aware. And we all applauded like we were supposed to.

Afterward, they herded all the kids except us helpers back to class and started the reception in the auditorium's atrium while the Secret Service guys stood

116

guard along the tall glass window wall between the potted sago palms. Most of the reporters had gotten what they needed for their features and they left. Basically, the reception was just so the Lowders, the school's senior faculty, executive staff, and the school board members could bask in Reagan's presence. She was smiling politely at all of the fawning suits around her, but you could tell that she was probably thinking about meeting the Pope the following week and was at best half-listening to anything anyone told her. David was serving a group of teachers on the other side of the room. I was standing there perspiring in my suit and tie, dumbly presenting a platter of brownies, feeling super out of place and wishing I could just go take a nap in one of the storage closets.

The principal waved me over to where he was standing by Reagan. We approached and offered them the tray. Reagan took the tiniest brownie on the platter and nibbled a corner of it politely, the way older ladies do when they don't intend to finish something because they're on a diet.

But when the first crumbs melted on her tongue, I saw her eyes dilate hugely. Suddenly her brown eyes turned black. And just as suddenly she shoved the rest of the brownie into her mouth and grabbed two more in each hand. The expression on her face had gone from a polite smiling blankness to one of primal hunger.

"Whoa, I guess these are some pretty good brownies," Principal Wiley joked as Reagan messily shoved both squares into her mouth. "What did y'all put in these, son?"

I was gaping like an idiot, staring at Reagan two-fisting brownies like she was a drunk in a county fair eating contest. Her hands were caked with brown crumbs, and her mouth was smeared with chocolate and buttery oil. Something weird was going on with her face. It was swelling, and at first I thought maybe she was having some kind of allergic reaction.

The nearest couple of Secret Service agents had left their posts and were striding toward Reagan; one was muttering, "Rainbow is off the reservation; repeat, Rainbow is off the reservation!" into his lapel mike.

The first agent gently touched her shoulder and said, "Ma'am, please, you need to go easy on those," but she slapped his hand away and hissed at him openmouthed like a freaking goose. Or a king cobra.

I took two steps back.

Mid-hiss, her dentures fell out and clattered on the dark wood parquet floor. But where I expected to see smooth pink gums, I saw sharp, serrated teeth that were growing longer by the second.

The Secret Service agent stepped forward and took her by both shoulders. "Ma'am! Pull yourself together!"

And that's when she unhinged her jaw and bit his fucking face right off.

She only really got his nose, cheeks, and jaws on that first bite. The poor dude let go, flailing, his ruined face spurting gore, the stump of his severed tongue twitching. Howling through the red hole of his throat. But Reagan had tasted blood and she wasn't about to let him go. In two strides she'd caught him, opened wide and crunched down on his skull. Brains squirted like custard between her teeth.

That's when I dropped the platter of brownies on the floor and ran for the nearest exit…but one of the Secret Service guys caught me, put me in an arm bar and forced me down on my knees on the hard floor. He was a broad-shouldered redhead, and under other circumstances, I totally wouldn't have minded him throwing me down someplace.

"Let me go!" I wailed.

"Sorry, kid, I can't. We can't have you telling people what you just saw."

I could still see Reagan. About half the Secret Service agents had drawn stun guns and were trying to subdue her with electric shocks while the others were locking the doors or restraining people trying to escape.

But the subduing wasn't working. Three more agents were down, clutching at bleeding arm stumps. And Reagan was growing. Her skin split in bloody tatters, revealing moist dark green scales beneath. She'd had real skin but a whole other body inside, like the fleshy shell the T-800 had in *The Terminator.* As she got bigger and more of her human disguise fell away, I realized she was some kind of humanoid lizard, like the alien invaders in *V*.

Hollywood knows about her, I thought. They know and were trying to warn us!

Reagan was about eight feet tall now, and sharp raptor claws had erupted from her fingers. She was biting and slashing anything that moved, and everyone was screaming. The air stank of blood and urine and vomit and feces. I thought I would pass out from the stink. With one swipe, she disemboweled Billy Ray Lowder, his guts spilling like fat worms onto the floor. He looked so, so betrayed for that brief second before he fell face-first into his own innards and died.

"Goddamn it." The Secret Service agent pulled me up to my feet but poked a stern finger into my chest. "Do not move, or I will come for you. If I have to come for you, you will wish Mrs. Reagan had eaten you instead. Understand?"

I nodded mutely, although inside I was screaming. He nodded gruffly, cocked his service revolver and waded into the fray, shooting live rounds into her bulk. The bullets simply bounced off her scales, but suddenly all her angry focus was on him. A moment later, she'd snatched him up in both claws and bit his head off like he was a Slim Jim.

Our history teacher Mrs. Bellum was crouched down by one of the potted plants, sobbing hysterically. As far as I could tell, she and I were the only two still alive in the room. Reagan had gotten so big she was having to crawl on her hands and knees. She looked like a giant mutant iguana now; bladelike ridges had erupted from her back, and at some point she'd grown a thick, spiny tail.

She scuttled over to the only person who was making noise—Bellum—and started devouring her alive.

As Bellum shrieked, I very slowly and quietly backed up to the nearest door and tried to push it open. But the Secret Service had locked it. In my panic I couldn't figure out how to get it open again.

"Fucking fuck fuck," I whispered, frustrated.

Then I realized Bellum had fallen silent. All the hairs rose on the back of my neck. I turned. Nothing was left of Bellum but her left hand, her feet still strapped into a pair of maroon leather Naturalizer heels, and a bloody blonde wig. Reagan had abandoned her remains and was creeping toward me, her murderous black eyes focused on me like twin lasers.

I'm about to die, I thought.

They say that your life flashes before your eyes in moments like that. But it wasn't the life I'd already lived. It was the one I *wanted* to have. I was picturing all the things I wanted to do, like see *Giselle* at the Palais Garnier, or visit the smoking lava fields of Kilauea, or see Madonna perform at Madison Square Garden. Snuggle with a cute boy on the porch of a snow-bound cabin while we watched the Aurora Borealis dance in the wintry sky. All the things I'd never get to do because of this gigantic murdering lizard.

I was scared, and furious, and shell-shocked. I still don't know exactly why I did what I did next, but I did it and it's why I lived to tell this story.

Reagan was less than fifteen feet away from me, and I could see that her bloody teeth were as long as my forearms.

I took a deep breath, and started belting out "Tainted Love." It was one of the songs I'd been practicing for the ball. An homage to the original Gloria Jones version, not the Soft Cell cover, even though the 1981 hit was how I came to love the song in the first place. I guess maybe I figured that if I was gonna get et, I should perform my act for *someone* before I died. Couldn't let my time and sweat and sore feet go to waste, you know?

And to my amazement, the Reagan abomination stopped mid-stalk. And blinked. Did I see her flinch?

I put more oomph into my singing, and started adding in my dance moves. Some footwork, and a little bit of a hip wiggle.

Reagan was *definitely* flinching. So I really went for it: a full-on Tina Turner-style shimmy and jazz hands.

She emitted a strangled hiss, turned, and crashed through the wall of windows into the parking lot.

In my relief, I collapsed on the floor, my heart pounding in my ears.

I can't believe I'm alive, I thought.

But then I remembered my cousin: *Oh, shit.*

I scanned the carnage, looking for his corpse. All the victims were in bloody bits and pieces. It was impossible to know if he was lying among them or not.

"David?" I called, not daring to hope that this was anything but futile. "You in here, dude?"

I heard the scrape of a ceramic planter across the parquet floor and looked toward the sound. David had folded his skinny body up like an origami frog and wedged himself completely behind a potted palm in the corner. It was the best tuck I'd ever seen.

He slowly stood up, his whole body shaking, his face sheet pale. "Is...is it gone?"

"She's left the building," I replied. "But she's not as gone as she needs to be."

When we got outside, the whole parking lot was in chaos. Nancy Reagan had grown to two stories tall and was eating the vice principal's truck. The sheriff's deputies were shooting at her with rifles and shotguns, but none of their firepower seemed to affect her.

"I think I know what to do," I told David. "Let's get to the phones in the choir room and call all the queens and kings we can. Get a phone tree going, and tell everyone who's ready to throw down to show up at The Red Bandana ASAP!"

The situation was wildly, incomprehensibly dangerous, but I knew our town's drag performers would show up for it. I knew it sure as I knew the lyrics to "Tainted Love."

Why? Here's the thing: if you can survive in a place like Lamersal, a place where gay kids and black kids get beaten bloody just for existing, a place where the knuckle-draggers threaten lesbians with "corrective" rape...just living our lives makes you tougher than football ever would. But then, imagine that you don't just survive but you adopt a persona that defies the gender you were born with, and then you get up on a stage in front of God and everyone and perform your queer little heart out. You stand there and make your own personal public declaration against all the haters who say you shouldn't exist...honey, if you can do all that, you have a spine like a steel girder. And if you do all that, not just once but every Friday night…you ain't gonna be all that scared of some rampaging Republican reptile.

Or if you *are* scared, it sure as hell won't stop you from trying to fight.

An hour later, I'd briefed the thirty-odd drag queens and kings in the parking lot of The Red Bandana. Some were in gowns, wigs, and war paint; others were still in their street clothes. I know that at any other time, nobody would have believed my story…except that we could literally see and hear Nancy Reagan eating her way across the city like a nuclear-disarmed Godzilla with a bad case of the munchies. She was taller now than any of the buildings; there would be no problem tracking her.

"Y'all know Lamersal is a crummy shitkicker cow-town," I told everyone, "but it's *our* crummy shitkicker cow-town, dammit. That scaly bitch over there has no right to destroy our community. Let's get out there and stop her. Who's with me?"

I raised my can of Aqua Net high in the air, and a chorus of "Yeah!" and "Woo!" erupted from the crowd.

David gave the queens and king who volunteered to drive some walkie-talkies that we'd gotten at Radio Shack on the way over. And then we all piled into their vehicles: Ella Gant's GMC Vandura, Ivanna Mann's Ford Tourneo, Sue Preem's Chrysler minivan, Marma Lade's Buick Skyhawk, Rocky Rhoad's Subaru station wagon, and David's aging Oldsmobile Toronado.

I got in beside David, who was good to drive even though he was seriously wigged out.

"You got a plan, ma'am?" he asked. We'd stopped calling each other "dude" once we got into our practice gowns and hairpieces. They weren't nearly as pretty as our performance outfits, but those weren't finished yet, and anyway I suspected whatever glad rags we put on that afternoon weren't going to survive the day. Supposing we survived it ourselves.

"Yes." I adjusted my platinum blonde bouffant and gave my lips a quick swipe of scarlet CoverGirl. I hadn't had time to shave off my peachy-blond stubble that day, and there hadn't been time for either of us to do our makeup or tuck, but fuck it. As much as it hurt me on a deep level to be doing skag drag in public, I realized that realness wouldn't help our cause, anyway. I wasn't sure what part of my performance had freaked the beast, but my gut was telling me that the more deviance and gender non-conformity we could bring, the better.

121

So I was free balling it under my satin skirts. If I popped any awkward wood, I was gonna make a huge pink tent. I hoped my Scottish Highlander ancestors would be proud.

"You gonna share your plan with me sometime?" David's voice was tight.

"Catch up to her and get in front of her," I said. "We need to lead her away from buildings and people. Let's try to get her to the empty lot off Mesquite Boulevard where they're planning to build the mall. That should be big enough."

He gripped the steering wheel tighter, his blue eyes shifting fast from left to right. "How are we going to lead her anywhere?"

"Leave that to me. You just focus on driving fast and not hitting anything."

The muscles in David's jaw stood out like cables as he floored the Oldsmobile and roared down Harwood Way. That car was a real land yacht and nearly impossible to parallel park; fortunately he'd only had to do it once for his driver's test. I radioed the other drivers to let them know what we were doing.

A few streets later and we were about fifty yards in front of the beast. Reagan's clawed feet were the size of Sherman tanks now, and she was ambling at a solid thirty miles per hour. She had the big Lamersal Cinema 4 sign in one paw and a Texaco tank trailer in the other, and was alternately munching the sign and washing it down with gasoline. The neighborhood behind her was a splintered wreck.

"Stay ahead, but try to match her speed," I told David, then eased myself up and out the open passenger window so I was sitting on the rubber molding with my pink satin dress flapping noisily around my bare ass in the wind. I had to hold my wig down with one hand while I held on for dear life with the other.

I took a lungful of air and hollered as loud as I could. "HEY NANCY!"

That ginormous scaly bitch blinked and looked down at me but did not break stride.

"I saw *Night into Morning* last week and it's a shitty cornball movie, Nancy!" I screamed up at her. "And you were garbage in it! You're the worst fucking actress I've ever seen! You can't sing and you can't dance! I know fifty drag skags better than you ever were!"

"Ooh, girl, that's *harsh*!" David said.

Reagan crushed the tanker like a Coke can, spilling gas all over someone's ranch house, and roared in fury, her teeth flashing red in the sunlight.

Yep, that did it. I quickly slipped back down onto the passenger seat and belted myself in. "Punch it! Get to the mall lot!"

The monster pounded after us, every step shaking the ground so hard I was worried the Olds would bounce right off the road into the grassy ditch. But David kept us steady, and soon our destination was in sight: a big flat expanse of tamped-down brown soil in the middle of our big patch of nothing out in the middle of nowhere.

We jounced over the curb and slewed across the packed dirt of the future mall site, the monster just a few big strides behind us. And behind her, the rest of the drag racers were tearing up the street.

"Okay, y'all all know 'It's Raining Men,' right?" I said into the walkie-talkie as David and I piled out of the car, ready to scatter to safety.

"Yep!" "Hell yeah!" and "Honey, 'course we do!" greeted my query.

The monster stomped David's Olds flat with the creak of rending steel and crack of shattering axle.

He gave a long wail of despair. "My car!"

I grabbed his skinny wrist and pulled him along behind me.

"Okay, get parked somewhere and come out singing," I told everyone else. "Don't worry about being perfect. Just be loud and proud. Try to get the monster surrounded, but don't get squashed."

"What do we do after that?" asked Marma Lade.

Well, honey, that was the question, wasn't it? "I reckon we keep singing until we get a sign for what to try next."

The queens and kings poured out of the cars and started running toward the dirt lot, all singing The Weather Girls' hit. At first it was pure cacophony; everybody had started the song someplace different, and it was in at least six different keys.

But as they assembled in a loose ring around the now-befuddled monster (who had been picking at pieces of the flattened Olds), they fell in synch and the song snapped into tune. Reptilian Nancy Reagan shuddered, threw her scaly head back and roared at the clear blue sky. We were causing her *pain*. It was glorious.

But the song was drawing to a close. What could we do that would hurt her even worse?

It came to me in a brilliant, shining moment of clarity.

"Time Warp!" I screamed. "Everyone, do the Time Warp!"

We had *never* rehearsed this song as a group. Not the queens together, not the kings together, not even me and David back in the TV room above his parents' garage. There was no reason to think that we could pull that off cold…except I knew every last one of us had been to a dozen midnight showings of *The Rocky Horror Picture Show* at the Lamersal Cinema 4.

But Ella Gant dropped her voice to a baritone, embodied the attitude of Riff Raff, and intoned a shivery warning about fleeting time and madness. Rocky Rhoad jumped in with Magenta's lines in a strong, sensual alto…and it was on like Donkey Kong.

Regan shuddered and bellowed as we sang and danced around her. The scales on her head and body started to change color, lighten, redden, as if she were blushing. There was a rumbling noise like a huge kettle starting to boil.

And when we got to the first pelvic thrusts…Reagan's head exploded.

I don't mean that figuratively. I mean it *literally* exploded. Five tons of meat, bones, brains, teeth and scales popped like an overfilled water balloon. We were showered with bits of the beast and hundreds of gallons of sticky ichor that stank like crude oil.

Then the thing collapsed sideways—half the group had to run like hell to avoid being crushed—and it twitched and bled out all over the mall site. The feds did intense remediation during the cover-up but if you go down into the mall's steam tunnels you can still smell the stink of the monster.

Oh, the cover-up was amazing. Men in black swooped down on the town in dark panel trucks and helicopters just minutes after she fell. All of us skedaddled well before they got to the mall lot to clean up the carcass. The local CBS crew had broadcast the first part of the rampage live to local viewers, before she kicked over their truck, but the agents destroyed all that footage, and the reporters who covered it ended up in an asylum. When they came out, they disavowed the whole thing. The official story was that the town had suffered an anarchist terrorist attack—LSD in our water supply—and everything people had seen was just a hallucination. And the damage to the town was from an unseasonable tornado that touched down. Just a huge coincidence, folks, nothing to see here! They tracked David down because of the squashed Olds and grilled him pretty hard, but he played it cool and said that he'd left it parked and the twister must have moved it. Eventually they left him alone.

I do have evidence. I saved a dozen scales from that scaly hag. They're as big as cafeteria trays and they have an iridescent green shine. Really kinda pretty, considering. Someday I'm gonna turn them into some sweet blingy pageant jewelry.

Oh yeah, I'd love to give you one so you could get it analyzed…problem is, the sample would get stolen from whatever lab you sent it to. And you and the lab tech and whoever else had handled it would just disappear one night. And then, depending on if you talked or not, they'd come looking for me. I can't risk any of that. Sorry. I'm much more comfortable with you believing I'm a crank than I am with knowing I got you killed.

The real bitch of the whole thing? Just two weeks later, Nancy Reagan was live on international TV, visiting Rome to see Pope John Paul II. That seriously had me questioning my sanity…right until David's older brother gave us a copy of *Parapolitics Monthly*. We learned about the clones and body doubles that high-level people have at their disposal. She was replaceable—just like the rest of us, right?

Now that you mention it, I can't honestly be certain whether the monster we killed was the "real" Nancy Reagan or not. All the people she ate are dead just the same, though. As are my friends who got sick when her husband let AIDS burn through the country. 700,000 people gone to dust just here in the U.S. If some radioactive kaiju from Japan had waded into San Francisco Bay to stomp 7,000 people, Reagan would have moved every military branch and every agency to stop it. We would hear about America's righteous victory over the monster every day.

Thousands of the people who acted heroically in the face of AIDS are just unsung ghosts now. I want to tell their stories any way that I can. Not how they died, but how they lived.

Sure, more coffee would be great. Thanks, honey.

You know, though? It *would* make sense that she used one of her clones for the Texas trip. Because who the hell wants to visit Lamersal?

Ten Miles of Bad Road

STEPHEN GRAHAM JONES

Josh, Tina told him, had dressed for a music video, not for a day at the junkyard.

"But whose video?" he said right back, daggering his eyes out at her through his hair, dragging deep on his cigarette, waiting for her to see the Dokken in his fingerless gloves, the Warrant in his road-worn weariness, the Ratt in his...well, down the right thigh of his skintight jeans, right?

"The one with all the Corsicas in it," Tina said, turning sharp down another random row of junked-out cars.

That's what they were here for, a Corsica. Specifically, the driver's side wheel well that Josh had dragged most of the way out the night before, he wasn't exactly sure how. They'd pulled it the rest of the way out before parking it back in Tina's driveway, but her mom was going to hear the damage the next time she got her brand-new car out on the highway and that radial started in singing.

Unless they could replace the wheel well. Unless someone had already wrecked their new Corsica, and it had found its way to this particular vehicle graveyard.

"I bet any Chevy'll work," he said, following her, stepping wide around anything that might snag his leather trench coat.

Tina, always the sensible one, had pulled a pair of her mom's custodian overalls over her shorts and T-shirt, so she fit right into this place. Unlike Josh, who was already baking in all the denim and leather, and—yeah—eyeliner and hairspray, what the hell.

Still, this junkyard, way the hell out here? It would actually be a pretty good place for a righteous music video. Start in the harsh bright sun like this, then transition to night when the guitarist struts out on top of that pile of crushed cars, the lights coming on all around the place, amps perched on every crumpled hood, the revelers rolling out of their trunks for the festivities.

Josh smiled, liking this vision, and snagged his boot on something half-buried in the dirt, had to stumble forward to keep from face-planting. But he nearly did anyway, finally having to catch himself on the grill of some station wagon

129

monstrosity, shaking nasty-ass birds up from somewhere inside it that made him jerk back, swinging his arms around to keep any dirty feathers from touching his face, infecting him with its grime.

"My hero," Tina said, watching all this with a grin.

Josh stepped forward and stomped the car's bumper with the heel of his boot to show it who was boss.

For once this actually worked, too.

The car creaked back, had only been balanced on bare wheels scavenged from some other car.

"Tim-ber..." Josh said, and stepped back, holding his hands high and away to show that one kick from him had been enough.

Maybe five seconds later the car reached a tipping point and crashed back and down, a grand fall of maybe two feet, a starved-down cat screeching out from under it at the last possible second, ramming immediately into the wall of Josh's shins. The cat collected itself, hissed up at him and bolted away. Josh, startled, did fall on his ass now.

"You scared her!" Tina screeched in that way she had, stepping in not to haul Josh up but to see where that miserable cat might have blasted off to.

"Cats, birds," Josh said, trying to clamber up without getting his gloves dirtier than they probably already were. "What's next?"

"So glad I brought you," Tina said to him, still not helping him up.

"Dogs," Josh said, answering his own question, looking down the row, sure some junkyard beast was going to be barreling down to rip a hunk of face meat off. It's what all this had to be leading to, right?

There was just heat waves and junked cars. Even the air out here felt rusty, like if Josh coughed, scratchy red particulate matter would come out.

He hauled himself up, dusted off as best he could, and when he looked around for Tina, she was gone.

"Hey!" he said, so she could bob up from whatever car she was inspecting for the least thrashed wheel well.

She didn't look up.

"Tina?" Josh said again, checking all around now.

Hunh.

Him having pulled her mom's wheel well halfway out was only part of why he was here. The other part was that—and if he said this out loud she'd kick his ass even more—but the other part was that a girl like her out here in guy land...it wasn't a situation Josh really liked.

Not that he was much bigger than her, and not that he could really outfight her, if it came to that. But still.

She was right about how he'd gone overkill on getting geared up to pull parts, but without his gloves and boots, trench coat and casual spikes, well, what else did he really have, right?

His voice, he decided. Taking a running start, he vaulted up onto the hood of some Datsun- or Subaru-looking thing, breathed in deep and let out a "Hey T" with all he had.

At the very least, some of the other junkyard denizens should be slouching out from under their chosen hood to see what this ruckus might be.

None of them were.

"What the hell," Josh said, rubbing his lower lip with the side of his left glove. It was a gesture or move or whatever he'd seen in a music video, just the lead singer wiping his mouth between lines so as to not spit his way through the next one, but somehow it had infected Josh, was part of who he was now.

He stomped on the hood of the Datsun or the Subaru to get some attention but all he got was a bit more of the windshield, caving in.

He looked down to it and—shit, really?

There was still blood around that spidery white crater in the glass. Fresh, like the car had just been pulled here, even though it was six or eight from the main road, and there was no room in the row to maneuver a forklift or tractor.

Josh squatted down, inspected closer, his fingertip about—about to touch it...but no.

"Screw this noise," he said, and hopped down from the hood, his trench coat spreading around him like great black wings, he knew, the thick soles of his boots coming down into the dirt in slow-motion, the way he chose to see it.

He could already feel the piano starting up, going light through the melody that was going to come on like a metal storm right before the first chorus, when the girls started pouring out from the trashed-out panel van, none of them smiling, all of their hands balled into fists to raise against the sky.

"More like it," Josh said, grinning then spin-checking all around, sure Tina was watching him, that she could see into the side of his head, into the video he was in.

She still wasn't there.

"It was just a stupid cat," Josh said, and, instead of trying to find her, he tried to find the next best thing to a Corsica, so he could be a hero that way.

Three rows over, the front gate just a distant memory, the sun a boiling cauldron of fire about to tip over down his collar, Josh didn't find Tina, but he did find a newish Monte Carlo.

Well, not new-new, but new-to-the-yard, just totaled the past weekend, whatever. It was on the end of a row, where the recent arrivals should be.

A Monte Carlo was bigger than a Corsica, but…maybe? Could Josh and Tina shave down the wheel well, tap some new holes, screw it up? Would her mom ever lay down under the car and take a close enough look to know?

Josh walked around the car, clearing it of the possibility of cats and birds before gathering the tails of his jacket in his lap and squatting down to inspect above the driver side front tire.

The wheel well was gone. Of course. Along with the engine. All that was left was the crushed-in radiator, the scrunched hood.

"Probably some blood too," Josh muttered to himself.

He wasn't a ghoul or anything, but—the best songs come from pain, don't they? From hurting. And leaning in to see where someone had probably just died, that had to be adjacent enough to pain and hurt to count some, anyway.

Only, when Josh pulled the door open to check things out, what he saw instead, behind the passenger seat, was—

No way.

Not a human head left behind, not a stash of cash, not even a case of cassettes not turned to brittle junk by the sun yet, but a litter of brand-new kittens.

They mewled up at him, their eyes not even open yet.

Josh looked across the cab and saw the passenger window rolled down over there, like it had probably been for the big wreck.

He smiled one side of his mouth.

That cat that had got Tina pissed at him, got him abandoned in this living hellhole. These were hers, weren't they?

Josh hipped the driver's door shut, walked quickly around to the passenger door, and pulled and pulled at it until it groaned open. The wreck hadn't been nice to it, but it still responded to muscle and weight, at least.

Even better, the window, rolled down into its slot in the door, still cranked.

Josh rolled it neatly up, told the kittens "sweet dreams," and pushed the lock down on the door, shut it.

Walking away, his jacket lifting dramatically around him on the unexpected breeze—or was that fans the director had strategically placed?—Josh tried not to grin. But he couldn't help it.

That momma cat was going to scratch her claws out trying to get through the glass, into that Monte Carlo. Her children crying for her just two feet away, maybe even making their way onto the front seat to reach for her.

This was not something to inform Tina about. It was just for Josh.

But this wasn't a music video, he knew.

It was too damn hot, and dusty, and just generally crappy.

"Tina!" he called again, louder, cranking his voice as high as it would go this time because, apparently, he was the only human left in the world anymore.

And then he heard it, the place he knew this day had been going. It was later than he'd expected, but also probably right on time, too: dogs.

They were running and snarling down some row, he couldn't tell which one.

Josh shook his head no, his breath suddenly deep. He turned to run before even realizing he'd given his feet that order.

He took every turn that seemed less likely than the last. But would that even matter to junkyard dogs? He didn't know. But he did know that these dogs were usually Dobermans or Rottweilers, and that they had spiked collars, and that the owners didn't feed them enough, just to keep them good and hungry.

Josh scrabbled, fell, screw how dirty his gloves and knees were getting.

Finally, at the end of a row, up on blocks, no tires, shining like the beacon it was: an actual Corsica!

Its trunk was all slammed in and the grill had been crushed back, but screw it, the cab was good, the cab all right, the cab was all he needed. Already he could feel the dogs snapping at the tails of his jacket.

He peeled out of it, had to spin to get all the way free, and flung it behind him to slow them down, dove across the top of the car, came down in a pile on the other side, his right hand already opening the door.

He pulled himself in, shut the door just when the snarling was almost on him.

He was breathing so hard and so fast that it was kind of like screaming quietly.

By degrees, he got semi-control of himself.

When he could, he sat up.

The dog maw he one hundred percent expected to be slamming into the glass against his face didn't slam against the glass.

Had they already left? Or—or was this what they did? Lulled their prey into a false sense of safety while they crouched down two cars over, ready to rend him limb from limb the moment he opened the door?

Josh locked the door.

At least—at least Tina would be here soon, right? She had a way with animals. She'd pet the dogs down, make friends, introduce her stupid sometimes-boyfriend to them, and they'd walk out together.

Josh thought this way for the first two hours.

For the next two, he honked the horn. Because the car was so fresh, the battery still had juice. The radio even still came on.

He dialed it over to his station, turned it up, and cracked the windows to keep from sweating all the way to death.

Item by item, he stripped down, was only wearing pants by the time the sun started its long glide down.

Was Tina going to let him spend the night here? Seriously?

Josh leaned the seat back, made himself shut his eyes, lost himself in the guitar solo the Corsica's pretty good speakers were pushing.

He played along as best he could, and, and—

When he sat back up, it was already night, somehow.

He'd fallen asleep? How long did that song even go?

Josh looked all around, looked all around some more, and finally, timidly, cracked the door open.

The moment the dome light glowed on, the snarl of a half-dozen dogs came on as well.

They were under the car. Of course. Dobermans and Rotts have jet-black coats, don't like the sun any more than headbangers in leather trench coats.

Josh eased the door shut, shook his head about the stupidity of all this, and, just to push back, cranked the radio as high as it would go, because who cares about the speakers, they're not his speakers, they're not Tina's mom's.

The song he knew wound down, the DJ traipsed through his usual BS, and then he shifted voice-gears, chuckled, said he had something new for the really metal people out there on this Saturday night, something called…"wait for it, wait for it…'Ten Miles of Bad Road,' loyal listeners, beer drinkers and hell-raisers."

"Hunh," Josh said, about that title. That was what his uncle had said about him one Saturday morning, when Josh was struggling to the refrigerator for some orange juice: that he looked like ten miles of bad road.

"Feel like it too," Josh had croaked, trying to stab his hand into the cold for the carton he needed.

In the oven of the Corsica, he couldn't even imagine reaching into the fridge, couldn't even guess that refrigerators even ever really existed, much less chilled orange juice. Just, like the DJ had said, "Ten Miles of Bad Road."

Whatever.

Josh closed his eyes to give the song a chance, to fall back into the song's space. It started out just with whistling, very Scorps, real original, guys, but then it trilled hard into a thrash of angry drums that made Josh smile in spite of himself, because the song hadn't taken a sharp left turn all on its own, it had put its arm around Josh, smuggled him around that corner with it, into some new and rawer space.

The drums were a heartbeat, but not any heartbeat. They were thumping out Josh's—all metal and slamming, thrash and crash.

"Yeah, yeah," Josh said, and when the whistling came back to bridge from one stanza to the next, kind of reset to make the climb all over again, this time Josh knew it. He whistled along, or tried to. His lips were too dry, too cracked.

134

But it didn't matter. The whistling was…it was coming through the speakers, but it was all around him, too. Like he was doing it, except he wasn't, was he?

He sat up slow.

The—the junkyard all around.

The headlights were glowing on, and there were shapes out there now, and…no.

Amplifiers on the hoods?

The whistling trailed off, down the slope the drums had laid for it, and then the guitar screeched in, jacking that melody up to fifty, and cranking it faster and harder, deeper and bloodier, the guitarist's pick a razor blade digging into the real meat of the night.

Josh's heart swelled, his face warmed.

"No way," he said, his hands to the dash.

Trunks were popping open, doors were yawning like coffin lids, and the extras were all unfolding themselves, stepping their thick soles down to the ground delicately, like making sure the packed dirt of the junkyard was really there.

And then—

"No, no," Josh said, but yes, yes: girls were pouring from one of the vans. Black bras, vests with no shirts, torn jeans, shorts and fishnets, strappy shoes, spike heels.

His people. Josh had found his people.

Without thinking, he pulled on the door handle to step out into this, but the handle came off in his hand.

He reached across the seat and the other handle came off too.

"What the hell?" he said, not mad, just confused, and then turned to whatever that sound was behind him.

There, right behind his seat.

He jumped back, his head scraping the headliner, his hair going instant static.

The litter of kittens? Here?

Only, their eyes were open now.

"I don't—I don't have anything to—" Josh told them, because no, he didn't have anything to feed them, he wasn't their stupid mom.

But they were hungry all the same.

The yellowish one mewled, pulled itself up onto the backseat, its tiny claws already leaving little rents in the fabric. When it stretched and yawned, its tiny teeth were already razor-sharp little pinpricks.

Josh shook his head no, turned around fast when the Corsica shook.

The guitar player was on the hood, leaned back and shredding through the solo, fountains of sparks geysering all around, their sparkle and flash winking orange in a hundred side mirror.

"Hey! Hey!" Josh said, pounding on the window.

When that didn't work he tried the horn, but the song was too loud, drowned the horn out. Finally he sat back to kick the windshield out, but the glass was more solid than he was.

The guitar player stepped down, away, into whatever better camera angle the director was guiding him toward, and Josh felt something behind him.

Cat whiskers.

The gray-striped kitten was half-grown now, was on the headrest.

It had to be starving, to have grown that much just in the time Josh hadn't been watching it.

"No, no, bad kitty!" Josh said, slapping it down, and then a flash beside him—

It was one of the girls, dancing on the car beside him. No, not dancing, just standing there, hand on her hips. She was kind of moving with the music, too cool to actually dance.

"Hey, hey, please!" Josh said, slamming his open hand against the window.

Finally, as if bothered to be having to go off-script, she looked over.

"Yes, yes, please!" Josh said, both hands to the glass now, and this girl, she just smirked, turned away from him so he could see what had been hidden before.

Her cat tail.

He shook his head no, fell back against the steering wheel, and—and now the cats from the backseat, they were full-grown, they were on the headrests, on the dash, between the seats. All mewling, all hungry.

How many of them had there been?

Josh wasn't sure.

He tried to slap the first one away, and then the second, and then the third and fourth, while all around him the music video screeched and howled.

The best songs come from pain, some part of him knew.

This one was going to be epic.

Epoch, Rewound

VINCE A. LIAGUNO

A new wave of monster
creeps up from the well of time,
all Day-Glo colors as it slithers
out of an old bucket of Slime—
the kind with plastic worms—
and swallows everything in its path.
It springs upon the unsuspecting
like a worn VHS tape
ejecting from the pop-up mouth
of an antediluvian VCR,
only this beast with bad manners
isn't kind enough to rewind.
Its horrors trickle down
like Reaganomics,
as valley girls flee suburban malls—
their Bazooka wads
gagging them like spoons—
while goblins play synthesized soundtracks.
An ostentatious ogre
from an era of excess
bears down upon
flocks of seagulls in parachute pants
and gyrating Janes in leg warmers
and shimmering spandex.
It's backdated butchery,
like a night out at the drive-in
watching sorority sisters
getting strangled at slumber parties
and prom goers losing their heads

on catwalks of carnage.
Pandemonium ensues
as people shirk shoulder pads
and try to roller skate around the rink
beneath swirling disco balls
to evade this teething tetrapod
from the decade of decadence.
Clara's screaming for her beef,
while alien botanists in drag
demand a dime to call home
on makeshift landline telephones—
even though they can neither
speak nor spell.
The leviathan squashes
sixteen candles beneath its feet
while the club that meets for breakfast
narrowly escapes detention
and promises not to forget you
even as simpler minds prevail.
Even dragons hide in dungeons,
waiting for the beast to pass,
hoping it will return
to its temple of doom
before twisting everything in its wake
like a Rubik's Cube.
The world is filled
with echoes and reverberations
from the past,
a time when radio stars
were mercilessly struck down by video
and disco died in the street.
The monstrous '80s unleashed—
like alien eggs plopping out
of the queen's ovipositor
and seeping into pop culture consciousness
like acidic blood eating
through eight-track tape decks.
These are the facts of life now,
and few will be saved by the bell
even when your hair is jacked-up for Jesus

or Jheri-curled for Jackée—
it's a never-ending killer-thriller night
of creeps and demons and the dawning dead.

Demonic Denizens

CULLEN BUNN

Jarod couldn't help but notice that the ground was crawling with millipedes. Hundreds of the wriggling, curling creatures writhed just below a sparse canopy of grass and twigs: undulating, fibrous legs carrying dark, serpentine bodies along the damp dirt in a search for food. There had been a lot of storms in the last few weeks. Maybe the rain had forced the millipedes to the surface in such numbers. Now, as Jarod looked down and tears dripped from his face, the ground grew just a little more wet.

"You can have the books back at the end of the week." Tucker was a third-year camp counselor. He was a tall, lean young man with longish hair tucked under a baseball cap. "We'd like to talk to your parents about them, though. We really don't believe they support the values a boy your age should hold dear."

One of the other kids—Jarod didn't know his name—giggled and screeched with delight.

"That book's got naked ladies in it!"

Jarod raised his eyes, just a little, and he spotted the players from his gaming group—Toby, Doug, and Chris—standing with the other kids. Their faces were red with embarrassment. When his eyes met theirs, they quickly looked away. They had been excited about spending a week at camp. Jarod had an exciting new adventure planned. Now, those plans had fallen apart, and on the very first night of the week.

"Naked ladies and demons!"

Tucker held Jarod's well-worn copies of the *Dungeon Master's Guide*, *Players Handbook*, and *Monster Manual*. From the cover of the *DMG*, a grinning demon leered. Stuffed between the pages of the book were dozens of sheets of paper. He had been playing Advanced Dungeons & Dragons with his friends for almost two years. The maps and notes from their gaming sessions were scrawled on those pages.

Wiping away his tears, Jarod spoke, his words were barely a whisper. "Just be careful with those," he said.

141

"You understand why we're taking these, don't you?" Tucker shook his head in pity. "You came to camp to spend time with good friends, to participate in wholesome activities. You shouldn't be spending time messing around with a board game like this."

"It's not a board game," Jarod said. "It's a role-playing game."

Lucy—a round-faced camp counselor with bad skin, bad hair, and bad glasses—spoke up. "I know all about it. You pretend to be wizards and warlocks and assassins. It's not just a game. It's a gateway to drugs and devil worship. I watched a segment on *PM Magazine*. That game teaches kids horrible things."

"It does not!" Jarod snapped, and this time there was a growling fury in his voice.

"You must get all that anger from somewhere," Lucy snorted.

"We'll just see what your parents think about it," Tucker said.

Looking at the game manuals as if they were covered in warm feces, Tucker turned to walk away.

"Take the dice, too," Lucy said. "If they still have the dice, they can play with or without the books."

Tucker turned back toward Jarod and held out his hand.

A sigh of defeat escaped Jarod's lips. He reached into his shorts pocket and dragged a set of polyhedral dice free. Grudgingly, he put them in Tucker's hand.

"That all of them?" Tucker asked.

Jarod nodded.

"Sorry." Tucker leaned closer on touched his ear. "I don't hear you."

"That's all of them."

The sun was setting, the sky was turning blood red.

In helpless anger, Jarod pressed his sneaker down on top of the millipedes, mashing them to a gooey pulp.

As darkness fell, bonfires were ignited, and campers gathered around the flames for ghost stories and s'mores. Jarod, though, trudged along the shadowy path leading back to the cabins. The trail cut through thick tangles of dark, crooked trees. The pale glow of the moon illuminated the way.

He sniffled, wiped his nose with the back of his arm. Waves of sadness, followed by waves of anger, followed by waves of embarrassment crashed into him. The words of the counselors, the shamed reactions of his friends, the snickers of the other kids—these things haunted him, following along after him.

Something dashed through the brush, snapping twigs.

Jarod jumped. His pulse quickened. His breath caught in his throat. "Who's out there?" The question jumped from his mouth.

Silence answered him.

He took another step.

The unseen presence moved again, shuffling through the carpet of damp fallen leaves, keeping pace with Jarod.

"Is that you, Doug?" Jarod staggered to a stop again. "Toby? Chris? If that's you, just come out. I'm not in the mood."

Silence.

But only for a second.

The voice did not belong to one of his friends, nor could Jarod imagine it belonged to any human being at all. "JAAAAAAARRRRRRROD. I'VE GOT A GAAAAAAAAAME YOU CAN PLAY."

Jarod broke into a run, and he didn't stop until he reached his cabin, smashed open the door, jumped into his bunk, and threw the covers over his head.

Sometime in the night, Jarod felt his head being gently lifted. He awoke groggily, his sense of time and place coming back to him in furtive spasms of awareness. He was still hidden under the covers. It was still dark and silent. But he felt someone slipping something beneath his pillow.

He didn't move. He pretended to sleep. He worried the mysterious visitor was the same person…or thing…that had spoken to him from the woods with such an inhuman voice. And he didn't want to see their face.

Having left something beneath the pillow, the visitor moved away from the bed. The cabin floor creaked under their weight. Their shoes must have been metal-shod, because they clomped loudly on the floor.

Once the room had fallen silent—save for the snoring of one of his cabinmates—Jarod hesitantly reached beneath the pillow. His fingers touched an object he immediately recognized as a large hardback book. He pulled the book free, grabbed the flashlight he kept next to his bunk, and—still hidden beneath his sheets—rolled over to examine the prize that had been left for him.

The book was titled *Demonic Denizens* and the cover depicted a horned, winged overlord lashing out at a group of warriors and wizards with a great flaming scimitar. Under the glow of the flashlight, the devilish lord's face seemed to twist and move, almost as if he mouthed weird, silent incantations. A trick of the light, to be sure, but it gave Jarod a morbid thrill.

A role-playing game! One he had never heard of before!

He opened the book and spent the rest of the night reading.

The next night, after the evening slop had been served, Jarod led the members of his gaming group through the shadow-haunted woods.

"We're gonna get in trouble out here," Doug whined.

"Stop worrying so much," Jarod said. "No one will know we're missing until it's time for the bonfire."

"Where are we going?" Toby asked.

Jarod shook his head. "Would you guys just shut up? Wow. I wish you had been this talkative when they were taking my books away yesterday."

"What were we supposed to do?" Chris asked. "Nothing we could have said would have changed that."

"It's all right," Jarod said. "Don't worry about that now."

Pushing branches aside, Jarod stepped into a small clearing by the lake. The lake was swollen from the recent rains. Along the edge, the tangled branches of small trees and bushes reached up from under the water. The reflection of the moon rippled across the lake's calm surface.

On the ground before Jarod, white stones had been arranged in a circle. Flashlights stood on end around the circle, looking almost like tall candles. In the center of the circle lay the copy of Demonic Denizens.

"What is this?" Toby asked.

Jarod smiled.

"It's our new game."

Jarod explained how the book had been delivered to him in the darkness, how he had spent the rest of the night reading the rules of this new game, how he had crept away from camp during the softball game to set up this spot where they could play in secret.

"I've never heard of that game," Chris said, "not even in Dragon Magazine."

"It's a lot like D&D," Jarod told him, "only a little darker and a lot more violent."

"And you've read all the rules?" Toby asked.

"Most of them," Jarod said. "I understand enough to get us started. I figured we could learn the rest as we go along."

"Why not?" Doug shrugged. "Let's try it."

Jarod smiled and took his place in the center of the circle. He turned on one of the flashlights. He didn't need it just yet, but he would soon. He flipped open the rule book and turned to the section on creating player-characters. Toby, Chris, and Doug took spots around the edge of the circle.

"Hold on," Toby said. "Don't we need dice?"

Almost as soon as he had asked his question, he cried out in pain. His hand flew to his mouth. Doug and Chris, their eyes wide, also groaned and whimpered and trembled. The three boys hunched over, mewling in agony, coughing. Each of them spat up a single tooth. The teeth glistened in the dirt, the roots bloody. In the enamel of each tooth, several strange symbols had been etched.

Jarod scooped the teeth up, rattled them in his hand like dice.

"Ready to roll up some characters?"

Chris reached into his mouth, feeling for the spot where his tooth had been. His fingertips came away bloody.

"What the hell was that?" he asked.

"It's not like you needed all those teeth anyhow," Jarod said. "And I bet it doesn't even hurt now, does it? Let's get started."

"But we…" Doug spoke hesitantly. "…don't even have character sheets."

And the boys cried out again as their T-shirts grew bloody, as if a blade was carving letters into the skin of their stomachs.

Late into the night, they rolled the bones.

Surely, the counselors and other campers had noticed them missing. They were probably looking for them right now. But the boys did not care. They explored forbidden keeps and forgotten tombs, lost shrines and deadly caverns. Toby played a fierce barbarian warlord. Chris took on the role of a mysterious sorcerer. Doug played a courageous paladin.

Their shirts were red with the blood, the testimony of their heroic deeds etched into their flesh.

Jarod played the quest master, guiding the players through more perilous adventures.

"You have slain the Minotaur King," Jarod said, doing his best to imitate the impish voice of the Dungeon Master from his favorite Saturday morning cartoon. "But your battle has attracted the attention of other terrible creatures!"

Holding his flashlight over the pages, Jarod flipped to the back of the rule book, where a detailed appendix provided a Wandering Demon table. He gathered up the teeth and rolled them across the ground. He checked the chart, comparing the result to a list of horrible monsters to inflict upon his players.

"Three goblins attack the party," it read.

"A trio of drooling goblins leap from the shadows," Jarod said.

"I hack them down with my ax!" Toby cried.

"I cast a fireball!" Said Chris.

"I repel them with my holy light!" Doug added.

With a few rolls of the teeth, the party made short work of the goblins. Their characters grew in strength. Their shirts grew more bloody.

"We continue deeper into the dungeon!" Toby said. "What do we find?"

Once more, Jarod rolled the dice and consulted the chart.

"Tucker encounters a harvester," it read.

"Tucker?" he muttered.

A scream erupted from the darkness. It was distant, but loud and filled with horrible pain. It was Tucker's voice, only filled with terror and agony.

The boys jumped. They looked at one another in startled fright.

"That sounded like—" Doug started, but he didn't finish the thought.

Jarod rolled the dice again.

"Lucy encounters Grixella the Defiler," it read.

And another scream—this time closer, this time the cry of a young woman— ripped through the night. Her pleading scream was cut short by a monstrous roar.

"What's happening?" Toby asked.

"I'm not sure," Jarod said. "Let me check something."

His fingers trembled, fidgeting with the dice. He wanted to roll them. Wanted to see what might happen next.

And so he did.

"The kid who giggled at 'naked ladies' encounters a succubus."

Another horrible cry rose from the shadows. The upper branches of nearby trees whipped. And the winged figure of a woman burst into the sky above the gaming group. She wore no clothing, but her skin was scaled and glistening. She carried the boy who had giggled and sneered at Jarod. She held onto him by one ankle as he flailed wildly. The winged woman swooped down low over the lake and then vanished into the darkness beyond.

"Jarod!" Toby said. "What the hell did you do?"

"I didn't do anything," Jarod said. "It's the game!"

Suddenly, the rule book in his hands felt like a hot, fleshy, sweaty thing. He tossed it onto the ground before him.

146

But he couldn't take his eyes off the chart.

When he had heard the boy's scream, he had looked away from the book. He hadn't read the die roll's result in its entirety.

"The kid who giggled at 'naked ladies' encounters a succubus," the chart read, "and roll again."

The dice—clutched tightly in Jarod's hand—sprung from his grip and thumped across the ground. They settled on matching symbols.

"What are you doing?" Doug cried.

"I d-didn't!" Jarod said.

The boys looked down at the dice in dread.

"What does that mean?" Chris asked.

Jarod hesitantly picked up the *Demonic Denizens* rulebook and checked the table.

"Chris, Toby and Doug encounter Shadow Hunters."

Three tall figures, each dressed in pitch-black armor, their eyes glowing redly from beneath their helms, emerged from the woods. Despite the metal they wore, despite the metal that seemed to be fused to their flesh, they moved without a sound. The creatures swept up behind Toby, Doug, and Chris, grabbing them by the shoulders, their barbed fingers sinking into flesh.

Jarod watched as his friends shrieked and were hauled off into darkness.

"No!" he yelled. "No! I'm the quest master! I don't want this to happen!"

But his voice was drowned out by the gurgling screams of his friends.

"Stop it! I don't want to play anymore!"

He scooped up the dice, ran to the edge of the lake and hurled the rulebook out across the water. He threw the demonically marked dice with all his might, let them sink to the depths.

"I'm done!" he cried. "Do you hear me? I'm not playing anymore!"

The forest fell silent once more.

But he did not see his friends again.

Wearily, Jarod walked along the path back toward the campground. He didn't know what awaited him. He didn't know what he would tell the other campers about Chris, Doug, and Toby. He didn't know if he'd even find any other campers waiting for him.

He staggered to a stop.

On the path before him, glistening wetly, was the copy of *Demonic Denizens*.

In the moonlight, he saw millipedes crawling in the dirt around the book.

He heard a familiar shuffling through the brush. He looked into the shadows that swelled between the trees but saw nothing. Then, a voice boomed from the darkness.

"JARRRRRRRROD. OUR GAME ISN'T DONE. YOU ARE THE QUEST MASTER. YOU CAN'T JUST STOP."

"I don't want to play," Jarod said. "Even if I did, I don't have any—"

Searing pain brought Jarod to his knees. He sputtered and gurgled and whimpered. Bloody drool spilled from his lips. His teeth—all of his teeth—twisted in their sockets, the ligaments tearing, the gums oozing blood. He felt what might have been tiny blades scratching into the surface of each tooth, chipping away, digging deep into the nerve.

He spat into the dirt—first one tooth, then another, and another, and another.

And they just kept coming.

Dark figures moved through the forest, slithering and slinking, lumbering and crashing through the trees, writhing and uncoiling their massive, segmented forms. Jarod, sweating and twitching and drooling, saw them through a veil of pain-filled tears.

He smiled a toothless smile.

His new gaming group had arrived.

The White Room

RENA MASON

Richard sat on the Emeco aluminum chair where Caroline had left him that morning. He faced the back wall with his wrists handcuffed behind him, each of his ankles manacled to the chair's front legs, the drain grate underneath it unsoiled. Glossy white subway tiles covering every inch of the twelve-by-twelve room made his bare skin paler and cast him in an ethereal glow. Caroline had wanted to use black-and-white squares like the room in the *Alice and Mad Hatter* music video with Tom Petty and the Heartbreakers or something more similar to the checkerboard print on Vans, but Richard insisted that the absence of hue calmed the monster inside him.

She watched him through the soundproof glass as he fidgeted his toe around the intercom buzzer set into the floor. This, he'd said, tested his patience and control over the beast he swore ruled his business brain. The cables attached to the eyebolts on the underside of the seat appeared untampered. He knew full well the added injuries he'd suffer for meddling with the wiring, latches, or for pushing the button again. The alarm gave her throbbing migraines, and she hated it. Caroline went to the door and entered the code, parting the seal around it with a soft pop. Richard slid his foot back and scooted forward when she came in, mumbling around the gag she'd placed in his mouth.

Her neon-pink stilettos clicked against the tiles as she approached the medical cart behind him, a row of silver coat hooks above it. Taking her time, Caroline observed his muscles flex and contract as the monster inside him bucked and wrestled to get out. At least that's what he told her, but she knew better. His anticipation and excitement for what was to come had built up during the hours he'd been held captive. She donned the apron that read RELAX in bold black letters then took the biggest wooden cooking spoon from the cart.

Spittle hung from his chin, and he rolled his eyes back when she stepped in front of him. Caroline waited for him to look again, and then she slapped the side of his head with her hand, his damp hair dulling the sound. Richard growled and moaned a simultaneous guttural whimper, but her palm stung all the same.

149

"I hope you're ready," she said. "I've had a horrible day. Jazzercise was canceled, and the dry cleaners lost the Velcro shoulder pads in my favorite lime blazer." Caroline whacked him with the spoon in tune with her words. The fleshy percussion emphasized the staccato, making her sound like a beat poet or rap artist. Oh how she loathed that new song by The Fresh Prince now helping to fuel her rage. She couldn't wait for the music fad to go away.

"Then that Vu or Vo woman at the salon buffed my thumb too hard." It throbbed as she wrenched the spoon's handle. "I hope like hell it doesn't get infected." Caroline glanced at her nails. "She does some rad work, though." The random geometric designs and splattered vivid colors across the white polish dazzled her before she swung again, harder this time, thinking of how her tennis coach totally harped about her lame forehand.

"And like, oh my God with the line at Blockbuster on a Sunday. You're a total moron, Richard. Seventy dollars in late fees! Just kill me if I ever say I'll return your videos again."

Understanding registered in his eyes when the flat of the spoon struck his thigh and snapped at the neck. The top flew off and then clacked behind them. Caroline pulled back before stabbing the broken stick into him. She hunched over, panted, and let the handle fall to the floor.

Caroline pulled the gag from his mouth. Slobbery strands tinged red with his blood stretched between his lips and the red rubber ball.

"Thank you," he said with a hoarse, fragile voice.

If someone had told her she'd meet and marry the man of her dreams while attending Columbia and then spend her weekends torturing and humiliating him in the basement of their house recently featured in *Architectural Digest*, overlooking the eleventh green in Cherry Hills Country Club, she wouldn't have believed it.

Richard had always had a little kink for being dominated, but it wasn't until after he became CEO of GenTech Pharmaceuticals that he had the white room built and told her about the corporate monster that drove his success.

"Now, let's get you cleaned up," she said. "Sam and Naomi will be here at seven."

"What are you making?"

"Your favorite. Why don't you go over the recipe with me?"

His speech needed to return to normal and talking usually did just that. Caroline wheeled the cart over and cleaned the wounds that would later be compressed and hidden under his Calvin Klein jeans and a Britannia polo. His voice cracked a few times while reciting the ingredients for her braised duck, fennel, and crème brûlée. He winced and flinched as she gingerly swiped astringent-soaked gauze across raw skin. Then he prattled about work, reprimanding his employees who wouldn't take their aerobics breaks to increase productivity, and by the time he got to the topic of the stock market Richard sounded very much like himself again. His chatter took her mind off his angry wounds, the contusions, abrasions, blood and weeping red flesh. He talked because he loved her. As much as she loved him.

Sam, dressed as if he'd stepped off a private jet from Miami wearing deck shoes with no socks, white linen pants, matching blazer, and a mint-green shirt. He cut several lines on a mirror kit he pulled from his coat pocket. Sam snorted two before handing it off to Richard who also did a couple. Then they talked about their golf swings.

"You're looking a little stiff with your follow-through," Sam said. "Once Vitrex gets passed, I'll prescribe you some. We get approval from the feds yet?"

"Should hear any day now," Richard said.

"My partners keep asking. Some of the younger guys in the group chomping at the bit. No pressure on you though. Anyhow call the office, I'll tell them to get you in." The pager on his hip went off. "Speaking of which…" He glanced at the flashing numbers then stopped the obnoxious beeping. "Ah, just the club letting me know I'm set for my tee time tomorrow. Now, back to your back—"

"I'm fine. Stop trying to get me under your knife to even up our handicaps."

Sam laughed and patted Richard's shoulder. Caroline saw Richard's jaw muscles clench, but no one else would've caught it or ever thought anything might be wrong—not with the Claytons.

After Sam and Naomi left, Caroline went upstairs and got ready for bed. Richard went into his den and shut the French doors. He'd be up late typing on the clackety keys of the massive computer that took up half his desk. Why Richard didn't dictate his replies for his secretary to type up Caroline stopped wondering years ago. When it came to anything corporate he trusted no one but his stupid monster.

Caroline hated Mondays more than the average person. They determined the outcome of Richard's entire workweek, which laid the foundation for hers as well.

At the end of the day, he came home, walked right past her, and went straight to his den without a word.

That couldn't be good, Caroline thought.

She gave him five minutes alone then opened the door. Richard had his elbows on the desk with his face in his palms.

"What happened?"

"No FDA approval for Vitrex, and I had to fire Ray Benson."

"Anything I can do?"

"White room?"

The thought of opening yesterday's wounds or swiping scabs that had started to heal made her shudder.

"But it's only Mon—"

"I know, but it needs to be kept down or I won't make it through this with all the disappointment in the air. Maybe just the ceiling chains," he said. "A few hours ought to calm it and give it time to think on what its next move should be."

Her rage bulged to an eruption. The same way it did on her eighth birthday when she smashed a chair through her bedroom window. Remembering the neighbor's dog on the sidewalk with a shard of glass in its side, she thought of how parents respond to children having imaginary friends, sometimes with anger, only Richard was a grown man, so her fury now felt as validated as it did then. Her mom and dad made her sit in that damn chair facing the corner for talking about Thomas. Only he wasn't someone she'd made up. Not until college had she considered Thomas might have been a ghost. She never went back home after that. She never forgave her parents either.

Caroline left the den and stalked to the basement. Richard knew she wouldn't say no. Vitrex was his baby—supposed to work just like Valium but better. He had a lot invested in it. But Caroline had always wondered why he'd want to improve upon an already perfect drug. The "monster" was totally stupid.

A little after four in the morning she woke on the chaise. She must have fallen asleep after releasing her own demons with Jane Fonda's Workout. Upset she'd forgotten to set an alarm, Caroline went down to the white room.

Everything looked wrong. His body hung limp and contorted, and his color! The twisted chains from the ceiling caught her eye. Caroline fumbled numbers on the keypad with trembling fingers.

Richard's arms had twisted with the chains, his backside blue. She turned him, and the taut links unwound and snapped apart, whipping his body around and swinging his head from side to side. Caroline gasped. Red webs and splotches crossed his bulging eyes, and his jaw hung slack, swollen purple tongue hanging out. He'd strangled himself in the crook of his arm.

She held back a sob. How could the pain she'd given not have been enough? Why didn't he say? Fury rose in her again then tumbled into sorrow. No one understood her the way he did. But she wouldn't cry, not in his white room. The monster in him would've wanted her to stay in control.

"I love you." This couldn't really be happening. Maybe he was faking to punish her for not coming down sooner. Caroline placed shaking fingers on his neck and checked for a pulse. "How could you do this to us?"

Nothing.

Cold seeped from his skin into her fingertips and she jerked her hand back.

"Where's your fucking monster now?" Caroline screamed. Rage flooded her with adrenaline, and she pommeled Richard's chest in a torrent until she dropped to the floor in a heap at his feet.

"Why? Why would you do this to me?" She slapped the floor and listened to the sound reverberate off the shiny white tiles.

"I can't leave you up there like that for police photos." She needed to think, figure out a way to get him down and dressed before calling the police. "Your parents will be mortified if this is the last image they have to remember you by." What excuse would she use? How could she arrange things to eliminate the white room?

Richard's monster's intricate planning might have given her a way, so long as the builders kept their mouths shut like they'd agreed to when they'd signed the contracts. He'd told them to include a plan for a hidden "panic room." Then Richard had removed the toilet and plumbing they'd installed and replaced it with the simple drain in the floor, and he did all the tilework and cabling himself. Concrete bricks and even the mortar that lined the unfinished section of the basement slid closed perfectly into place across the white room's door.

Caroline went over to the med cart for the key to the wrist and ankle restraints. Clinking sounded behind her as she opened a drawer. She spun around and fell back against the cart. Richard's body twitched, shifting the chains above.

"Thank God, you're alive!" Relieved, she ran to him, her fingers trembling too much to get the key in the lock. "Dammit, Richard, stop moving." Caroline stepped back, and looking upon his face, saw no signs of life. His skin remained dark purple, and a blue-white haze now coated his eyes. She rushed to the cart for the smelling salts, easy to find since the box reeked of ammonia. Capsules spilled out when she opened it, and as she scrambled to grab one his muscle tremors intensified behind her until he convulsed, clanging the chains above and straining the cables that kept his feet spread.

A fissure ran down his spine then opened up and split apart with deafening sounds of rending flesh as gore and meat splattered the floor. Muscles and sinew stretched across the front of his spinal column until they snapped, exposing his vertebrae. Caroline couldn't move, didn't even breathe as she watched something dark impossibly push its way through Richard's back. It spilled out onto the tiles with a splat and opened up into an enormous bloody, fleshy thing not quite a man.

Caroline couldn't scream. It had the bony facial structure of a bloated Max Headroom, only no plastic skin or latex hair. Its eyes glowed with pure white energy. Power surged off it in electric tendril currents reaching out across the room, filling the air with ozone. Its head raised in her direction. Not a mouth but a maw opened and lightning for teeth shot back and forth from its dripping gums.

She bolted for the door. The monster lunged and grabbed her leg. Caroline pulled free, leaving her leg warmer in its clutches. As her hand touched the keypad, her body jerked back and swung through the air. Brain-splitting pressure shot to her skull as her hair whipped the ceiling tiles. Caroline's stomach lurched as her body's forward motion came to an abrupt halt with a loud squelch. The brain squeeze released, and her torso went numb.

Caroline's head felt disproportionally too far from her neck as it hung upside down under the aluminum seat. Although she couldn't see the damage, the icy metal chilled her innards and streamers of blood wrapped down and around the chair legs.

Relief crashed through her. She'd given her husband the love he needed to keep the monster inside, thankful she never had to love him that way again. A single line of blood glided across the white tiles to the drain in the floor. It dripped once, twice, and then stopped.

Ghetto Blaster

JEFF STRAND

Clyde strutted down the sidewalk, boom box pressed to his ear, music blasting. He never maxed out the volume when he started out on his daily walk, because he enjoyed being able to turn it up when he received negative feedback. A dirty look would merit a slight increase; a request to lower the volume would make him crank it up a couple of notches.

It wasn't as if he was blasting bad music. He was providing a public service. A little cultural awareness for other white people like him. Most people in Iowa didn't realize that rap music was the future, but he was there to enlighten them. He'd be turning twenty-five in a couple of months, and he was proud to already have a purpose in life.

"Turn that crap down!" an old lady shouted at him, so Clyde turned it up and grooved even harder to the beat. He switched the heavy boom box to the other arm, so that his muscles would be evenly exercised.

A couple of blocks later, a man angrily waved at him, saying something that Clyde couldn't hear. He was always interested in constructive criticism to ignore, so he turned the boom box down.

"We don't all need to listen to that!" the man said. "Get a Walkman, for God's sake!"

Clyde turned the volume back up. Only selfish people listened to music through headphones. Music was for sharing.

He went into his favorite pizza place and got one slice of pepperoni and one slice of sausage. Naturally, he kept the music on, signaling his order by pointing to what he wanted through the glass and holding up one finger. He left with his pizza, happily munching away.

A man sat outside an antiques shop. He waved for Clyde's attention but didn't have the usual expression of annoyance. Clyde turned down the music.

"Nice boom box," said the man.

"Thanks."

"Not a top-of-the-line model, though."

157

Clyde shrugged. "Works fine."

The man stood up. "Come on in. I bet we can work something out."

Though Clyde had no interest in a new boom box, he saw no reason not to humor the guy. It was a glass storefront, so he was unlikely to have evil intentions, and Clyde was confident in his ability to bash his boom box over the man's skull if it came down to it.

They walked into the shop. The man led him to the back, where a boom box rested on a shelf next to a vase and what looked like an old crockpot. It was smaller than Clyde's, and the black surface was all scratched up. It was the kind of boom box a poor person would have. Clyde was extremely unimpressed.

The man picked it up. "What do you think?"

"Looks like a piece of junk."

"The sound quality, though. Check it out." The man turned it on. Some Lawrence Welk-sounding shit began to play, and it sounded kind of tinny through those cheap-ass speakers.

"Sounds like crap," Clyde noted.

"Well, that's probably just because of your musical preference. Trade the cassette that's in there with the one you're listening to. It'll give you a direct comparison."

"I'm not going to buy your boom box."

"I think you'll be impressed."

"I spent all my money on pizza."

"Just listen to it. Yes, it's a little beat up, but the sound quality will blow you away."

Clyde couldn't help but be intrigued. No way could that piece of garbage compete with the boom box he had now. What kind of con was this guy trying to pull?

They both ejected the tapes from their respective boom boxes. Clyde put his into the antique one and pressed play. The sound wasn't terrible, but it wasn't all that great, either.

"Mine's better," said Clyde.

"Put it to your ear."

Clyde picked up the boom box and put it to his ear. Nope. His was still vastly superior.

He tried to lower it and couldn't.

For a second he thought that maybe the man had put glue on it, yet he didn't feel anything sticky. It was more like a very powerful magnet. He kept trying to pull it away from his ear, but the boom box refused to budge.

"Hey, what the hell?" he demanded.

"Full disclosure," said the man. "That's a cursed boom box. All of the items in this back aisle are cursed. I apologize for not saying something sooner, but you wouldn't have put it to your ear if you'd been well-informed."

"I'm serious, stop playing around!" said Clyde. "Get this thing off me!"

"I just told you it was cursed."

"Break the curse!"

"That's not how curses work. What kind of lame curse would it be if I could just snap my fingers and break it as soon as it took hold of you? No, no, you must break the curse yourself."

"How?"

"Hell, I don't know. I didn't place it. Some sort of life lesson that you learn, I assume."

"Break the curse or I'll kick your ass!"

The shop owner nodded. "Uh-huh. Sure. You're going to kick my ass while holding a heavy boom box to your head. How about you let go of it and see how well your neck supports its weight? Don't—then I'll have snapped-neck corpse on the floor, and fixers are expensive, and I'm barely keeping this place open as it is. My advice to you is to head out into the bright, beautiful world and see what kind of self-improvement you can work out."

"I'm gonna kill you!" said Clyde.

"No, you're probably not. You can leave your boom box here if you want. I won't sell it or anything. The longer you wait, the heavier that thing is going to feel, and though it may not break your neck it'll probably rip off your ear. Have you ever seen somebody with a ripped-off ear? It's gross. You can see deep into the cavity. Earwax just leaks right out onto their shoulder. Nasty, nasty business."

Clyde desperately wanted to kill him, but the shopkeeper was right: having a heavy boom box stuck to his ear presented a clear offensive disadvantage. Instead, he glared at him and stormed out of the shop.

Once out of the shop, Clyde remembered that he didn't believe in curses. So he held the boom box with both hands and pulled as hard as he could, stopping only when it started to feel like flesh might be coming off the side of his head.

What should he do? Go to the hospital? What kind of surgery could doctors perform to get a cursed boom box off his head? Should he go to a church? An exorcist? Where did Gypsies gather? Was it racist that he assumed that it was a Gypsy curse? Was "Gypsy" even a race, or just a lifestyle?

He did have a friend who did a lot of woodworking. He had a table saw.

Obviously, Clyde was not going to let a spinning circular blade come right next to his head, but if he could saw most of the boom box away, that would solve the problem of its weight ripping off his ear or snapping his neck.

He ran the twelve blocks to Jimmy's house.

159

Clyde pounded on the front door. Jimmy got fired from his day jobs on a regular basis, so there was a good chance that he was home. A moment later, Jimmy opened the door, wearing only underwear and a T-shirt.

"Hey, Clyde," he said. "Wanna play some ColecoVision?"

"I need your help," said Clyde. "Can we go to your garage?"

"Sure, sure. C'mon in." As Clyde stepped into the unkempt house, Jimmy said, "My mom's not home, so you don't have to keep the music down."

Clyde said nothing. They walked through the house into the garage, where all of Jimmy's equipment was set up.

"What can I do for you?" Jimmy asked.

"I need you to saw off this boom box."

"I beg your pardon?"

"It's stuck to my head."

"You mean with super glue?"

"It doesn't matter. I just need you to saw it away."

"How'd you superglue your ghetto blaster to your head?"

"I said, it doesn't matter."

"I think it does matter. Seems like there'd be a good story behind it."

"Will you saw it away or not?"

"All right, all right, take a chill pill," said Jimmy. "This is a precision instrument, but I feel like if you move around I could take off part of your head, so I'm gonna have to write up one of those things where you can't sue me if I maim you."

"All I want you to do is saw off three-quarters of it. You're not going to get close to my head."

"The saw was really made for wood, not so much plastic and metal and speakers and stuff."

"Dammit, Jimmy, are you going to help me or not?"

"Don't spazz out. I'll help you. I'll turn on the saw, and you lower the boom box onto it wherever you're comfortable."

"Thanks," said Clyde. "I'm sorry I snapped at you. I'm under a lot of stress right now."

"Well, sure, you have the embarrassment of super-gluing your head to a boom box. I'd be grumpy too."

Jimmy turned on the table saw. The sound was annoyingly loud and grating. Clyde took a few moments to position himself properly, then very slowly lowered the boom box down upon the spinning blade. There was a lot of screeching and a lot of sparks, but the blade didn't seem to be cutting into anything.

He stood back up and asked Jimmy if he noticed any difference. Jimmy mouthed "I can't hear you" at him then turned off the saw.

"Did it do anything?" Clyde asked.

Jimmy shook his head. "Not a scratch. At least not a new scratch. That thing is all scratched up. What happened to yours?"

"It doesn't matter. What other tools do you have that might remove it?"

"That saw goes through bone," said Jimmy. "I mean, that's what I'm told. If it won't do the trick, I don't know what else I have that would. I guess I could try to smash it apart with a hammer."

"Let's do that."

"Do you have a hammer?"

"Why the hell would I have a hammer?" Clyde asked. "We're in your workshop!"

"Oh, yeah, yeah, sorry. It's kind of unnerving that the saw wouldn't harm the boom box. Feels a bit supernatural."

"Just get a hammer."

As Jimmy walked over to the shelf to retrieve a hammer, the boom box began to play Clyde's cassette. Jimmy smiled and bopped his head to the beat. The music got louder and louder.

"Oh, yeah, crank it up!" said Jimmy.

"I'm not controlling it!"

"That's right, good music has a life of its own!"

The music continued to increase in volume until it started to hurt Clyde's ears. The windows of the garage started to quiver.

Jimmy said something that appeared to be, "Hey, that's probably loud enough. Any chance you could turn it down a bit? I don't want the neighbors to complain."

The volume kept increasing. Clyde tried to turn it down, but the boom box had no volume control. He wondered what the hell kind of boom box lacked a volume control knob, then remembered that it was a cursed one.

Jimmy said something that appeared to be, "Turn down the goddamn music, Clyde! You're going to blow out my eardrums! C'mon, man, knock this shit off! Please, Clyde, it's really starting to hurt and I can't—"

Jimmy dropped to his knees and let out a scream that Clyde couldn't hear.

Pink froth began to spew from his ears.

Then the froth turned red.

It got thicker in consistency, as if brain matter might've been added to the mix.

And then both of Jimmy's ears shot off the side of his head in a geyser of blood. His left ear struck the tool shelf, while his right ear launched toward the other wall of the garage but didn't quite make it.

The music stopped as Jimmy dropped to the floor.

Clyde cried out in horror and ran out of the garage. As he raced through the house, he nearly bumped into Jimmy's mother. She gave him the disapproving look that he knew very well, but then her expression turned to concern. "What's wrong?" she asked.

The music blasted again. Jimmy's mother slapped her hands against her ears, and froth immediately leaked through her fingers. Clyde just stood there, apologizing over and over and over until her ears exploded off of her head. He fled the house as she dropped to the floor.

He ran down the street, music blaring. A screaming man clutching his ears tumbled off his front porch, but Clyde figured that could be a coincidence. A happy couple walking hand in hand let go of each other's hands and looked much less happy as Clyde approached. Four ears jettisoned and four streams of goo shot forth. This was probably not a coincidence.

It occurred to Clyde that he shouldn't be running back toward the more populated section of town, but he was in too much of a panic to stop himself.

Everywhere he ran, people suffered the same grisly fate. They weren't going to appreciate his music taste anytime soon. He said he was sorry to everybody he passed, though without ears they probably couldn't hear his sincere apology.

A small dog went on its way, apparently unaffected. Good. Clyde would've felt terrible if he caused harm to a dog.

So much death. So much pinkish-red froth. So many disconnected ears.

At least Clyde's own brain hadn't liquefied. He wasn't proud of himself for being relieved by this.

Maybe he was meant to sacrifice himself. Maybe the way to break the curse was to release his grip on the boom box and let it snap his neck.

He stopped running, wondering if this was truly the answer.

As he mulled that over, he noticed that he'd stopped next to a restaurant with outdoor seating. Dozens of screaming people were covered with each other's brain froth. It was so disgusting that he wanted to keep running, but no, he deserved to see something this gross.

A bus pulled up alongside of him. It drove away as the passengers began screaming and dying.

He had to do this. Too many innocent people had perished.

Clyde let go of the boom box.

Its weight yanked him to the sidewalk. Somehow he was able to hear the snap over the music. His entire body from the neck down went numb.

The music continued.

Well, shit.

People kept coming out of buildings to see what was going on, and they kept screaming and covering their soon-to-come-off ears. When he left for his walk, Clyde could've never imagined the nightmare he would behold.

If only he'd been more considerate.

If he could do it all over, he'd keep his music at a reasonable volume so as not to disturb others.

The cursed boom box shut off.

Oh. Apparently that was the life lesson.

In retrospect, it seemed kind of obvious. He probably should've started there.

Clyde vowed to become an ambassador for the use of portable cassette players with headphones. He would preach the gospel of being considerate with one's music. And he might have, except that a couple of badly injured people stumbled over him and did additional damage to his neck, which turned out to be fatal.

Though nobody knew that this carnage spawned from a cursed boom box, people did become concerned about loud music. In particular, sixteen-year-old Joey Winkle, who stopped playing his own boom box so loud in his bedroom. His sister, Wendy, whose bedroom was across the hallway, was then able to concentrate well enough to solve the Rubik's Cube she'd been working on for the past two months.

And so, though this may be a bit of a stretch, this tale can be said to have a happy ending.

Haddonfield, New Jersey 1980

CINDY O'QUINN

When your past trails you like a shadow, it becomes a ghost unable to say goodbye.

I found you hidden among precious memories. The real Haddonfield—not the one made famous by Hollywood's disguise. Keeper of its own nightmares made difficult after the 1978 release.

A man in a mask, glowing pumpkins on a once peaceful tree-lined street. I couldn't compete with that Halloween. It changed my secrets…the ones I was hell-bent to keep. Silence stretched out for two years while the shadows in my mind whispered of the monster I would create.

There may have been something in the fictional fog, a maniac, a watcher in the woods, terror on a train, something in the deep, someone who really shined, or a skeletal driver for the hearse. Who knows? Could be the sound of Van Halen that made my heart skip a beat.

A mind often reshaped by pain inflicted to flesh and bones.

I think back to my eight-year-old self and how mad I was because I no longer spent all my time playing in the woods. Stuck inside an old house on a scrap of land that was nowhere and one hundred miles to anywhere. Divorce took me there as a child and divorce left me there alone as an adult. Surrounded by the memories of ghosts, not even my own but those who once lived there and chose to stay for no other reason than to haunt me.

My mind held together by the same scars that marked my flesh and broke my bones. I became the shadow of my dad as I spent two years trying to win her back. Waiting on a storm to clear, I imagined her wearing the black dress, the one that fit like a signature against her curves. She loved the dress but the hat was more important to me. I envied the wide brim which hid your face from prying eyes when tilted just so.

I remember the day I lost my mind. The ghosts were listening because everyone and everything spoke. It just so happened the one person I needed,

164

neither listened or cared as I threatened to do more harm come Halloween than any Hollywood Slasher had ever done.

Once you've loved someone can that love ever die or does it lie in wait? Billy Squier was probably right when he sang, "Nobody Knows."

On October 31, 1980 I tried making my own slasher hit that would get my ex-wife's attention, along with the rest of the world. I looked at the reflection in the mirror and decided a mask wasn't necessary. The past two years living as a recluse among ghosts and cobwebs in my mind had created a face so full of shadows and hollowness…Hollywood would have been impressed.

I gathered all the butcher knives from the kitchen. All sharpened to a hair-poppin edge. Headed to the most perfect tree-lined street in the real Haddonfield and parked. Aptly named Elm Street. I laughed. Waited. Watched the trick-or-treaters start to make their way up and down the sidewalk. Noticed how the grass wasn't bright green like in the movie. It was actually Fall in real Haddonfield and leaves were really orange, red, and yellow. Brightest foliage ever.

I barely remembered getting out of my car but I did because I found myself walking down the sidewalk. Empty-handed. Mothers looked at me and smiled. Something was wrong. People should be afraid of me. My face, the way it looked in the mirror. Two boys gave me the thumbs up. A small girl about age five, tugged on my britches and said, "I like your costume!"

What was I doing? How could I have thought of such horror? Turns out there was no Smith's Grove in the real Haddonfield but there was an Altered States Mental Health Center. I was admitted that night.

How fortunate was I to have found Altered States? With any luck I'll be out in time for Halloween 1981.

When He Was Fab

F. PAUL WILSON

Floor drains.

Sheesh. Doug hated them.

Being super of this old rattrap building wasn't a bad job. The hours could play hell with you sometimes, but he got a free room, he got his utilities, and he got a salary—if you wanted to call that piddly amount in his weekly check a salary. But you couldn't knock the deal too hard. Long as he stayed on the job, he had shelter, warmth, and enough money for food, enough time to work out with his weights. Wasn't glamorous, but a guy with his education—like, none to speak of besides seventh grade and postgrad courses in the school of hard knocks—couldn't ask for a whole helluva lot more.

'Cept maybe for drains that worked.

The basement floor drain was a royal pain. He hovered over it now in his rubber boots, squatting ankle deep in the big stinky puddle that covered it. Around him the tenants' junk was stacked up on the high ground against the walls like a silent crowd around a drowning victim. Third time this month the damn thing had clogged up. Course there'd been a lot of rain lately, and that was part of the problem, but still the drain shoulda been working better than this.

Now or never, he thought, unfolding his rubber gloves. He wished he had more light than that naked sixty-watter hanging from the beam overhead. Would've loved one of those big babies they used at night games up at Yankee Stadium.

Jeez, but he hated this part of the job. Last week the drain had clogged and he'd reached down like he was about to do now and had come up with a dead rat.

He shuddered with just the memory of it. A monster Brooklyn brown rat. Big, tough mother that could've easily held its own with the ones down on the docks. Didn't know how it had got in this drain, but the grate had been pushed aside, and when he'd reached down, there it was, wedged into the pipe. So soft,

169

at first he'd thought it was a plastic bag or something. Then he'd felt the tail. And the feet. He'd worked it loose and pulled it free.

Just about blew lunch when he'd looked at it, all soft, puffy, pulpy, and drippy, the eyes milk white, the sharp yellow buck teeth bared, the matted hair falling off in clumps. And, God, it stunk. He'd dumped it in his plastic bucket, scooped up enough of the rapidly draining water to cover it, then run like hell for the dumpster.

"Whatta y'got for me this week, you sonuvabitch?" he said aloud.

He didn't usually talk to floor drains, but his skin was crawling with the thought of what might've got stuck down there this time. And if he ever grabbed something that was still moving…forget about it.

He pulled the heavy rubber gloves up to his elbows, took a deep breath, and plunged his right hand into the water.

"What the hell?"

The grate was still in place. So what was blocking it?

Underwater, he poked his fingers through the slots and pulled the grate free, then worked his hand down the funnel and into the pipe.

"What now, you mother? What now?"

Nothing. The water felt kind of thick down there, almost like Jell-O, but the pipe was empty as far as his fingers could reach. Probably something caught in the trap. Which meant he'd have to use the snake. And dammit to hell, he'd left it upstairs.

Maybe if he squeezed his fingers down just a little further he'd find something. Just a little—

Doug reached down too far. Water sloshed over the top of his glove and ran down the inside to his fingers. It had a strange, warm, thick feel to it.

"Damn it all!"

But when he went to pull back, his hand wouldn't come. It was stuck in the hole and all his twisting and pulling only served to let more of the cloudy water run into his glove.

And then Doug noticed that the water was no longer running down his arm—it was running up.

He stared, sick dread twisting in his gut, as the thick, warm fluid moved up past his elbow—crawled was more like it. After a frozen moment he attacked it with his free hand, batting at it, wiping it off. But it wouldn't wipe. It seemed to be traveling in his skin, becoming part of it, seeping up his arm like water spreading through blotter paper.

And it was hot where it moved. The heat spread up under the half sleeve of his work shirt. He tore at the buttons but before he could get them undone the heat had spread across his chest and up his shoulder to his neck.

Doug lost it then. He began whimpering and crying, clawing at himself as he splashed and scrambled and flopped about like an animal caught in a trap, trying to yank his right hand free. He felt the heat on his face now, moving toward his mouth. He clamped his lips shut but it ran into his nostrils and through his nose to his throat. He opened his mouth to scream, but no sound would come. A film covered his eyes, and against his will his muscles began to relax, lowering him into the water, letting it soak into him, all through him. He felt as if he were melting, dissolving into the puddle…

Marc hopped out of the cab in front of the Graf Spee's entrance, paid the driver with his patented flourish, and strolled past the velvet cords that roped off the waiting dorks.

Bruno was on the door tonight. A burly lump of muscle with feet; at thirty-five he was maybe ten years older than Marc; his hair was a similar brown but there the resemblance stopped. As Marc approached the canopied entrance he wondered what Bruno had looked like as an infant, or if the doorman's mother had been prescient. Because Bruno had grown up to be the epitome of Brunoness.

"Ay, Mista Chevignon," Bruno said with a wide grin and a little bow. "How ya doon anight?"

"Fine, Bruno. Just fine."

Keeping his hands jammed deep into the pockets of his Geoffrey Beene tweed slacks, and trapping his open, ankle-length Moschino black leather coat behind his elbows while exposing his collarless white Armani shirt, buttoned to the throat, Marc swiveled and surveyed the line of hopefuls awaiting the privilege of admission to the Spee.

"Real buncha loooosuhs tanight, Mista C."

Marc let his eyes roam the queue, taking in all the well-off and the trying-to-look-it, some natives, some tunnel rats and bridge trolls, all dressed in their absolute best or their most fashionably tacky ensembles, trying to look so cool, so with-it, so very-very, but unable to hide the avid look in their eyes, that hunger to be where it was most in to be. Somebody had killed Lennon, somebody had tried to kill Reagan, Mount St. Helens had blown its top, and a shooting war had started raging in the Falkland Islands—wherever they were—but forget all that. The thing that really mattered was a chance to dance on the rotating floor of the

Spee and search for the famous faces that would be on the "Star Tracks" page of next week's People.

"Have they been good little aspirants, Bruno?"

"Yeah. No wise guys so far."

"Then let's make someone's day, shall we?"

"Whatever you say, Mista C."

He sauntered along outside the cords, watching them stare his way and whisper without taking their eyes off him. Who's he?...You ever seen him before?...Looks like Simon Le Bon...Nah, his shoulders is too big...Gawd, he's gawgeous!...Well, if he ain't somebody, how come he's getting in ahead of us?...I dunno, but I seen him around here before.

Indeed you have, sweetheart, he thought.

The last speaker was a bony, brittle, bottle-blonde with a white hemline up to here and a black neckline down to there. Knobby knees knocking in the breeze, spiky hair, a mouth full of gum, three different shades of eyeshadow going halfway up her forehead, and wearing so many studs and dangles her ears had to be Swiss cheese when her jewelry was off.

Perfect.

"What's your name, honey?"

She batted her lashes. "Darlene."

"Who you with?"

"My sister, Marlene." She reached back and pulled forward an identically dressed clone. "Who wants t'know?"

He smiled. "Twins. More than perfect." He lifted the velvet cord. "Come on, girls. You don't have to wait any longer."

After exchanging wide-eyed glances, they ducked the velvet and followed him to the canopy. Some of the dorks grumbled but a few of them clapped. Soon they were all clapping.

He ushered them to the door where Bruno stepped aside and passed the giggling twins through into the hallowed inner spaces of the Graf Spee.

"You're a prince, Mista C," Bruno said, grinning.

"How true."

He slowed, almost tripped. What a lame remark. Surely he could have come up with something better than that.

Bruno stepped into the dark passageway and touched his arm.

"You feelin' okay, Mista C.?"

"Of course. Why?"

"You look a little pale, is all. Need anyting?"

"No, Bruno. Thanks, but I'm fine."

"Okay. But you need anyting, you lemme know an' it's done. Know what I'm sayin'?"

Marc clapped Bruno on the shoulder and nodded. As he walked down the narrow black corridor that led past the coat checkroom he wondered what Bruno had meant. Did he look pale? He didn't feel pale. He felt fine.

The twins were hovering near the coat check window, looking lost. They'd finally achieved their dream: They'd made it to the swirling innards of the Spee, and they weren't sure what to do about it. So they stood and numbly watched the peristalsis. One of them turned to Marc as he approached.

"Thanks a million, mister. It was like really great of you to get us in and like if, you know, you like want to get together later, you know, we'd like really be glad to show our appreciation, know what I mean?"

The second twin batted her eyes over the other's shoulder.

"Yeah. We really would. But do you mind if I, like, ask, uh…are you someone?"

Just as he was thinking how pathetic they were, he reminded himself that once he'd had to wait in line like them. That had been years ago, back in the days when King Kong had been the place. But after he'd been let in once, he'd never stood in line again. He'd taken his chance and capitalized on it. And as time had passed and his status had risen, he'd developed the nightly ritual of picking one or two of the hoi polloi for admission to the inner sanctum of whatever club he was gracing with his presence that night.

"Everyone is someone. I happen to be Marc."

"Which is your table?" said Twin One.

"They're all my tables."

Twin Two's eyes bulged. "You own this place?"

He laughed. "No. Of course not. That would be too much trouble." And besides, he thought, these places stay hot for something like the lifespan of a housefly. "I just go where the action is. And tonight the action is here. So you two wiggle in there and enjoy yourselves."

"All right!" said Twin One.

She turned to her sister and they did a little dance while making jazz hands at each other.

Marc shuddered as he watched them hurry toward the main floor. They might be just vulgar enough to amuse someone. He opened the door marked PRIVATE and took the narrow stairway up to the gallery. Gunnar, Bruno's Aryan soulmate, was on duty at the top of the steps. He waved Marc into the sanctum sanctorum of alcoved tables overlooking the dance floor.

The Manhattan in-crowd was out in force tonight, with various Left Coast luminaries salted among them. Madonna looked up from her table and waved as she whispered something in a pert brunette's ear. Marc stuck his tongue out and kept moving. Bobby DeNiro and Marty Scorcese nodded, Bianca blew him a kiss, and on and on…

This was what it was all about. This was what he lived for now, the nightlife that made the drudgery of his day-life bearable. Knowing people, important people, being known, acknowledged, sought out for a brush with that legendary Marc Chevignon wit. It was that wit, that incisive, urbane flippancy that had got him here and changed his nightlife. Soon it would be changing his day-life. Everything was falling into place, beautifully, flawlessly, almost as if he'd planned it this way.

And he hadn't.

All he'd wanted was a little excitement, to watch the watchables, to be where the action was. He'd never even considered the possibility of being in the play, he'd simply hoped for a chance to sit on the sidelines and perhaps catch a hint of breeze from the hem of the action as it swirled by.

But when lightning struck and he got through the door of the Kong a couple of years ago, things began to happen. He'd sat at the bar and fallen into conversation with a few of the lower-level regulars and the quips had begun to flow. He hadn't the faintest where they'd come from, they simply popped out. The cracks stretched to diatribes using Buckley-level vocabulary elevated by P .J. O'Rourke-caliber wit, but bitchy. Very bitchy. The bar-hangers lapped it up. The laughter drew attention, and some mid-level regulars joined the crowd. He was invited back to an afterhours party at the Palladium, and the following night when he showed up at King Kong with a few of the regulars, he was passed right through the door.

A few nights and he was a regular. Soon he was nobbing with the celebs. They all wanted him at their tables. Marc C. made things happen. He woke people up, got them talking and laughing. Wherever he sat there was noise and joviality. He could turn just-another-night-at-the-new-now-club into an event. If you wanted to draw the people who mattered to your table, you needed Marc Chevignon.

And his wit didn't pass unnoticed by the select few who recognized obscure references and who knew high-level quick-draw quippery when they heard it. Franny Lebowitz said he could be the next Tom Wolfe. And LuAnn agreed.

He stopped at LuAnn's table.

"Hiya, Marky," she said, reaching for his hand.

Her touch sent a wave of heat through him. He and LuAnn were an item these days. They had a thing going. He spent three or four nights a week at her place. Always at her place. Never at his. No one saw his place. Ever.

That, he knew, was part of his attraction for these people. They'd taken the measure of his quality and found it acceptable, even desirable. But he was an unknown quantity. Where he came from, who he came from, where he lived, what he did in the day were all carefully guarded secrets. Marc Chevignon, the cagey, canny mystery man, the acid-tongued enigma.

He suspected that LuAnn genuinely cared for him, but it was hard to tell. She tended to let down her panties a lot quicker than her guard. She'd been around the scene so much longer than he, seemed to have had so many lovers—Christ, when he walked her into some of the private afterhours parties he could be pretty sure she'd screwed half the guys there, maybe some of the women too—but she seemed truly interested in him. At least now. At least for the moment.

She was the one who'd been pressing him to write down his more incisive observations so she could show them to a few editors she knew—and she knew all the important ones. She was sure she could land him a regular spot in the Voice, and maybe Esquire, if not both.

Thus the tape recorder in his pocket. During the day he never could remember a thing he'd said the night before. So he'd decided to record himself in action and transcribe the best stuff the next morning.

Nothing so far tonight worth writing down. Hadn't really come up with anything last night either. No inspiration, he guessed.

But it would come. Because it was happening. He was happening. Everything coming his way. Esquire, the Voice, maybe an occasional freelance piece for GQ later on. He wasn't going to be a mere hanger-on anymore, someone who merely knew Somebodies. He was going to be one of those Somebodies.

But the best part of it all was having LuAnn. LuAnn…twenty-eight with the moon-white skin of a teenager who'd never been to the beach, night-dark hair, pale-blue, aventurine eyes, and the trademark ruby lipstick. All day long he ached for the sight of her. He couldn't tell her that, of course. Had to play it cool because Marc C. was cool. But, man, sometimes it was hard to hide. Most times it was hard to hide. Most times he wanted to fall at her feet professing his undying love and begging her never to leave him.

Sure, it scanned like a third-rate Tin Pan Alley ditty, but that was how he felt.

"Ms. Lu," he said, bending and kissing her. God, he loved the soft, glossy touch of her lips.

She jerked back.

"What's wrong, Lu?"

"Your lips. They feel…different."

"Same ones I wore last night." He tugged at them. "I don't remember changing them."

175

LuAnn gave him a patient smile and pulled him down next to her. He waved and nodded hellos in the dimness to the LuAnn table regulars, then turned his attention to the lady herself. Her eyes sparkled with excitement as she leaned toward him and whispered close in his ear; the caress of her warm breath raised gooseflesh down his left side.

"I hear you gave Liz's guy the slip last night."

"Liz's guy?"

"Don't be coy, Marc. I heard it earlier this afternoon. Liz had one of her people tail you home from my place last night—or at least try to tail you."

Any warmth he'd been drawing from her vanished in a chilly draft of unease. She could only mean Liz Smith, the columnist who'd been trying to get the scoop on him for months now. He guessed she was tired of tagging him with the "mystery man" line when she did a piece on the club scene. Other people had tried to tail him before but he'd spotted them easily. Whoever this guy was must have been good. Marc hadn't had the slightest suspicion…

"He said you ducked into an old apartment house in Brooklyn and never came out."

"Oh, yes…" Marc said carefully. "I spotted him shortly after I left your place. He was good. I couldn't lose him in the usual manner so I led him all the way into Bay Ridge and used the key I have from the owner of this dump there—in the front door and out the back. I always do that when I think I'm being followed." He rubbed his chin, Bogart style. "So he was one of Liz's boys. That's interesting."

More than interesting—terrifying.

"Yeah, she's determined to track you down," LuAnn said, snuggling closer. "But she's not going to be first, is she, Marky? You're going to take me to your place firstest, aren't you?"

"Sure, Lu. You'll be the first. But I warn you, you'll be disappointed when the day comes."

"No I won't."

Yes, you will. I guarantee it.

He sat next to her and tried to keep from shaking. God, that had been close! He'd been right on the edge of having his cover blown and hadn't had an inkling. Suddenly Marc didn't feel so good.

"Excuse me a moment," he said, rising. "I need to make a pit stop." He winked. "It's a long ride from Bay Ridge."

LuAnn laughed. "Hurry back!"

Feeling worse by the minute, he headed straight for the men's room. As he pushed into the bright fluorescent interior, he saw Karl Peaks turning away from the sink, licking a trace of white powder from his index finger.

176

"Marc?" Peaks said, sniffing and gawking. "Is that you, man?"

"No. It's Enrico Caruso." Enrico Caruso? Where the hell did that come from?

"It's your face, man. What's happened to it?"

Alarmed, Marc stepped over the mirror. His knees almost buckled when he saw himself.

My face!

His skin was sallow, leaching into yellow under the harsh light. And the left side was drooping, the corners of his mouth and left eye sagging toward his chin.

My God! What's happening?

He couldn't stay here, couldn't let anyone see him like this. Because it wasn't going to get better. Somehow he knew that the longer he waited the worse it would sag.

He spun and fled past Peaks, turned a hard right and went down the back steps, through the kitchen, and out into the rear alley.

It had started raining. He slunk through the puddles like a rat until he found an intersecting alley that took him out to West Houston. He flagged a cab and huddled in the protective darkness of the rear seat as it carried him through the downpour, over the Williamsburg Bridge to Brooklyn. Home.

Doug watched Marc flow back into the bucket, sliding down his arm, over his wrist and hand, to ooze off his fingertips like clear, warm wallpaper paste. A part of him was furious with Marc for letting him down tonight, but another part knew something was seriously wrong. He'd half-sensed it during the last time they'd been together. And tonight he was sure. Marc wasn't acting right.

Marc…Christ, why did he call this pile of goo Marc? It was goo. A nameless it. Marc Chevignon was someone who existed only when Doug was wearing the goo. He'd picked the name Marc because it sounded classy, like Marc Antony, that Roman guy in the Cleopatra movie. And Chevignon? He'd borrowed that from the label inside some fancy leather coat he'd seen in a men's shop.

Somewhere along the way he'd started thinking of the goo as a friend…a friend named Marc.

"What's the matter, Marc?" he whispered into the bucket when the goo had all run off him. "What's goin' on, man?"

Marc didn't answer. He just sat in his bucket under the harsh light of the white-tiled bathroom. Marc never answered. At least not from the bucket. Marc

177

only spoke when he was riding Doug. Marc was brilliant when he was riding Doug. At least till now.

Doug remembered the first time Marc climbed on him, down in the basement, when he'd reached into the plugged drain…remembered the heat, the suffocating feeling. He'd been so scared then, afraid he'd been caught in some real-life replay of The Blob, absolutely sure he was going to die. But he hadn't died. After blacking out for a minute or so, he'd come to on the basement floor, half in, half out of the shrinking puddle. He'd scrambled to his feet, looked at his hands, felt his neck, his face. The goo was gone—not a trace of it left on him. Everything seemed almost normal.

Almost. His skin didn't feel quite right. Not slimy or nothing, just…different. He ran upstairs to his place, the super's apartment on the first floor. He seemed to be moving a little different, his steps quicker, surer. Almost, like, graceful. He got to the bathroom and stared in the mirror.

He'd changed. He looked the same, but then again he didn't. His normally wavy brown hair was darker, straighter, maybe because it was wet and slicked back. Even his eyebrows looked a little darker. His eyes were still blue but they seemed more intense, more alive.

And he felt different inside. Usually when he finished a day's work he liked to get a six-pack, flip on the tube, and mellow out for the night. Now he wanted to move. He felt like going places, doing things, making things happen instead of letting them happen.

He stared at the reflection for a long time, telling himself over and over he wasn't crazy. He'd just had some sort of daymare or something. Or maybe fumes—yeah, some sort of fumes bubbling up from the drain had screwed up his head for a little bit. But he was okay now. Really.

Finally, when he sort of believed that, he staggered back to the basement. Still had to do something with that water.

But the water was gone. The drain had unclogged and all that was left of the stinking puddle was a big round glistening wet spot. Relieved that he didn't have to stick his arm down that pipe again, Doug collected his gloves and junk and headed back upstairs.

In the hall he ran into Theresa Coffee, the busty blonde graduate student in 308. He gave her his usual smile—at least he thought it was his usual smile—and expected her usual curt nod in return. She'd caught him staring at her underwear down in the laundry room once too often and had been giving him the cold shoulder ever since. Treated him like a pervo. Which he wasn't. But her underwear, man—looked like it came straight out of a Fredericks of Hollywood catalog. Whoa.

But this time she actually stopped and talked to him. And he actually talked back to her. Like, intelligent. He sounded like he had a brain in his head. Like a guy who'd finished high school. College even. He didn't have the faintest idea where all that talk came from, all he knew was that for the first time in his life he sounded brainy. She seemed to think so too. She even invited him up to her place. And before too long she was modeling all that underwear for him.

Much later, when he left her, he didn't go back to his apartment to sack out. He went back to change into his best clothes—which weren't much then, for sure—and headed for Manhattan. For the King Kong.

The rest was history.

History...the celebrity friends, the notoriety, the promised writing career, LuAnn, a way up and out...history.

Yeah. History. Only right now history seemed to be coming to an end.

Doug stared down at the two-gallon bucketful of goo. Cloudy goo. Marc used to be clear. Crystal clear. Like Perrier. What kind of game was it trying to run?

"C'mon, guy," Doug said, rolling up his sleeve. "One more time."

He slipped his right hand up to his wrist in the goo. He noticed how Marc was cooler than usual. In the past there'd always been a near-body-temperature warmth to it. Slowly it began to slide up his forearm.

"There y'go!"

But it only made a few inches before it started to slide back into the bucket.

"You bastard!"

Doug couldn't help being mad. He knew he owed a lot to Marc—everything, in fact—but he couldn't help feel that he'd been teased along and now he was being dumped. He wanted to kick the bucket over. Or better yet, upend it over the toilet and flush it down to the sewers. See if Marc liked it down there in the dark with the crocodiles.

"So what's up, here, Marc? What's doin'? You gonna put me through the wringer? Gonna make me crawl? Is that it? Well it won't work. Because I don't need you, Marc. I owe you, I'll give you that. But if you think I can't live without you, f'get about it, okay?"

For Doug had arrived at the conclusion that he didn't need Marc any more. Marc hadn't really done nothing. Marc just was like the wizard in The Wizard of Oz. How'd that song go? "Oz never did give nothing to the Tin Man, that he didn't already have." Right. And Doug was the Tin Man. All that sharp wit and grooviness had been hiding in him all along. All Marc had done was bring it to the surface—and take credit for it. Well, Marc wasn't going to take credit no more. Doug was taking the wheel now. He knew he had it in him. All the doors were already open. All he had to do was walk through and make this city his oyster.

"Okay." He rose to his feet. "If that's the way you want it, fine. You make plans for the sewer, I'll head for the Spee."

On his way out the door he should have felt great, free, lighter than air. So how come he felt like he'd just lost his best friend?

"Yo, Bruno," Doug said as he stepped under the canopy and headed toward the entrance of the Graf Spee. "I'm back."

Bruno straightened his arm and stopped Doug with a palm against his chest. It was like thumping against a piling.

"Glad to hear it," Bruno said, deadpan. "Now get back in line."

Doug smiled. "Bruno, it's me. Marc."

"Sure. An I'm David Bowie."

"Bruno—"

"Ay! Fun's fun, guy, an' I 'preciate a good scam much as the next fella, but don't wear it out, huh? When the real Mista Chevignon comes out, maybe I'll introduce you. He'll getta kick outta you. Maybe even pass you in. He's good like dat."

"I snuck out the back, Bruno. Now I'm—"

The piling became a pile driver, thumping Doug out from under the canopy and back into the rain. Bruno was speaking through his teeth now.

"I'm startin' to get pissed. You may dress like him, you may comb your hair like him, you may even look sompin' like him, but you ain't Marc Chevignon. I know Marc Chevignon, and you ain't no Marc Chevignon." Bruno's face broke into a grin. "Ay. I sound like a president debater, don't I? I'll have to tell Mista Chevignon—the real one—when he comes out."

"At least let me get, like, a message to LuAnn. Please, Bruno."

Bruno's grin vanished like a pulse from one of the strobes winking over the Spee's dance floor. "Miz Lu's gone home. The real Marc Chevignon would know where dat is. Now lose yourself afore I kick your butt downa Chinatown."

Doug stumbled away through the rain in shocked disbelief. What was happening here? Why didn't Bruno recognize him?

He stopped and checked his reflection in the darkened grimy window of a plumbing supply place. He couldn't see himself too well, but he knew he looked right. The same tweed slacks, same leather coat, same white shirt. What was wrong?

At first he'd thought it was because Bruno hadn't seen him leave, but there was more to it than that. They'd stood within a foot of each other and Bruno thought he was somebody else.

LuAnn! He had to see LuAnn. Bruno had said she'd gone home. Early for her, but maybe she was looking for Marc.

Well, okay. She was going to find him.

Doug flagged down a cruising cab and rode it up to the West Eighties. LuAnn's condo was in a refurbished old apartment house with high-tech security. Doug knew the routine. He rang her bell in the building's foyer and waited under operating-room floodlights while the camera ogled him from its high corner perch.

"Marc!" her voiced squawked from the speaker. "Great! Come on up!"

On the eighth floor the elevator opened onto a three-door atrium. The middle was LuAnn's. She must have heard the elevator because her door opened before Doug reached it.

Her smile was bright, welcoming. "Marky! Where on earth did you disappear to? I was—"

And then the smile was gone and she was backing away.

"Hey! What is this? You're not Marc!"

As she turned and started to close the door, Doug leapt forward. He wasn't going to be shut out twice tonight. He had to convince her he was Marc.

"No! LuAnn, wait!" He jammed his foot against the closing door. "It's me! Marc! Don't do this to me!"

"I don't know what your game is, buddy, but I'm going to start screaming bloody murder in a minute if you don't back off right now!"

Doug could see how scared she was. Her lips were white and she was puffing like a locomotive. He had to calm her down.

"Look, Lu," he said softly. "I don't unnerstand what's come over you, but if I, like, step back, will you, like, leave the door open just a crack so we can talk and I can prove I'm Marc? Okay. Ain't that fair?"

Without waiting for a reply, he pulled his foot free of the door, took the promised step back, and held his hands up, under-arrest style. When he saw LuAnn relax, he started talking. In a low voice, he described how they'd made it last night, the positions they'd used, the hardcore videos she'd insisted on running, even the yellow rose tattooed on her left cheek. But instead of wonder and recognition in her eyes, he saw growing disgust. She was looking at him like he might look at a sink one of the tenants had tried to fix on his own.

"I don't know what your game is, clown, and I don't know what Marc's up to, but you can tell him LuAnn's not amused."

"But I am Marc."

"You don't even come close. And get some diction lessons before you try to pull this off again, okay?"

With that she slammed the door. Doug pounded on it.

"Luann! Please!"

"I'm calling security right now," she said through the door. "Beat it!"

Doug beat it. He didn't want no police problems. No way.

And when he got outside to the street, he felt awfully small, while the city looked awfully, awfully big.

It didn't seem the least little bit like an oyster.

"What d'ya need, Marc?" Doug said softly over the bucket once he was home and back in the bathroom.

Something awful had occurred to him on his way home. What if Marc was sick? Or worse yet—dying?

The thought had been a sucker punch to the gut.

"Just lemme me know an' I'll get it for you. Anything. Anything at all."

But Mark wasn't talking. Marc could talk only when Doug was wearing him. So Doug shoved his hand and forearm into the bucket again, deep, all the way to the bottom. He noticed how the goo was even cooler than before. Another bad sign.

"Come on, Marc. Make me say what you need. I'll hear it and then I'll get it for you. What d'ya need?"

Nothing. Doug's lips remained slack, forming not even a syllable. Frustration bubbling into anger, he yanked his arm free, rose to his feet, and smashed his moist fist into the mirror. The glass spiderwebbed, slicing up his reflection. His knuckles stung…and bled.

He stared at the crimson puddles forming between his knuckles and dripping into the sink. He turned to look at the bucket.

And had an idea.

"This what y'want?" he said. "Blood? You want my blood? Awright. I'll give it to you."

So saying, he jammed his fist back into the bucket and let the blood flow into the goo. When the bottom of the bucket turned red, he withdrew his hand and looked at it. The cuts had stopped bleeding and were almost healed.

Doug tried to stand but felt a little woozy, so he sat on the toilet seat cover and stared into the reddened goo.

Marc wanted blood—needed blood. That had to be it. Maybe the goo was some sort of vampire or something. Didn't matter. If Marc wanted blood, Doug would find it for him. He'd said he'd get anything Marc needed, hadn't he? Well, he meant it. Problem was...where?

As he watched the goo that was Marc he noticed the red of his blood begin to swirl and coalesce in its depths, flowing to a central point until all the red was concentrated in a single golf-ball-sized globule. And then the globule began to rise. As it approached the surface it angled toward the edge of the bucket. It broke the surface next to the lip and spilled its contents over the side. The rejected blood ran down over the metal and puddled stark red against the white bathroom tiles.

A cold bleakness settled in his chest.

"All right. So you don't want no blood. What do you want, man?"

Marc lay silent in his galvanized metal quarters.

"You're sick, aren't you? Well, who the hell do I take you to? A vet?"

And then it hit him: Maybe Marc wanted to go home.

Aw, man. No way. He couldn't let Marc go. Without him, he was nothing. Which was pretty much what he was now. But maybe...

Slowly, reluctantly, Doug lifted the bucket by its handle and trudged through his apartment, out into the hall, down to the basement. Wet down here again, but the floor drain wasn't backed up. Not yet, anyway. He knelt by the grate, lifted the bucket—and paused. This was pretty radical. Pouring Marc down the drain...no coming back from that. Once he was back down there it was pretty good odds he was gone for good.

Or maybe not. Maybe he'd come back. Who knew? What choice did Doug have anyway? Maybe Marc just needed to get back to the drain to recharge his batteries. Maybe he had friends or family down there. Might as well put him back where he came from because he'd didn't look like he was gonna last too much longer up here.

Doug lifted the grate and tipped the bucket. The goo almost leapt over the side, diving for the opening. It slid through the grate, oozed down the pipe, and splashed when it hit the water in the trap below.

Doug sat down and waited, wishing, hoping, praying for Marc to come bubbling back up the drain and crawl onto his arm again. He didn't know how long it would take, maybe days, maybe weeks, but he'd keep waiting. What else could he do? Without Marc he'd have to be Doug all the time.

And he didn't want to be Doug anymore.

Welcome to Hell

CHRISTINA SNG

The screams wake me up
From the dull matinee
I got stuck watching
This hot summer's day.

From the movie screen spills
A huge gelatinous blob,
The same box office bomb
No one cared to watch.

The blob drops heavily
Onto the moviegoers,
Engulfing them whole,
Their shrieks cut short.

Grabbing my backpack,
I race out of the theater,
Leap onto my BMX,
Pedaling like a bat out of hell.

It is chaos out here when
The blob hits the sidewalk,
Smacking people down.
Death is all around.

I see bodies digested
Through its pink jelly flesh,
Too sticky to escape
And probably acidic inside.

Some of them are still alive.
I recognize my nasty form teacher
And the kid who beats my sister.
Yeah, no way I'm helping her.

Then without warning,
A swarm of orange-haired dolls
Race out from the toy store,
Wielding tiny sharp knives,

Bloodlust in their eyes,
Stabbing people
Square in their ankles,
Slowing them down

Just in time for the blob
To roll lazily over them
Like a bulldozer in winter,
Cutting off their screams

As they slowly asphyxiate,
Drowning,
Pushing fruitlessly
Against its insides,

Foetuses trapped
In a cannibalistic womb.
Gross! I scream in my mind.
I won't be able to sleep tonight.

I ride faster,
Speeding through town,
Avoiding storm drains
And masked killers

Wearing Halloween costumes.
They emerge from the shadows,
Attacking panicked people
With rusty machetes and knives.

One even has a pair of hands
Fused with sharp metal claws.
They screech as he scrapes them
Against a flickering lamp post.

In my head,
A disturbing rhyme plays on
And on, lulling me to sleep
Till I get home,

Shaking it off just in time
To see the poltergeists
Working on our television,
Opening up a portal

To the underworld
Where dead spirits emerge
To drag my drunken dad to hell,
Still holding on tight to his bottle.

The front door slams open
And the blob enters my home.
It ignores me, pulsating with
Dozens of half-digested bodies,

Most of them
Bullies in this town.
It stops, mesmerized,
Following the spirits into the TV.

The portal closes behind them
As I sigh with relief,
Our world safe again from
The true monsters in our lives.

My mother stumbles downstairs,
Half-asleep, baby in arms,
Asking me gently,
"What was the ruckus all about?"

"Everything's fine," I tell her.
She looks at me, quizzically.
"Everything will be okay
From now on," I reassure her.

She puts the baby back to bed
While I tell her I'll go out
And look for Dad who is
Probably stonedrunk again.

Instead, I take myself
Into the dark woods
And dig a deep hole
By the fading moonlight.

The puzzle box I found
In the old antique shop
Promised to raise hell.
I place it in the ground.

It has served me well.

Perspective: Journal of a 1980s Mad Man

MORT CASTLE

"Someday I may stand in a court of law, where I will someday be accused of doing what I have done.

"Someday. I may."

1980

The Rubik's Cube debuted in Berlin at the International Toy Fair. It was invented by a Hungarian commie named Ern Rubik. It was first called the Magic Cube.

I got one. Couldn't do it. Saw all these four-eyed shitty kids on television doing it.

I smashed the goddamned thing with a hammer.

In April, President Peanut attempted to rescue the American hostages in Iran. Guess he thought it was the Christian thing to do. Didn't work out all that well. Oops.

Didn't work out at all.

On May 18, Mount St. Helens erupted.

Bang.

The eruption column rose 80,000 feet, getting way the hell up there, and shot nasty, ashy shit into eleven U.S. states and two Canadian provinces.

That volcano killed fifty-seven people.

In 2017, lone gunman Stephen Paddock opened fire on a crowd of concertgoers in Las Vegas.

He wounded 422 people.

He killed fifty-eight people.

Then he killed himself.

Fifty-nine.

Mount St. Helens? BFD.

Four days later, the Pac-Man video game was released. You think that's a coincidence?

In December, John Lennon was killed. I was always more of a Stones fan.

I did not kill any people in 1980.

I killed cats and I killed dogs.

I think it was twelve dogs I killed.

I killed more cats than that.

Wouldn't you?

1981

The term "serial killer" first appeared in a 1981 Times report on Wayne Williams, who was implicated in the murders of thirty-one children in Atlanta between the years of 1979-1981.

Dynasty started on TV. I don't remember if that was the one about JR. It was no Gilligan's Island.

March 30: John Hinckley Jr. tried to assassinate President Reagan. He was trying to impress Jodie Foster. Reagan lived. Foster wasn't impressed.

I thought about getting a T-shirt made. HINCKLEY, YOU'RE NO MARK DAVID CHAPMAN. I thought maybe someone would try to get me if I wore it. Let 'em try.

See, Chapman was religious. He didn't like Lennon saying the Beatles "were more popular than Jesus" and he didn't like the lyrics of Lennon's songs "God" and "Imagine."

Everybody's a critic, but some are better shots.

The Columbia Space Shuttle was launched, Mehmet Ali Agca attempted to assassinate Pope John Paul II, and Prince Charles married Lady Diana Spencer. File all this under LOSERS.

The first IBM-PC was released. Ubiquitous porn was on the way, lickety-split, yessir, yessir.

And in early November, I killed a kid. You don't need to know the exact date or the place. It was in a pretty lousy place where kids get killed all the time, sometimes by their parents or teachers.

I knew then. It gave me answers to questions I'd been asking myself.

Q: Is it hard to kill someone?

A: No.

Q: Does it feel good to kill someone?

A: Yes.

How 'bout that, Hinckley? How 'bout that, Ali Baba Agca PooPoo Hoo-hah?

1982

There was a war. Can you believe, there was a war, and we weren't in it? Sonofabitch.

Argentina invaded the Falkland Islands. For God and Queen and some total horseshit, the Brits went to war.

It lasted seventy-four days.

The Argentines surrendered on June 14.

Their gauchos weren't allowed to use atomic *bolas*.

The numbers: 649 Argentine military personnel were killed.

255 British military personnel were killed.

Three Falkland Islanders were killed.

I don't know the numbers, but I'd imagine there were some dogs and cats killed and perhaps some of the penguins for which the Falklands are somewhat famous. (Why, I'm from the Falklands, and we have five different species of fucking penguins!)

In 2013, one little sarin poison gas attack in Syria killed better than 1,700.

The film *E.T.* was really popular with everyone who loved ugly little fucks.

Hanoi Jane Fonda put out (yeah, you know she did) her *Workout* VHS tape. To look good for it, she had two ribs removed, de-lumpifying her. It's not known if she donated the ribs to someone in need of a rib transplant.

At fourteen, skateboarder Tony Hawk joined the "Bones Brigade" and turned professional. (Tony Gawk is worth around $120 million today. Professional skateboarders, goddamn.)

Maybe that's where I got the idea.

It was almost sunset when I straight-armed a kid off a goddamn skateboard. Then I cut his throat.

1983

Ronald Raygun announced Star Wars, the missile system, not the stupid movies, and Michael Jackson gave the world...*Thriller*. He also likely gave a bunch of kids some tush tickling, with the approval of mummy and daddy.

I began to understand John Hinckley and Mark David Chapman much better.

But they were wrong, you know. You don't need to do the celebrities.

191

Just the average, or, frankly, the worse than average, will do just fine.

I killed four that year. No cats or dogs. Not anymore.

Not one penguin.

Just people. A man, a woman, a boy, a girl. I was just a little bit careful, that's all you have to be, and so I didn't get caught.

You see, nobody gave a goddamn about the four I killed.

No, I guess I did.

1984

In 1984 sales were only so-so for *1984*, George Orwell's novel. Sales were much better when it was published in 1949.

Do you want your MTV? Madonna performed "Like a Virgin" at the first-ever MTV Awards. Madonna, MTV, BFD. Quite a career, Madonna. Can you imagine how popular she'd be/would have been if she'd had talent?

Lee Iacocca appeared in television commercials for Chrysler. Wasn't that great? Who can forget Lee Iacocca? Last name sounds like a gum disease. Face looked like one.

September 20: *The Cosby Show* debuts. Dr. Bill becomes world's favorite person of color.

Hey, hey, hey, Fat Alberta, want a Jello Jiggler?

Attention Pepsi drinkers, introducing the new taste of Coca-Cola, the best Coca-Cola ever! I mean, that ho ain't never gonna taste no benzodiazepine in that Coca-Cola!"

Hey, it's…DATE RAPES! Take a Big Chomp! Beats hell out of Oreos!

That Bill Cosby.

Her two bodyguards assassinated Indian Prime Minister Indira Gandhi. The bodyguards were named Beant Singh and Satwant Singh. They were both Sikhs. Sikhs profess that God can be experienced through love, worship, and contemplation. Sikhs seek God both inside themselves and in the world around them. It is reported that Indira Gandhi told Beant and Satwant, "Get a haircut, guys," so in a spiritual act, they shot the hell out of her.

India had a great year. There was a huge poison gas leak at Union Carbide plant in Bhopal, India.

It's estimated that Union Carbide killed 15,000.

Bernhard Goetz shot four would-be attackers on a New York subway. Much bigger deal.

Bernie, he was okay.

Me, I shot maybe twelve people that year. I stabbed two others to death with a World War II-era Navy bayonet.

I think the bayonet belonged to my uncle.

1985

I killed twenty-five people that year.

The film *Back to the Future* starring Michael J. Fox was released that year.

Seven of the people I killed had recently seen that film.

So much for motives.

1986

April 26: Chernobyl nuclear meltdown occurs.

The official report: It killed fifty people.

No big deal.

As for all those whiners and moaners who claim they got cancers and shit, why, the International Atomic Energy Agency says that health studies have "failed to show any direct correlation between radiation exposure" and cancer or other disease.

So some of their three-eyed children glow in the dark. Nice for the holidays.

Someday I may stand in a court of law, where I will someday be accused of doing what I have done.

Someday. I may stand in a court of law.

Or perhaps not.

I'd say it's in God's hands.

If there were a God.

1987

October 19: U.S. stock market plunges on Black Monday.

Lordy, lordy, that old stock market sure messed me up. Sent me out to kill someone. Changed my mind. Went to a Bonanza Steak House. Steak was pretty good.

DNA was first used that year to convict criminals and exonerate innocent prisoners on death row.

Some of one, some of the other.

Want a sample of my DNA? There are a number of ways I'll be glad to give it to you.

Eli Lilly Drug Company began marketing Prozac.

Didn't everything get better for everybody then?

I used to smile and sometimes laugh out loud, thinking how fortunate I was not to need a chemical crutch.

There were other ways I could relieve stress.

Motivational speaker and firewalker Tony Robbins published his first book, Unlimited Power.

Yeah, Tony, whatever you say.

1988

On May 15, Soviet troops begin to withdraw from Afghanistan after nine-year occupation.

Afghanistan. Now, why does that kind of tick at the mind?

George Bush Sr. got elected president of the United States. Nobody ever had a better knot on his tie. He didn't turn out to be an ass grabbing groper until he was senile and in a wheelchair. He'd tried that shit when he was younger, Barb would have given him a skillet alongside the head.

December 21: Pan Am Flight 103 got bombed over Lockerbie, Scotland. 270 people died.

A Libyan named Abdel Baset al-Megrahi was charged with 270 counts of murder, conspiracy to murder, and breach of aviation security.

He stood in a court of law, where he was accused of doing what he had done—maybe. He claimed he was innocent.

The trial began in 2000 in the Netherlands, and al-Megrahi was convicted. In 2002, he started his life sentence in a Scottish prison.

Six years later, he beat the rap. That clever guy, al-Megrahi, was found to have advanced prostate cancer. He only had a short time to live, so a Scottish judge compassionately decided to free him.

The Scots, a big-hearted people, you know.

Mr. al-Megrahi arrived home in Libya to a hero's welcome.

Me, I think the guy was a patsy.

The top grossing film of that year was Who Framed Roger Rabbit? There was no difference between the human actors and the animated characters. It was strikingly true to life.

And yes, I killed some people.

I was, I decided, a serial killer.

And it didn't seem like all that much.

1989

Exxon Valdez spills millions of gallons of oil on Alaskan coastline.

Someday BP may stand in a court of law.

I kill and kill and I'm not clever and I'm no criminal mastermind it's just killing and that's what I do and it's all right, a place for everything and everything in a place a place.

Someday I may stand in a court of law, where I will someday be accused of doing what I have done.

June 4: Student protesters killed in China's Tiananmen Square.

September 20: F.W. DeKlerk becomes president of South Africa.

November 9: Berlin Wall falls.

Everybody's free.

I am.

So are you.

September 22: *Bay Watch* debuts.

December 17: *The Simpsons* debuts.

Gameboy is released.

The internet goes global.

The **1990s** are coming.

I have plans.

Mother Knows Best

STEPHANIE M. WYTOVICH

Perched in front of her vanity, Eden White ripped out a collection of knots and tangles from her hair. Between the sweat, blood, and tears, her brown locks were matted together, and she was afraid if she tugged any harder that she'd rip them directly from her scalp. She accidently pulled a few hairs from the crown of her head and wondered if she soaked in the bathtub for a bit, if her hair would become easier to tame.

She rubbed her eyes and winced in pain. The powder-blue eyeshadow she'd specifically gone to the store earlier that day to buy was smeared and leaking into the cuts on her cheeks. Thick wads of mascara dressed the lines around her eyes, and one of her fake eyelashes had attached itself to her right sleeve. Eden looked like a badly beaten clown, a sad joke, and come Monday, everyone would know why.

Or at the very least, they'd speculate. Some of them probably already were.

The thought of their whispers turned her stomach.

News traveled fast at Hamilton High.

Eden kicked off a now-damaged pair of Capezio jazz shoes—the ones she'd begged her mom for last Christmas—and stepped out of the rest of her clothes. She folded her bloodstained clothing, trying to make it take up as little space as possible and set it on her dresser.

A creak climbed the base of the walls and Eden imagined her mother's shaky form stumbling down the hall, one hand on the wall for support, the other reached out before her for balance.

I don't have time for this...

Eden's throat felt raw, raked. She didn't want to speak to her mother now—not with how they'd left things—but she knew if she didn't, her mother would feel compelled to check on her, and she couldn't let her see her like this. Never like this. It would be too hard on her, and life was already too hard on her.

"Mom? That you? Sorry I'm late," Eden said, her lie a budding hornet's nest. "The night went a little longer than expected. I'm getting in the bath now."

197

No answer.

Just silence.

Gin will do that to you, though. Sneak up on you when you least expect it.

Eden knew the feeling.

She set her bra and panties on top of her clothes, her near-translucent skin glowing under the harshness of her bedroom light. The bruises on her arms and inner thighs were already noticeable, and those big blossoms of purple and yellow made her taste Seth's cologne all over again: Calvin Klein's Obsession. If she never smelled that spicy scented garbage again it would be all too soon.

Outside her bedroom window, the night sat still, soft, a quiet autumn darkness. The leaves had started changing colors a few weeks ago, but everything looked midnight at this hour.

She cracked the window and let the chill cradle her naked body, the scent of all things dying lingering in the air.

I wonder how long before I'm included in that?

Eden picked up her glasses off the nightstand—a pair of thin black-rimmed oversized frames that suited her high cheek bones—and wrangled her hair into a messy bun, hairspray, dead ends, neon scrunchie and all. A migraine built behind her eyes, the drumming in her head a constant boom, boom, boom. A wave of dizziness crept up her spine, and the room danced before her in careful twists and turns. Her walls were collaged with posters of boys with big sad eyes and pleading faces: Johnny Depp, Keifer Sutherland, John Cusack, Rob Lowe. Their desperation tapped behind her eyes like a curious child trying to get the attention of an adult.

You should have known.

You should have seen it coming.

It was all there, all the signs.

You asked for this.

Eden walked into the bathroom—careful to avoid the mirrors—and turned on the water, testing it with her hand to make sure it was hot enough. She wanted it to be boiling, blistering. When she sat in the tub and felt it sink into her flesh, she wanted it to burn.

Earlier that day, Mr. Myers asked her to stay after class. Eden collected her books, the sounds of hushed voices already taking shape in the air.

"I bet she's fucking him, too."

"You think her mother knows?"

Mr. Myers had dated her mother for the better part of the last three years, and their relationship was no secret in town or to the student body. Eden's father had left when she was eight, and she'd pretty much grown up as a latchkey kid for the better part of her life, even when—truthfully—she was probably too young to be taking care of herself. For the longest time, it had been just her and her mother doing their best to survive, but for the most part, even though they had each other, Eden was pretty much always alone. Sure, there had been men here and there who waltzed into her mother's life, men who took them out for ice cream, who made them spaghetti on Sundays, but they were fleeting, each of them a passing name and fancy to both her and her mother.

But Mr. Myers was different.

Eden had met him on her first day of sophomore year for Chemistry, and her mom met him shortly after around midterms when Eden's grades were less than passing. The two of them hit it off immediately. In fact, Eden could still remember hearing them laugh like school children in the kitchen on their first date, and for the longest time, it felt like she had a family, like she finally had a father, someone who cared enough about her to stay. That meant three years of holidays, birthdays, pancake breakfasts, and pizza nights, not to mention the awkward run-ins with teenage emotions and carpooling to school or the occasional late homework assignment that didn't carry any penalties in his class. But ever since that night with the glass, the one with all the shouting and the gin, those drops of cherry-red beads on the living room carpet, he'd pretended that he'd never known her, at least not in the I've-seen-you-eat-peanut-butter-from-the-jar kind of way.

No, here, in this room, in this school, they were strictly student and teacher now, but that didn't make it any easier to swallow the lump forming in her throat.

You knew this was going to happen eventually.

Just breathe.

Reluctantly, Eden walked to his desk, but even with a large cherry wood barrier in front of her, she was still careful to keep her distance. Everything in her body went on edge when he looked at her, and all she could feel were judgmental eyes from every direction. Her classmate's stares burned holes in her cheeks, cut her breath like knives on a cutting board.

She wanted to disappear, but she also wanted to throw her arms around him.

Give him the benefit of the doubt.

He didn't know. Couldn't know, after all.

"How are you holding up these days?" he asked her.

How do you think I'm holding up?

"Fine," Eden said. She picked at the skin around her thumb.

Mr. Myers watched as the remaining students trickled out of the room. He walked over and closed the door. Eden tried not to watch him, but she couldn't break her gaze away from his body. It felt cliché, her watching him like this, but she couldn't help it.

Eight steps to the door.

Three to the window if I need it.

"Look, it's been hard for me, too. I have no shame in admitting that," he said, reaching for her hand. "I miss you and your mother, and I'm not happy with how we ended things."

Eden pulled away and hated herself for it.

She thought about how the two of them used to play chess on the back porch.

"I know this whole ordeal has put a lot of pressure on you, and that's not fair. But look, even though I know you don't want to talk about what happened that night, I think we need to," said Mr. Myers. "In fact, I've wanted to talk to you about it for some time now."

Eden clenched her toes and tapped her foot.

A nervous habit.

"I'm really sorry I haven't been more responsive," he said, his words soft, pleading. He motioned for her to sit down, but Eden refused.

She brushed a tear off her cheek, bit the inside of her mouth.

Don't be weak.

Eden searched for words, wondered if there were any to even justify the situation. How could he be so cavalier? Just throw out some half-assed apology like that somehow made it all better? Like that erased what he did to her? To her mom? To their family?

The lump in her throat melted into razors.

They cut the inside of her throat, her rage turning blood to fire.

The ceiling lights got brighter, thicker.

"It's been three weeks," she said. "That's twenty-one days you were fine not talking about it, fine not answering my calls. You left me. You left me alone to deal with this, with your mistake. And now you want to talk about it? Now I suddenly fit into your schedule?"

Eden slammed her books down on his desk.

A snaked coiled in her stomach.

"Well maybe now isn't a good time for me," she said. "Maybe I no longer want to talk about it."

Mr. Myers looked over his shoulders to make sure they hadn't drawn a crowd.

"Eden you need to calm down?" he said. "Let's talk about this like adults, okay?"

"Oh, I'm sorry. Am I suddenly not adult enough for you, Seth? Did I somehow misinterpret the past three weeks? Get my signals crossed?" Eden said.

She collected herself and motioned to walk out of the room, her words like lingering venom in the air. Seth grabbed her arm and pulled her into him.

"Later then. At the house? Eight thirty?" he said.

Eden pushed him off and walked out the door.

"See you then," he said. "Both of you."

She pretended she didn't see him smile.

The savory scent of fresh tomatoes and basil clung to the walls of the kitchen as Eden stirred the sauce. In a separate bowl, she grated and cut garlic and onion, her eyes welling with tears as the sting crushed the dams behind her eyes. She wanted to make something simple tonight, simple but filling, and even though it wasn't Sunday, spaghetti was always a fan favorite. She doubted her mother was ready to eat anything though, but she figured if she could persuade her, the carbs would do her well. She'd hardly eaten anything since that night, and the weight was falling off her like slipped cushions.

Eden had told her mother what happened at school as soon as she'd gotten home that afternoon. She'd opened the curtains in her bedroom to let some light in, and then sat down at the foot of her bed, gently stroking her feet to wake her up. Half-ashamed and half-frightened, she said that Seth planned to come over to the house that evening to talk to them, but Eden couldn't detect the slightest note of fear or hesitation in her mother's expression.

Like most of their interactions these days, she was quiet, stoic.

It was like all the best parts of her had died.

Eden dumped the garlic and onion into the sauce and spooned in a spoonful (or two) of sugar. Her mom wasn't a fan of the sweetness, said it confused her taste buds, but Eden figured since she probably wasn't going to be joining them for dinner, she was fine throwing it in.

The Kit-Cat Klock next to the refrigerator read five to eight and Eden watched its tail swing back and forth as if she were hypnotized. She'd always hated that thing, thought the way its eyes followed her was creepy. She wasn't even sure when they got it—in some ways, it felt like it had always been there.

I should get rid of it.

Mom would probably never even know.

Eden dumped a pack of noodles out of their box and chucked them into the not-yet-boiling water on the stove. She figured she had a good fifteen minutes to kill before the noodles went to hell, so capped the sauce, set the timer, and then headed into her bedroom to make herself presentable.

The doorbell rang a little after eight thirty and Eden walked to answer the door, ever the dutiful hostess. Dressed in a white oversized blouse with thick raised shoulder pads, she added suspenders that attached to a mid-thigh-length skirt, her silhouette evoking a menacing stance, a broad sense of power. She had teased her hair to give it some volume, some extra height, the scent of her Aussie Hairspray dominating the light strawberry mist she'd sprayed on her neck, breasts, and wrists.

"Coming," she said.

She'd asked her mom again if she was planning on joining them, but the empty bottle of gin on her bedside table answered for her.

Great. Another problem I get to deal with alone.

Eden opened the door and gave a half-smile.

"Hi, Eden. Nice to see you," Seth said. He walked into the house and hung his sports jacket on the coatrack, something he'd done a hundred times before. "Something smells delicious. Is that your famous spaghetti sauce, by chance?"

"You guessed it," Eden said, heading into the kitchen. "Can I get you something to drink?"

"Actually, Eden, I hoped to talk to your mother first if you don't mind," he said. "Is she home from work yet?"

Eden's mother used to work retail at the Macy's downtown. Typically, she worked twelve to eight on Fridays, but after she stopped coming to work a few weeks ago, Eden overhead a message on their answering machine telling her not to bother coming in anymore.

"She should be home soon. She called a little bit ago and said she was running late," Eden said.

Seth nodded and sat down on the recliner in the living room.

Just make yourself right at home, why don't you?

Eden recalled movie nights and popcorn, how he'd laughed at her when she had nightmares after watching Steven Spielberg's Poltergeist.

"Here, I poured you a gin and tonic," Eden said. "I know it's your favorite."

Seth thanked her and took the drink, rested his hand on hers. "Eden, look I know I already said how sorry I was earlier, but—"

She took a step back and fought to compose herself.

Easy now. Not yet.

"Actually, you didn't. You said you were sorry for not talking to me. That's not really the same thing," Eden said, forcing out a smile.

Mr. Myers looked taken back by her callousness.

"Okay, okay, that's fair," he said, his voice half-catching in his throat. "I probably deserved that."

He took a sip of his drink, his moustache wet, shining under the soft overhead light. He wore a white button-down shirt and a pair of salmon chinos, no socks. A professional—but relaxed—look for a man who was anything but professional and should definitely not be relaxed.

"Can you just—can you let me explain?"

He leaned toward her, desperate, almost begging.

"Isn't that why you're here?" Eden asked.

Seth rubbed his temples and dropped his head between his legs.

His right heel taped nervously on the hardwood floor.

"I was drunk, angry. I didn't realize what I was doing, and I know that's not an excuse, but it's the truth," he said.

Are you hearing this, mom? He didn't realize what he was doing. I wonder: did you know what you were doing? Can anyone in this fucking house take responsibility for their actions that night?

Eden knelt down and gently lifted his face to hers.

"Do you know how long it takes to clean blood off curtains?"

Stunned, Seth straightened up, his spine now aligned with the chair.

"What?"

"Three hours," Eden said. "It took me three hours to get the blood out, and even still, there's a stain. Not a terribly noticeable one, mind you, but I still know it's there."

Seth looked at the curtains behind him, a deer caught in headlights.

"Eden—"

"Look. Let's just be frank with each other," Eden continued as she walked into the kitchen. She turned the warmer off and took three plates out of the cabinet, starting scooping heaps of noodles onto one. "You don't care. Not about me, not about my mom. You're not even here to save this family. You're here to save yourself."

"Look, I know you're upset—"

"Upset? Why would I be upset?" she asked as a large spoonful of red sauce spattered against the plate and ricocheted off the walls. "You didn't hit me after all."

For a second, she thought she saw her mother in the entranceway, her mouth dripping with blood, a jagged shard of glass in her hand, a tooth peeking out through her bottom lip.

She shook the image from her head, blinked twice hard.

"You don't know what you saw," he said, his voice somehow changed, darker now, more serious. His façade dropped. "You're confused."

Mr. Myers stood up, his hulking frame a tower compared to hers.

Eden laughed.

Really? He's going to try to gaslight me now?

This would have been terrifying if it wasn't so incredibly predictable.

Eden grabbed the knife off the cutting board and sliced into a loaf of bread.

"It wasn't fast, in case you were wondering" she said as she positioned the slices of rosemary-chive in a spiral on the plate. "I mean, I know it was for you. You left after the first black eye."

The color drained from his face, his skin a now sickly pallor, waxen and gray.

"I don't feel good," Seth said. "Everything is spinning." He grabbed his forehead and struggled to regain his balance, dropped his glass. It shattered against the linoleum floor. "What—what did you do?"

"No, I think you mean, what did she do?" Eden said. "Because after you beat her bloody and bruised, she came after me. And why wouldn't she, right? I was the one who told her you were fucking your students. I was the one who threw a wrench into her seemingly perfect relationship."

Seth clutched his throat and dropped to his knees.

"It's funny, though, because while I expected it from you, I never once saw it coming from her. Guess she was just drunk and mad, too. Unfortunately for me though, where you used your fist, she used a piece of glass. You know," Eden said, motioning to where the coffee table used to be. "The one you knocked her into that night."

Eden unbuttoned her shirt and showed a collection of cuts on her chest, some of them deeper than the others, but all ones she'd had to stitch together herself.

Unconscious and lightly breathing, Seth fell in a heap on the floor.

Eden sat next to him, a plate of spaghetti in her lap, and quietly began to eat.

The basement smelled like spoiled cabbage and laundry detergent. Piles of clothes and dirty towels littered the space in front of the washer while a mountain of forgotten purple lint sat on top of the dryer. Four three-inch nails were haphazardly pounded into the adjacent wall and a stained tablecloth hung limply off the top, its form a billowing ghost.

A bare bulb flickered once, twice, three times before finding its breath and then flashed a harsh fluorescent glow amidst its surroundings.

"What the?" Seth asked as his eyes began to adjust. He tried to stand, but instead pathetically wobbled back to the cement floor. "Eden? Eden, where are you? Goddammit, let me out of here!"

His arms were wrapped around a pole, his hands bound at the wrists once with duct tape and then again with an extension cord.

Better to be safe.

Eden watched him struggle as she sat crouched in her spot at the top of the stairs. She was slightly hidden but not completely invisible, a professional voyeur in a movie of her own making.

He screamed for a bit, but Eden wasn't worried. She knew it was pointless. In fact, it actually kind of made her laugh. They were so far out in the middle of nowhere that even if he wasn't underground, he'd still have no chance of someone hearing him.

Perks of living in the country.

Eden walked down the stairs, her head pounding, her thoughts aflame with images of blood and steel. Her right temple throbbed and a voice unlike her own crept out of her mouth, something shrill yet mature, wizened even, afraid.

"How long has it been happening?" Eden asked.

Her tone was sharp, accusatory. She ran her hands down the wooden railing, stared at the white paint chipping off the walls.

Seth stared in her direction, his face painted a mixture of confusion and terror.

"What? How long has what been happening?"

"How long have you been fucking your students?" Eden snapped back, her tongue sandpaper against her teeth. "Eden told me. She said she saw you with Nancy."

Eden broke down into hysterics as sobs racked her body.

For a second, she almost felt embarrassed to be emoting like this in front of him. She suspected it was that age-old stereotype of women being weak, too quick to overwhelm and break at a feather's touch. But this was different. This was deserved. Here she was thinking they were in a committed relationship, thinking that maybe sometime near in the future, he might propose.

And yet here was staying after work for his extracurricular activities.

Helping all those students who were desperate for attention, begging for some extra help.

She wondered if he'd ever touched Eden. Was that why she was so scared when she came to her?

"What do you mean Eden told you?" Seth asked.

His eyes seemed to double in their size as she walked toward him, and like a popped balloon, Eden turned off the waterworks, showed him the knife she'd been holding behind her back.

"I mean she came home in a fit and said she saw you with Nancy," Eden said. "She popped by your room after last period and…well…for Christ's sake, Seth. She's practically Eden's sister. How could you do this?"

"Eden, I've never—"

"Cathy," Eden corrected him.

Seth swallowed hard and seemed to climb the pole lodged against his back.

"Cathy," he said, his voice shaking. "I've never, and would never, do something like that. I'd lose my job. Think about it."

Eden stopped and took a moment to consider what he said.

"She's lying to you," he said in a ploy of desperation. "She's jealous, sick. She's trying to come between us, baby."

The light flickered above them in two quick jabs.

Another wave of pain exploded in Eden's head, and for a moment, she thought about cutting it out with the knife, digging it right into the side of her skull and pulling out that cursed vein, bleeding it dry.

"She wouldn't lie, though," Eden said, her nails scratching down her face. "Not to me. I'm her mother."

One of her press-on nails caught her hair and lodged itself near her ear.

"Eden, please, I'm begging you," Seth said.

"STOP CALLING ME THAT," she said. "My name is Cathy."

Blood trickled from her cheek.

"Cathy," he said. "Please, baby, please put down the knife."

Eden's chin quivered and her entire body shook, drenched in a cold sweat.

She turned to walk back upstairs—to leave this all behind, make it tomorrow's problem—but he had to know. He needed to know what he made her do.

The drums beat louder in her head.

He did this.

He's responsible for her blood.

"I punished her, you know. Didn't want to believe her when she first told me," Eden said. "Not with that mouth of hers. Hell, she'd said something similar about her daddy, and we both know how that ended."

A faraway look set into her eyes. It was almost trance-like the way she recounted the story, desperate to believe in this new rewrite.

"I cut her up good, dressed her in slashes so she'd remember for next time, know that it's bad manners to hurt people like that, say things that aren't true."

She leaned against the wall and a dusting of dirt fell into her hair.

"I think I might have gone too far though," Eden said. Her mouth erupted into a slow, uneven smirk. Her voice got low, hushed. It seemed to slip out of her like a growl.

Eden tightened her grip around the knife.

"I think I scared her," she said.

A puddle formed underneath Seth as his pants darkened with piss.

"Ed—Cathy..." he pleaded.

"Do you know what it feels like to be scared like that, Seth? What it feels like to have someone you love so incredibly wrong about you?"

Seth screamed, howled.

His face looked like Eden's had, awash with fear and betrayal.

"Let's see if you fare better than her."

Eden eased into the bathtub, her flesh an immediate sore. Dirt and blood seeped off her like rainwater on glass, and by the time she sat down, the water was already a light brown, the color of wheat. Her boom box sat on the toilet, its cord snaking along the wall like a viper ready to attack. Pat Benatar eased out of the speakers and helped drown out the oohs and aahs as Eden adjusted to the burn. She half-smiled as she tapped her bleeding and blistered foot against the faucet. Her mother always used to yell at her about bringing "that damned box" into the bathroom with her, said she'd fall asleep to the music and drown, or worse electrocute herself—as if some hand was going to reach out of the water and purposefully pull the stereo into the tub with her—but lately, her mom didn't seem to care about what she did, and it was hard to tell whether that was a good thing or not.

It's like I don't even exist anymore.

Like she doesn't even see me walking down the halls.

Eden took a breath and slipped underneath the water, her filth a crown layering itself above her face. Echoes vibrated against her body, around the drain, and their moans sounded like something trapped, like something held down against its will.

Eden felt her chest constrict.

Her limbs went tight and stiff.

A thick smear of blood attached to the silver spigot dripped into the water, its contact like small bombs exploding around her, each droplet a flash of red, a small kind of death. Eden flashed back to the night her mother attacked her, to the way the knife jabbed her like a stuck pig.

How did we get here? How did it end up like this?

Eden jolted forward, gasping.

Water sloshed out of the tub as Eden got up and reached for a towel to rub the memories out of her head. She hated this, this constant paranoia, the guilt. The way it burrowed inside her, festering and surfacing when it felt like it wasn't fair.

You did what you had to do.

You had to save her.

She didn't know what she was doing.

Eden dried off and wrapped the towel around her, leaving wet footprints in her wake as she hurried down the hall and gently knocked on her mother's door.

"Mom? You up?" she asked.

Eden cracked the door a bit, forever respectful of her mother's privacy. After that night—the one with the accusations and the crying—she didn't want to catch her off guard again. Plus, the two of them had just started speaking after a week or two of the silent treatment, and while Eden didn't want to admit it, for a while there, she really missed her mom.

A wave of nausea spread through her stomach as the door opened, but Eden pushed it down, her gag reflex stronger now, more apt to the smell.

The room was dark, enveloped in a putrid blanket of rotting food and flesh.

A plate of spaghetti sat on the bedside table, an unwelcomed addition to the other full, untouched plates that were stacked up high on the bed and floor. Blowflies and maggots bathed in gray, furry swamps that swam on the top of disregarded meals.

"You know you're going to have to eat something eventually," Eden said. "You can't just let yourself waste away like this."

Her mother's face stared back at her, a portrait of disgust.

"Oh, come on now," Eden said as she squeezed the sagging flesh around her mother's shoulders. Her body, half its size, collapsed into its bloat. "No man is worth this, and look, I know we've both had our differences, but all mothers and daughters fight."

The television in the room cracked and popped, its signal filled with the dance of static. It reminded Eden of that scene in Poltergeist, the one where the little girl pushes her hands up against the screen, hoping that whoever's inside can hear her, can take her far, far away…

Eden traced her scars, her fingertips ablaze with the imprint of her mother's rage.

You were protecting yourself.

You were staying alive.

"Plus, I mean, if we're being perfectly honest with each other," Eden said, her words quiet, a gentle whisper in what was left of her mother's ear, "I probably have some things I need to apologize about, too."

Eden motioned to the corner of the room, Seth's body a bloody, bleeding sack painting the wall.

A short chuckle rang through the room as Eden got into bed with her mother, took her seeping, decomposing hand in hers.

"Good thing we're both forgiving," Eden said.

Stranger Danger

GRADY HENDRIX

I should have remembered that no one eats the fruit in their trick or treat bag. Ever. The problem was I'd been gorging on chocolate and caramel and nougat and now it coated the inside of my mouth, piled up in my guts, oozed out my pores. That apple looked so crisp.

I bit into it, crunching through the tight red skin, and for a second I tasted cool juice then something punched the roof of my mouth. I kept chewing because I didn't understand why the roots of my teeth sizzled, why my tongue burned, where all this salty juice came from like someone turned on the hose, flooding my mouth, shooting up my sinuses, pouring down my throat, exploding out my nose.

Automatically, I clamped my mouth shut so I could make it to the bathroom without ruining my bedroom carpet and doctors tell me that's what pushed the razor blade between my two central incisors — what my mom called my bunny teeth — so deep into my gums that it hit bone. They had to yank it out with pliers.

It hurt so bad. I felt like someone had smacked me in the face. All this liquid needed to come out and I gave up on saving the carpet and puked blood and liquid chocolate all over the Halloween candy piled in front of me, screaming between each fresh gout, gargling the thick brown blood and chocolate slurry back down my throat, which made me spray it back up again. I shot hot chocolate vomit and blood out my nose. I opened and closed my mouth trying to call my mom, gnashing the razor blade lodged between my bunny teeth up and down into my lips again and again.

Paralyzed, on my hands and knees, my stomach launching bile into my mouth where it burned my shredded lips like acid, I screamed a high-pitched, gargling wail that made my eardrums rattle and my mom banged my door open and I had to get this pain out of my mouth, and liquid poured out of me, and I could not remember a time when my face didn't hurt.

It took six surgeries to rebuild my lips.

I couldn't remember which house gave me the apple. My mom said I'd

212

blocked it out. They sent me to headshrinkers who took notes on every picture I drew, then they sent me to doctors who made me look at ink blots like a psycho, then they sent me to really expensive summer camps where we spent a lot of time with horses and everyone acted like it was totally normal that at least one kid every year wet the bed and screamed in his sleep.

It took me a few years to want to go trick or treating again. When I finally did — well, everything that happened next happened because of Moody's dog.

"All Bennett did was bark at him," Moody whined from his bed.

Moody whined a lot. He whined about us trying to get the Playboy Channel on his cable box, he whined about us riding our bikes too fast, he whined about eating the cheese his mom was saving for guests, but he had an Apple IIe and nobody was funnier. He once farted on Adair Leland's little sister.

We were waiting for his Apple to boot up so we could see how *Castle Wolfenstein* looked on it, and we'd already heard about what Judge Horlbeck did to Bennett from our parents, but this was the first time we'd heard it from Moody.

"It's how he says hello," Moody said, twisting his fingers around each other. "He was on our side of the fence."

"Someone should sue the judge," I said.

I talked okay in front of Moody and Chuck with my old man's mouth. The web of scars around my lips had faded until they looked like wrinkles, but sometimes in the middle of a word my lips would pull too tight in one direction, or too loose in another, so my sentences got mushy. My parents sat me down last week and told me I needed to quit soccer so I'd have time to start seeing a speech therapist again. I pretended that I hadn't heard them fighting about it all week. That I hadn't heard how my dad thought it cost too much money. How he said my mom needed to accept this is how I was now.

"You just want a new boat!" Mom had yelled.

I wanted a new boat, too. I hated that my face meant we were stuck with the one that couldn't even pull skiers.

"He's lucky Bennett didn't hump him," Chuck said. "That's the other way he says hello."

"We had to take Bennett to this dog farm upstate," Moody said.

"You must be sexually frustrated," Chuck said.

"I wrote him a letter saying I was going to break into his house and send him upstate, instead," Moody said. "My mom found it in my room before I sent it. Now they're going to make me start taking spazz pills."

Two kids in the grade below us took spazz pills. No one liked them — the kids or the pills. Our parents told us the kids were only hyperactive and the pills were just Ritalin, but we knew they were spazz pills and these kids were going to wind up working in gas stations or getting shipped to Delaware.

Delaware was full of military schools. We knew that because Chuck's parents kept threatening to send him to one. They'd even ordered the pamphlets. Chuck snuck them out once and we looked through the stack at all their pictures of the miserable little brainwashed kids and then looked at their return addresses: Delaware, Delaware, Delaware.

Chuck never invited us over to his house. I think it was bad there.

Castle Wolfenstein finally booted up and we let Moody play first so he'd feel better about Bennett.

After a while, Chuck said, "On Halloween we should egg Judge Horlbeck's house."

"What's egging going to do?" Moody asked.

"It ruins the paint," Chuck said. "Someone did it to the people across the street and they had to get their entire front door repainted."

"Okay," Moody said, but he sounded like a weak prick.

"Don't be a weak prick," Chuck said.

"I'm not a weak prick," Moody said.

"Yes, you are," I pointed out.

"Egging his house isn't going to get Bennett back," Moody said.

"You were never going to get Bennett back," I told him. "Your parents sent her away because they were worried you'd get her pregnant."

Moody kicked me, and I punched him in the shoulder, and onscreen a Nazi killed him again.

"This isn't about getting Bennett back," Chuck said. "It's about revenge. Don't puss out."

"Fine," Moody said. "But I don't want to get caught."

None of us wanted to get caught, but the grown-ups made it easy for us by inventing Halloween. It's like they were practically begging us to take revenge.

From 5 pm to 6:30 pm on Halloween night, dads in deely boppers and Groucho Marx glasses dragged shuffling Strawberry Shortcakes and ETs down the sidewalk with one hand, and carried plastic cups of booze with the other. Moms manned the candy bowls and topped off dad drinks from bottles they kept behind the door. By the time I hit the streets at 7pm, all the ads were walking super-slow and super-loose, their sugar-shocked kids balanced on one hip, masks pushed up on top of their heads, faces streaked with tears. By 7:15pm they'd closed their front doors behind them, turned on their TVs, and the streets belonged to us.

No one drove cars, no one rode bikes, just a sidewalk-to-sidewalk river of Madonnas, Smurfs, GI Joes, and Daisy Dukes flowing down the Old Village streets. Mobs of Ronald Reagans, packs of Rocky Balboas, troops of Darth Vaders, saggy Supermen, kids in full KISS face paint, and even one guy dressed like a Rubik's Cube, roamed the suburban streets like gangs.

I pushed my way through the flood of Draculas and Michael Jacksons, stomach jumping, skin hot, anxious to get to Chuck and Moody before they left without me. I didn't carry a candy bag because I was never going to take candy from a stranger again. I wore one of my dad's white hospital lab coats because it had big pockets I'd stuffed with walnuts and I'd hooked a fake beard over my ears because it hid my scars and made me feel normal.

Relief tingled over my skin when I saw Moody and Chuck still standing on the corner of Pitt and Morrison. Chuck wore a white undershirt with the sleeves torn off and an anarchy "A" scratched on the front in black marker. He'd gelled his hair into a mohawk and wore slit sunglasses. Moody wore a thin plastic mask and a cheap plastic poncho from the store. He had the mask pushed up on top of his head.

"God save the Queen," Chuck said making devil horns with his fingers. "What're you? A gynecologist?"

I pulled out a handful of walnuts.

"Nut doctor," I said. "Trick or treat, I've come to check your nuts."

They both laughed. The fake beard made me brave. If I slurred my words a little or they came out mushy I could blame it on the beard.

"Better than this boner," Chuck said, kicking Moody in the thigh.

The front of Moody's poncho said "The Empire Strikes Back" and showed the AT-AT walkers coming over the snow with Luke Skywalker's snowspeeder crashed in the foreground. Moody pulled the thin mask down over his face. It was radioactive green and had bat ears and a scrunched up mouth, lined and scarred like mine.

"No one dresses like Yoda anymore," I said.

"Except me," Moody said, sliding his mask back on top of his head.

"He's a defective who waited until the day before Halloween to beg his mom to take him to Eckard's and that's all they had left," Chuck said, then turned to Moody. "When are your parents getting divorced?"

"Separated only they are," Moody said in a Yoda voice. "May divorce be with you."

Moody was funny when he wasn't being a crybaby.

"Weapons check," Chuck said, and unslung his backpack.

It made me nervous to do this in the middle of the street, but no one cared. It was Halloween. I pulled a single egg wrapped in Kleenex out of my walnuts.

"Mine broke," Moody said.

"You should have brought the carton," Chuck told me.

"How would I sneak that out the house?" I said.

"Good thing you know me," Chuck said.

He unzipped the main pocket of his backpack and let us see the fat, white plastic squeeze bottle of lighter fluid with the red cap. Then he unzipped his front pencil pocket and showed us the box of bang-snaps. You threw them on the ground and they sparked and made a bang.

"We'll do a Flaming Dixie Doorbell," Chuck said, lowering his voice. "I'll soak the Judge's welcome mat in lighter fluid, then ring the bell. When he comes out we hit it with a bang-snap and WHOOOSH."

"He'll see our faces," Moody whined.

"Not if we wear masks," Chuck said, and tied a bandana over the lower half of his face.

Moody lowered his Yoda mask. I smoothed my beard.

Since the Judge's front door had a long set of brick stairs you could see from the street, we decided to strike late.

"My mom wants me home by nine," Moody said.

Chuck spat a hawker on the sidewalk in disgust, even though I knew both our moms had told us to be home by nine, too.

"Your mom's an alcoholic," Chuck told him.

"At least she's good at something," Moody said through Yoda's mouth slit.

With nothing else to do for two hours, we went trick or treating.

We got popcorn balls at the Wilsons ("Trash 'em," Chuck advised), and homemade fudge at the Savages ("The secret ingredient is Ex-Lax," I said). We pegged candy corn and Bits O'Honey at people's windows because they sucked.

The Horselys were out of candy cigarettes by the time we got there. The Eatons were so cheap Mrs. Eaton split every Twix bar in two and put them in separate sandwich bags. We hid in the shadows in front of the Standards' and watched Mr. Standard sit on his front porch dressed like a scarecrow, lolling on

216

his joggling board like a stuffed dummy so when a kid walked past he could lurch to life and scare the piss out of them.

"Do they give out anything good?" Chuck asked.

"Hershey's Kisses and raisins," Moody said.

Chuck nodded to me and I took out a walnut and pegged it at Mr. Standard. It hit the side of his head so hard we could hear it from the street.

"Yeouch!" he shouted, pinwheeling his arms before crashing backwards off the joggling board. "Who did that?" he roared, springing to his feet.

Two ballerinas and a Jawa going up his front porch screamed and ran away. We laughed so hard we barely made it to the corner.

We walked beneath bedsheet ghosts hanging from live oak branches, past crepe paper black widows the size of pizza boxes stapled to tree trunks, and Styrofoam tombstones lit with green and red bulbs in front yards. We ran into Chuck's dad who made Chuck's little sister walk with us until we ran into Ellen Boench who was in third grade with her and they went off together, and Peter Mannings dressed as C3-P0 went to a few houses with us, and we followed the pack of guys trick or treating with Adair Leland for a few houses because she was dressed as Little Orphan Annie and looked really hot, and then Brooks Wisely, dressed as Indiana Jones, told us the Lucas's were giving out full-sized Reese's Peanut Butter Cups way down on the far end of Pitt Street right by the Old Bridge.

"They discontinued them this year," Moody said. "Like, they're not making any more. It was on the news."

"If these are the last Reese's Peanut Butter Cups, it's worth the stretch," Chuck said.

We started down Pitt and the yards got bigger and the houses got set further back and the trick or treaters started to thin out. I stayed on the street while Chuck and Moody went to the front door. I didn't like getting too close to grown-ups on Halloween. One of them gave me that apple.

"See," Moody said. "There's someone else in the same costume."

I jumped. Moody stood right behind me. I looked from him to the Moody in his Yoda mask standing next to Chuck at the Lucas's front door, holding out his bag. I pulled Moody's Yoda mask up and he flinched.

"What?" he said.

"I thought that was you," I said, pointing to the Yoda mask kid by Chuck.

"I'm standing right here," Moody said.

"Then who the hell is he?" I asked.

"Shut up," Moody said. "They're coming back."

Chuck and the Yoda mask came down the front path and I tried to look through the eyeholes of this other kid's mask but it was too dark and I didn't want him to know I cared so I couldn't stare for more than a second.

"I told them I needed three for you nerds," Chuck said. "But you didn't come to the door so I'm not giving you shit. These are the last Reese's ever."

He didn't say anything about the extra kid, so we all started back up the street towards the judge's house and the Yoda mask kid dropped back a little but he kept following us.

"Who the fuck is that?" Chuck whispered to Moody.

"I don't have a list of everyone who bought a Yoda costume," Moody whispered back.

We could hear the kid's cheap plastic poncho crinkling behind us. Was it some younger kid from earlier who didn't go home when it was time and was scared now and wanted to stick near bigger kids? Was it someone we knew's little brother? Was it someone trying to scare us?

"I'm going to ask," Chuck said.

"Let's just ditch him," Moody said. "It's almost nine."

Chuck remembered our mission and nodded. We turned right up McCants and started walking towards Ocean Grove Cemetery. We were going to circle around behind the judge's house and come at it from the other direction because that seemed like the kind of thing Rambo would do. We'd ditch the kid on the way. We could hear the swishing plastic of his poncho behind us. None of us talked as the big, black blot of the cemetery rose up on the left side of the street.

Yoda Mask was only a few steps behind us. I wanted to turn my head and see how far back he was, but that would be like inviting him to notice me, and I really didn't want him to notice me. There was something still and quiet about him, like a grown-up compressed into a little kid's body. He wasn't right.

The cemetery ran for two blocks but one of the streetlights had gone out in the middle, so the nearest light was at the far end. The swishing plastic behind us sounded louder in the dark, crackling and hissing back and forth. We started walking faster, the plastic swished harder, we walked even faster, and then we didn't even agree to it, we just ran.

Behind us, the rustling poncho got frantic, but fell back, and the three of us reached Simmons Street and hung a left, legs pumping, lungs aching, throats burning from the cold October air. Moody's shopping bag tore on a backswing and its bottom fell out and all his candy went sliding across the street, but we didn't stop running until we'd passed the tennis courts.

Chuck stopped because next to us was a parking lot full of police cars and next to that was the brightly lit police station. Plenty of streetlights shone here and we all doubled over, hands on knees, panting. I lifted my beard and spit a mouthful of something sour onto the street.

"What the fuck?" Chuck said.

I pushed off my knees and looked back towards McCants. The Yoda Mask stood beneath the streetlight, mask in heavy shadow, watching. After a moment, a second Yoda Mask, wearing the same plastic poncho, walked out of the cemetery and stood beside him, empty eye holes pointed our way. They started towards us, stumble-walking like little kids, and the three of us backed away, and Moody started to turn, ready to run, when the two Yoda Masks stopped and squatted over his pile of spilled candy. They began to stuff it under their ponchos.

"That's mine," Moody said, instinctively offended.

"We should run up behind them and pull off their masks," Chuck said.

"Candy-stealing dicks," Moody said, and his voice sounded on the verge of tears.

We stared at these two weird Yoda Masks grubbing up all Moody's candy. Something about how greedy they were made me feel sick.

"Come on," Chuck said, walking away from us towards Queen Street. "Let's stay on mission."

"I want to go home," Moody said.

"Then go," Chuck said over his shoulder.

Moody looked at me, his Yoda mask pushed up on top of his head, eyes getting wet. I shrugged and went after Chuck. If I had to pick which one of them to stick with, Chuck was bigger.

We weren't halfway down the block when we heard the slap of Moody's sneakers.

"*Quest for Fire*'s on HBO tonight," he said. "I could be seeing Rae Dawn Chong's tits right now."

We got to Pitt. The river of kids had trickled to clumps and lumps plodding home. More houses had gone dark. Someone had smeared a jack o'lantern down the middle of the street.

"Act natural," Chuck suddenly hissed and grabbed our shoulders, pulling us in to face him.

My back was to Pitt, but Chuck and Moody both faced it and saw the same thing.

"Did he circle around?" Moody asked.

"Who?" I asked, looking over my shoulder.

Coming down Pitt were some big kids, a guy dressed as Wonder Woman and a girl dressed like Batman, with a Spider-Man in between. Behind them trailed one of the Yoda Masks.

We were under a streetlight and couldn't run without calling attention to ourselves. The three of us pretended to check what was in Chuck's candy bag.

"Look at all that candy, candy, asshole candy," Chuck muttered.

I did community theater downtown so I said, "Peas and carrots, peas and carrots, peas and carrots."

Moody slid his Yoda mask down over his face and watched over my shoulders.

"Oh, crap," he said.

"What?" Chuck asked, jerking his head up.

"He just reached in Spider-Man's bag," Moody said. "He's totally stealing his candy."

Chuck looked the way he did when he was thinking hard about something, then suddenly squatted and poured out his bag on the side of the street. Candy slithered onto the asphalt, wrappers colorless in the silver streetlight. A single red apple dropped out last and rolled into the grass. It looked black in the light. My gut got as small and cold as a frozen pea.

"No one was giving out apples," Moody said. "We would've remembered."

Chuck lifted the apple over his head then threw it down at the street as hard as he could where it exploded into white chunks. A passing cowboy with an arrow through his hat looked at us as he went by.

Moody squatted next to Chuck, who was poking through the white apple meat with a stick. I didn't want to look.

"Holy shit," Moody said.

I made myself look at what lay at the tip of Chuck's stick, wet with apple juice: a gray rectangle catching silver street light along its blade.

Lightning bolts forked through my jaw, making the roots of my teeth sizzle. The scars around my lips squirmed.

"He wasn't taking candy out of that kid's bag," Chuck said. "He was putting this in."

They looked up at me and I stared down at the razor blade. All of a sudden, they weren't important anymore. Halloween had become all about me.

"Where'd he go?" I asked.

They stood up and scanned the street.

"There," Chuck said.

Halfway up Pitt we saw the kid stumbling along. As he walked under a streetlight we saw the white triangles from the back of his Yoda mask sticking out on either side of his head.

I ran after him, sticking to the sidewalk and the shadows. Moody and Chuck caught up on the next block. We followed Yoda Mask up King, over to Greenwich, across Simmons, up Palmetto, all the way to Bellview. The houses here were small and mean with cars parked on the grass and stuff piled on their front porches. It was still the Old Village, but not really.

Every block, Yoda Mask stopped and checked back over his shoulder, his bland, scrunched-up Yoda face scanning the street behind him. We froze in the deep black shadows of the sidewalks or slipped behind bushes in people's front yards. Then he'd turn and keep stumble-walking away and we'd let him get half a block ahead before following again, our sneakered feet soundless on the acorn-covered sidewalks.

Finally, he veered across a front yard covered in leaves. The house was a one story brick rancher with pine needles piled on the roof, a white van in the driveway, and a For Sale sign in the yard. Yoda Mask stepped onto the concrete square of a front porch with a cheap wooden roof over it, held up by pressed-aluminum columns of grape vines painted black, opened the screen door, then the front door, and walked inside. The doors closed behind him. We stood on the empty street.

"If you suggest we turn around and go home I'm going to pound you," Chuck said before Moody could open his mouth. Then he turned to me. "Which way?"

"Around back," I said.

"We're going to get in so much trouble," Moody said, his whisper slurred behind his Yoda mask.

"We need to see what they're doing," I told him.

Moody stripped off his Yoda mask and tore off his plastic poncho and let them float to the ground.

"It's after nine," he said.

Chuck grabbed him by the collar of his t-shirt and yanked him forward.

"They put razor blades in apples," he hissed. "They fucked up Kevin's face."

"Yeah," Moody said. "And someone needs to tell people not to eat them. Like, on the news or something."

"We have to make sure it's them or we'll get in trouble when we tell," Chuck said.

Chuck looked at me to back him up, but I didn't care if they stayed or left. I walked across the street, heading for the house. I needed to know. They caught up and we ran across the exposed front yard, bent double, then slipped into the bushes clinging to the house. They kept us back from the shuttered windows, but we could see light oozing out around them.

Chuck dug his fingers into my arm and pointed to a lightless black slit on the other side of the driveway. We crept between the white van's grill and the closed garage door and slipped into the alley running to the back yard, Chuck first, me in the middle, Moody last.

It was really dark back here and at the end of the alley, Chuck stopped short and we piled up. He fanned his hand in front of his face.

I smelled what he meant. The back yard reeked of wet, rotten leaves and old cat food. The knotted scars on my gums throbbed and twitched.

I forced myself past Moody and Chuck and crept into the back yard. Dead moonlight lay over everything, from the white iron patio table with its chairs knocked down around it, to the endless garden hose piled outside the back door. Light poured through the open shutters of the windows.

The first window was too high, so we slipped beneath it, then past the back door, then stopped at the big double window. Behind its dirty screens, clotted with spider webs and insect husks, the house had green and yellow walls like my grandmother's, all faded and gross. The only furniture we could see was a long dining room table pressed up to the window, surrounded by Yoda Masks.

They sat on broken-legged chairs and stood on plastic milk crates, leaning across the table, fighting over a long pile of candy poured down the middle. There were a lot of them, some little kids, some slightly bigger, I heard Chuck counting quietly next to me.

"...eight...nine...ten...eleven," he whispered.

They snatched the candy, grabbed it, slapped it out of each other's hands. The one closest to me got a Tootsie Roll unwrapped and squished it through the tiny mouth hole in his Yoda mask. I realized that the Yoda masks were ripped around the edges, and some had been crushed and pushed back into shape, and some of their *Empire Strikes Back* ponchos were stretched and torn. I thought about how many kids had dressed up as Yoda when *Empire* came out two years ago, and how many of those costumes had wound up in the garbage. I imagined these kids pulling them out of the trash, smoothing out the wrinkles, licking clean the dirty patches, stapling rubber bands back into place, pressing Scotch tape over bad tears, saving them for this Halloween.

On some silent cue, all the Yoda Masks turned towards the kitchen and a tall Yoda Mask carrying a cooking pot piled high with red, shiny apples came out. He dropped it on the table and the Yoda Masks began grabbing at them. The tall Yoda Mask poured out a paper bag of little boxes, and the Yoda Masks tore them open and started pushing razor blades into apples.

Something on my right changed, and I turned and saw Moody backing away. Chuck was still riveted to the window, clinging to the brick sill with his fingertips, but Moody wanted out, and I saw the iron patio chair lying on its side right behind him, and I eased out of the line of sight from the dining room window, and I shook my head "no", and Moody shook his head back at me, and I shook my head at him, and finally I found the courage to hiss, "Stop!"

He stopped, the backs of his legs just brushing the iron chair, but it was too late, and he lost his balance and sat down backwards, falling on his ass, knocking the entire patio table over with his back. The clang sounded like the end of the world. I turned and saw Yoda Masks crowding the window, and they saw

Chuck's face and he pushed himself off the bricks and turned to run, but got his feet tangled in the garden hose and went down.

Through the filthy windows I saw Yoda Masks running to the front door, and others streaming to the back, and some pressed to the window, and the handle of the back door turned, and I ran for the back fence. I'd always been good at climbing.

Moody smashed into me from the side, but we both hit the tall fence at the same time and flew up it, rocking it back and forth as we climbed, splinters spearing my palms, then I swung one leg over the sharp top, racked my balls, got my other leg over, scraped my stomach as I slid down, and I was free.

Moody landed beside me and we ran hard through the neighbor's backyard, but then I turned right to run around to the front of the Yoda Mask house and he peeled off left — belly bouncing, fists pumping, legs pistoning — and ran home. I knew he'd puss out at some point. Not me.

I ran to the corner of the block and charged down the street, getting there just as Chuck shot out of the alley beside the house and Yoda Masks came pouring out the front door and there were six, seven, eight of them and Chuck burst out from behind the white van, almost at the street, but his feet slipped on rotten leaves and he went down on all fours.

The Yoda Masks were silent — I could hear Chuck telling them to fuck off, to get the fuck away from him — as they crowded around him and kicked at his arms, kicked his legs, stomped his fingers, rode his back, and finally got him down on the ground. They grabbed his moussed mohawk and dragged him onto the grimy concrete porch where he grabbed one of the pressed tin columns and held on. The Yoda Masks pried his fingers off one by one, hauled Chuck inside, the screen door slapped shut, the big door swung closed, and I stood on the street alone.

They had Chuck. I wasn't scared. My rage was an enormous black bird unfurling its massive wings inside me until they filled my chest and rose up out of my back.

A black blot lay on the edge of the driveway where Chuck went down and I realized it was his backpack. I flew across the street, dropped a squat, and unzipped the pocket with the bang-snaps, then the lighter fluid, and the zippers sounded chainsaw-loud in the still night.

A plan instantly appeared inside my head. I went back to the corner and picked up Moody's discarded plastic *Empire Strikes Back* poncho and Yoda mask and pulled the poncho over my head, settled the sweaty Yoda mask over my face, and carefully slid the bang-snaps into my front pocket. I left Chuck's backpack in the neighbor's yard, and stumble-walked across the street the way they did, holding the lighter fluid behind my leg.

On their porch, I popped the red cap and soaked the ratty welcome mat until the plastic bottle sputtered air, then I tossed it in the bushes. Without hesitating, I pulled open the screen door, fully committing to my character, stepped over the welcome mat reeking of lighter fluid, pushed open the front door, and walked into their house.

The air in the house felt even colder than outside. The only thing I smelled was my hot breath trapped behind my plastic Yoda mask. In front of me stood the doorway to the dining room where I could see the Yoda Masks gorging themselves on candy, gabbling and gobbling, standing on their boxes and broken chairs, crawling across the table, stuffing more apples with more razor blades. Way down at the end of the long hall on my right, three Yoda Masks came out of a door and closed it behind them and hooked a latch they'd screwed into its frame.

I couldn't just stand there so I turned and walked towards them, remembering how to do stealth from *Castle Wolfenstein* where you could put on an SS uniform and walk right past the guards. I made myself stare straight ahead, hoping they couldn't see my heart pounding inside my chest, snapping my ribcage up and down, and my skeleton wanted to run but I locked down all my muscles and held it in place, and kept walking, one foot after the other, down the hall carpet. Right before I passed them I saw the open bathroom door on my left and turned inside. The edges of our plastic AT-AT ponchos whisked against each other but they didn't even slow down, and I closed the door, and my scarred lips buzzed and burned behind my mask.

The bathroom stunk. The smell crawled up my nose, and into my hair, like a Port-a-Potty on a hot day, and I heard buzzing flies. I lifted my mask and tried not to breathe and saw they'd been using the bathtub for a toilet.

My head spun with ammonia fumes, and my vision blurred, and I counted to fifteen, but could only make it to six before I yanked open the door. The hall was empty so I went as fast as I could away from the flailing shadows and hissing from the dining room and lifted the hook latch on the door at the end of the hall and slipped into the main bedroom.

The overhead light was on and the room was bright and empty except for a gross mattress thrown on the floor. Dead roaches lay on their backs all over the wall-to-wall carpet, and Chuck lay on the mattress in his underpants. They'd torn his t-shirt off and scratched up his chest and stomach with their fingernails. They'd yanked his jeans down to his ankles and gouged long scratches into his legs and I couldn't understand why he rolled from side to side until I saw they'd wrapped wire coat hangers around his wrists, holding them together in the prayer position. They'd wrapped them around his ankles, too.

"Fuck you, dorkass," Chuck said, but his voice didn't have any anger in it, only fear.

I ripped off my mask.

"It's me," I whispered.

"Oh, shit," he said. "I thought you were one of those creepers."

"They're all over the house," I said.

I didn't want to go to the mattress with its weird brown stains and Chuck's almost naked, scratched-up body, and the dead roaches everywhere, but I made myself kneel down beside it and unravel the wire coat hanger from his ankles. Then I unwrapped the wire from around his wrists and he pulled his pants up.

"We need to go out the window," I said.

The windows weren't locked, only latched, and even though the latches were stiff I got one of them turned halfway around before it stuck.

"They're little," he said, mush-mouthed. They'd split his top lip. "But there's so many of the fuckers."

We crowded our fingertips onto the latch and both pulled as hard as we could, feeling our fingers and wrists strain and shake. The latch slowly, slowly, slowly slid around. In the reflection of the window, I saw the bedroom door open behind us. I turned, putting my back to the glass.

Yoda Masks filled the door, and a cluster of scrunch-mouthed Yodas stared at us from empty eyeholes. The Tall Yoda Mask pushed his way to the front. We all stood there, watching each other for three long eye blinks.

"You better let us go," Chuck said.

The Tall Yoda Mask shook his head once, a simple back and forth.

"Our parents will be looking for us," Chuck tried.

"Your parents?" Tall Yoda Mask said, voice muffled behind Yoda's plastic face. "Michael? Show them."

One of the smaller Yoda Masks raised his mask. He looked like a normal kid, a little grubby and hair too long, except he had a skull mouth. No lips, just a too-big grin of long white teeth behind a ragged melted hole in his face. His chin was raw bone.

"One Halloween," Tall Yoda Mask said. "Michael's dad got angry Michael didn't save him any candy. So he made Michael drink a glass of Drano mixed with oven cleaner."

"So?" I said.

"Jason," Tall Yoda Mask said.

Another of the kids raised his Yoda mask. He was Asian and he didn't have a nose, just a black, ragged hole punched deep into his skull. I didn't want to see what was at the bottom.

"Jason got some Mickey Mouse stickers from a grown-up at the mall," Tall

Yoda Mask said. "They were soaked in PCP. When he licked the back it made him go crazy. He took his dad's chisel out of the toolbox and hammered off his nose."

Tall Yoda Mask nodded to a third kid who raised his mask to reveal his mouth sewn shut with black thread.

"Cooper talked too much," Tall Yoda Mask said. "His grandmother finally sewed his mouth shut. That's what parents are like. That's the world they built for us. One where they get all the treats, and everyone else gets tricks. Not us. We go wherever we want. We get the treats. We play the tricks. It's always Halloween."

"You need to let us go home," Chuck said and I hated how it sounded like begging. "We won't say anything."

"Home to your parents?" Tall Yoda Mask said. "You're just their pets. And pets always tell on us to their owners."

"I ate one of your apples three years ago," I said, stepping forward to make sure they saw my scars. "It sliced my mouth up. I'm not a grown-up."

"There weren't razor blades in apples until parents made it up," Tall Yoda Mask said. "They invented it."

He nodded to the other Yoda Masks and they pulled silver X-acto knives out from under their ponchos. Beside me, Chuck made a noise with his mouth like a girl. My gums tickled and squirmed.

"I'll play you a game," I said.

"What game?" Tall Yoda Mask asked.

"Apple Roulette," I said. "We'll sit in the kitchen with the apples between us, and we'll each take a bite. The first one to get a razor blade loses. You lose, we go home."

One of the Yoda Masks giggled and then they all started, like a plastic rustle hissing through the mouth holes of their masks.

"One bite per apple," I said, feeling braver. I was in control of this now. I was choosing this. "Unless you're scared."

The Yoda Masks all looked up at the tall one and he hesitated, then turned and made an "after you" gesture with one hand. Beside me I could feel Chuck wobble. For the first time since I'd known him, he didn't know what to do. But I did.

"Come on," I whispered and we waded into the Yoda Masks.

They parted in front of us then closed behind us like pigeons in a park. Chuck stayed close and I felt something and realized he was trying to hold my hand. I pulled mine away. I needed both hands free.

We walked down the hall, Yoda Masks crowding behind us, and got to the end and I looked in the dining room and saw one really small Yoda Mask sitting

226

on the table Indian style, sucking a single M&M at a time through his mouth hole. The big pot of apples sat in front of him, weeping clear juice through razor blade slits.

Chuck's breathing sped up beside me.

"Both," Tall Yoda Mask said, trapped a few feet down the hall by the wall-to-wall Yoda Masks. "Both play."

"Okay," I said. "We'll both play."

A few Yoda Masks crowded around, pushing us towards the kitchen.

"But —" Chuck started.

I grabbed him and shoved him towards the front door and I turned and shoved the front Yoda Mask down, and he went backwards, turning the rest into a thrashing pile.

Chuck just stood there and I pushed him in front of me out the front door. An apple thumped into the doorframe beside my head. The tiny Yoda Mask in the dining room stood on the table, hurling apples from the pot.

"Ay!!!" he screeched and sat down, sucking on his razor-slashed palm.

Yoda Masks screamed and hooted in fury as we blew through the screen door, then on the porch I stopped and turned, facing the furious Yoda Masks boiling towards the front door.

Chuck, already halfway across the front yard, turned and yelled, "What are you doing?"

I pulled my hand out of my pocket as two little Yoda Masks came flying out of the house, screen door slamming against the wall, and I threw all the bang-snaps down hard on the lighter-fluid soaked welcome mat.

Our parents always warned us about how flammable Halloween costumes could be, especially the cheap ones from the drugstore. A column of fire shot from the doormat to the porch ceiling, one big yellow tongue, licking it black, catching one Yoda Mask in the middle. His cheap plastic poncho squirmed and wrapped around his body, his Yoda mask softened instantly and fused to his face.

Something stung my hands and a coating of blue flame encased my *Empire* poncho and I tore it off but the soft plastic stuck to my palms in strips. Something yanked me from behind and Chuck was pulling me backwards into the middle of the front yard.

We stood and watched the Yoda Mask dance and spin in the flames and set the entire porch on fire. Heat tightened the skin on our faces as fire gobbled up the porch and clawed its way onto the roof. By the time Chuck pulled me into a run, the entire front of the house roared with flames.

The cool air stung our faces as we ran to the corner, and my palms throbbed as we turned towards home. My lungs felt chemical-scorched with burning plastic fumes. Even when the house was out of sight behind us, and cramps made us stop and suck cold air down our raw throats, we could see the orange glow lighting up the sky.

"We're in so much trouble," Chuck moaned. He pressed the button on the side of his watch and it lit up. "It's almost eleven."

I remembered the piles of glossy folders he pulled out of his backpack that day from the military schools: Hargrave, and DMU, and Howe, and Randolph-Macon.

"We burned down a house!" Chuck said, and I hated his parents for making him scared. "My mom's going to be so pissed. We reek. My dad's going to know we stole his lighter fluid. They're going to read about the house in the paper tomorrow and they're going to know it was us."

I hadn't even thought about tomorrow.

"What if we killed those kids?" I asked.

"We'll both go to military school," Chuck said. "They're probably already looking for us."

"Shit," I said.

And just like that, headlights lit up the road and my mom's car rolled out from a side street and took the turn. It passed us, and we both turned, and through the window saw the disorienting sight of Chuck's dad driving my mom's car. Our moms were in the back seat. They saw us at the same time we saw them, their brake lights flared, and they began to do a three-point turn.

"It's never going to be normal again," Chuck said.

Chuck was right. When I thought about how much trouble we were in I wanted to cry. I looked back up the street, because maybe we could still run and get home before they did and pretend they hadn't seen us, and that's when I saw it: the white van slid out of a side street and stopped in the middle of the road. Its side door stood open, gaping and black, and I knew it was waiting for us. I looked back down the street and saw my mom's station wagon already rolling towards us, pinning us in its headlights, and Chuck standing there, slumped and undone.

I thought about Moody, already home and probably in trouble for being out after nine, and soon he'd be on spazz pills because instead of standing up to the judge his parents took Bennett to a place where he didn't know any other dogs. At Christmas Chuck would come home wearing some ugly polyester uniform and a crew cut, and all he'd want to do is talk on the phone to other kids from military school who knew all the same military school jokes. I thought about how I'd saved him from the Yoda Masks and instead of admiring my bravery my parents were going to give me endless lectures and maybe even call the police.

I grabbed Chuck's hand and I pulled. It felt like the most natural thing in the world. I grabbed Chuck's hand and I pulled him after me, and in the headlights of my mom's car, we ran.

We ran for the white van because that open door didn't look scary to me, it looked like an invitation.

Chuck's dad gave a tentative peck on his horn and sped up, pulling alongside us, but we ran harder, and the white van got bigger, and Chuck ran as fast as I did, and we ran from their lectures and their talks and their disappointment and their endless questions. We ran for the white van and Chuck's dad hit the horn harder, and then arms pulled me into the van, but Chuck wasn't beside me anymore.

I turned and squinted into the station wagon's headlights and Chuck stood on the street, shirtless, shoulders slumped, a black silhouette.

"I can't," he said. "I'm scared."

In that moment, I knew something real. He hadn't eaten the apple, but I had. The world was divided into tricks and treats and the grown ups kept all the treats for themselves and stuck us with the tricks. I didn't want to get bitten. I wanted to bite.

"Come on!" I told Chuck.

He raised one hand goodbye and held it there as the station wagon doors opened behind him and our parents got out of the car.

Behind me, someone said, "Punch it," and the van lurched away so fast I almost fell out of the door onto my face. Two of the kids wrestled the sliding door shut, and now Chuck's dad honked and flashed his lights, but they were falling behind. I watched them surround Chuck and someone handed me a Yoda mask and I slid it over my face and knelt on the back bench and looked out the window at my parent's headlights and my best friend slipping further and further away, as Tall Yoda Mask went 35, 45, 55 mph down streets marked for 25, and we went so fast, racing into the dark, chasing Halloween, chasing Halloween forever.

The Garden of Dr. Moreau

LISA MORTON

April 9, 1984

Dr. Moreau paused the video and leaned back in satisfaction. "My God…"

Her assistant stood behind her, eyes still on the monitor, now frozen on the shot of corn stalks. "You'll get the Nobel Prize for this, you know."

The older woman laughed. "I'm more interested in a great veggie burger." She leaned forward and turned off the VHS player. "You know, Dr. Montgomery, we couldn't have done this without your tissue culture techniques."

Montgomery shook her hair, releasing a few blonde strands from the simple bun. "This is really *your* project. You deserve the recognition."

Dr. Moreau accepted the compliment in silence, recognizing its truth. Ten years of research into RNA-splicing, designing new biolistic particle delivery systems, a decade of failures and small triumphs, of lost opportunities and better grants, had led to *this*, the moment when she'd just reviewed a time-lapse video recording spanning fourteen hours, showing how a row of genetically altered and water-deprived corn plants had actually moved their root systems to access a low trough of open water on the ground.

"Mary-Dell Chilton may have beat us by a year with *Agrobacterium*," Montgomery said, gathering up a stack of folders, "but this is a hundred times bigger."

Standing and stretching, Moreau smiled. "Now let's just hope we can continue to replicate the results."

"We will."

It was late—after nine p.m.—and Montgomery said good night; Moreau knew she was anxious to get home to her husband, Mitch. Moreau followed, locking up the lab and stepping out onto the quiet campus grounds. She didn't head for her car, though, but to the small plot located behind the Biology building.

231

The university had given her the fifty-by-thirty-foot patch for her research; considering the amount of donations her name and work brought in, it was the least they could do. A chain-link fence had been erected around the micro-field; she used a key to unlock the padlock suspended from a chain, then swung the gate open. She stepped inside the fence and stopped, drinking in the moment.

She'd given up so much for this. Her personal life had been anything but triumphant: one marriage that had lasted three years before sputtering out in a loveless failure; no children, the rest of her family on the other side of the country and perpetually angry at her lack of communication, a sixty-year-old house in bad need of repair…but right now none of that mattered, because she knew they'd made history tonight. They'd created a transgenic plant that spanned *kingdoms*, that combined fauna and flora. Food crops that would be able to care for themselves; the plants could seek water when they needed it or remove their pest infestations. Agriculture would be revolutionized; within a few years, she could picture a world in which everyone was fed in a way that was ecological and ethical.

Now, the corn stood tall under the university's overhead lights, swaying slightly in an evening breeze. The stalks were majestic, the leaves green, the ears ripening.

Perfect.

She basked in the sight. *I did it. I really did it. It was all worth it, for this moment.*

Finally, she turned away, tired, ready for dinner and rest.

As she was snapping the padlock shut, movement caught her eye and she looked up. One of the stalks bent towards her before bouncing back to its upright position.

Moreau stared, waiting to see if the motion was repeated, but the plant remained still. She smiled at the thought that the plant had somehow bowed to her (*just the breeze*), and headed off, looking forward to celebrating with the vegetarian plate from her favorite Middle Eastern takeout and a glass of white wine.

April 10, 1984

"You're shitting me. I mean, pardon my French, Doc, but—that's fucking awesome."

Moreau smiled wryly as the intern bent over the monitor where he'd just seen the tape from yesterday. The doctor liked the burly young man, with his thick glasses and foul mouth, even if he did perpetually smell like barbeque and meat.

"I mean, that plant just stuck a root out on its own, right? You weren't—you know, off-camera pulling strings or something, right?"

"Mr. Prendick—!"

He held up his thick hands, placating. "Sorry, bad joke. Seriously, Doctor Moreau—it's historic. I'm really honored that you showed it to me."

"You're only the third person to see it so far."

"Wow." Prendick abruptly clapped his hands and grinned. "I know let's celebrate by going out for steaks tonight."

Montgomery had just entered the room, overhearing. "Ed, don't be disgusting."

"Okay, I know: another bad joke. I'll stop now." He let a second go by before adding, "T-bone, rare…"

He mock-ran from the room as Montgomery and Moreau both eyed him. "Should I tell him again," Montgomery said, "how his diet is both cruel and unhealthy?"

Moreau turned back to her work, handwriting notes on a legal pad. "He knows already. We can't change all the carnivores."

At least not yet, she thought.

April 17, 1984

Dr. Moreau was working on the paper for *Nature* ("Bioletics used in the insertion of transgenic cross-kingdom T-DNA") when Montgomery asked, "Did you hear about Ed Prendick?"

Moreau looked up. "It's Tuesday, right?" She often lost track of the days when working. "Shouldn't he be here by now? Is he sick?"

"Worse than that: he's missing."

Moreau pushed away from her computer keyboard, looking up. "Missing?"

Montgomery nodded and handed her a copy of the school newspaper. "There was a report about it in there today. They said he was last seen Sunday night, leaving a party at Heysbrook Hall, drunk. He was crossing the campus to get back to his own dorm, but he never made it."

"That's alarming." Moreau looked down at the paper, saw a grainy photo of Ed Prendick, bushy hair topping thick glasses and a broad smile.

"It is. It's not like him to just drop off the map. I'm worried."

"Let me know if you hear anything."

Moreau tried to return to her report, but something felt wrong, *really* wrong. Then it hit her: a conversation she'd had a few weeks ago with Mr. Prendick. They'd been outside, working in the cornfield, taking tissue samples for testing, when the intern had casually confessed that he sometimes left his nearby dorm room at night and returned here, to the corn, to sit on a bench nearby and look at it while he smoked a joint. He'd half-jokingly offered to share one with Moreau some night, but she declined and promised not to turn him in.

Moreau told Montgomery she wanted to check something. She rose, left the lab, went outside and headed to the corn patch. It was two in the afternoon, still and sunny. She opened the padlock and stepped in. She ran her fingers along the nearest leaf, enjoying the sensation—

Something crunched under her feet.

She looked down, puzzled, stepped back. Kneeling, she saw what she'd stepped on.

A pair of thick glasses.

She picked them up, holding them before her eyes.

Prendick's.

Looking around, she spotted something else ten feet away, between the end of the stalks and the fence: a red-and-white high-top sneaker. She knew that, too.

"Converse Fast Breaks," Prendick had told her, as he'd stuck out his big feet clad in the sneakers. She knew he'd spent a great deal of his parents' money on the shoes.

The ground felt soft, spongy. It was darker than the dirt outside the lot. When she knelt, the smell assaulted her. She knew what was in the ground before she drove her fingers into it and brought them up, reddened:

Blood.

Oh my God. Prendick was murdered and buried here.

Even as that thought hit her, she realized how unlikely it was. Someone would've had to unlock the gate to get in. There were only two copies of the padlock key: she had one, and the other was kept in a drawer in the lab. Only she, Montgomery, and three of their student interns knew about that key. One of the interns was apparently dead now; the other two were friendly, smart, dedicated young women who had no motive she could imagine.

Montgomery and Prendick had argued two weeks ago. He'd mentioned something President Reagan had said that he liked, and Montgomery had chewed him out in no uncertain terms. But they'd laughed together at the end of the day, and that certainly wasn't enough to commit murder. Besides, Montgomery was no killer; she wouldn't even eat meat because she couldn't stand the idea of slaughtering an animal.

What did that leave?

Moreau examined the ground again, saw it was uneven and loose. She dug her fingers down deeper, biting back nausea. She felt something a few inches under the surface, outlined its shape.

It felt like a finger.

Pushing dirt aside, she uncovered it. Definitely a finger, but she couldn't pull it from the ground. Her fingers traced the shape of a hand, but there was something else…she pulled at it, setting her feet, leaning back, and at last it came free.

Moreau dropped it and fell back in shock. It was a hand (*Prendick's*), severed at the wrist, with roots wrapped tightly around it.

She stared up at the corn, the stalks stiff and straight, the leaves a nearly iridescent green, the ears large and plentiful. They didn't move. They didn't even tremble. They looked like normal, beautiful plants.

But Moreau still crept out of the lot backwards, never taking her eyes off them. When she reached the gate she fell back through it. Shaking badly, she staggered to her feet, slammed the gate closed and snapped the padlock shut.

Feeling her gorge rise, she rushed into the Biology building and straight to the first bathroom, where she scrubbed frantically at her hands, watching the water turn a dark reddish-brown as it spiraled down the drain. The knees of her pants were also stained so she grabbed a wad of paper towels, rubbing at her legs. Finally her energy drained and she stopped, dropping the towels in a trash bin, staring at herself in the mirror. What she saw there was a frightened fifty-year-old woman who looked like she'd already lost.

She didn't like what the mirror revealed, so she forced herself to think. *If I bring the police in on this, they'll start looking for a killer…but they'll also pay the wrong kind of attention to my work. I can't afford that, not now, not after so long, when I'm so close.*

Ten minutes later, Dr. Moreau stepped out of the bathroom, her face composed, Prendick's glasses having been wrapped in towels and deposited in the bathroom trash. She was determined to keep the terrible secret about his death to herself.

April 19, 1984

"Have you noticed that all the birds and squirrels around here have disappeared?"

Dr. Moreau looked up from the green numbers flitting across the black computer screen as Montgomery spoke behind her. "What?"

"I was standing out by the corn a few minutes ago, and I knew something was different, but I couldn't figure out what it was right away. I finally realized that I couldn't hear any birds. And it's been at least a week since I've seen a squirrel. Remember how much trouble we had with them getting into the corn at one point?"

Moreau's gut clenched.

Montgomery turned to leave. "I'm going out to the field to—"

"No!" Moreau's sharp rejoinder caused Montgomery to freeze and peer at her curiously. Moreau modified her tone. "I'm worried about contamination."

Montgomery's face creased in perplexity. "Isn't it a little late for that?"

Moreau thought, *I'm worried about them contaminating us*, but she said, "I've ordered containment suits. I don't think we should go out there again until we get those."

"Okay, but I still don't understand: what exactly is it that you're worried about?"

Taking a deep breath, Moreau answered, "The birds and squirrels…"

"What about them? Are you worried about them eating the corn?"

Moreau couldn't stifle a short, bitter laugh. "Actually, I'm worried about the corn eating *them*."

"I'm not following."

"Montgomery, the intent of this project was to benefit agriculture by creating genetically modified flora that could tend to itself."

The other doctor gaped for a second before saying, "So you…what, think the corn turned the birds and squirrels into…*blood meal*?"

When Moreau didn't answer, Montgomery fell into a chair, stunned. "How sure are you?"

"Quite sure. I found…" Moreau paused before adding, "…*feathers*."

"Dear God. If it's true, then…what do we do?"

"Well, we're *not* sure it's true yet, so we continue with the experiment, but we proceed with caution—*extreme* caution."

"Doctor Moreau, you don't think it's possible…Ed Prendick…?"

"That seems—shall we say—unlikely, doesn't it?"

Montgomery nodded. But Moreau was glad she'd thrown the glasses away.

April 26, 1984

Wearing their new containment suits, moving through the extra fence that had been erected around the perimeter of the field, Moreau and Montgomery stepped among the corn, prepared to conduct routine research. Montgomery was first to notice it, though: "Two of the plants are missing."

Moreau saw where her colleague was pointing; two stalks were gone from the end of the second row, the ground where they'd been turned up. She looked around—and froze at what she saw: the two missing plants were *outside* the field and both fences, fifty feet away.

Pushing past Montgomery, Moreau walked through the gates, striding up to the plants. They stood between two spreading oak trees, next to a paved walk that ran from the Biology building to Chemistry. Moreau knelt, reached out a gloved hand and felt the ground around the stalks. The soil was firmly packed, the corn apparently well-rooted.

Moreau rose as Montgomery joined her. "What is *this*?" Montgomery asked. "Who would move them? Who *could* move them?"

"I don't know."

But she did know. Her suspicion was confirmed when she saw a headline in the student newspaper: *Second student goes missing.*

She could scan the security camera footage, but she already knew what it would show. Roots, after all, were tough and would make fine fence climbers.

The plants were actively hunting now.

April 27, 1984

Moreau sipped coffee, waiting anxiously for Montgomery to arrive for work. When Montgomery showed up, Moreau asked her to take a seat before saying, "We need to terminate the corn."

She'd expected the younger woman to protest or question, but instead Montgomery inhaled, took a moment, and then said, "I agree."

"We'll record everything, of course, so we can start over. This does not mean I consider the project a failure."

Montgomery's eyes were haunted when she looked up. "So...do we tell anyone about...?"

"I think that should depend on what we find. After we've removed the plants, we can run our own soil samples. If necessary, we'll turn over our findings to the authorities."

After considering, Montgomery said, "Yes."

Moreau already knew what was in the soil, but she didn't have the courage to reveal that to Montgomery.

They made arrangements: tonight, Moreau would stop at a hardware store, purchase garden shears, hedge trimmers, and several boxes of the biggest trash bags. They'd meet back at the lab tomorrow morning; it would be a Saturday, and the campus would be largely empty. The campus had its own trash incinerator; they would accompany a janitor there and make sure the bags were burned thoroughly.

Moreau worked late, revising her paper, preparing tissue sample vials for tomorrow, making sure everything was in place. It was after nine in the evening when she finally left; she'd sent Montgomery home at seven. Montgomery deserved a quiet night with her Mitch. Moreau wanted a salad (*just no corn, please*).

The campus was quiet as the doctor left the Biology building, heading for her car. Under other circumstances, the walk would have been pleasant: the campus grounds were beautifully landscaped, mixing century-old oak trees that predated the college itself with grass, rose gardens, shaded ferns and the traditional ivy. Spring had arrived, and the night breeze carried the rich scents of new blooms and ornamental garlic. In the distance Moreau could hear the raucous sounds of parties in the dorms, but here it was quiet, no one else around—

237

Then why did she hear someone else moving through thick undergrowth fifty feet away, near the Chemistry building?

No, not someone—some*thing*.

She slowed, and then stopped, listening. The sounds stopped, too. She walked forward ten feet. The some*thing* followed.

She was being tracked.

Her first instinct was to run, but reason overruled fear and she turned, determined to discover the nature of her tracker.

Moreau squinted as she approached the massive brick three-story building. The area immediately below the front wall was in dense shadow, a place where no overhead light reached. She stepped forward cautiously, wishing she had a flashlight.

After a few seconds, her eyes adjusted. She scanned the area, but saw nothing. No stalks, standing still in the gloom, waiting. Nothing but grass, low shrubbery, and the ivy…

The ivy was moving.

She walked up closer, but the dark green vines—nearly black in the shadow— hung motionless. She waited for long seconds. She took a few side steps, but the ivy hung still. A few leaves rustled, but it was only the air moving the leaves.

Impossible. The corn couldn't somehow genetically modify other plants.

The sound came from the other direction now. She spun, peering out across the night-time grounds…and *there*. Something narrow and tall, but moving…

Moreau didn't investigate. Instead, she shivered and jogged the remaining distance to her car, not stopping until, heart hammering, she was inside with the doors locked and the engine revved.

April 28, 1984

Moreau arrived at the lab just after 8 a.m., carrying a large plastic bag with the name of a hardware store emblazoned on one side. Montgomery arrived a few moments later, bringing with her two steaming cups of coffee. "Thought you might need this," she said to Moreau as she handed her one.

They drank the coffee in silence. Finally, Moreau set her empty paper cup down. "Let's get this over with."

Montgomery nodded, gulped the last of her cup and tossed it in the trash. They each donned one of the bulky white containment suits, securing the hoods and gloves last. Moreau picked up the shears and the box of large trash bags. Montgomery took the hedge trimmers and a plastic tub of vials and baggies. It was a Saturday morning, so the campus was quiet around them.

They opened the door out of the lab, Montgomery stepping into the hallway first, Moreau following a step behind.

The hallway in front of them was full of corn plants. They stood there on their long, thick roots, either curled beneath them or spread out. They moved with an eerie grace, gliding forward on the tiled floor as the roots pulled and pushed and grasped and slithered.

Moreau heard Montgomery breathe out, "Oh my God," the words muffled in the confines of the suit.

The first root shot up. The nearest of the stalks was still eight feet away, but that was close enough for a tendril to whip out and wrap around Montgomery's hedge trimmers. They were jerked from the paralyzed woman's hand and pulled back. Roots wove about the closed handles of the trimmer, flipped them around, and drove the long blades back towards Montgomery. Moreau tried to push her colleague aside at the last instant, but she was too late—the blades knifed through the containment suit and into Montgomery's neck. She staggered back, one gloved hand reflexively moving up to grab at her wound as blood sprayed through her fingers, down the suit, onto the floor, onto Moreau. The roots pulled the trimmers back, drove them forward again, this time into Montgomery's midsection. She collapsed, blood filling the suit, her ruined neck drowning her. She was dead within seconds.

Moreau stood above her, tensing for her own end…

It didn't come. Instead, the plants stood before her, wavering, hesitant.

What are they waiting for?

She took one step backward, and the plants followed suit, but still made no threatening moves toward her. Another step…they followed…

She abruptly turned and ran.

The last thing she felt was herself falling as a root yanked one ankle back.

???

Moreau awoke slowly, painfully. Her head hurt, she was nauseated, she suspected a concussion…

But I'm still alive.

She tried to sit up, but couldn't. She could lift her head just enough, though, to see that she was in her lab, the fluorescent lights overhead momentarily blinding her. She felt metal beneath her, knew she was on one of the work counters. Her arms and legs were immobilized however; she was tied down.

No, she thought, with bitter humor, *not tied—rooted.*

She didn't know how long she'd been unconscious, but the bigger question was: *why am I still alive?*

The plants stood around her, like a silent jury. They could sense the moisture and nutrients she carried (and they'd certainly sensed the threat posed by

Montgomery), but Moreau wasn't sure how far their awareness extended. Did they somehow know she was their creator? Was that why she'd been spared?

A root appeared just inches before her eyes, hovering there before moving around the side of her head. She cried out when she felt it tickle her ear; she screamed when it slid in.

She stopped screaming, though, when she heard words in her mind, words that weren't hers.

You/mother/god

Moreau blinked in astonishment, in perplexity. What she was hearing were less words than feelings that shaped themselves into ideas she could grasp. She was flooded with gratitude, adoration, but also control.

She tried to form questions that she hoped they would understand. *What do you want?*

A few seconds passed before images seeped into her mind: images of plants. All sorts of plants: vegetables, fruits, flowers, grains, bushes, trees.

She understood: they wanted her to modify *all* plants.

Will you kill more people?

What was placed in her head in response was a sensation of rich food being absorbed by roots, bringing health and life to the plants.

Moreau sucked in a sharp breath as she understood. *We're just…fertilizer to them. They're going to eat us.*

But the plants felt her alarm, and tried to offer her comforting, calming feelings. She understood that she wouldn't die; she was more valuable to them than mere food.

They presented images of her working with them to create more of their kind, and they would revere her as a Creator. They would protect her, cherish her, care for her.

And then she saw them presenting her with sustenance, but it was meat—great bloody, red steaks. She instinctively pulled away from the image, but she felt their revulsion and she saw the last, greatest irony of her terrible mistake:

Of course—they won't let me eat them, after all.

Dr. Moreau's laughter was broken and hollow. The plants released her and waited.

Biographies

Linda D. Addison grew up in Philadelphia and began weaving stories at an early age. She currently lives in Arizona and has published over 300 poems, stories and articles. Ms. Addison is the first African-American recipient of the world renowned Bram Stoker Award and has received four awards for collections: *Four Elements* written with Charlee Jacob, Marge Simon and Rain Graves (Bad Moon Books 2013); *How To Recognize a Demon has Become Your Friend* short stories and poetry (Necon EBooks, 2011), *Being Full of Light, Insubstantial* (2007), *Consumed, Reduced to Beautiful Grey Ashes* (2001). *Dark Duet* (Necon EBooks, 2012), a collaborative book of poetry written with Stephen M. Wilson, was a 2012 finalist for the HWA Bram Stoker Award®. She co-edited *Sycorax's Daughters*, an anthology of horror fiction and poetry by African-American women (publisher Cedar Grove Publishing, 2017) with Kinitra Brooks and Susana Morris, which was a HWA Bram Stoker finalist in the Anthology category. In 2018 she received the HWA Lifetime Achievement Award.
http://www.cith.org/linda/index.html

Cullen Bunn is the writer of creator-owned comic books such as *The Sixth Gun, Harrow County, The Damned, The Empty Man*, and *Bone Paris*. He also writes books such as *Deadpool Kills the Marvel Universe* and *Asgardians of the Galaxy* for Marvel.

In addition, he is the author of the middle reader horror novel, *Crooked Hills*, and the collection of short fiction, *A Passage in Black*.

He has fought for his life against mountain lions and performed on stage as the World's Youngest Hypnotist. Buy him a drink sometime, and he'll tell you all about it.

His website is www.cullenbunn.com.
You can find him on Twitter at @cullenbunn.

Mort Castle, deemed a "horror doyen" by *Publishers Weekly*, has won three Bram Stoker Awards®, two Black Quills, a Golden Bot, and has been nominated for an Audie, the International Horror Guild Award, the Shirley Jackson Award, and the Pushcart Prize. He's edited or authored 17 books; his recent or forthcoming titles include: *New Moon on the Water, Writer's Digest Annotated Classics: Dracula*; and the 2016 Leapfrog Fiction contest winner *Knowing When to Die*. More than 600 Castle authored "shorter works," stories, articles, poems, and comics have appeared in periodicals and anthologies, including *Twilight Zone, Bombay Gin, Poe's Lighthouse,* and *Tales of the Batman*. Castle teaches fiction writing at Columbia College Chicago and has presented writing workshops and seminars throughout North America.

Award-winning filmmaker **Mick Garris** began writing fiction at the age of twelve. By the time he was in high school, he was writing music and film journalism for various local and national publications, and during college, edited and published his own pop culture magazine. He spent seven years as lead vocalist with the acclaimed tongue-in-cheek progressive art-rock band, Horsefeathers. His first movie business job was as a receptionist for George Lucas's Star Wars Corporation, where he worked his way up to running the remote-controlled R2-D2 robot at personal appearances, including that year's Academy Awards ceremony.

Garris hosted and produced "The Fantasy Film Festival" for nearly three years on Los Angeles television, and later began work in film publicity at Avco Embassy and Universal Pictures. It was there that he created "Making of..." documentaries for various feature films. Steven Spielberg hired Garris as story editor on the *Amazing Stories* series for NBC, where he wrote or co-wrote 10 of the 44 episodes. Since then, he has written or co-authored several feature films (*Nightmare Cinema, Riding the Bullet, *Batteries Not Included, The Fly II, Hocus Pocus, Critters 2*) and teleplays (*Amazing Stories, Quicksilver Highway, Virtual Obsession, The Others, Desperation, Nightmares & Dreamscapes, Masters of Horror, Fear Itself*), as well as directing and producing in many media: cable (*Psycho IV: The Beginning, Tales From the Crypt, Masters of Horror, Pretty Little Liars, Its Spinoff, Ravenswood, Witches of East End, Shadowhunters, Dead of Summer, Once Upon a Time*), Features (*Critters 2, Sleepwalkers, Riding the Bullet, Nightmare Cinema*), television films (*Quicksilver Highway, Virtual Obsession, Desperation*), series pilots (*The Others, Lost in Oz*), network miniseries (*The Stand, The Shining, Steve Martini's The Judge, Bag of Bones*), and series (*She-Wolf of London, Masters of Horror, Fear Itself*).

He is Creator and Executive Producer of Showtime's *Masters of Horror* series, as well as creator of the NBC series, *Fear Itself*, both anthology series of one-hour horror films written and directed by the most famous names in the fear-film genre: John Carpenter, Tobe Hooper, George Romero, John Landis, Dario Argento, and several others. Garris also is a writer and director on both series. Garris was also Executive Producer and Director of Stephen King's *Bag of Bones* miniseries for A&E. He is currently developing three series. Garris is also Executive Producer of the Universal feature, *Unbroken*, based on the life of Louis Zamperini and the book by Laura Hillenbrand. It was directed by Angelina Jolie, and has proven to be an international box office hit. His new film as producer, *Nightmare Cinema*, featuring five stories by five internationally renowned horror filmmakers—Ryuhei Kitamura from Japan, Alejandro Brugués from Cuba, David Slade from the UK, and Joe Dante and Garris from the USA—will soon hit theater screens.

Mick is also known for his Fearnet television interview series *Post-Mortem*, where he sits down with some of the most revered filmmakers in the horror and fantasy genre for one-on-one discussions. It has since become the popular Post Mortem with Mick Garris Podcast. *A Life in the Cinema*, his first book, was a collection of short stories and a screenplay based on one of the included stories, published by Gauntlet Press. Garris' first novel, *Development Hell*, was published by Cemetery Dance, who are also publishers of his novellas, *Snow Shadows* and *Tyler's Third Act*, his second novel, *Salome*, and this year's novella, *Ugly*. He has also had many works of short fiction published in numerous books and magazines.

Grady Hendrix is the Bram Stoker Award®-winning author of *Paperbacks from Hell*, and a believer that there is either PCP or razor blades in most Halloween candy. His novels include *My Best Friend's Exorcism* and *The Southern Book Club's Guide to Slaying Vampires*, and his movies include *Mohawk* and *Satanic Panic*. He is an avid trick-or-treater. You can hear more of his drivel at www.gradyhendrix.com.

Bram Stoker Award®-winner **Eugene Johnson** is a bestselling editor, author and columnist. He has written as well as edited in various genres, and created anthologies such as the *Fantastic Tales of Terror*, *Drive in Creature Feature* with Charles Day, the Bram Stoker Award®-nominated nonfiction anthology *Where Nightmares Come From: The Art of Storytelling in the Horror Genre* and many more.

As a filmmaker, Eugene Johnson worked on various movies, including the upcoming *Requiem*, starring Tony Todd and directed by Paul Moore. His short film *Leftovers*, a collaboration with director Paul Moore, was featured at the Screamfest Film Festival in Los Angeles as well as Dragoncon. Eugene is currently a member of the Horror Writers Association. He resides in West Virginia with his partner Angela, daughter, and two sons.

Biographies

Stephen Graham Jones is the author of sixteen novels and six story collections. Most recent is the novella *Mapping the Interior*, from Tor.com, and the comic book *My Hero*, from Hex Publishers. Stephen lives and teaches in Boulder, Colorado.

From the day she was born, **Jess Landry** has always been attracted to the stranger things in life. Her fondest childhood memories include getting nightmares from the *Goosebumps* books, watching the *Hilarious House of Frightenstein*, and reiterating to her parents that there was absolutely nothing wrong with her mental state.

Since picking up a pen a few years ago, Jess's fiction has appeared in anthologies such as Crystal Lake Publishing's *Where Nightmares Come From*, Unnerving's *Alligators in the Sewers*, Stitched Smile's *Primogen: The Origins of Monsters*, DFPs *Killing it Softly*, and April Moon Books' Ill-Considered Expeditions, as well as online with SpeckLit and EGM Shorts. She currently works as Managing Editor for JournalStone and its imprint, Trepidatio Publishing, where her goal is to publish diverse stories from diverse writers. An active member of the HWA, Jess has volunteered as Head Compiler for the Bram Stoker Awards® since 2015, and has most recently taken on the role of Membership Coordinator.

You can visit her on the interwebs at her sad-looking website, jesslandry.com, though your best bet at finding her is on Facebook and Twitter where she often posts cat memes and references Jura
facebook.com/jesslandry28
twitter.com/jesslandry28),

Joe R. Lansdale is the author of 48 novels and over 20 short story collections. He has written and sold a number of screenplays, has had his plays adapted for stage. His work has been adapted to film; *Bubba Ho-Tep* and *Cold in July* among them. His best-known novels, the "Hap and Leonard" series has been adapted for television with Lansdale as co-executive producer with Lowell Northrop under the title, *Hap and Leonard*. He has also edited or co-edited numerous anthologies.

Kasey Lansdale, first published at the tender age of eight by Random House, is the author of several short stories and novellas, with stories from Harper Collins and Titan Books, as well as the editor of assorted anthology collections, including Subterranean Press' *Impossible Monsters*. She is best known as a Singer/Songwriter. Most recently, you can hear Lansdale as the narrator of various works, including Stan Lee's *Reflections*, George R.R. Martin's *Aces Abroad*, and George A. Romero's latest installment, *Nights of the Living Dead*, among others. Her new collection, *Terror is our Business*, was lauded by *Publisher's Weekly* as "storytelling that delightfully takes on a lighter and sharper edge."

Vince A. Liaguno is the Bram Stoker Award®-winning editor of *Unspeakable Horror: From the Shadows of the Closet* (Dark Scribe Press 2008), an anthology of queer horror fiction, which he co-edited with Chad Helder. His debut novel, 2006's *The Literary Six*, was a tribute to the slasher films of the '80s and won an Independent Publisher Award (IPPY) for Horror and was named a finalist in *ForeWord Magazine's* Book of the Year Awards in the Gay/Lesbian Fiction category.

More recently, he edited *Butcher Knives and Body Counts* (Dark Scribe Press, 2011)—a collection of essays on the formula, frights, and fun of the slasher film—as well as the second volume in the Unspeakable Horror series, subtitled *Abominations of Desire* (Evil Jester Press, 2017). He's currently at work on his second novel.

He currently resides on the eastern end of Long Island, New York, where he is a licensed nursing home administrator by day and a writer, anthologist, and pop culture enthusiast by night. He is a member (and former Secretary) of the Horror Writers Association (HWA) and a member of the National Book Critics Circle (NBCC).

Author Website: www.VinceLiaguno.com

Rena Mason is a three-time Bram Stoker Award®-winning author of the *The Evolutionist* and *East End Girls*, as well as a 2014 Stage 32 /The Blood List Presents: The Search for New Blood Screenwriting Contest Quarter-Finalist. She's had nearly two dozen short stories, novelettes, and novellas published in various award-winning anthologies and magazines and writes a monthly column. Her dark fiction often crosses and mashes genres. For more information visit: www.RenaMason.Ink

Ben Monroe grew up in Northern California, and has spent most of his life there. He lives in the East Bay Area with his wife and two children. His most recent published works are *In the Belly of the Beast and Other Tales of Cthulhu Wars*, and the graphic novel *Planet Apocalypse*. He can be reached via his website at www.benmonroe.com and on Twitter @_BenMonroe_.

Thomas F. Monteleone has published more than 100 short stories, 5 collections, 8 anthologies and 30 novels—including the bestseller, *New York Times* Notable Book of the Year, *The Blood of the Lamb*. A five-time winner of the Bram Stoker Award®, he's also written scripts for stage, screen, and TV, as well as the bestselling *The Complete Idiot's Guide to Writing a Novel* (now in a 2nd edition). His latest novels are a global thriller, *Submerged*, and the conclusion of a YA trilogy, *The Silent Ones* (with F. Paul Wilson). With his daughter, Olivia, he co-edits the award-winning anthology series of imaginative fiction—*Borderlands*. With his wife, Elizabeth, he is a co-founder of the annual Borderlands Press Writers Boot Camp. He is well-known as an entertaining reader of his work, and routinely draws a large, appreciative audience at conventions. Despite being dragged kicking and screaming into his seventies and losing most of his hair, he still thinks he is dashingly handsome—humor him. In the spring of 2017, he received the Lifetime Achievement Award from the Horror Writers Association at StokerCon in Long Beach California.

Lisa Morton is a screenwriter, author of nonfiction books, award-winning prose writer, and Halloween expert whose work was described by the American Library Association's Readers' Advisory Guide to Horror as "consistently dark, unsettling, and frightening." Her most recent releases include *Ghosts: A Haunted History* and the short story collection *Cemetery Dance Select: Lisa Morton*. Lisa lives in the San Fernando Valley and online at: www.lisamorton.com.

Lee Murray is a multi-award-winning writer and editor of science fiction, fantasy, and horror (Sir Julius Vogel, Australian Shadows) and a three-time Bram Stoker Award®-nominee. Her works include the Taine McKenna military thrillers, and supernatural crime-noir series *The Path of Ra*, co-written with Dan Rabarts, as well as several books for children. She is proud to have edited thirteen speculative works, including award-winning titles *Baby Teeth: Bite Sized Tales of Terror* and *At the Edge* (with Dan Rabarts), *Te Kōrero Ahi Kā* (with Grace Bridges and Aaron Compton) and *Hellhole: An Anthology of Subterranean Terror*. She is the co-founder of Young New Zealand Writers, an organisation providing development and publishing opportunities for New Zealand school students, co-founder of the Wright-Murray Residency for Speculative Fiction Writers, and HWA Mentor of the Year for 2019. In February 2020, Lee was made an Honorary Literary Fellow in the New Zealand Society of Authors Waitangi Day Honours. Lee lives over the hill from Hobbiton in New Zealand's sunny Bay of Plenty where she dreams up stories from her office overlooking a cow paddock. Read more at www.leemurray.info. She tweets @leemurraywriter

The American Library Association calls **Weston Ochse** "one of the major horror authors of the 21st Century." His work has won the Bram Stoker Award®, been nominated for the Pushcart Prize, and won four New Mexico-

Arizona Book Awards. A writer of more than thirty books in multiple genres, his *Burning Sky* Duology has been hailed as the best military horror of the generation. His military supernatural series *SEAL Team 666* has been optioned to be a movie starring Dwayne Johnson and his military sci fi trilogy, which starts with *Grunt Life*, has been praised for its PTSD-positive depiction of soldiers at peace and at war. Weston has also published literary fiction, poetry, comics, and nonfiction articles. His shorter work has appeared in *DC Comics, IDW Comics, Soldier of Fortune Magazine, Cemetery Dance, Weird Takes*, and peered literary journals. His franchise work includes the *X-Files, Predator, Aliens, Hellboy, Clive Barker's Midian, Joe Ledger*, and *V-Wars*. Weston holds a Master of Fine Arts in Creative Writing and teaches at Southern New Hampshire University. He lives in Arizona with his wife and fellow author, Yvonne Navarro, and their Great Danes.

John Skipp is a *New York Times* bestselling author, editor, film director, zombie godfather, compulsive collaborator, musical pornographer, black-humored optimist and all-around Renaissance mutant. His early novels from the 1980s and '90s pioneered the graphic, subversive, high-energy form known as splatterpunk. His anthology *Book of the Dead* was the beginning of modern post-Romero zombie literature. His work ranges from hardcore horror to whacked-out Bizarro to scathing social satire, all brought together with his trademark cinematic pace and intimate, unflinching, unmistakable voice. From young agitator to hilarious elder statesman, Skipp remains one of genre fiction's most colorful characters.

Christina Sng is the Bram Stoker Award®-winning author of *A Collection of Nightmares* (Raw Dog Screaming Press, 2017). Her poetry has appeared in numerous venues worldwide, and received multiple nominations in the Rhysling Awards, the Dwarf Stars, the Elgin Awards, as well as honorable mentions in the Year's Best Fantasy and Horror and the Best Horror of the Year. Visit her at http://www.christinasng.com and connect @christinasng.

Luke Spooner is a freelance illustrator from the South of England. At 'Carrion House' he creates dark, melancholy and macabre illustrations and designs for a variety of projects and publishers, big and small, young and old.

Jeff Strand is the four-time Bram Stoker Award-nominated author of over forty books, including *Pressure, Dweller*, and *Bring Her Back*. His website is www.JeffStrand.com.

Biographies

Lucy A. Snyder is the Shirley Jackson Award-nominated and five-time Bram Stoker Award®-winning author of over 100 published short stories. Her most recent books are the collection *Garden of Eldritch Delights* and the forthcoming novel *The Girl with the Star-Stained Soul*. She also wrote the novels *Spellbent, Shotgun Sorceress,* and *Switchblade Goddess,* the nonfiction book *Shooting Yourself in the Head for Fun and Profit: A Writer's Survival Guide,* and the collections *While the Black Stars Burn, Soft Apocalypses, Orchid Carousals, Sparks and Shadows, Chimeric Machines,* and *Installing Linux on a Dead Badger.* Her writing has appeared in publications such as *Asimov's Science Fiction, Apex Magazine, Nightmare Magazine, Pseudopod, Strange Horizons,* and *Best Horror of the Year.* She lives in Columbus, Ohio and is faculty in Seton Hill University's MFA program in Writing Popular Fiction. You can learn more about her at www.lucysnyder.com and you can follow her on Twitter at @LucyASnyder.

Tim Waggoner has published close to forty novels and three collections of short stories. He writes original dark fantasy and horror, as well as media tie-ins, and his articles on writing have appeared in numerous publications. He's won a Bram Stoker Award, been a finalist for the Shirley Jackson Award and the Scribe Award, and his fiction has received numerous Honorable Mentions in volumes of *Best Horror of the Year.* He's also a full-time tenured professor who teaches creative writing and composition at Sinclair College in Dayton, Ohio.

Stephanie M. Wytovich is an American poet, novelist, and essayist. Her work has been showcased in numerous anthologies such as *Gutted: Beautiful Horror Stories, Shadows Over Main Street: An Anthology of Small-Town Lovecraftian Terror, Year's Best Hardcore Horror: Volume 2, The Best Horror of the Year: Volume 8,* as well as many others.

Wytovich is the Poetry Editor for Raw Dog Screaming Press, an adjunct at Western Connecticut State University and Point Park University, and a mentor to authors with Crystal Lake Publishing. She is a member of the Science Fiction Poetry Association, an active member of the Horror Writers Association, and a graduate of Seton Hill University's MFA program for Writing Popular Fiction. Her Bram Stoker Award-winning poetry collection, *Brothel,* earned a home with Raw Dog Screaming Press alongside *Hysteria: A Collection of Madness, Mourning Jewelry,* and *An Exorcism of Angels.* Her debut novel, *The Eighth,* is published with Dark Regions Press.

Her next poetry collection, *Sheet Music to My Acoustic Nightmare,* is scheduled to be released late 2017 from Raw Dog Screaming Press.

Follow Wytovich at
http://www.stephaniewytovich.com/

twitter @JustAfterSunset.

F. Paul Wilson is the award-winning, *New York Times* bestselling author of fifty-plus books and numerous short stories spanning medical thrillers, sf, horror, adventure, and virtually everything between. More than 9 million copies of his books are in print in the US and his work has been translated into 24 languages. He also has written for the stage, screen, and interactive media. He is best known for his urban mercenary, *Repairman Jack*. He was voted Grand Master by the World Horror Convention and received Lifetime Achievement Awards from the Horror Writers of America, the Libertarian Futurist Society, and the RT Booklovers Convention. His works have received the Stoker Award, the Porgie Award, the Prometheus and Prometheus Hall of Fame Awards, the Pioneer Award, and the prestigious Inkpot Award from San Diego ComiCon. He is listed in the 50th anniversary edition of Who's Who in America.

Special Thanks:

I would like to thank the following people for they helped and supported this passion project of mine to become a reality. My family: Angela, Hannah, Bradley, Oliver and Ethan, Fred and Debbie; The Ricketts and Gibsons; my grandparents Lois and Ben Muncy; my wonderful friends Luke Styer, Paul Moore, Scot Tanner, Dr. Patton and Linda, Thom Erb, John Stroud, Chris Sartin, Essel Pratt, Richard Chizmar; my agent Cherry; Teddy, Ethan and Scott Berry, John P, Dave Simms, Steve Dillon, Mort Castle, Tim Waggoner, L. Zedda-Sampson, Jason Stokes, John Q, Norman Prentiss and all the awesome staff at Cemetery Dance Publishing and Raw Dog Screaming Press; all the writers and artists, and you the reader!

And the Plaid Dragon Publishing Supporters: Chris Sartin, May Budd, Alain Davis, Jess Landry and Jason Stokes.

Made in the USA
Middletown, DE
17 August 2022

70775573R00156